What Reviewers Say
About Cari Hunter's Work

Alias

"The storyline, following the main character as she tries to work out who she is and why she came to in a crashed car on a mountain road, is incredibly engaging. …As the main character is suffering from amnesia, she learns about herself at the same pace as the reader, which adds another interesting aspect to the story. …This book has a great storyline with an excellent mystery to solve, and is well worth a read."—*Books at the End of the Alphabet*

"*Alias* is written in first person from the point of view of the amnesiac woman which gives us perfect access to her headspace. …Along with the characters, the reader slowly brings the pieces of the puzzle together. We suffer and get frustrated with the slow progress in reconstructing the events, the plot teasing us with incomplete memory flashbacks. Even though we know all that the character learns about herself, and without playing tricks on us, Ms. Hunter manages to deliver a twist at the end."—*Lez Review Books*

"[O]ne thing you can count on is that when you pick up a book by Hunter it is going to be awesome."—*The Romantic Reader Blog*

The Dark Peak Series

"Gruesome and compelling, mostly snowing and refreshingly English. They don't drink 'tea,' they 'make a brew' in this book. Sometimes they have 'a chippy' for supper. When it gets bad, they

have a kebab. Use caution when reading the first 20% of any of the Dark Peak books right before bed, they start with a bang. Not a literal bang, but a pretty gruesome murder. You have been warned."
—*She Sighed Blog*

A Quiet Death—Lammy Finalist

"This cracking good mystery also has a thorough respect for the various ethnic subcultures it explores. I learned things, which is never bad for a reader. Moreover, it has a distinctly British flavour, not pandering to American tastes. Of the three of Hunter's books I've read and reviewed for this blog, this has got to be my favorite. Interesting plot, great characters, muscular prose—I'm more than chuffed. I'm potty about it. And that's no bollocks."
—*Out in Print*

"[A]n awesome book, not to mention a kick butt thriller and mystery."—Danielle Kimerer, Librarian, Nevins Memorial Public Library (MA)

"Cari Hunter is a master of writing credible suspense laden crime detective stories that feel realistic. Sanne and Meg are extremely ordinary, two women trying to live quiet lives on their beloved Peaks, caught up in a dreadful ring of crime and, as always, doing their ordinary best to help those who need them. ...Once again I cannot recommend this series enough. If you like crime, thriller, and suspense with a cast of real life everyday folk and unassuming heroes, written with excellent if unpretentious style, you really cannot do any better than this."—*Lesbian Reading Room*

immediately as a captive woman makes her bloody escape and then—Well, this is not a romance, dear reader, so brace yourself. …Our heroines are Detective Sanne Jensen and Dr. Meg Fielding, best mates forever and sometimes something more. Their relationship is undefinable and complicated, but not in a hot mess of drama way. Rather, they share unspoken depths, comfortably silly moments, rock-solid friendship, and an intimacy that will make your heart ache just a wee bit."—*C-Spot Reviews*

Tumbledown

"Once again Ms. Hunter outdoes herself in the tension and pace of the plot. We literally know from the first 2 pages that the evil is hunting them, but we are held on the edge of our seats for the whole book to see what will unfold, how they will cope, whether they will survive—and at what cost this time. I literally couldn't put it down. *Tumbledown* is a wonderful read."—*Lesbian Reading Room*

"Even though this is a continuation of the *Desolation Point* plot, this is an entirely different sort of thriller with elements of a police procedural. Other thriller authors (yes, I'm looking at you Patterson and Grisham) could take lessons from Hunter when it comes to writing these babies. Twists and turns and forgotten or unconventional weaponry along with pluck and spirit keep me breathless and reading way past my bedtime."—*Out In Print*

Desolation Point

"[*Desolation Point*] is the second of Cari Hunter's novels and is another great example of a romance action adventure. The story is fast paced and thrilling. A real page turner from beginning to end. Ms. Hunter is a master at an adventure plot and comes up with more twists and turns than the mountain trails they are hiking. Well written, edited and crafted this is an excellent book and I can't wait to read the sequel."—*Lesbian Reading Room*

"Cari Hunter provides thrills galore in her adventure/romance *Desolation Point*. In the hands of a lesser writer and scenarist, this could be pretty rote and by-the-book, but Cari Hunter breathes a great deal of life into the characters and the situation. Her descriptions of the scenery are sumptuous, and she has a keen sense of pacing. The action sequences never drag, and she takes full advantage of the valleys between the peaks by deepening her characters, working their relationship, and setting up the next hurdle."—*Out In Print*

Snowbound

"[*Snowbound*] grabbed me from the first page and kept me on the edge of my seat until nearly the end. I love the British feel of it and enjoyed the writer's style tremendously. So if you're looking for a very well written, fast paced, lesbian romance—heavy on the action and blood and light on the romance—this is one for your ereader or bookshelf."—*C-Spot Reviews*

Visit us at www.boldstrokesbooks.com

By the Author

Snowbound

Desolation Point

Tumbledown

Alias

Breathe

The Dark Peak Series

No Good Reason

Cold to the Touch

A Quiet Death

BREATHE

by
Cari Hunter

2019

BREATHE
© 2019 By Cari Hunter. All Rights Reserved.

ISBN 13: 978-1-63555-523-3

This Trade Paperback Original Is Published By
Bold Strokes Books, Inc.
P.O. Box 249
Valley Falls, NY 12185

First Edition: September 2019

Credits
Editor: Cindy Cresap
Production Design: Susan Ramundo
Cover Design By Sheri (hindsightgraphics@gmail.com)

Acknowledgments

Thanks and an Uncle Joe's Mint Ball to the whole gang at BSB, especially my editor, Cindy, for her feedback and support, and for knowing which veggies float and which sink. To Sheri for getting the cover absolutely right. To Kel for her "Crock Om Boosh"—I can't believe I managed to sneak that in! To all the folks who read my books, send feedback, bake their own bara briths, and happily chat about daft stuff online. To my funny, permanently knackered, and loving family in green, both present and past. And to Cat, who spends hours working on these books with me, helps me chase through fields after lost lambs, and loves me no matter what.

Dedication

For Cat

Always

CHAPTER ONE

"Oh God, don't let me die. Help! Please help me!"

The wind tore at the man's thin wail, breaking it into pieces, half of his entreaty heading south to the Manchester Ship Canal and the other half whipping across Barton Bridge. Lying flat on her front, her boots hooked over the rim of the hard shoulder and her elbows in a puddle, Jem trained her torch on the hapless bloke and tried not to look at the water swirling a hundred feet below.

"Bloody hell," she said. Trevor, her crewmate for this latest run of weekend nights, stalked toward their ambulance, his curt request for assistance drowned out as the rope suddenly slipped and the man shrieked.

"I'm falling! Tell Bella I love her!"

Jem rechecked his position: he wasn't falling. He was dangling in midair a few inches lower than he had been, but he wasn't falling.

"Try to keep still," she shouted.

He gave her an incredulous look as the wind spun him in a slow three-sixty. "Fucking brilliant advice! Any other bright ideas?"

"No, not really," she muttered and then jumped as a hand clapped her on the shoulder and a policewoman in a scarlet beanie hat and a high-vis jacket squirmed into a prone position beside her.

"What've we got?" the officer asked, apparently oblivious to the puddle she was now sharing with Jem. She peeked over the ledge and snorted. "Oh, for fuck's sake. I'm guessing he's the groom?"

"The L-plate would certainly imply that," Jem said.

The "Learner" tag, and the loincloth to which it was attached, were the man's sole items of clothing. His friends had stripped him before tethering him to the stanchion and leaving him to it, and although they probably hadn't intended his current predicament, a combination of slip knots, high winds, greasy metal, and a shitload of alcohol had been a recipe for disaster.

"My mate's requesting Fire and Hazardous Response," Jem said.

The officer shook her head. "We're stuffed there. A warehouse went up in Ardwick about an hour ago, and every man and his dog are otherwise engaged." She eyeballed Jem. "How are you at abseiling?"

"What?" The question squeaked out, and Jem felt her palms begin to sweat. "No, no, we can't! You don't understand. This kind of thing, it doesn't—not for me..." She couldn't explain. She could barely raise her voice above the traffic on the motorway and the rain that had started to batter the tarmac. "We need to wait for backup," she said, but the officer brushed off her feeble plea.

"It'll be fine. Trust me." She shuffled forward and called down to the man. "Hang in there, pal. We'll be back in a jiffy."

"Stop taking the piss!" he yelled, twirling again, the L-plate flapping to reveal exactly how cold he was. He was still ranting as the officer tugged Jem's hand, encouraging her to her feet.

"I've got a tow rope in my car," she said. "Do you have anything we can make a harness out of? For him, not for us. I was joking about the abseiling."

Jem's instinct for career preservation made her falter, but she was already thinking, imagining a rough design fashioned from lifting belts and stretcher straps. "Possibly," she conceded, dragging the word out. "Give me a couple of minutes."

"Fab."

They parted at the kerbside, the officer rummaging in her car boot while Jem headed to the ambulance. She found Trevor hastily crushing a fag beneath his boot.

"HART gave an ETA of ninety minutes, and control reckon that's optimistic at best," he told her, none too subtly blocking the rear doors.

"Right."

When she went to step around him, he parried her move.

"No," he said. "Whatever you're planning, just—no."

He was older than her but less experienced, and in terms of qualifications she outranked him. Given her reputation, though, she understood his reticence.

"We can't leave him there for ninety minutes," she said. "He's already panicking. He'll do something stupid and end up in the canal."

"Or *you'll* do something stupid, and then it'll be our fault." Trevor seemed to ponder this for a moment and then smiled sweetly. He reached for his radio with one hand and unlocked the ambulance with the other. "Okay, okay, go ahead. I'll have a word with our dispatcher."

With no time to worry about ulterior motives, Jem scrambled into the back and started to pull equipment from the cupboards. Trailing luminous strips of plastic, she met the officer on the hard shoulder and sat with her on the kerb to clip and tie and rearrange their kit until they had something resembling a scaffolder's harness, if they squinted at it and used a lot of imagination.

"Think it's big enough?" the officer asked, holding the rig in front of her to check its size. She only had an inch or so on Jem height-wise, but she was slimmer around the waist and backside, and two of her would have comfortably fitted into it.

"Try it against me instead," Jem said, and felt a flush of heat in her cheeks as the officer's gaze wandered over her.

"Yeah, as if you're a fair comparison." The officer widened the left leg, seemingly on a whim, and slung everything across her shoulder. "Your mate going to lend us his muscles?" she asked as they walked to the side of the bridge, careful not to trip on the rope they'd secured around a lamppost.

Jem glanced back at the ambulance. She could see the puff of smoke marking Trevor's position on the far side of the vehicle. Out of sight, out of mind. She had literally taken the rope, and he was hoping she'd hang herself with it. Ignoring a renewed bout of fear, she coughed through the wheeze that had started to accompany her every breath.

"I think we're on our own," she said.

The officer shrugged, unfazed. "We'll manage. I bet you're stronger than you look."

Jem smothered another cough. Nothing could be further from the truth. On a good day she could dead lift the defib and the response bag, but not when she was scared shitless and needed her inhaler. She wanted to run to the ambulance, lock herself in the cab, and wait for the experts. Instead, she concentrated on breathing through her nose and knelt by the officer at the side of the bridge.

"You still with us, pal?" the officer shouted, directing her torch at the man. Jem realised how young he was: twenty-five at most, and sober enough now to appreciate his predicament.

"Hey, what's your name?" she called. "I'm Jem, and this is…" She looked at the officer.

"Rosie." The officer raised a hand to underscore her introduction.

"Sean. My name's Sean."

"Okay, Sean." Jem took the strap attached to the harness and began to feed it down. "Without loosening anything that's holding you, we need you to grab this and get into it."

He watched the multicoloured contraption descend, his eyes so wide that they flashed like twin moons against the darkness surrounding him.

"Don't be fucking stupid. How am I supposed to get into that?"

"One leg at a time," Rosie suggested helpfully. She pulled on a pair of leather gloves and gathered the lamppost rope.

"He's giving it a go," Jem told her. Despite his protest, Sean had wriggled a foot through the first loop, and she was manoeuvring the guide strap to inch the second loop into position. He caught it with a toe and yanked it up his leg. Jem saw Rosie's stance widen as she took the strain, and she sprinted across to help her, grasping the section in front of Rosie and hauling on it.

"Keep going," Rosie said, her breath puffing warm on Jem's neck. "Keep going, you're doing great."

Jem nodded, gritting her teeth as her muscles burned. The rope shifted in fits and starts, grinding around the concrete lamppost. She waited for it to snap, for the scream as Sean plunged to his doom, for her own inevitable capitulation. What she saw instead was Sean's hand flailing, trying to find purchase. She gave a yelp of encouragement, and she and Rosie tugged harder, invigorated. Caught up in their heads-down, heels-dug-in rhythm, they launched him over the railing, and he landed in a heap on the tarmac, his arse quivering and his limbs tangled.

"Holy shit," Rosie gasped. "It worked."

Jem's hands were shaking. She dropped the rope and bent double, struggling to draw in a full breath. "Didn't…didn't you think…it would?"

Rosie laughed, a joyous, raucous sound. "Fuck no, did I hell. I have bollock-all luck with this kind of thing. Hey, maybe you're like a, a—what do you call 'em?" She clicked her fingers, searching for the word. "A talisman?"

Jem coughed and gave in, sucking on her inhaler, no longer bothered about keeping up appearances. "I really doubt that," she said once she could speak without the accompanying bagpipes. "I'll get him a blanket."

On her own in the ambulance, she leaned against the oxygen cupboard and closed her eyes. Her knees were knocking.

"Come on, you're being a berk," she whispered. She found a blanket and clasped it to her chest for a moment before reopening the back door. The door stuck, the step catching as it dropped, so she pushed harder, throwing her weight behind it when it met unexpected resistance. She heard a cry and a scuffle, followed by the sound of screeching brakes, and she peered around the door in time to see Sean bouncing off a car's windscreen. He landed with a thud, rolled back onto the hard shoulder, and came to a stop in front of Rosie's boots.

"Jesus wept!" Rosie said.

Dumbstruck, Jem froze on the top step as Trevor ran across to them.

"Have you *killed* him?" he shouted. "I bloody knew it! I *knew* something like this would happen."

She shook her head convulsively, unable to move. One thought was rolling through her mind on a loop: *please no, please no.*

"He's not dead, you pillock," Rosie snapped, and Sean gave a groan, attesting to the fact. "The car was only doing five miles an hour. Stop gobbing off and help him." She went over to Jem and touched her arm gently. "Hey. You okay there?"

"I'm fine," Jem managed through a renewed bout of wheezing. "I need to—" She gestured toward Sean.

"You need to sit down," Rosie said. "You look like you've seen a ghost."

Jem's laugh bordered on hysterical. "Not this time," she said as Rosie stared at her. "Not this time."

CHAPTER TWO

Kev Kerrigan uncapped his Biro and fished his notepad from his pocket, performing a long-suffering double take when he saw its *Dora the Explorer* cover. Mumbling something about "those bleedin' kids," he flicked to a clean page, past crayon drawings of sheep and pigs, and a more abstract scribble that resembled a blue hedgehog.

"Let me get this right." He shifted his chair closer to Jem's, bringing with him a faint waft of baby sick. A suspicious white stain obscured the pips on his left epaulette. If anyone asked him about his family, he'd say he came to work for a break. "You and Officer..."

"Rosie," Jem said.

"Officer Rosie." He shrugged and wrote it down. "You managed to pull this lad up, just the two of you?"

"Yes."

"And where was Trevor while you were tug-of-warring with Barton Bridge?"

"Um." Jem focused on the wall behind Kev's head, suddenly intrigued by a flu vaccination poster. "Uh, he was liaising with control."

"I see." Kev's tone told her he wasn't fooled. "So you yank the lad out of the void, and then minutes later you somehow chuck him into the path of a Fiat Panda."

"I didn't chuck him, I bumped him with the back door. And everyone was rubbernecking, so the car was going dead slow."

"'Bumped him…with the back…door,'" Kev said, scribbling it down verbatim.

"It got stuck," she added. "On the step, and I didn't know he was standing behind it. How could I?"

"'Stuck,'" Kev was still writing. "Dare I ask what the damage was?"

She sighed. "Dislocated shoulder and road rash. I gave him plenty of morphine, if that helps any."

"It might," Kev said. As her immediate manager, it wasn't the first time he'd had this sort of chat with her. "Look, it could've been worse, so things will probably go no further."

She bowed her head, tears brimming in her eyes. "That's good. Thanks."

"Trevor's gone off sick," he continued, pretending not to notice as she dried her eyes. "Stress, he reckons, so you're solo. I can't see the resource manager doing anything with you at this hour. Head back to station when you're ready."

"Okay. Okay, I'll do that." She stayed where she was until his footsteps had faded down the A&E corridor, and then she straightened in slow, halting increments. Her back and arms ached, and her palms were red raw where the rope had slid through them. She flexed her fingers, wincing at the sting.

"Damn," a familiar voice said quietly, somewhere off to her left. "I had spare gloves in the car, but I never thought."

Jem squinted up as Rosie set two plastic cups on the hand gel dispensers and crouched by her side. It was warm in the corridor, and Rosie had taken off her hat, freeing waves of auburn hair streaked through with blond and cut into a choppy bob, as if the style had wanted to conform but rebelled at the last minute. If she'd chosen it to match her personality, it was damn near perfect.

"I fell off a tyre swing when I was seven and ended up with paws like these." She took hold of Jem's wrists, assessing the damage. "My mam—she was never really one for first aid—smothered them in butter and bandages and left them to cook for two days of a nineties heat wave. They got infected, and I nearly lost a pinkie."

Jem waited a few seconds for a punch line that never came. "That's quite an upsetting story."

"Yeah, but it has a happy ending. Look." Waggling her intact little fingers, Rosie plonked into the chair Kev had vacated. She reached to retrieve the brews, her coat sleeve riding up to reveal a black tattoo of a Manchester bee. "I wasn't sure if you were a tea or a coffee gal, so I made one of each. Take your pick. I'm not fussy."

"Tea, thanks." Jem cradled the cup, smiling at the paper towels Rosie had insulated it with.

"Did he read you the Riot Act?" Rosie asked, thumbing in the direction of Kev's departure.

"Not really. How about you?"

Rosie ticked the misdemeanours off on her fingers. "I should have requested an urgent assist, tow ropes aren't designed for search and rescue, the lamppost hadn't been risk assessed, and Traffic should have closed the motorway. There's probably a few more I'm forgetting, but the lad's bride-to-be and his dad all but declared their undying adoration for me in front of my sarge, so I'm still gainfully employed."

Jem raised her cup in a toast. "To gainful employment."

"I'll drink this nasty NHS coffee to that." Rosie took a slurp from her brew. "I don't believe we were properly introduced. Rosie Jones—pleasure and all that."

"Jemima, but my mates call me Jem."

"Jemima..." Rosie trailed off expectantly, and Jem sighed, bracing herself for the usual slew of jokes.

"Pardon. My surname's Pardon."

"Jemima Pardon." Rosie sounded it out slowly, hitting the syllables as if testing their rhythm. "I like it. It's unusual."

"It's a pain in the arse," Jem said, too much on the defensive to appreciate the compliment. "Everyone takes the piss."

Rosie drained her cup and pushed out of her chair. "Jealousy results in very tiresome behaviour, Ms. Pardon. Us plain-monikered folk can be a bitter bunch."

The surface of Jem's tea rippled as she laughed. Rosie might be borderline bonkers, but she certainly brightened a night shift.

"That's more like it," Rosie said. "Don't let the buggers grind you down."

The fierce note of solidarity prompted Jem to lower her cup. "I try not to."

"Good. Sorry, just a sec." Rosie adjusted her earpiece, listening to her comms as she fastened her jacket. "Bollocks, I've got to run. There's a riot kicking off at McTucky's in Beswick."

"Sounds like fun."

"Yeah, assault with a spicy chicken wing. This city is ridiculous at times."

Jem watched Rosie hare down the corridor, narrowly avoiding an elderly bloke heading for the toilet.

"Be careful out there!" she shouted after her.

Rosie paused halfway through the door and raised a hand in acknowledgement. "You too!"

The door slid shut behind her, and seconds later, flashes of blue marked her passage from the hospital grounds, the light growing distant and then disappearing altogether. The man doddered from the loo, one hand grappling with his open gown, the other slapping the wall as he struggled for balance.

"Here." Jem offered him her arm. "Which bed did you come from, love?"

"Fifty-four."

There were twelve bays on Majors. "Aye, that's what I thought," she said, and led him around to the nurses' station.

"Incoming! Duck, Kash!"

Rosie dodged the man's swinging fist as Kashif heeded her warning, diving out of harm's way.

"Chicken, technically," Kash said, and clobbered the shins of their would-be assailant with his baton. Enraged, the man sucked in a deep breath and spluttered, spraying spit onto the Formica. He lashed out with his arms, not caring whom he caught in the crossfire but coming nowhere near the table Rosie had taken shelter behind. She watched, bemused, as his movements gradually lost coordination. His eyes bulged, and his face turned first scarlet and then a funny shade of dusky blue as he grappled at his clogged throat with both hands.

"Shit. Kash? *Kashif!*" Rosie waved frantically, but Kash was too busy disarming a lad brandishing a flick knife and a spork, and the shop's proprietor had disappeared behind the deep fat fryer. "Bloody Nora!"

She darted to the shop counter, creating enough space for a run-up, and threw herself at the bloke's back. Blindsided, he went down like a sack of spuds, bouncing hard onto his beer belly, and she followed him to the floor, straddling his hips as he retched and spat half a chicken drumstick across the lino.

"Get off me, you fat bitch!" he yelled once he'd caught his breath.

"You're welcome," she said. "And that's muscle, not fat, you cheeky git. I go to the gym three times a week. Now, you do not have to say anything—"

"Fuck off." He jerked his arse sideways, trying to throw her, and she gripped harder with her thighs, reaching for her cuffs.

"But it may harm your defence," she continued, snapping the cuffs into place, "if you do not mention when questioned—"

"They're fucking hurting me. I'll do you for police brutality."

"The more you struggle, the tighter they'll get, but I'm assuming you know that already." She dismounted, letting him flop around on the floor. He was old enough to be her dad, and he stank like a brewery. "Where were we? Oh yes: something you later rely on in court."

He rolled until he could glare at her. "I'll see *you* in court, when I have you done."

"Mm-hm." She pointed at the camera fixed to her stab vest, its circular lens illuminated by a bright red ring. "Got it all recorded, mate, including the bit where I stopped you from choking to death."

"You never did. You lying sla—" His denial cut off as she toe-poked the chicken bone from its puddle of drool.

"Didn't your mum ever tell you to chew your food?" Leaving him to seethe, she returned to the counter, where McTucky's grateful owner was plying Kash with milkshakes and buckets of chicken. She frowned at the smear of red on Kash's cheek, until she realised it was ketchup. "Van coming for these idiots?"

"Ten minutes," he told her. "Chocolate or vanilla?"

"Chocolate, please." She stuck a straw through the milkshake lid and sucked hard enough to give herself brain freeze.

He sat with her at the cleanest table and popped the top off a bucket. "That was a nifty Heimlich. Slightly unorthodox, but very effective."

She laughed around her straw. "What can I say? Sometimes you just have to improvise. Been a bit of a night for it."

"Yeah, I heard about Barton. First shift in months that they make us run solo, and I miss out on all the fun."

"And a cute paramedic," she said, blowing bubbles into her shake.

He paused, drumstick poised at his lips. "Your team or mine?"

She deliberated for a long moment. "Indeterminate. No specific vibes either way, but she was...she was..." Rosie exhaled slowly. "Anyway, I liked her."

"Did you get her number?"

"No, no, nothing. Christ, Kash, we'd only just met, and we were a tad distracted. I think she works out of Darnton. I'll probably never see her again."

"On the other hand, maybe you'll bump into her all the time, now they've mucked around with our shift pattern."

She shrugged. "It's a possibility, I suppose."

"*Their eyes met across a naked man,*" he said in his best film trailer voice. "*They found a rope...*"

"Sod off." She flicked shake at him.

"*And against all the odds...*"

"The van's here," she said. "Grab your bucket and stop being a twerp."

❖

Jem entered the garage code and lined the ambulance up to reverse park. The driving aspect of the job had been her Achilles' heel when she first joined the service. As a twenty-year-old nervous newbie who'd never driven anything bigger than a Micra, she'd clipped countless wing mirrors, cracked several lights, and suffered the indignity of having "L" and "R" penned on her hands to ensure she could follow the satnav without watching its screen. Now, twelve years later, she eased the Mercedes Sprinter into a bay designed for much smaller vehicles, the wing mirrors never in jeopardy and the rear lights well clear of the garage wall. With ninety minutes left on her shift, she emptied the clinical waste bin, changed the defib battery, and wiped down the saloon surfaces. She briefly considered washing the exterior, but the garage was cold, a wet Manchester winter having given way to an even wetter spring, and she stuck her hands beneath her armpits as she headed for the kitchen instead, craving tea and toast and a catnap.

A cackle of laughter from the crew room slowed her walk to a tiptoe. She'd parked in the farthest bay along and hadn't spotted the seven o'clock shift vehicle, but its crew were obviously on station. She knew that Dougie and Bob, who usually ran the line, had booked the nights off, and she cursed herself for not checking who'd been put on their shifts. Sometimes forewarned was forearmed. Nearing the door, she recognised the voices and hugged herself a little harder.

"Don't be mard," she told herself, quelling the impulse to hide in her ambulance until the crew got a job. If they were on their rest break, she could be standing toast-less in the draughty garage for another twenty minutes. It was the toast-less part, not the chill, that brought her to a decision, and she shoved the door open. Her appearance stopped the conversation dead, both the young women in the room turning to stare at her as she walked in.

"Hey," she said, keeping her tone light so they wouldn't suspect she might bolt at the slightest provocation. "Anyone want a brew?"

Caitlin—six foot something, with tattooed eyebrows and teeth bleached to dazzling whiteness—hid a smirk behind her sleeve and nudged her half-empty mug. "Got one, thanks."

"Amira?"

"No, ta."

Jem went into the kitchen, out of sight but still within earshot, and heard muted giggles erupt in her wake. In their early twenties and fresh out of university, Caitlin and Amira were paramedic reserves, newer staff members still waiting for a permanent shift pattern and duty-bound to fill the rota gaps in the meantime. As the East Manchester group included three different stations, they didn't always work out of Darnton, but they made their presence felt whenever they copped for a shift there. Dougie, who rarely had a bad word to say about anyone, had christened them the "Witches of Ardwick."

With the toaster ticking over and her tea nowhere near stewed enough, Jem stacked a mass of mucky pots in the dishwasher and scrubbed something that might have been curry sauce from the countertop. The sign asking staff to do their "own bloody dishes" had fallen behind the microwave again, which apparently rendered it null and void.

"So, Jem," Caitlin said, raising her voice to ensure it carried, "is it true you *accidentally* shoved a patient under a van and broke his neck?" More stifled laughter punctuated the question, and there was a dull thud, as if one of them had slapped the arm of the other.

Jem buttered her toast, picking the shreds from her marmalade, though her appetite was fading fast. Her first slice dropped to the floor as she started to butter the second. It flipped and landed jammy side down.

"Bloody typical," she muttered, scraping it up and dumping it in the bin.

"Come on, Jemima," Amira said, taking up Caitlin's thread. Unlike Rosie, she had the knack of making Jem's name sound like an insult. "You can tell us. We won't breathe a word, we promise."

"Cross our hearts," Caitlin added.

Jem's mouth was too dry for her to answer, and she took her time screwing the top back on her jam. Despite the mouse that lurked in the dishwasher, the ants that regularly paraded across the top of the fridge, and the unidentifiable ooze between two of the floor tiles, the kitchen felt like a sanctuary compared to what awaited her in the crew room. Annoyed that she was allowing the pair of them to hound her on her home station, she drank a few fortifying sips of tea and rattled the spoon against the mug, giving the impression she'd just finished making it. Then, almost sure that she wouldn't reveal her nerves by dropping anything, she carried her supper through and sat two seats away from them.

"No, it's not true," she said quietly. "That wasn't what happened, and he was discharged about an hour ago." Gauging the disappointment in their expressions, she bit into her toast, enjoying its buttery crunch now that she'd taken the wind from their sails. If they wanted the full story, they could ask someone else.

"He didn't need emergency surgery?" Caitlin asked, her eyes narrowing as she tried to catch Jem in a lie.

"He needed his shoulder popping back in and a couple of plasters." Jem finished chewing her crust. "Would either of you like a piece? I'm going to do another, so it's no bother."

"No, thank you," Amira said. "I'm gluten intolerant."

You're generally intolerant, Jem thought, and hid her relief behind her mug as their radios went off.

"Why can't they all just stay in fucking bed?" Caitlin said, grabbing the vehicle keys and stomping to the door. She'd only been a paramedic for a year, and her university diploma course had somehow failed to prepare her for the nonstop barrage of water infections, falls, overdoses, snotty kids, and the worried well. She was already talking about finishing her degree and getting a better paid job in a Minor Injuries unit, an ambition that Bob had been actively encouraging.

Jem listened for the start of the engine, the creak of the garage doors, and the sirens that were blaring before the ambulance had even left the yard. The din faded with distance, the whoop and wail replaced by the occasional rumble of a passing HGV and chirps from the dawn chorus's more zealous members. Jem set an alarm on her phone and sank into the closest armchair, too worn out to care that its headrest was greasy from years of use and that it smelled like an unwashed old man. Her eyes burned when she closed them, and even curled up she couldn't get warm enough. She needed a hat like Officer Rosie's, she decided: something woolly enough to withstand the winds at the highest point of Barton and stop her hair from blinding her. And if it happened to be as flattering as Rosie's, that would be fine too. Shaking her head at the memory, she tugged her jacket tighter and dozed off, smiling.

CHAPTER THREE

Watery sunlight peeking beneath the blackout blinds, along with a weird smell that might have been offal and orange, woke Jem before her alarm got its chance. She slapped a hand on the button to deactivate it and buried her face in her quilt.

"Fergus!" Her summons was muffled by her fifteen-tog winter warmer, so she held her nose, ducked out her head, and tried again. "Ferg! Get your arse in here."

He appeared five minutes later, a contrite six-foot-three, flame-haired Scot wearing a stained apron and a liberal dusting of flour. Stopping short of the threshold, he proffered a mug of tea and a bacon barm like a flag of truce.

"Get over here, you big idiot," she said, ruffling his curls as he shoved onto the bed with her and helped himself to a bite of her butty. "What bloody concoction have you got on the boil down there? Slaughterhouse and potpourri?"

"Kidney à l'orange. It sounded like such a winning combination in my head."

"And in reality?"

He grimaced. "It tastes like death and Del Monte."

"Oh dear." Although she'd aimed for sympathetic, her plate began to shake as she suppressed a laugh, and a rasher of bacon gave the game away by sliding out of her barm. As chief recipe developer at Pie Hard and its sister shop Pie Harder, Fergus was living his dream, and none of his ardent fan base needed to know about the occasional spectacular misses that occurred in pursuit of the much clamoured-after hits. "Back to the drawing board with this one, then?" she asked.

"Aye. Sometimes discretion is the better part of valour." He crossed his legs at the ankles and tapped the tip of her nose. "Sleep okay?"

"Like a log."

"Shift okay?"

"Yeah, not too bad," she said, rescuing her errant rasher and avoiding his gaze.

"Thought as much. Mr. Murphy pushed a note through to say you'd parked at the wrong house again."

"I did? Buggeration." She sagged against her pillows, racking her brain for details of her journey home. The Murphys lived two doors down, but she couldn't remember parking on their drive. She couldn't even remember leaving station.

"How bad," Ferg asked, "on a score of one to 'See You in Coroner's Court'?"

"Only about a three. Could've been worse. Trevor did quite well, considering. He lasted almost eight hours before he went off sick, so I'll be solo tonight."

Ferg tugged her upright, her plate and mug clattering as he set them on the bedside cabinet. "You're better off without that knob. Get in the shower. I'll shift your car and rally the troops, and you can tell me all about it."

He shut the door behind him, and Jem gifted herself a moment to finish her butty, listening to the blue tits squabbling with the robins around the feeders she'd hung in the small backyard. She and Ferg had shared the terraced house for the past three years. He'd been an A&E nurse at the time of signing the lease, and they'd bonded over their mutual love of pastry, cakes, and all things calorific. She patted her arse as she rolled out of bed. The cheeks wobbled slightly beneath her palms, and she wondered how much of their current expanse was a direct result of being a prize baker's taste-test stooge.

"Most of it, at a guess," she said, waiting for the shower to show willing and produce a hint of steam before she stripped off.

The full-length mirror caught her naked body in profile, and she turned slowly to face the glass. She knew she'd never be rake-thin, and in truth she was quite fond of her curves. Her breasts were chipper enough, she didn't have bingo wings, and while her tummy definitely wasn't a six-pack, it hadn't reached the level of keg.

Using one hand to clear the mirror of mist, she gave her bedhead the evil eye and tugged on one of its tufts. Though she might be at home with her body, her hair was another matter entirely. It was stringy, mud brown, and best displayed beneath a cap, and she had always hated it. With no solutions of her own apart from shaving it all off, she kept the same style to appease her hairdresser, a myopic sixty-year-old who still thought basin fringes and backcombing were the height of fashion.

"Balls to it," she said, and stepped beneath the spray.

Reconvening with Ferg on the driveway, she abandoned her attempts to kirby-grip her fringe into submission and greeted the frantic menagerie of mutts Ferg had collected.

"Hallo, pups," she said, squatting to hand out treats. She untangled three of the leads, dividing the load equally between her and Fergus, and clicked her tongue. "Right-o, best foot forward."

The rain had cleared as she slept, leaving puddles on the pavements, and the smell of fresh grass in Abbey Vale. Stretching across several miles of wetland, fields, and woodland, the nature reserve was high and open enough in places to give views of the Pennines and the monument atop Stanny Pike in one direction, and the city skyscrapers in the other. Jem had spent hours exploring its trails, and she walked the dogs more for pleasure and exercise than financial gain. Children were shrieking on the main playground, lured outside by the first clear weather in days, and two no-fixed-abodes had hung their sleeping bags to dry from nearby trees. They raised their lager cans in greeting as Jem steered her dogs by.

"Seen rats in 'ere bigger than them," one said. "Best watch out if you go near the lake. The seagulls will have 'em."

She ignored him, and Ferg's amused snort.

"Sod off, I can't help it," she said, once they'd rounded the corner. Nothing over knee height, that was her rule, and that meant her knees, not Ferg's. She'd pushed the limits of her comfort zone by accepting a marginal beagle from an elderly gent with a bad hip, but she'd firmly drawn the line at the Murphys' boxer.

Ferg touched the smaller of two scars below her left eye. "I know, hen. I'm not really taking the piss. Besides which, toy dogs are brilliant for meeting women." He scooped up Delilah, the tiny Chihuahua struggling to keep the pace, and nodded and smiled at a pretty thirty-something blonde who'd slowed her jog to coo at their Pomeranian. Barely acknowledging Ferg, the woman beamed at Jem before accelerating away. He shrugged, not offended in the slightest. "I rest my case."

"I met someone last night," Jem said, too shift-addled to consider how the statement might be interpreted. "No, *no*, not like that," she stuttered, as he gaped at her. "She's a police officer, and there was this lad, dangling, he was dangling off Barton Bridge, and we pulled him up together, and then the lad got dinged by a car, and she came to the hospital and made me a cup of tea." She ran out of air, coughing as she tried to inhale and exhale simultaneously.

Ferg steered her to the closest bench and waited until the rasp in her chest became less audible.

"Better?" he asked.

"Yes. Thanks."

"That little escapade going to cause you any trouble?"

"No. Kev didn't seem to think so."

He tickled Delilah beneath her chin, making her tongue loll out. "And what might be the name of this police officer who's got you in such a tizzy?"

"Her name is Rosie. And I'm not in a tizzy. She was nice enough, but she was nuttier than a fruitcake." She and Ferg leaned back in unison, considering the pack of diminutive pooches milling around their ankles.

"So, basically you're made for each other," he said at length.

She slapped her knees and stood. "Absolutely. She's the Thelma to my Louise, the Butch to my Sundance, et cetera, et cetera."

"You do realise all four of those went over a cliff."

She thought that one over, perturbed that even her subconscious tended toward pessimism. "Hmm, yeah, good point. Butch and Sundance survived, though. Well, for a while."

A fine drizzle began to fall, misting over the lake and gathering on her eyelashes. She dabbed them dry and held out a hand to pull Ferg up.

"If you're Sundance, exactly how butch was this Officer Rosie?" he asked, in a blatant attempt to lighten her mood.

She let out an exaggerated breath. "Off the scale, mate. Hard as nails. She'd make mincemeat out of you."

He yanked his dogs to a halt and looked at her. "Really?"

"No."

He snorted and slung an arm around her shoulders. "Okay, fair enough, I asked for that. Fancy a brew and a cake at the cafe?"

"Are you buying?"

A quick slap of his jeans pocket made coins jingle. "Yes, unless those all turn out to be pennies."

"I'm sure we'll manage. We can always get one tea and two straws if we're really desperate." She squeezed his hand. "If we end up sharing a scone, though, I'm having the jammy half."

If Rosie looked hard enough, she could see the odd mark on the wallpaper where she'd Blu-Tacked her favourite posters. The bunk beds were the other way around now, and her old desk had been replaced by a new unit for the television she'd always begged for and never been allowed, but otherwise the room was the same claustrophobic little box room she'd spent most of her formative years in.

Humming along to an earworm Kash had inflicted on her the night before, she was about to reach for her mug of coffee when a shriek stilled her hands.

"You nipped my ear, Rosie! You proper cut me. Is it bleeding? I bet it's bleeding. I won't tell Mam if you give me a fiver."

Rosie held the scissors aloft, examining them carefully for claret and chunks of lughole. "You're a dirty fibber, Janelle Badu. Hold still so I don't make a cock of your fringe."

Janelle—thirteen going on forty-five—folded her arms and scowled, her jaw working furiously as she chewed her bubblegum. "You don't get to boss me about just cos you're a copper."

"No, I get to boss you about because I'm older than you and bigger than you, and because Dad said I could."

"*Step*dad," Janelle said, wafting at the falling hair so she could continue to glower upward. "He's only your stepdad, and he likes me the best."

Re-angling the scissors, Rosie sent more black curls spiralling into Janelle's lap. "Hmm, I don't know. I think Samuel has the edge. They both like footy, fishing—"

"Farting," Janelle added, and laughed so hard Rosie had to stop cutting. The laugh was infectious, a throaty, full-bellied roar that caught her up in its sheer enthusiasm. Janelle could be a pain in the arse at times, but she was good fun when she wasn't setting the world to rights.

"Boys, eh?" Rosie said, winking at her in the mirror.

Janelle wiped her nose, smearing snot and loose hairs across the sleeve of Rosie's smock. "Mam reckons they're only good for one thing."

"Yeah?" Rosie closed her eyes, wondering what the hell Janelle had overheard. "What's that?"

Janelle blew a bubble and left Rosie in suspense until it popped. "Getting the lids off stuff. Are we done yet?"

"Just about."

A liberal application of curl-defining gel rounded things off, and Rosie held up a smaller mirror, displaying the back and sides of Janelle's new style for her approval.

"Love it." Janelle tore off the smock and kissed Rosie's cheek. "Tammy wanted hers doing as well."

"Tammy will have to wait. I'm on shift in an hour and a half." Rosie caught the hood of Janelle's sweater. "Hoover, missy. Mam's got enough to do without cleaning up after you."

"It's like having two bleedin' mothers," Janelle muttered, her fondness for swearing still eclipsed by her reluctance to get in trouble over it. When Rosie tugged on one of her curls, she smiled shyly, the stroppy teenager morphing into the sweet baby half-sister who had made everything all right with Rosie's new dad, and who had come to rely on Rosie for a good deal of her parenting when two further children had followed in rapid succession.

Lured downstairs by a heady aroma of roasting meat and spuds, they walked into a kitchen filled with steam, the cloud all but obscuring Maggie Badu as she slid a tray of Yorkshire puddings from the oven.

"Whoa, easy, Mam." Rosie grabbed an oven glove and caught the tray as it began to tilt, drawing a relieved but frazzled smile from her mam, who placed the tray on the counter with one hand and rapped Janelle's knuckles with the other.

"Ow! Jesus Christ."

Swearing earned Janelle another smack, and she dropped the pilfered Yorkie to stick her reddened fingers in her mouth. Their mam ruled the roost, despite being a short, unassuming woman, and even her husband gave her wooden spoon a wide berth.

"It'll be ready in five minutes," she told Janelle. "Go and help Tammy set the table. Rosie, be a love and carve the beef. I think your dad's watching the footy with Sam."

"That sounds about right," Rosie said, taking up the knife and stabbing the thick joint with a fork.

Her mam was busy with the mashed carrots, pepper flying everywhere as she gestured with the grinder. "It keeps them out of my way, and they'll be doing the washing up while I finish that nice bottle of plonk you brought."

Rosie put a hand on her heart, aghast. "It's not *plonk*. I'll have you know it's a very fine"—she checked the bottle—"Australian Shiraz."

"Lidl or Aldi?"

Rosie chuckled. It was impossible to pull the wool with her mam, and their respective budgets rarely stretched beyond the value supermarkets. "Lidl. They were two for six quid."

"Pity you're working tonight. We could've watched *Strictly* and got sozzled."

"I'd need to be bloody anaesthetised to watch that crap. I'd rather be scrapping with a nowty scrote." Rosie hefted the plate of meat and balanced the Yorkies on top. "Right, we're good to go. Grab the gravy and corral the kids. I'm on a deadline here."

Speed eating was a skill most emergency service workers perfected in their first year. Those who didn't tended to return to a nice nine-to-five, where lunch came bang on twelve o'clock, lasted an hour, and didn't give you an irritable bowel. Six years as a response officer had made Rosie a past master, and she was finishing her cherry cobbler as her mam shared out seconds in Yorkshire puds between the children.

"Tammy's got a boyfriend," Sam announced to all and sundry, lofting his entire pudding on his fork and biting into it. "And she kissed him round back of Kumar's."

From the corner of her eye, Rosie saw Tammy flush beetroot red and stop chewing.

"No, I never," Tammy said. "I don't even like boys."

"That's my girl," Rosie said. "You keep your options open, love. There's plenty of time to make these difficult life choices at a later date."

Tammy frowned, the advice flying right over her ten-year-old head. "Whuh?"

"Never you mind," their dad said, his deep voice almost a growl. Although he tolerated Rosie's flexible approach to her sexuality, he'd never quite managed to throw off the yoke of his strict Christian upbringing. Thanks to his wife's ardent liberalism, he no longer developed a twitch when Rosie brought a girlfriend over for tea, but he'd never be a card-carrying PFLAG member.

Rosie dabbed her lips with a tissue and then stood and kissed his bald head. "It's been a pleasure, as ever, but duty calls."

"There's a parcel of leftovers in the kitchen," her mam said. "Mind how you go out there."

"I will." Rosie leaned down and hugged her. "Thanks for tea. Text me if you need anything." Straightening, she eyeballed the kids. "Behave yourselves, rabble."

A chorus of farewells followed her to the doorstep, where she swapped the muggy warmth of the small terrace for the nip of Manchester in mid-March as she jogged across to her car. A quick check of her watch gave her fifteen minutes for her twenty-minute journey. With the following night's tea safely stashed on the passenger seat, and the radio blaring out a song she almost knew the lyrics to, she turned onto the main road and stuck her foot down.

CHAPTER FOUR

The skin on the woman's arms chronicled her advanced years and poor state of health. The surface was rippled into dehydrated ridges, and it was covered in old bruising and white scars marking previous falls or careless nudges against sharp-edged furniture. She mumbled something nonsensical as Jem tightened a tourniquet around her arm, but she made no attempt to pull away or otherwise acknowledge what Jem was doing. Jem shrugged out of her fleece and used a paper towel to wipe the sweat from her own forehead; the small bedroom was stifling, its air thick with the smell of incontinence and poor personal hygiene.

"Sharp scratch here, Dorothy." She gave the warning more out of habit than any expectation of a reply. The vein blew the instant the cannula pierced it, and she swore beneath her breath, pressing gauze over the rapidly spreading bruise. "It's always the ones who bloody need it," she said, ripping tape with her teeth whilst contemplating her next target.

Two courses of antibiotics hadn't touched Dorothy's urinary tract infection, and the carers at her residential home had taken a few hours to realise that her violent shivers were due to a high temperature and that the extra blankets they'd piled on her weren't actually helping. She was septic, her blood pressure low, her pulse and respiratory rate sky-high. She needed time-critical transfer to A&E for IV antibiotics, blood cultures, and fluid resuscitation. Instead, with ambulances queuing in hospital corridors and a stack of 999 calls still waiting for vehicles, Jem was managing alone with a single tank of oxygen and IV saline that she couldn't find a vein for.

For the most part, Jem didn't mind shifts on the rapid response vehicle. The single-manned cars had been introduced to hit government targets designed to get the sickest patients an ambulance within seven minutes. They stopped the clock and ensured essential aid could be rendered, but they couldn't transport a critically ill patient to the hospital. Jem usually enjoyed the challenge of solo working, and with no regular mate on her line, the RRV could be a welcome break from an ever-changing parade of newbies and numpties. On nights like this, however, when the service was operating at DEFCON 6, the RRV became a nightmare, trapping her on scene for hours without backup, no matter how unstable the patient. At least there were no relatives breathing down her neck this time, just three well-meaning but harried staff members who had a full house of demented residents demanding their attention and who had been only too happy to entrust one of them to her care.

"Sorry about this, love." She swabbed a fresh patch of Dorothy's arm and downgraded the size of her cannula, guided by the logic that any access was better than no access. It was a sound theory, and relief made her feel giddy as she flushed the line and taped it into place. "There we go. All done."

Using the door and a coat hanger as a drip stand, she set the saline running wide open and hit the voice button on her radio for the third time.

"Do I have an ETA on a crew?"

"That's a negative, Jem." Ryan, her usual dispatcher, sounded as despondent as she felt. "We still have thirty-four calls in the stack."

"Not your fault, pal. Just do your best, eh?"

A tentative knock interrupted his reply. She hurried to the door, grabbing the IV to prevent it pulling loose.

"We contacted her son, but he's at an office party so he's not coming over," the carer said. "He'll call in the morning to see how she is." The grim look Jem gave her must have been answer enough, because she sighed and ran a hand through Dorothy's patchy hair. "She has a 'Do Not Attempt Resuscitation' form. I'll get it out of her file for you."

"That'd be really helpful, thanks," Jem said. Under no illusions as to the outcome of the job, she had positioned the defib in readiness at Dorothy's side, but the DNAR removed the prospect of having to manage a cardiac arrest on her own if Dorothy finally succumbed.

"Can I get you a brew, love?" the carer asked.

"Maybe something cold?" Jem said. "Water or juice? If it's no bother."

"None at all. I'll see if I can find you a few biccies."

Jem's mouth watered at the prospect of food. It seemed as if days had passed since the cake she'd shared with Ferg in the Abbey Vale cafe. She rechecked Dorothy's observations, patted each of her pockets until she found her reading glasses, and made a start on her paperwork.

Eighty-three minutes, two custard creams, and a glass of apple juice later, the roar of a Merc's engine and the sound of boots on the gravel drive stopped her worrying about her depleted oxygen supply and the saline she was about to run out of.

"Hey, Spence," she said as the paramedic poked his head around the door. "It's good to see you."

"Likewise. Been here a while?" he asked, taking stock of the empty IV bags and raising an eyebrow at the blood pressure reading on the defib.

"Couple of hours. That BP's the best I've had."

"Crikey. We'd better get a wriggle on, for what it's worth. The hospitals are slammed. We've just done three hours on the corridor at West Penn."

"Joyful." She helped him and his mate slide Dorothy onto the stretcher. "Let's hope my next one's a bag of shite I can flirt off to a doctor, or I'll be stuck with them till the end of my shift."

She walked down to the ambulance with the crew, handing Dorothy's details over as they steered the stretcher through the maze of corridors, and swapping oxygen cylinders and saline at the vehicle. Spence smiled at her as she stowed the tail lift for him.

"I'd wish you good luck, but I'd be wasting my breath," he said, and laughed when she punched his arm. He'd spent six months working on a temporary line with her before he'd transferred to the Hazardous Area Response Team, which was five months more than anyone else had managed. "Take it easy, Jem."

"Yeah, you too."

The EMT hit the blues at the gate, the strobes illuminating sporadic spots of rain that had become a fully-fledged downpour by the time Jem reached the RRV. She stopped in the middle of the driveway and turned her face skyward, relishing the coolness against her heated cheeks and letting the droplets rinse the smell of Dorothy's room from her hair. Feeling less desperate to go back to station for a shower, she stowed her kit and settled into the driver's seat. Ryan reacted to her "clear on scene" message within seconds, simultaneously sending her a job and voicing her on the radio.

"We've got nothing else for this one," he told her, as she scrolled through the inputted information. "Are you okay to assess or would you rather wait for backup?"

"I'm okay to assess," she replied, pulling out of the car park and accelerating on the main road. "Are the police running?"

"Notified, but nothing available. Update us from scene."

"Wilco." She released the radio's lever, glancing again at the job's description. *Male. Approx 17 yoa. Unconscious with multiple injuries. Caller to meet crew on Ellery Lane.*

"Shit," she said, her sweaty palms slippery against the steering wheel. The address had been given as *Abbey Vale Nature Reserve*, with an almost apologetic addendum, *River near the lake*, which didn't really narrow it down. There were three lakes, interconnected by numerous rivers and streams, and Ellery Lane tapered out well short of them. For all she knew, the caller was the patient's assailant, and she had just agreed to follow him into the middle of nowhere.

Slowing for a red light, she hit the sirens and then crept through the junction, checking each lane was clear of traffic. She would be off the main roads in less than a mile, weaving through the back streets until she finally joined Ellery, a rutted, unlit track that few visitors used for access. She dried her left hand on her trousers and hovered over the talk request button, getting as far as putting her thumb on it but without exerting any pressure. What the hell would she say? "I've had a bit of a think and I've changed my mind. I'd rather sit on my arse at a rendezvous point and leave the lad to freeze or bleed to death"? She was no martyr, eager to rush headlong into danger for glory's sake, but she had an emergency button on her radio, a hefty torch, a waterproof jacket, and—thanks to an almost magnetic attraction for this kind of job—ample experience.

"Once more unto the breach," she said, and took a left onto Ellery Lane.

Any hopes of the call being a hoax disintegrated the instant she saw the man waving at her, a frantic two-armed windmill impersonation that had "bad job" written all over it. As she threw on her high-vis jacket, he ran to her car.

"Where's the ambulance?" he said, peering beyond her into the darkness.

"I'm it." She passed him her torch and yanked the boot open, collecting as much equipment as they could carry between them. "Grab this. And this. Sling that on your shoulder, it's easier." She studied him as she spoke. He looked familiar, although she couldn't place his face.

"You're the little dog lady," he said, neatly solving the head-scratcher as she slammed the boot shut. He dropped one of the bags she'd given him and snatched it up again before it could topple into a puddle. "From earlier in the Vale. I was with my mate."

"Ah, that's right," she said, realising he was one of the homeless lads and feeling marginally safer. He'd seemed harmless that afternoon and still seemed harmless now, his expression tight with fear and worry. A smell of damp earth and stale beer rolled off him, but his clumsiness was probably due to nerves rather than intoxication.

They set off together, skirting potholes and puddles as they left the lane and entered the wood, the torchlight bouncing around to pick out tall pines and deciduous trees still barren after winter.

"How far?" she asked, already out of puff beneath her burden and struggling to match his pace.

"Dunno, miss. A mile or so? It's hard to say."

"Okay." She tried to distinguish landmarks, anything she could use to describe the route and guide people in, but all she saw was the forest looming above her and the quagmire coating the ground. If there was a path, it had long ago been hidden by leaf litter. Twenty minutes later, with no sign of them closing in on their destination, she voiced Ryan and requested he mobilise Mountain Rescue, though she had no idea where to send them.

"Get them to Ellery, at least," she said, attempting to keep the strain from her voice. "I'll send someone back for them." Her feet slid sideways, and she lost her grip on her radio, Ryan's affirmative muffled by the mud.

The man stooped and retrieved it for her. "Not far now," he told her.

"Cheers. What's your name? I'm Jem."

"Brian, but I go by Bear." He touched the bristles of his thick beard and used the same two fingers to give a high-pitched whistle. At the answering yell, he altered his course slightly, and she heard the swift rush of water seconds before her torch picked out his companion crouching at the side of the river. Finding a burst of energy from somewhere, she sprinted toward the second man, and dropped her bags by the young lad he was attempting to shield from the worst of the rain. He'd used one of their sleeping bags to rig a shelter in some low branches and the other to cover the lad, but the wind was whipping across the nearby lake, driving rain in from all angles, and the river was swollen enough to have edged beyond the confines of its banks, saturating the ground she knelt on.

"Hey," she said. "How's he doing?"

"He stopped moaning," the man whispered, the words choked and distraught. "He were moaning at first, but he couldn't say owt."

She lifted the sleeping bag and trained her torch on the lad's face. He was younger than she'd expected, fifteen at most, scrawny and deathly pale, the visible parts of his body marred by bruises and lacerations. Twigs and strands of vegetation were tangled in his hair, and the rich smell of copper mingled with that of churned-up muck.

"Was he in the water?" She unzipped her response bag, her mind a whirl as she tried to order and prioritise her actions.

"Yeah, caught up on that tree." Bear pointed at a stooped trunk, its branches skimming the river's surface. "We couldn't leave him in there."

"You did fine." She fastened a hard collar around the lad's neck and secured an oxygen mask. On the monitor, his heart rate was sluggish and irregular at forty, and a flick of her pen-torch showed a blown left pupil. When she pulled her gloved hands from the back of his head, they were covered in fresh blood and small lumps of spongy tissue.

"Shit," she said, her heart sinking. She took off her high-vis and spread it on less sodden ground. "Help me lift him onto this. Gently, good, that's great."

The men handled the lad as if he were made of bone china, hovering close by once they'd repositioned him but evidently floundering without direct instruction.

"Can one of you go back to Ellery?" she asked, using her fleece to dry the lad's chest so she could attach the defib pads. "Wait for Mountain Rescue or whoever gets there first, and show them where we are."

"I'll go," Bear's mate said. He looked green around the gills, and when she nodded at him he scarpered as if afraid she might change her mind.

The crash of his footsteps was still audible when the lad's respiration rate abruptly dropped and his pulse took a similar nosedive. Jem positioned the ventilation bag and used it to support his faltering breaths.

"I need help out here," she shouted into her radio, too stressed to go through the proper channels. "This lad's about to arrest and I can't move him on my own."

"Police are en route," Ryan said. "No ETA."

"Thank fuck for that," she muttered. Then, louder, "Cheers. Better than nothing." She let the radio go, reaching for the suction as the lad gagged and coughed, the bag and mask falling aside to allow a thick spray of blood and vomit to splatter across her shirt.

His hands flew up without warning, ragged nails clawing at her arms and clothing.

"Shh, it's all right," she said, fighting to keep him still. "You're all right. I'm a paramedic. No one's going to hurt you."

A thin wail sent goose pimples rippling across her skin, and for an irrational moment she thought he might wake, until the noise cut off as if a switch had been hit, his hands falling limp, his body tensing and then relaxing. She watched, horrified, as eight breaths became five, then two, then stopped altogether.

"Shit." She looked at the monitor, its screen now showing an irregular mess of rapid spikes. "Bear, move! Get clear."

She hit *charge* on the defib as Bear stared, open-mouthed. The shock she administered made the lad's limbs jerk in unison and turned the spikes into an ominous flat line. She immediately started CPR, counting out the rate as she pushed on his bony chest, and wincing at the flex and crack of a rib beneath the heel of her hand. Thirty compressions to two breaths: she repeated the cycle without pause, willing the monitor to show even the slightest sign of recovery, but there was nothing except the beat she created, the line falling flat every time she stopped to give a breath. Time passed by in a blur of pumping first his chest and then the bag, as the rain continued to pour and further bursts of river water washed toward them. The exertion stopped her from feeling the cold, but she could feel the muscles in her arms beginning to shake, and she knew she had to rest.

"Bear, can you help me? Here, like this." She positioned his hands and started the metronome on the monitor. "This'll keep you to a rhythm. Don't push too hard. That's perfect."

Holding the torch in her mouth, she dragged her bag closer and found the IV pouch. Hypothermia ruled out a peripheral line, so she tried for the external jugular, letting out a short gasp of surprise when she hit it first time.

"Adrenaline's in," she said, marking the time on her glove.

Bear nodded as if he understood and then cocked his head to one side, his compressions faltering. "I can hear someone shouting," he said. "Should I go and fetch them?"

"Yes, go. I've got this." She readied her hands again, swapping roles smoothly as he scrambled to his feet.

"Won't be long, miss."

He quickly vanished from sight, swallowed up by the fog swirling off the lake. The metronome continued to tick, its measured beat a stark contrast to the frantic pounding of her pulse. Thirty to two, thirty to two, over and over, even though she knew it was hopeless, that it had already been too long and nothing she could do for the lad would fix him. Thirty to two. Thirty to two. Biting down on her lip, she bowed her head and persevered.

The snap and crunch of twigs sounded like firecrackers, sharp little explosions approaching at speed. Already twitchy after her half-mile trek through the woods with Grizzly Adams's less kempt brother for an escort, Rosie stopped dead and saw Kash reach for his Taser.

"The fuck?" he whispered. "Can you hear that?"

"Of course I can. You watch too many bloody horror films," she said, but then put her hand on her own Taser as she saw a large bearded man sprinting toward them. He stopped a couple of metres in front of them, his feet skidding in the wet leaves.

"This way," he said. "Come on, come on. Mickey, you go back to the road and wait for the rest of 'em."

Spurred by his urgency, they followed their new guide without question, hurdling fallen trees and splashing through boggy patches of grass. Mist rose and fell as they ran, and from a distance Rosie spotted a small, huddled figure, arms outstretched and tight as bowstrings as they pressed down repeatedly on a body.

"Shit. We'll need Major Crimes and SOCO here ASAP," she said. They hadn't been told much about the job, just that it was an injured male in the woods, with a medic requesting assistance. There had been no further updates en route, so no one had warned them about blundering into a possible crime scene.

Kash keyed his radio mike, leaving her to go ahead of him as he relayed the information and made the necessary requests. She closed the remaining distance with more care, panning her torch across the ground to ensure she didn't stomp on potential evidence. Engrossed in the resuscitation effort, the paramedic didn't react to Rosie's approach until the torch beam hit her. Then she looked up, shielding her eyes with one hand as she searched for the light's source.

Rosie swore quietly, almost flinging her torch into the river in her haste to avert its glare.

"Jesus. *Jem?*"

"Hey." Jem scarcely shaped the word. She was soaked to the skin and visibly exhausted, her hair plastered to her face, her movements stiff and automatic and accompanied by fitful coughing.

"Where's your inhaler?" Rosie snapped. She'd seen Jem use it on the bridge, and Jem obviously needed it now.

"In my fleece," Jem said. "It's on his legs."

Frigid water splashed up as Rosie knelt and began to search. She shivered, feeling the chill seep into her boots and clothing. Jem was wearing only a short-sleeved shirt, having wrapped both her coats around the lad, but she seemed oblivious to the cold, or simply past caring.

"Here you go," Rosie said, softening her tone. "Take a break for a few minutes. I can do this."

Jem nodded, coughing around the mouthpiece but still poised to work the ventilation bag.

"How long have you been here?" Rosie asked. An IV line was sticking out of the lad's neck, and glass syringes littered the ground. The job had already been thirty minutes old when it was passed through to her and Kash.

"I'm not sure," Jem answered in a hoarse whisper. "An hour? More, probably. Feels like forever."

"I'll bet. What the hell happened to him?"

"I don't know. Those blokes pulled him from the river. He was alive when I got here, but the back of his head's caved in…" She trailed off as Kash crouched beside them.

"Mountain Rescue and two Emergency Response docs are about ten minutes from Ellery," he said. "What can I do to help?" He directed this last to Jem, who gave him the ventilation bag.

"Two breaths when the defib tells you. I'm going to try to intubate him, but I need to get my stuff sorted first."

"Allah," he murmured, and Rosie saw him swallow nervously. She'd been with him on his first dead-in-bed call; he'd thrown up in the old chap's wastepaper basket. "Okay. Okay, right."

"Kash, this is Jem," she said to distract him. "Jem's the para from Barton last night. We only seem to meet in puddles."

Jem gave a small smile and a wave, and Kash spluttered a little before disguising his reaction beneath a theatrical throat clearing.

"You two are on a hell of a streak," he said.

"Tell me about it." Jem finished laying out her kit and took the bag back. "Tube first, the long, pale blue one. Then the syringe and this holder thingy." Almost lying on the ground, she cranked the lad's mouth open with a metal blade and peered along the blade's length. "Tube," she said. "Rosie, just stop compressions for a tick. Perfect, go again. Syringe."

Rosie watched as Jem secured the tube, her brow furrowed in concentration until she seemed satisfied that everything had gone to plan. Her quiet assurance was a far cry from the timid uncertainty she'd shown the previous night.

"That's better," she said, mostly to herself. "Thanks, Kash."

"No problem." He abandoned his attempts to stay dry and sat on the grass. "Major Crimes and SOCO are also en route," he told Rosie. "I'll have a scout around and see what I can see. Where exactly was he found?"

Jem aimed her torch toward the river, circling its beam on a tree with spindly branches. "He was stuck in there."

Kash walked carefully in the direction she'd indicated, examining the ground for signs of a struggle or evidence the lad had been anywhere but the water. As he followed the path of the river, his dark outline merged into the shadows and the driving rain, the occasional bob of his torch beam the only proof he was still out there.

"Do you want to swap?" Jem asked Rosie. "It's tiring after a while."

Rosie shook her head, despite the ache across her back. "I'm all right."

"We'll never get him out of here. Not like this." Jem stroked a muddy strand of hair from the lad's forehead as if in apology. "Helimed don't fly at night, and we won't be able to do CPR properly while we carry him. The docs will probably call it on scene."

"He's just a kid," Rosie said. She pressed down harder, doing her best textbook CPR, as if that alone might somehow change the outcome.

Jem's shoulders were slumped in defeat. She used her free hand to rub her face. "It's been too long, and his skull's in bits. Even in a hospital, I doubt he'd have come back from this. Stuck here, he's had no chance."

"Shit," Rosie whispered.

Jem nodded. "Yeah. Yeah, it is."

Jem couldn't feel her hands. A small heating pad sat in each of her palms, but she couldn't detect their warmth or grip them properly. Through sheets of rain, she watched the two Emergency Response doctors confer with the detectives beyond the perimeter established by the Scene of Crime Officers. A white forensic tent was rapidly being erected, but she could still see the lad's body, its face angled toward her by the weight of the ventilation bag she had only just relinquished. Even in death he didn't look peaceful. His half-lidded eyes glared when the torchlight caught them, and the tube curled his lips into a snarl, as if in defiance of the team's decision. She shuddered and turned at the sound of approaching footsteps, grateful for any distraction but even more so when Rosie crouched by her side.

"Will these help?" Rosie held out a large pair of gloves. "I pinched them off Kash. His hands are bigger than mine." Without waiting for an answer, she tugged one onto Jem's left hand and slid the pad beneath the leather. It was a snug fit, pressing the heat close, and Jem whimpered in relief, encouraging Rosie to repeat the process on her other hand. "Better?"

"Much, thanks." Jem made a tentative attempt to curl her fingers. "Puddles and sore hands: there's a definite theme developing for us."

They exchanged weary smiles, and Jem shuffled over on the plastic kit box, making space for Rosie to sit, and attempting to share the foil blanket one of the Mountain Rescue blokes had wrapped around her. They huddled closer, the foil crinkling and curling in the wind.

"What's going on over there?" Jem asked.

"Usual rigmarole," Rosie said. "The body will stay in situ while SOCO do their thing. He didn't have any ID on him, so we need to find out who he is. Given his age, it's likely someone will report him missing, and then it'll be a case of tracking his movements, speaking to his family and friends, and trying to establish whether this is murder, manslaughter, or simple misadventure." She shifted slightly so she could meet Jem's eyes. "One of the docs wanted a word with you, and DS Merritt has asked me to take you to Clayton for forensics and a statement."

"Forensics?" Jem said, struggling to connect the dots. She didn't know if it was stress or hypothermia or an adrenaline crash, but she felt as if someone had replaced her brain with putty, obliterating her ability to concentrate or follow simple logic.

"SOCO will need your uniform and your boots," Rosie said slowly, as though sensing there was a problem. "And swabs from the scratches on your arms."

"Oh." Jem had forgotten about the gouges the lad had inflicted. They'd still been oozing blood when an officer covered them in film to preserve trace evidence.

"Is he from your patch?" Rosie jerked her head toward the only other paramedic who had made it to the scene. Jem vaguely recognised him as local to Manchester, though he didn't work in her group. The pips on his epaulettes marked him as an Advanced Paramedic, and he hadn't yet bothered to introduce himself.

"Sort of," she said. "I think he's based in the city centre, but don't hold me to that. Rumour has it he's a bit of a knob."

"The rumours are right on the money. He took the docs to task for calling it."

"Really?" Jem's eyebrows almost hit her hairline. "How did that go down?"

Rosie chuckled. "Like a mug of cold sick. The lady doctor told him to wind his neck in and to get here sooner next time if he wanted to be involved in the decision-making."

Jem wished she'd been privy to that discussion. She might not know the AP, but she was very well acquainted with the "lady doctor" in question, and Harriet Lacey did not suffer fools.

"Speak of the devil," Rosie said, and Jem looked up to see the AP stalking across the small clearing. He was younger than her, and his ill-advised moustache and goatee combo spoke of a thwarted desire to mask his baby face. She knew his type well: excellent in paramedic theory but craptastic in practice.

"Jemima Pardon?" he said.

"Yes." Jem stayed seated, despite the authority he was trying to project. "Well, Jem. I go by Jem."

"I need to speak to you about all this." He gestured offhand toward the body. "Are you in tomorrow?"

"No, I'm back on a day shift on Wednesday."

He entered a note on his mobile. "Darnton, isn't it?"

"Yes, I work the six-six line."

"I know. I've heard all about you." There was no humour or kindness in the comment, just a snide undertone that made her bristle.

"I'm fine, by the way. Thanks for asking," she said, and he stared at her as if she'd slapped him. She didn't care. If his role here wasn't to support her and act as her advocate, then he was surplus to requirements. He scratched his beard, seeming simultaneously ill at ease and irritated by her insubordination.

"Wednesday morning, then. I'll arrange for you to be taken off the road."

"Fill your boots," she said, but he was already striding away, his radio bleeping for attention. "Tosser," she muttered.

Rosie leaned into her in a subtle show of support. "Ignore him," she said, and gave her an Uncle Joe's Mint Ball.

They sat in silence, sucking their sweets and waiting for permission to start the long walk back to Ellery. The scene grew brighter as a generator rumbled to life and then quieter as people dispersed to fingertip-search the immediate area. Jem was half-dozing, mechanically crunching the last of her mint, when a touch on her shoulder startled her. Harriet Lacey was standing in front of her with her arms folded, radiating authority in a manner the AP could only have dreamed of. If the mud allowed, she'd probably have been tapping her foot.

"Do I need to take a look at you?" she asked, and clipped a probe on Jem's finger regardless.

Jem squinted at the numbers. Pulse at one hundred and two, and oxygen saturations of ninety-five percent. Not brilliant, but acceptable by her standards.

"Apparently not," she said, and stuck out her tongue as Harriet narrowed her eyes.

"Warm shower, dry clothes, hot drink, and something to eat," Harriet told her, and then switched her attention to Rosie, who appeared to be on the verge of saluting. "Officer Jones, could you please call me on this number if Jem decides not to follow my advice?"

Rosie opened her mouth and snapped it shut again, taking the card Harriet held out. "Uh, okay, Doc. Yep, will do."

Jem didn't blame her for acquiescing. Harriet had an enviable knack of getting her own way. They hadn't seen each other for a while, but the circumstances and the adverse conditions hadn't diminished her take-no-prisoners countenance.

"Excellent," Harriet said. "Detective Sergeant Merritt said you're clear to go to Clayton, and you're to let her know when you've finished with everything there. Jem, I've spoken to your resource manager and told him you're indisposed for the rest of the shift. He's arranging for someone to collect the RRV."

"Thank you," Jem said, wondering how improper it would be to kiss her. Quite, she decided, and squeezed her hand instead.

"You're welcome." Harriet pocketed the probe. "Go on, get going."

Rosie waited until Harriet was well out of earshot before she spoke. "Bleedin' hell. There's no way I'm pissing *her* off. It's a hot shower and sustenance for you, young lady."

Jem gathered up the foil blanket. "No arguments from me. That sounds lovely."

They stood together, Jem wavering slightly as a head rush hit her. She had no idea how long was left on her shift. The hours she'd spent with Dorothy in the residential home seemed like several lifetimes ago.

Rosie flicked on her torch. "Ready?"

"Yep." Turning to leave, Jem glimpsed the raised flap of the forensic tent, a shock of white against the surrounding blackness. Someone lowered it almost at once, concealing the tent's contents, and Jem concentrated on picking her route over the irregular ground. She didn't look back.

Ellery Lane had never seen so much activity. Police vehicles— marked and unmarked—and two Mountain Rescue four-by-fours were parked at haphazard intervals, their drivers having attempted to avoid the divots and waterlogged ruts. SOCO and uniformed officers were hurrying between the vehicles, toting equipment or chattering into their radios. Glad to be heading in the opposite direction, Rosie steered Jem through the melee, aiming for her own patrol car, as an officer on sentry duty noted their departure.

"I'll ruin the seat," Jem said, her hand poised to open the passenger door. They were the first words she'd spoken since leaving the scene, barring the odd murmur to acknowledge hazards that Rosie pointed out. Slogging through the woods in torrential rain and a strengthening wind hadn't been conducive to a casual chat.

Rosie fished a large plastic sheet from her pocket. "Not to worry. SOCO gave me this for evidence preservation. Sadly, their generosity only stretched to one, so whoever drives this car next will be getting a wet arse."

Settling onto the plastic, Jem leaned her head back and closed her eyes, a blissful expression spreading across her face as Rosie started the car and banged the heating on full. Cool air blasted from the vents, but even that seemed preferable to being outside.

"It shouldn't take long to get warm," Rosie told her. "Have a nap if you want. I don't mind."

"I'm awake." Jem yawned and failed to open her eyes.

"Fibber. You sound like my dad. Fast asleep in front of the telly, but woe betide anyone who changes the channel."

"'Hey! I were watching that!'" Jem mimicked, her baritone grumble sounding so much like Rosie's dad that Rosie slapped the steering wheel and drove them into a pothole.

"Yours too?" she asked, bouncing them out the other side.

"All the bloody time. And it was always something crap like *Escape to Victory* or *The Dam Busters*."

Rosie slowed at the junction, giving a quick wave to the patrol unit waiting to turn. "Footy or *Songs of Praise* for mine. He loves booming along to the classics."

"Until he nods off mid-chorus."

"Exactly."

"Are you from around here?" Jem sat up straighter, curiosity seeming to banish her weariness. "Only, your accent's a bit hodgepodge. Sort of Manc, but then I don't know...Oldham? Rochdale?"

"Good ear," Rosie said, impressed. "I was born in Hathershaw, Oldham, but my parents split when I was seven, and me and my mam moved to Newton Heath. Eight years later, she remarried, and I ended up with two sisters and a brother."

"That must have been a shock to the system."

"I hated it, and I hated my stepdad." Rosie slowed the car, surprised by her admission. At the time, she'd taken to smoking dope, drinking cheap booze on the streets, and shagging around, but she'd never been brave enough to tell her mam why. Later she'd been too ashamed, and that shame had followed her into adulthood. She shook her head, still mortified. "For so long I'd had my mam to myself, and then I had to share her with this complete stranger who looked funny and talked funny and ate weird shit. He's from Ghana, and fuck me, I thought it was the end of the world."

"You were a teenager, Rosie. Everything's the end of the world at that age. And I'm guessing you got over yourself."

There was no condemnation in Jem's reply, and Rosie loosened her death grip on the steering wheel.

"I got over it, slowly but surely," she said. "Janelle—the first of the kids—was a godsend. She was such a sweetheart, I couldn't help but fall in love with her. She's a right little bugger now, but back then, cute as a button."

The bright pink of a takeaway sign lit Jem's smile. She'd relaxed during the journey, regaining a hint of colour to her cheeks and looking less like she might warrant a diversion to the nearest A&E.

"I can't count all my brothers and sisters," she said at length, as if she'd held a mental debate before broaching the topic. "I was fostered for years, and I saw kids come and go all the time."

"Oh." Rosie didn't quite know what to say, so she defaulted to candour. "That must've been shit."

"It certainly had its moments," Jem said with wry understatement. "I was lucky, eventually. I got adopted. Not many kids in care find a family as late as I did."

"How old were you?"

"Almost ten, but my mum and dad had been fostering me for two years by then." Jem tugged on her earlobe. She'd turned toward the window again, casting her face into shadow. "I don't know what they saw in a seven-year-old with knackered lungs who could barely write her own name, but I know I'd have been lost without them." She cleared her throat uneasily. "Sorry, I don't—I think I'm just tired."

Rosie concentrated on driving, not wanting to make things awkward. "We'll be there soon. And rest assured, what's divulged within the confines of this manky and very damp patrol car stays within its confines."

Jem faced forward, no longer tormenting her ear. "Okay, then. Let's talk about cheerier things."

"Like what?"

"Good question," Jem said as if momentarily flummoxed by the concept of joviality. "Uh, footy team? Pets? To dunk or not to dunk?"

Rosie began to tick her answers off on her fingers. "Man City. Fluffy the bearded dragon." She paused, digits still outstretched, to address Jem's muffled laugh. "Is something amusing you?"

Jem shook her head. "Nope, not at all. Carry on. It's a fine name."

Rosie did her best to look askance but gave up when she almost clipped the kerb. "Bugger, apologies." She overcorrected and clobbered a couple of cat's eyes instead. "I inherited Fluffy from the family of a dead smack rat, and he sort of answers to it, so we're stuck with it. Now, where were we? No to dunking, because I'm rubbish at it and I don't like crumbs floating in my tea. How about you?"

"Bolton, for my sins," Jem said. "No pets of my own, but I walk other people's dogs, and ditto on the dunking. I have on occasion sucked my tea up through a Twix, though."

"Well, that's disgusting," Rosie said. "You must teach me how to do it." The taxi in front of them dawdled up to a traffic light and sped through at the last second, leaving her to slam her brakes on for the red. "Arse," she muttered, tempering her road rage in deference to Jem.

"I'd have blasted the stupid sod," Jem said, apparently not as mild-mannered as Rosie had assumed. Her stomach rumbled, and she clapped a hand atop it. "God, sorry. I get proper nowty when I'm hungry."

Rosie thought of the leftovers her mam had packed and the promise she'd made to the doctor. The light changed, and she accelerated smoothly through it.

"If you can hang on for another ten minutes," she said, "I've got just the thing."

CHAPTER FIVE

The forensics tech dropped the bloodied swab into a plastic bag and sealed the bag's edge. "Sorry about that," he said, handing Jem a piece of gauze to dab against the scratch. The wounds were superficial, already crusted and closed, but he'd seen a speck of something in the corner of one and dug in deeply, aggravating it enough to make it bleed.

"Have you finished?" Rosie asked him. Her arms were full of paper evidence sacks, and although she'd waited on the sidelines while he meticulously dated and annotated multiple swabs, her patience was clearly running thin.

"Yes, I've finished," he said. "I'll come back for your uniforms in half an hour."

"Great." Rosie all but shoved him out of the locker room and bolted the door behind him. She stopped a metre away from Jem and rearranged the sacks in an arbitrary order, as a faint flush began to colour her throat. "Right. I'll, um…I'll close my eyes if you want."

Despite an almost overwhelming urge to agree, Jem shook her head. They were both professionals and in circumstances beyond their control, so they didn't need to feel awkward about this extremely awkward situation where they were going to have to get half-naked in front of each other. Besides which, it could have been worse: she could have been stripping off in front of the tech. Aware that standing around in wet clothing wasn't doing either of them any favours, she squared her shoulders and bit the bullet.

"I have to warn you," she said, "my knickers and bra don't match."

"Disgraceful!" Rosie opened the first bag. "I'm shocked and appalled in equal measure."

"Sod off." Jem began to unfasten her trousers, sliding her belt and radio clip free and emptying her pockets. "I bet yours don't either."

Rosie peeked beneath her own shirt and popped the button on her trousers. She made a show of deliberating before cocking her head to one side to deliver the verdict. "If by 'match' you mean 'clash in spectacular fashion,' then yes, they match."

Her audacity proved contagious, prompting Jem to strip off her trousers without fretting about the shape of her arse or how untoned her thighs were. She handed the trousers over and unbuttoned her shirt, folding it inward and placing it in the bag Rosie held ready.

"That's all they'll need," Rosie told her. "You get to keep the rest."

"How very generous of you."

"I am magnanimous to a fault." Rosie gave Jem a third bag. "Could you do the honours?"

"Certainly." Jem opened the bag wide, scrutinising the lockers behind Rosie's head as Rosie wrestled her legs from trousers that— judging by the amount of swearing—were clinging to her damp skin. Jem counted seven lockers in the first row, each decorated with an average of four photos, with pets outnumbering babies by three to one.

"Fer fuck's—Jem?"

Jem tore her gaze from a picture of a hamster perched in a shoe and followed the appeal downward, to find Rosie sitting on the floor, one leg free and the other trapped by a concertina of material at the shin.

"How on earth have you managed that?" she said.

Rosie hoisted her ensnared ankle. "It took a fair amount of skill."

Jem crouched in front of Rosie and felt her ears go hot. Rosie had already taken off her shirt, giving Jem a full-on view of a pastel blue bra and a well-defined torso. She tried to avert her eyes, only to end up gawping at a pair of red cotton briefs.

"Told you they clashed," Rosie said, sounding more amused than abashed.

"Yep." Jem was back to studying the lockers.

"Jem?"

"What?"

"You're mostly naked as well."

"I know that," Jem said. She still had her T-shirt on, though.

"I don't think we can do this if you're determined to stare at that hamster."

"How the hell did you—?" Jem gave up; she knew she'd been rumbled. She let her shoulders sag. "It *is* a very cute hamster."

"Are you really going to leave me to the mercy of that forensics bloke?" Rosie asked, sotto voce, the intimacy enough to make Jem's ears tingle again.

"Uh, no." Jem licked her lips and tried for something more emphatic. "Definitely not. Point your toes like a ballet dancer."

The trousers capitulated without much of a fight, and Jem tucked them into the bag, as Rosie stood and performed a neat pirouette en route to collect a pile of spare clothing.

"Gift from the custody suite," she said.

Jem took the grey outfit the tech had supplied. "He seems to have overlooked my top half," she said, displaying a single pair of jogging bottoms.

"More fool him," Rosie murmured, and then clapped a hand over her mouth. "Oh, fuck, I didn't mean…Well, obviously I *did* mean—but I didn't. Fuck. I'm just going to stop talking."

Jem's snort of laughter shot straight out of her nose. Now beyond any sense of modesty, she used her soggy T-shirt to wipe the snot from her face, peeling off the shirt when she was finished and dropping it onto the plastic.

Giving it a wide berth, Rosie headed for one of the lockers and returned with a pair of oversized hooded tops.

"Here, I keep a couple of emergency spares." She rubbed her hands, all business again, and ushered Jem toward the bathroom.

"There's shower gel and shampoo in there, and fresh towels. Come on, hop to it, or you'll catch your death."

Jem hopped to it, stripping off completely and then standing beneath the water for a while, letting her fingers and toes thaw as the force of the spray eased the stiffness from her muscles. Feeling less decrepit, and mindful of Rosie waiting in the locker room, she washed and dried quickly, throwing on her borrowed outfit to preserve any residual warmth. She propped each foot in turn on a low stool, folding up the overlong cuffs of her jogging bottoms and scowling at her hair in the foggy mirror. She couldn't do a thing to tame it without a brush.

"Rosie? Have you got a comb?" she shouted from the safety of the bathroom, too embarrassed to stick her head out of the door.

"Yeah, hang on. You decent?"

"Yes, but—"

Rosie was in before Jem could finish the sentence, brush in one hand and a choice of combs in the other.

"Ahhh," she said, drawing out the sound. She surveyed the disaster in front of her with a speculative eye rather than the derision Jem had feared, and then set down the brush and one of the combs. "Do you want me to…Look, my mam's a hairdresser, and she's taught me a few tricks. C'mere." She pulled up the stool and ushered Jem onto it.

"I can manage," Jem protested, entirely without conviction. Half expecting Rosie to whip out a pair of scissors, she relaxed when Rosie stuck to teasing out the tangles with the comb.

"If you take it this way, it follows the natural parting, see?" Rosie said. "And then your fringe falls like so, which complements the shape of your face."

Jem peeked up to see whether Rosie was taking the piss, but she seemed quite serious.

"Think it'd be better a bit shorter?" Jem asked. Rosie had achieved a minor miracle with her fringe in less time than it usually took Jem to swear at it.

"Definitely. If I were you, I'd get rid of most of the length. Go for a bold pixie cut, with a splash of colour. Auburn highlights would bring out the hazel in your eyes."

"'A bold pixie,'" Jem said. "My regular hairdresser would probably translate that as 'gormless goblin.'"

"In which case, Ms. Pardon, book in at Salon Chez Croquembouche—"

Jem started to laugh. "Rosie, that's a big pile of choux buns."

Rosie waved off her protest. "Yeah, but it's French so it sounds dead classy. Now, where were we? Right, yes: book yourself in and I'll get you sorted for a very reasonable fee."

"You will?" Jem touched a tuft by her ear, part of her scared to death of committing, part of her swept along by Rosie's confidence, and a tiny secret part whispering that this would be a good excuse to keep in touch with her. "Okay, then. Name your price."

Rosie twirled and pocketed the comb. "I am very partial to any and all kinds of chocolate biccies. And Special Toffee. Original or treacle, I'm not fussy."

Jem pushed her glasses to the top of her head, the pen slipping from her fingers and landing on her statement. Busy recounting the night's events, she hadn't really been listening to Rosie pottering about in the kitchen adjoining the small staffroom, and had assumed a brew and hopefully toast might be on the horizon. The ping of the microwave, however, heralded a smell far richer than that of toast, one redolent of winter Sundays at home, heaped dishes filling the table as sleet battered the windows.

"Voila." Rosie slid a steaming plate onto Jem's paperwork. "Try not to get gravy on that, eh?"

Jem stared at the roast dinner, afraid it might vanish like a mirage if she dared stick her fork in it. "Where the hell did you magic this from?"

"Leftovers from last night's tea at my mam's. Sorry, there's only half a Yorkie. The kids can eat their own weight in those buggers."

"Not a problem," Jem mumbled around a perfectly crisped spud. "God, has she done these in goose fat?"

"As if there's another option." Rosie waggled a fork-speared sprout. "How are you getting on with your statement?"

"Just about finished. I can't promise coherence, but the sequence of events should be fine."

"It's half-five in the morning, Jem. I'll be impressed if you've managed to spell your name right."

Jem mopped up her gravy with a piece of beef. "And yet here we are, eating dinner."

"We are merely following doctor's orders. If you clean your plate, I won't have to phone her and report back on you."

"Don't worry, I'll text her later and give an update."

"Excellent," Rosie said, a little too cheerfully. "That gets me off the hook." She looked like she wanted to say more, but she changed the subject instead. "Do you have plans for your day off? Tomorrow, that is. I'm assuming you'll be asleep for most of today."

Jem carefully divided a parsnip baton into three equal pieces. While she was glad to shift the focus from Harriet, this topic wasn't exactly an improvement. Stacking the parsnip onto her fork, she debated lying through her teeth and then wondered why telling the truth seemed like such a betrayal.

Rosie took a measured sip from a mug of coffee as she waited for Jem to answer. She wasn't blatant in her scrutiny, but Jem was nevertheless reminded that Rosie's career depended on her ability to read people. To make matters worse, Jem was generally rubbish at telling fibs.

"I have a date," she said, deciding to pull the metaphorical sticking plaster straight off the wound.

"Fab. Tell me all the gruesome details," Rosie said, seeming genuinely intrigued. She leaned closer to the table, her eyes glinting with mischief. "Is it one of those swipe left, swipe right affairs?"

"Christ, no," Jem blurted, and then worried she'd sounded like a prude. For all she knew, Rosie spent her free time searching online swiping sites for potential partners. She set down her fork, the parsnip forgotten. "I've never used one of those. Have you?"

"Oh, all the time. I can't get enough of them. I have to leave my phone on silent, or the notifications drive Kash berserk. I can't help it, I'm insanely popular." Rosie held Jem's gaze for a beat before cackling and stabbing another sprout. "And if you believe that, I've got a bridge I'd like to sell you."

"How much are you asking?" Jem said, dead serious.

Rosie choked and wiped her eyes with her fork hand, launching her sprout into oblivion. "Fuck me," she said, halfway beneath the table on a rescue mission. "I think I've hit night shift hysteria." She reappeared, sprout intact. "So, who's the lucky chap or chappess? Delete as appropriate."

"Chappess," Jem said, reasonably confident that wouldn't come as a shock. "Her name is Sylvie, and she's a friend of a friend of my housemate, Ferg. I'm guessing he's not told her much about me, because she said to wear 'something comfortable, with trainers.'"

"Hmm." Rosie cradled her mug, deep in thought. "Could be one of those spa day and cream tea fandangos."

"That'd be nice." Jem hadn't considered the possibility. She'd been too preoccupied conjuring up images of assault courses and boot camps, whilst planning to succumb to a migraine first thing Tuesday morning. "I wish I was sportier," she admitted. "I walk the dogs as often as I can, but I can't seem to find another exercise that suits."

"You mean one that doesn't set your chest off?"

Jem took up her mug and swallowed a mouthful of tea. She was full and cosy and just the right side of sleepy, and chatting to Rosie felt as comfortable as sitting in her pyjamas in front of the gas fire, though she wasn't sure what Rosie would think about the analogy.

"Yeah, see, I like swimming, but the cold water doesn't like me," she said. "And the one and only time I went jogging, an octogenarian who'd lapped me twice made me sit on the park bench and almost called an ambulance." She picked at a loose piece of the tabletop. "Maybe I should get a bike or something."

"Or a wetsuit," Rosie suggested. "If the cold is the only thing stopping you from swimming."

"I'd stand out like a sore thumb in a public pool."

"That bothers you, doesn't it? Standing out?"

Jem didn't shy away from the question. Her childhood had been a constant confusion of blending in and fighting for attention. Each new group home or temporary family had required her to toe the line and find her place within them, while the social workers pushed her to make herself unique, to give prospective parents a reason to want her. Even as a child, it hadn't taken long for her to realise she stood out for all the wrong reasons.

"I'd rather be part of the crowd. It's easier. But most of the time that doesn't really work for me either." She drained her mug and pulled out her statement. She didn't want to seem pathetic, and neither did she want Rosie to think she was angling for sympathy. "I should get this finished."

"Aye." Rosie gathered the empty plates. "If you've got any space left, there's cherry cobbler for dessert."

Jem patted her belly. "I shouldn't really. Are you having any?"

Rosie gave her a look. "We did CPR for ages and walked miles in the rain. Yes, I'm having pudding." She waited a few seconds, as if sensing Jem's crumbling resistance. "There's custard," she added.

"You swine," Jem said, entirely without malice.

Rosie grinned, all teeth and triumph. "Hold that thought. I'll be back in a jiffy."

CHAPTER SIX

The vibration of Rosie's mobile was as irritating as a low-flying wasp, its insistent drone dragging her from a nightmare whose sole distinct image had been a pallid, lifeless hand. She woke to more rain beating on the roof tiles, her mouth parched and her pulse drumming in her ears. The buzzing cut off before she could enter her passcode, but Stephanie Merritt's number was top of the phone log, and Steph answered Rosie's return call within two rings.

"Morning, sunshine," she said, bright as a button. "What would you say to a bit of overtime?"

"What?" The word barely made it past the dryness in Rosie's throat. She ungummed her lips with the back of her hand and tried again. "What time is it?"

"Half-twelve. Sorry, did I wake you?" Steph didn't sound at all remorseful. "I thought you'd be up by now."

Unlike Rosie, Steph had an enviable ability to function on four hours' sleep. She would have been to the gym on her way home, slept like a log, and woken perked to perfection. Rosie wanted to reach down the phone line and throttle her.

"I only got home at nine. I had to take Jem across to Darnton, so I hit all the traffic." She heard tapping in the background, as if Steph was typing, and then the ring of another phone. "Are you in work?"

"Yes." The tapping stopped. "The shit's hit the proverbial after the post-mortem on our lad from last night. The pathologist ruled the head injury as cause of death but couldn't determine whether it was inflicted deliberately. He found other injuries consistent with an assault, though, and the tox screen was positive for alcohol, cannabis, and spice."

"Fucking hell. Have you ID'd him?"

"Within the last hour. My lot are opening out the overtime for house-to-house, and I was hoping you might come and search the family manse with me and Ray before we get saddled with some knob who'll drive us both to distraction."

Rosie rolled over and stared at the ceiling. She really wanted to go. The case had the potential to be massive, and being involved at such a critical stage would put a tick in all the right boxes, should she ever take the plunge and apply for the National Investigators' Examination. On the downside, she felt like death warmed over and didn't want to risk making a mistake because she had a night shift hangover.

"Are you bringing the coffee?" she asked.

Steph didn't miss a beat. "Latte with a double shot of espresso and two sugars. Get here for half-one and I'll have it waiting for you."

Rosie made it to Clayton ten minutes later than arranged, but Steph held up her end of the bargain, throwing in a couple of pastries in lieu of breakfast. As predicted, she didn't appear troubled by scant sleep and a stressful case. She'd curled her dark hair into a pristine knot, her shirt was crisp and pressed, and her makeup was flawless. Sitting in the passenger seat of the pool car, Rosie dabbed crumbs from her uniform trousers but could do little else to improve her sleepwalked-through-a-hedge-backwards look.

"Ray's meeting us after he's organised the door-to-doors," Steph said as she waited at the car park barrier. "Kash is coming along as well, so you two can start the search while we interview Mum and siblings." She fished in her leather-bound, official-issue Major Crimes binder and pulled out a sheet of paper with a school photo clipped to its top corner. "Here you go: Kyle Parker, fourteen years old. A mate of his PM'd the Manchester Met Facebook page this morning when we ran a report and a description of Parker on our wall. He had a distinctive scar from an old fracture, so we hit the jackpot early. According to the message, the friend hasn't seen him for two, maybe three weeks."

Rosie looked at the image, finding it difficult to reconcile the smirking lad—cowlicked hair, cockeyed school tie, freckles across the bridge of his nose—with his traumatised body.

"He seemed smaller last night," she said. "It's weird, isn't it, how big a part personality plays."

"Without that, we're just meat and bones." Steph flicked her visor down, blocking out a rare glare of sunshine that was bouncing off the wet road. She sounded far more sanguine than Rosie, but then she hadn't spent an hour pounding on the child's sternum.

"Has he been missing from home or skipping school?" Rosie asked.

"Both, apparently." Steph turned the page in Rosie's hand. "There's a transcript of the first contact with Mum halfway down. The rumour mill on Curzon beat the official death message visit, and she phoned within ten minutes of us receiving the Facebook PM. Needless to say, I can't wait to meet her."

Rosie read through the transcript, reached the end, and reread it to let it sink in. Deborah Parker—"Call me Debbie"—had opened the conversation by declaring she'd always known her eldest son would "go and do something fucking stupid." Having declined to attend the mortuary to identify his body—"I'll send my dad. I've got to collect my bennies at eight"—she had ended the call with an enquiry about "doing one of them press conferences like what you see on the telly."

"She sounds delightful, doesn't she?" Steph said. She turned off the main road and braked for the first in a series of speed bumps designed to stop joy riders from haring round the estate.

Rosie clung to the armrest and watched rows of grim, grey-washed houses pass by. Thanks to her years on response, she knew the Curzon estate like the back of her hand, knew which of the flats had been colonised by addicts and alcoholics, and where the worst of the recidivists lived. Red door: twenty-eight-year-old male hanging. White door with the scuff marks: domestic assault, vic refused to press charges. North of the precinct, the houses were largely owned by right-to-buy residents, people who had lived on the estate for years, raised their children, scraped together enough for a mortgage, and then watched the area disintegrate around them. Burglaries and car thefts were their main complaints, as they were repeatedly targeted by those on the south side. The crimes reoccurred like clockwork, timed to hit insurance payouts, with the replacement televisions and computers disappearing almost as soon as they entered the houses. The luckier families could afford to move away, but most were stuck fixing bars to their windows and installing alarm systems that everyone ignored.

"Are we, perchance, heading to the south?" she asked.

"Battersby Walk," Steph confirmed. "Smack bang in the deepest, darkest, southernmost corner."

"Bleedin' hell," Rosie said. "I should've stayed in bloody bed." She and Kash had once spent a particularly lively set of nights on Battersby racking up an assault with a deadly weapon, two heroin overdoses, and a fatal leap from a third-floor balcony, in one record-breaking thirty-six-hour stretch. Even the stray dogs went around there in pairs.

"Aw, come on, no pouting," Steph said in a tone Rosie recognised all too well. It was the one Steph had used to wrap Rosie round her little finger, to get her to stay out for "just one more drink" or to call in sick when Steph fancied a duvet day. It had lost its efficacy in the end, but now, with Rosie's guard crumbling beneath three hours' sleep, it sent a flutter of sensation down her spine that wasn't altogether unpleasant.

"How many Parker kids are there?" she asked, making a determined return to the business at hand.

"Five now. Girls at eighteen months and eleven, and lads at four, six, and nine. They'll all be at home, so we should be able to have words with the two eldest, if they're in any fit state. I've written up an interview plan with Social Services, and one of the family liaison officers will be sitting in with us. We'll probably have to go back tomorrow to finish everything up."

Rosie nodded, glad that her contact with the family would be indirect, limited to sifting through their possessions rather than dealing with their emotions, whatever those emotions might be. There were countless ways in which people reacted to a loss, and she knew Debbie Parker's disdain for her son was liable to evolve at a moment's notice, with the usual processes of anger, denial, and grief all on the cards. Rosie had seen people punch holes in walls and throw televisions through windows. When cast in the role of messenger, she had taken a few punches herself, assaults that often ended with her assailant collapsed in her arms, their sense of loss so complete that it stole everything from them. She had wept with grown men, held on to children, and gripped the hands of bereaved mothers more times than she could count, but she had never tried to save a child one day and had to look his mum in the eye on the next.

"Here we go. Number thirteen. Christ, unlucky for some, eh?" Steph said, parking outside a dour, pebble-dashed house. Its front lawn, mostly taken up by a large trampoline, had been stomped into a muddy pulp, and overflowing bins stood like sentries along a crazy paving path.

Rosie's legs felt leaden as she got out of the car, the stench of nappies and rotting dog food like a slap in the face after half an hour of breathing Steph's designer perfume.

Steph joined her on the pavement, briefcase in hand and binder readied. "Cocktails at the Blue Door tonight. My treat."

Rosie murmured her accord without committing. She'd always found it easier to keep the peace and think of an excuse later than to immediately derail one of Steph's plans. "After you," she said, holding open a gate that almost fell off in her hand. They navigated the path in single file, aware of curtains twitching in neighbouring houses, and setting a dog barking before Steph could knock.

"Who is it?" a woman yelled. "If it's the press, you can fuck off!"

Steph readied her warrant card. "It's DS Merritt, Ms. Parker. We spoke on the phone."

The door opened a crack, allowing a woman with straggly bleach-blond hair and mascara-smeared cheeks to glower at them. Her hand shot out, grabbing Steph's ID and pulling it closer.

"It's Debbie," she said. "Not Ms. Parker, just Debbie."

"This is PC Jones," Steph said. "She's going to help with the search."

"You were the one what found Kyle?" Debbie directed the question at Steph, stepping clear of the door and escorting them into an uncarpeted hallway strewn with shoes and school bags and small coats.

Steph paused to pick up a pink jacket, draping it over the banister so it wouldn't get trodden on. "No, Ms.—Debbie. I was called to the scene by PC Jones, who did everything she could to help Kyle."

"Yeah, whatever." Debbie sniffed in apparent contempt, but she was chewing a ragged path through the gloss on her bottom lip.

"I'm sorry we couldn't do more," Rosie said. She shook her head at the inadequacy of the sentiment. "We tried our best, we really did, but nothing worked." She shuddered, hit by an unwelcome flash of Jem, drenched and freezing, struggling alone in the dark with a dead child. Something of the horror of that night must have shown in her expression, because Debbie sobbed and quickly covered her mouth to stifle the sound.

"Mam?" A girl's voice, young and fearful, carried from behind one of the closed doors. "Mam, you okay?"

"I'm fine, Lily." Debbie wiped her face and straightened her shoulders, steel returning to her posture and voice. "Get Maisie's milk ready and put them beans on for you and Harley."

"All right, Mam." Pans clanged, and Rosie heard bare feet pattering across a tiled floor. "I'll do toast with the beans."

"Good girl. Cut them crusts off for Harl," Debbie told her.

"I know, Mam. I'm not stupid," Lily yelled, and Debbie managed a wan smile as a hint of normality bled back into their lives.

Steph cleared her throat, obviously reluctant to intrude but needing to get her side of the proceedings underway.

"In here." Debbie opened the living room door and paused on the threshold, turning to Rosie. "Kyle's room is the second left off the landing. I've not—I went in there this morning, sat on his bed, but I didn't move anything."

"That's not a problem," Steph said before Rosie could respond. "If PC Jones needs to take an item to assist the investigation, it will be logged and returned to you if at all possible."

Rosie didn't catch Debbie's reply; the door was already closing behind them, leaving her alone in the hallway. Concerned for the eleven-year-old fending for herself and her siblings, she pushed cautiously at the kitchen door and peered through the small gap. Warm air washed over her, carrying the scent of toast and tomato sauce, and she could see Lily and two younger children sitting on cushions on the floor, their dishes on their laps, their attention fixed on a wall-mounted television. The gas stove was off, no one was running with knives, and the baby's fingers were nowhere near any of the plug sockets.

"Atta girl," Rosie whispered, as Lily held her toast with one hand and the baby's bottle with the other. The scenario was so familiar that Rosie could almost feel the rhythmic tug on the bottle as the baby suckled. She closed the door as quietly as she had opened it and walked upstairs.

Jem handed her dad a mug of tea and settled on the carpet by his chair, her arm tucked around his leg and her cheek pressed against his thigh. She closed her eyes as his fingers stroked through her hair. She had never been a lap child, so sure of her place that she could curl up on an adult's knee whenever she needed comfort. The floor seemed safer somehow, close but not close enough to be considered presumptuous, and despite her dad's best efforts to reassure her that this family—her new family—was forever, she had never broken free of all her old habits.

"Do you want to tell me about it?" he asked. He always bought the early edition of the *Manchester Evening News*, and one glance at its headline had prompted him to phone her. She couldn't count the number of her jobs that had made the front page. Her mum had kept a scrapbook for a while, until things had started to get ridiculous.

"Not really," she said. She knew the lad's name now and what he had looked like before someone assaulted him and left him to die. She raised her head so she could see her dad, and he smiled down at her, crinkling more lines into his forehead and dimpling his cheeks. He touched the skin beneath her eyes, his fingertips rough with calluses. He'd been digging in the garden when she arrived, and he still smelled like damp soil and lavender.

"You look tired, Jem."

"I am. I didn't sleep much."

"Me neither. Our latest arrival saw to that."

"How old?" she asked. The foster child was with Jem's mum at a doctor's appointment, so she hadn't met him yet.

"Eight months. Emergency domestic violence placement. He came to us in the wee hours with a swollen cheek and a busted lip."

"Poor little mite." She took her dad's hand and squeezed it. "He'll settle once you've worked your magic."

He chuckled. "Wasn't magic with you, love. We spiked your Horlicks with brandy."

"You never did!"

His mug wobbled as he laughed, and he put it down for fear of spilling his tea. "No, but we were very tempted, especially when you were up all night coughing your socks off."

"Fair point," she conceded. "Might've worked better than my inhalers." Stretching her legs out, she leaned back on the chair, trying to alleviate a stubborn niggle across the base of her spine. She had woken stiff and miserable after three hours of broken sleep, and the paracetamol Ferg had propped by the kettle had barely taken the edge off.

"Here."

A plump cushion dropped onto the floor beside her. She tucked it under her bottom without protest, too weary to be stoical, and watched the flames licking over the kindling and coals on the open fire. This little snug, sequestered at the back of the Victorian semi with a view over the fruit trees and the frog pond, had always been her sanctuary. Her mum had never paid it much mind, allowing Jem's dad to cram it with mismatched armchairs, antique wooden furniture, multicoloured throw rugs, and old ships he'd half-built from model kits. As there had invariably been more children than bedrooms, Jem had taken to hiding away in here, spending hours with her dad while he read to her, beat her at Monopoly and Go Fish, and repaired the damage wrought by an education in constant flux. Whenever she came home for a visit, it was the first place she checked, if her dad wasn't in his greenhouse.

"You sure you don't want to talk about it?" he asked quietly.

She drew her knees up again and wrapped her arms around them. "There's not much to say. I did what I could, but it wasn't enough, and he died."

"The report said you were on your own out there."

"Aye, for a while. Then Rosie came, and she helped a load."

She heard him sip his tea, and the satisfied sigh that followed his first taste of a decent cuppa. His favourite method of contemplation was slow and steady, with a brew in hand.

"Is Rosie one of yours? I don't recognise her name." He kept the enquiry light, but there was curiosity simmering below the surface.

"She's a police officer. We met on a couple of jobs over the weekend, and she took my statement this morning."

Her dad nudged her bum with his toe. "Your ears are pink."

"They are not!" She clapped a hand over one, full of righteous indignation until she felt the heat there. "Bloody hell."

"The cat has scarpered from the bag, Jemima. Elaborate," he said with uncontained glee. He loved gossip almost as much as he loved growing oversized competition veggies, which, given his impressive trophy cabinet, was saying a lot.

She threw up her hands. "Okay, okay. I like her. She's funny and pretty, and daft as a brush, and she gave me gloves and half her roast dinner."

Her dad toe-poked her again. "When's she coming for tea?"

"She's not. She promised to cut my hair for me, I promised to pay her in toffee, and that's all there is to tell. Besides which, I have a date with 'wear something comfortable' Sylvie tomorrow."

"Ah, that's tomorrow, is it?"

"Yeah." Jem twisted a tassel on the cushion. "I don't think anything will come of it, Dad. Nothing ever does."

"Now, now." Her dad leaned forward and unravelled the cotton before it could turn her finger white. "That's absolutely not the spirit, Jem."

"I know. I can't help it." She rarely talked about this with him. She knew how much it upset him. "I just—it's easier not to get my hopes up."

"Balderdash," he said, scratching his thin growth of whiskers. "So, we have two winsome ladies in contention, eh? If I were a betting man, my fiver would be on the enigmatic Ms. Rosie."

She slapped his foot, glad to play along. "Sod off."

"Sylvie doesn't make your ears blush."

Jem spun round and chucked her cushion at him. "I've never even met her. She might be The One, for all I know."

"She might well be," he said, his tone implying the opposite. "We are fickle fools in the face of this thing called love."

She puzzled that one out for a moment. "Shakespeare?"

"Fortune cookie. We had Chinese the other night." He guffawed and held up his empty mug. "Come on, let's find those posh biccies your mum bought and hid away somewhere."

"You really don't know where she stores all the loot?" Jem asked. She had found her mum's stash six months after moving in, and assumed everyone else had figured it out as well.

"No, I do not." He gaped at her, and then his eyes narrowed with cunning. "Name your price."

They stood slipper to slipper in front of the fire, her efforts to outstare him thwarted by her inferior height. "No teasing me about Rosie, and you don't mention her to Mum," she said.

"Done." They shook on it. "Spill the beans."

"Spill the bran flakes, more like. You didn't hear this from me, but check out the box," she told him. "There's never been any cereal in it. She just knows you bloody hate those things."

CHAPTER SEVEN

A flick of a switch changed the circle around Rosie's body cam from luminous green to red. It was a simple visual, designed to remind even the drunkest or stupidest perp that their actions were being recorded for posterity, and yet it outwitted them in their thousands.

"Search of thirteen Battersby Walk," she stated. "Starting in the bedroom of the deceased, Kyle Parker."

From her position just across the threshold, she turned to capture an establishing shot of the tiny room. A bare bulb swung from a central ceiling fixture, its sallow glow illuminating a grubby Manchester City quilt thrown over a threadbare mattress, and three drawers wedged at angles in a chipboard chest. A desk was shoehorned under the window, its surface strewn with DVDs, computer games, and takeaway cartons.

"Do you want me to take the desk?" Kash asked, peering round her shoulder. He had slept better than she had, and his enthusiasm was getting on her wick.

"Be my guest." Her latex gloves snagged on her sweaty fingers, the tips ballooning until she smoothed them down one at a time.

"You okay?"

"Fine," she snapped, and then shook her head in apology. "I'm fine, Kash. Let's just get it done."

Everywhere she looked, she saw traces of the lad Kyle had been: the empty bottles and crisp packets that told of a fondness for chocolate milk and pickled onion Monster Munch, and the chewed pens tossed alongside a school assignment. She checked the submission date at the top of the homework: February 5th. He'd missed the deadline by six weeks. He didn't have many schoolbooks, but a collection of dog-eared Harry Potter novels was stacked by his bed, as if he dipped into them when he couldn't sleep. Their garish covers, designed to appeal to children, were a stark contrast to the gore-soaked sleeve art on the DVDs he had amassed.

Kash lifted the lid of a pizza box and recoiled at the mould-furred crusts. "I'm guessing Debbie's not much of a cook."

Rosie was rummaging through the detritus in the top drawer: sweet wrappers, football stickers, filthy shin pads, and school timetables, all burying the photos Kyle had torn from an ancient porn magazine. "Kashif Ahmed, are your teenage years so distant you don't remember eating your tea and being starving again half an hour later?" she said, tucking the photos into a sticker album in the hope that Debbie wouldn't find them.

Kash scoffed. "You haven't met my mum, have you? If you ever finished a supper of hers and wanted so much as a wafer-thin mint in the next twelve hours, she'd consider it a personal insult."

Rosie paused, album still in hand, to look him up and down. "How on earth do you maintain your fantastic figure?"

"I chase around after three kids, and I married a woman with a sense of moderation." He carried a tower of polystyrene containers to the corner of the room, clearing his access to the desk's only cupboard. "This is a nice bit of kit," he said, pulling out a PS4 so new it was still boxed.

She shut the door and came to crouch beside him. "How the hell did he afford that? The family don't seem to have two ha'pennies to rub together."

"Back of a lorry?" Kash suggested. It was the most likely explanation. The majority of the loot nicked from the north side ended up traded on the south.

"Maybe." She ran a finger over the security seals. "Unusual for it to come with its packaging intact, though."

She went back to the drawers and emptied the middle one of underwear and T-shirts, unpairing the socks and refolding the shirts

Kyle had screwed up and jammed into any available space. The bottom drawer was more of the same, except themed around jeans and sweaters and creased school uniforms.

"You find anything else over there?" she asked, jerking the drawer closed along a dodgy runner.

"No." He tossed her half a bag of Maltesers. "I might nip out for a breath of fresh air before I make a start on Debbie's boudoir."

She hadn't realised how hungry she was until the scent of chocolate hit her. She tipped a couple of Maltesers into her mouth. "Thought you were quitting," she said, knowing full well what he was actually nipping out for.

"I am. I bought one of those bong things."

"E-cig, Kash," she said hurriedly, for the benefit of the camera.

"Yeah, that's the one." He patted his pockets, checking where he'd put his fags. "I'll be back in five."

Deciding they'd both earned a break, she switched off her body cam and sat on the floor, nibbling the chocolates and resting her head against the wall. The room was stuffy and smelled fusty, and now that she'd stopped, everything seemed to be humming. She closed her eyes, but dots still floated across her vision, amplifying the drunken feeling that traditionally followed a night shift.

"Our Kyle'd buy me sweets."

The quiet statement came out of nowhere, the voice close enough to make Rosie jump. Her eyes shot open, and she dropped the Maltesers into her lap.

"Shi—oh hey," she said, trying to pretend she wasn't having an internal conniption fit. The girl she had seen in the kitchen shoved herself onto the bed and kicked her bare feet. "It's Lily, isn't it?"

"Yeah. Lily-Mae really, but I don't like it. What are you looking for?"

That was a good question. "I'm not sure. I'm hoping we'll know when we find it." Rosie held out a hand. "I'm Rosie, so we're both flowers."

Lily stopped scrubbing at the tomato sauce on her cheeks and shook Rosie's hand. "I think I'm in charge now, cos our Kyle's gone."

"You are? What about your mum?"

"She gets busy with her stuff," Lily said, back to worrying at the sauce. "With her friends and Terry—that's her new boyfriend—and she goes out a lot." She pointed at the Maltesers. "Can I have one?"

"Of course." Rosie poured a generous helping into Lily's waiting palm. "What sweets would Kyle buy you?" she asked, wishing she'd never turned her camera off, but reluctant to spook Lily by restarting it.

Lily spoke around three Maltesers, her cheeks bulging like a hamster's. "It weren't just sweets. He'd get us crisps, pop, some toys. When Mum were cross with him, I'd text him to tell him she were gone, and he'd come round."

"Did he buy you a phone, then?" Rosie put no weight behind the question, and Lily nodded immediately, reading nothing into it.

"Yeah, a really nice one, only I can't show it to Mum."

"Gosh. He must've won the lottery or something."

The look on Lily's face made Rosie feel like the class dunce. "No, duh. He got a job."

Rosie's ears pricked up. "Doing what?"

"Dunno. He never said. He showed me a twenty quid once. Have you ever seen a twenty quid?"

"Not very often, no." She gave Lily the bag of Maltesers. "When did you last see him?"

Lily clasped the bag in her fist. "I can't remember. He got nowty and all sneaky and didn't come round much, and he wouldn't answer my texts." She looked up at Rosie, her eyes wet with tears. "He won't ever come round again, will he?"

"No, love. He won't."

"I wish he would. I don't want him to be dead." Lily began to sob, her chest heaving with misery, and covered her face with both hands.

Rosie went to sit beside her on the bed. She wanted to tell her that everything would be okay, that the grief and loss would become easier to bear, given time, but the promises rang false, and Lily made no attempt to seek comfort from her. So they stayed like that, close but not touching, on a quilt that stank of a dead child's unwashed socks.

❖

A two-for-one happy hour and a fault on the local tramline had packed the Blue Door to capacity, and Rosie was struggling to make her order heard above a woman's shrill laughter and the freestyle jazz blaring from a nearby speaker. She bit the skin at the side of her thumb as the barman fiddled with mint leaves and lime wedges. She hated the place. Hated its trendiness, its well-heeled clientele, and its tendency to serve bar snacks on trowels. More than anything, she hated its choice of music, and when the barman had finally finished mucking about she threw a tenner at him, abandoning her change in her haste to escape to a quieter corner.

"Here," she said, sliding Steph's mojito in front of her and taking the opposite seat. "Cheers." She raised her pint and drained half of it in one chug. She might have caved in to Steph's wheedling, but she'd be damned if she'd drink some frou-frou monstrosity with a brolly stuck in it.

"Where did Kash end up?" Steph asked.

"He has a home to go to. And he's teetotal."

"Ah, yes, of course," Steph said as if she had forgotten that when she invited him to tag along. "I've got a mind like a sieve."

Rosie opened a bag of scampi fries and offered them to Steph, who grimaced in a manner that could only be described as satisfying.

"God, Roz, put them away. You know I can't stand them."

Rosie crammed in a handful and washed them down with ale. "Sorry," she said, wishing she'd bought two packets. "I guess we both have minds like sieves."

"On that note…" Steph paused to drink her mojito with her pinkie raised. "Social Services are not happy with you. They want to know why you interviewed Lily Parker without a chaperone present."

The froth on Rosie's pint went up her nose as she inhaled sharply. She swallowed her mouthful and set the glass down, waiting out a burst of saxophone and the spike in her blood pressure. "It was hardly a bloody interview, Steph. We spoke for about five minutes. What would they rather I'd done? Ignored the kid and sent her on her way? She was distraught, and she obviously needed someone to talk to."

"*I* was there to talk to her," Steph said. "In an official capacity, in a structured interview."

Rosie chewed that one over for a couple of seconds. The alcohol had hit her empty stomach hard and given her a quick, pleasant buzz, which allowed her to face down Steph's self-righteous indignation with unusual equanimity. "Did Lily say much? When you talked to her officially, with the chaperone present?" The question was rhetorical; she'd overheard Ray ranting about the wasted hour before he stomped off to recall the door-to-doors. She watched the colour rise on Steph's cheeks, pink darkening to a florid red.

"Fuck off, Roz," Steph said, slamming emphasis on the nickname she knew Rosie loathed. "Nothing she told *you* was on the record. It's all inadmissible."

"She's not our perp, Steph," Rosie said quietly. "She's an eleven-year-old who's just lost her big brother, the brother who bought her stuff he shouldn't have been able to afford, who flashed twenty-pound notes at her and had a brand new PS4 hidden away in his room. From what Lily said, their mum doesn't know anything about this, and it's an important lead, so does it really matter how we came by the information?"

"It matters that we follow the fucking rules," Steph said. "That may be an unfamiliar concept to you, but I can't afford to step outside the lines whenever the fancy strikes me."

"Ouch." Rosie finished her pint and reached for her coat. "That was below the belt."

"Aw, c'mon." Steph raised both hands, as if calling a ceasefire now that she'd prevailed. "You know I didn't mean anything by it. Please don't go."

Rosie fastened her zip right up to her chin. The bar was hot and airless, but she was still cold. "It's been a really long day. You stay. I'll get a taxi."

Steph caught hold of Rosie's hand but released it again when Rosie stiffened. "Yours was the only break we got today," she admitted. "Debbie knew fuck-all. She's got herself a new boyfriend, and she's barely seen Kyle in the last three months. She doesn't have a clue where he's been or who he's been with. And yes, I'm pissed off that you got more from an illicit five-minute chat than I got from five hours of interviews. Wouldn't you be?"

"Probably. But I might not be such an arsehole about it."

Steph's laugh was a little too loud. It was unusual for Rosie to fight back to this extent, and she seemed thrown by it. "Okay, okay, I'm an arsehole. You're not really going to leave me here, are you?"

Rosie pocketed her scampi fries and pushed her chair back, distracted by thoughts of a brew in bed with biscuits and a hot water bottle. "Yes, unless you want to save me the taxi fare."

The false bonhomie vanished from Steph's face, and she fished out her car keys. "I'm not going to win this one, am I?"

"No," Rosie said. "You're not."

The stairs creaked as Jem tiptoed up them, her torch guiding her path so she didn't have to switch the big light on and disturb Ferg. She strode over the wobbly top step, somehow managing not to spill her mug of Horlicks or upend the plate of banana cake balanced atop it, and made a beeline for her bedroom, where she stowed her supper and huddled back beneath her quilt.

"Bloody Nora," she whispered, trapping her hands between her thighs to defrost them. It wasn't even that cold outside, but the old terrace had draughty windows, high ceilings, and a landlord disinclined to fit more efficient central heating. She was alternating sips of Horlicks with bites of cake when her phone vibrated with a WhatsApp message from Rosie. *Just checking in to see how you're doing.*

Jem wiggled her fingers to get the blood flowing and then tapped out a reply. *I'm all right, thanks. Wide awake, eating cake and watching* Supervet. *You?*

The response was almost instantaneous. *I'm missing* Supervet*??* *Which channel?*

4seven. It's a repeat. Bet you've already seen it.

Jem retrieved her mug as her phone timed out and its screen turned black. Thirty seconds into the first advert break, it vibrated again, not with a message this time but an incoming call. She fumbled to answer it, inexplicably nervous about speaking to Rosie outside of work.

"No spoilers," she said, cutting off anything Rosie might say. "I'm very worried about the Pom with the slipped disc, but I need to let it play out."

Rosie snuffled a laugh. "I don't know why I watch it. Even the reruns make me bawl." A pause as she slurped a drink. "You couldn't sleep either, then?"

"No. I dozed off for about an hour, but a car alarm woke me and that was that. I've resorted to Horlicks."

"Hell's bells, these are desperate times."

Jem picked a chunk of dark chocolate from her cake and dipped it in her drink, letting it melt a little before she ate it. "On the plus side, Ferg made a fab banana loaf."

"Lucky you. Fluffy and I are sharing bourbon biccies and hot chocolate."

"Hey, don't knock bourbons. They've seen me through many a night shift." Jem licked her fingers. She wanted to ask about Kyle, but it seemed too frivolous to broach the subject with chocolate on her hands. "Did you see the headline in the *Manchester Evening News?*"

"I saw it," Rosie said, and Jem heard her put her mug down. "Steph persuaded me to work overtime this afternoon, and I searched Kyle's house with Kash."

"Steph?" Jem couldn't place the name. "Have I met her?"

"Sorry, yes, she was there last night. Dark hair, tall. DS Merritt? She's taking the lead on the case."

"Ah, right. Mate of yours?" Jem was no detective, but Rosie's awkward, arse-backwards explanation suggested she and the DS were more than passing acquaintances.

"Long story," Rosie said, although she sounded quite upbeat about it.

Jem held up a hand, even though Rosie couldn't see her. "Say no more. Are you allowed to tell me what happened at the house?"

"Probably not, but I don't think you're the type to blab, are you?"

"Nope."

"Did you just do that thing where you lock your lips and throw away the key?"

"Nope," Jem said again, but then laughed. She'd been tempted.

"Okay, so the Parkers reside on the south side of Curzon, and Kyle has been largely absent from home for about three months."

Jem stared at the muted television as Rosie described the state of his bedroom, and her impromptu exchange with his eldest sister.

"Steph bollocked me for speaking to her, but I don't know what else I could've done. Turned her away? 'Look, love, I get that you're upset, but all this shit needs to be on the record'?" Rosie's voice had steadily risen, her frustration and anger unmistakable. Jem heard her take a breath and then another. "Sorry, Jem. I didn't mean to rant on at you."

"Feel any better for it?"

Rosie paused. "I do, now you mention it."

"Good. And for what it's worth, I don't know what else you could've done, and I'd have done the same thing."

"You would?" There was an uncommon note of uncertainty in Rosie's question. For the short time Jem had known her, she had always seemed larger than life, full of beans and brimming with an enviable confidence. It was odd to hear her so obviously in need of reassurance.

"Yes, I would," Jem told her. "Has this been keeping you awake?"

Rosie yawned. "Possibly."

"Are you any less worried about it now?"

Another yawn. "I think so."

Assured that the Pom was on the way to a full recovery, Jem switched off the telly and snuggled under her quilt. "Are you going to sleep, then?"

"Mm." Rosie already sounded halfway there. "I need to brush my teeth."

"Me too, but I'm too cosy to move, so I'll wait till I need a wee."

"Sounds like a plan. Is your date still on for tomorrow?"

"Yes. Thanks for reminding me." Jem tried not to look at the clothes she'd set out in readiness, but they crept into her peripheral vision regardless.

"Text me all the gruesome details. And shout if you need rescuing."

Jem stopped in the middle of turning over and frowned. "Rescuing?"

"Yeah, you know, 'Goodness, my friend's just phoned me. My cat's stuck up a tree. I really have to go!'"

"Ah, right, gotcha. If I need you to fake a cat emergency, I will be sure to text you."

"Just don't tell her you haven't got a cat, or it won't work."

"Okay, enough." Jem aimed for stern but spoiled the effect by giggling. "Go to bloody sleep."

The rustle of bedding and a pillow being thumped suggested Rosie was settling down.

"Night, Jem. Sweet dreams."

"You too," Jem said, and ended the call.

CHAPTER EIGHT

The headlights of the Audi A3 convertible flashed once to acknowledge Jem's wave, and its driver performed a neat parallel park to place its passenger door within touching distance. Jem had taken a wary step forward, unsure whether to let herself in, when the driver's door opened and a woman jogged around to greet her.

"Jem? Hiya, I'm Sylvie." She pumped Jem's hand in both of hers, her enthusiasm overcompensating for the initial flit of disappointment in her expression.

"Hiya," Jem said, determined not to write the date off in the first twenty seconds. "You made good time."

Sylvie patted the car's soft top. "This doesn't half shift when you put your foot down. What do you drive?"

Jem thumbed toward her Skoda Fabia. It was a good car: reliable, economical, and snot green, which meant she'd got it for a steal.

"Okay." Sylvie dragged the word out, her polite smile now more of a rictus. "Shall we go in mine? Here, let me put that in the boot for you." She took Jem's rucksack, as if afraid Jem might offer resistance if she didn't keep things ticking along. Jem stayed on the pavement, taking stock as Sylvie whirled around her. Though Sylvie matched her in height, the similarities ended there. Dressed head to toe in figure-hugging designer sportswear, she was lithe and tanned, and her sandy hair was secured in an intricate French plait. She moved with a self-assurance that made Jem's teeth hurt.

"Christ, what've you got in here?" Sylvie asked, hoisting the rucksack into the boot.

"Oh, y'know, bit of everything." Jem had packed and unpacked it three times, preparing for every eventuality—swimming, cycling, Nordic walking, maybe sky diving at a push—and squeezing in a novel at the last minute. It made the bag weigh a ton, but she always felt better if she had a book with her. At Sylvie's urging, she got into the car and was almost folded in half as the bucket seat sucked her arse toward the road. Thrown off balance, she knocked a large protein shake askew as she fastened her seat belt. Three wholesale boxes of whey powder on the back seat suggested Sylvie either had a serious addiction or sold the stuff on eBay.

"Terrific for building muscle mass," Sylvie said, catching her in the act of gawping. "I have one for breakfast, one for lunch, and a proper tea."

"That sounds…" Jem floundered. It sounded revolting, but politeness was an issue. "Committed?" she ventured.

Sylvie lifted her T-shirt and bounced a palm off her washboard abs. "It certainly requires discipline, but the results speak for themselves. Remind me to give you an information pack." She sped through a light that was more red than amber and accelerated past a lorry. "I'd love to do your job, zipping around on blues all day. It must be exciting."

"It has its moments," Jem said, clasping her armrest. She was used to being thrown about the cab by giddy new starters, but they had a siren to alert other road users, and a legal exemption to exceed the speed limit.

"I'll bet." Sylvie chugged her shake at another traffic light, slapping its cap back on as the taxi in front set off again. "What's the worst thing you've ever seen?"

Jem rubbed her forehead with the heel of her hand. If someone had given her a quid every time she'd been asked that, she'd have her own house by now. No one wanted an honest answer, though. They didn't want to hear about the heroin addict who'd fallen asleep on her newborn and smothered him, or the lad who'd just been told the bursitis in his hip was actually a metastatic tumour that would kill him within weeks, or the kids torn apart by a suicide vest full of metal shards. They wanted gore without the horror behind it, consequence-free splatter they could widen their eyes at and tell their mates about.

Pushing away the memory of Kyle Parker's battered corpse, she fell back on her tried and tested response. "We see all sorts. I had this lad once who'd been knocked off his bike, snapped his femur right here"—she patted the middle of her thigh—"and his leg was so twisted he could've turned his head and nibbled his own toenails."

As usual, it did the trick. Sylvie pulled the requisite face of awed disgust and rocked against the steering wheel. "Holy shit! What did you do?"

"Filled him full of morphine and straightened the bugger. We couldn't take him in with it wrapped around his ear hole."

Indicating right, Sylvie slowed to wait for a gap in the oncoming traffic. She revved the engine, nudging the car back and forth. Even when stationary, she was moving. "You should write a book."

Jem had heard that one before as well. "It's tempting, but people would think I was making it up." She delivered the standard line by rote, her attention fixed on a sign at the junction that read Manchester Climbing Centre. "Bollocks," she mouthed, hoping she was wrong but sure she was right.

Sylvie had also spotted the sign. "Damn, busted. I didn't know that was there. I usually come in the other way. Are you surprised? I was hoping you'd be surprised."

"I am. Very." Jem couldn't have been more surprised had Sylvie announced they were going cage diving with great whites.

Apparently fed up of waiting, Sylvie sped across the junction, earning a blare of horn from an oncoming petrol tanker. Jem saw the whites of the driver's eyes, but Sylvie didn't even blink, chattering on without pause. "Have you been here before? I bet you have. Ferg told Mandy you loved climbing in the mountains."

"Ah, well. Sort of." Jem wondered how much of that conversation had been lost in translation. Most of it, she guessed, given her current predicament. "I, uh, I think the message has got a bit mixed there. I'm more of an armchair mountaineer, really. My dad used to tell me loads of stories—the history of the Great Walls, first ascents, that sort of thing. I go to the Alps every summer if I can, but only to hike."

"Right. Shit. I must've got my wires crossed." Sylvie pulled into the climbing centre car park and drummed her fingers on the wheel, clearly considering her options. "I've booked us a session each."

Jem shook her head in apology. "I can pay you back. It's not a prob—" She broke off as Sylvie dismissed the offer with a wave of her hand.

"Don't worry, I know all the staff here. I'm sure they'll switch you to the beginners' wall, and we can meet up for lunch afterward. There's a cafe in Hulme that does a fantastic vegan omelette."

The latter concept left Jem so flummoxed that she was rousted from the car and standing at the climbing centre's reception desk before she could mount a protest.

"That's great. Thanks, Kel," Sylvie was saying to the receptionist. "Can we get her a pair of shoes as well? I don't think her trainers will cut it."

Jem scuffed her feet on the hardwood floor, her chest tight with apprehension and embarrassment. She felt like the kid who'd forgotten her PE kit and got stuck with the class hand-me-downs. "Sorry," she said to no one in particular. "I don't have any…" Her explanation withered to nothing as she watched Sylvie stride toward the changing room. Kel put a hand on Jem's arm, keeping her at the desk.

"Here, hon, these are brand new out of the wrapper." Kel placed a spotless pair of climbing shoes on the signing-in book. "I'll give Rob a shout. He's brill with newbies, and you can take things at your own speed, so don't look so scared, okay?"

"Okay," Jem said, easing her grip on the inhaler in her pocket. "Thank you."

Shoes in hand, she entered the changing room, where Sylvie was pacing the floor, decked out in all the right clobber.

"There you are," Sylvie said. "I'm going to make a start on the Beast. It's the advanced wall at the far end, if you fancy watching when you've had enough. It's got some awesome overhangs on it." She flexed her fingers, cracking most of her knuckles. "Have fun, and I'll see you in a couple of hours."

And then she was gone, the door swinging in her wake, and the changing room silent aside from the occasional squeak of Jem's breathing. Jem sat on the central bench and opened her rucksack. Her book was balanced on top of her towel and toiletries like a siren on a rock, its cover bright and alluring, promising two hours of entertainment that wouldn't involve falling from a great height and snapping something vital. It would be easy for her to hide in one of the cubicles, while away some time, and then see how Sylvie was faring with the Beast. She pulled the novel out and set it in her lap, toying with the frayed edge of its bookmark. She'd read it more times than she could count, but there was comfort in its familiarity, like spending time with good friends who arrived with no expectations and never outstayed their welcome. The thought brought Rosie to mind, and Jem's eyes strayed to the climbing shoes. Rosie would tell her to go for it, to put the damn book away, put the damn shoes on, and haul her arse up the damn wall. It was only a beginner's wall, after all. How high could it be?

The shoes were a perfect fit, removing her final excuse to procrastinate. She slinked out of the changing room, immediately overwhelmed by a hubbub of shouted instructions, cries of encouragement, and the occasional yelp of failure. A tall bald chap spotted her within seconds, dodging around a line of teenagers bedecked with ropes and carabiners to greet Jem by name.

"Kel asked me to look out for you. I'm Rob, and you have me all to yourself for"—he checked his mobile—"the next hour and fifty. Shall we make a start?"

"Okay," Jem said, mesmerised by the sheer scale of the walls surrounding her. The climbing centre had been built inside a converted Victorian church, and a beautiful stained-glass window rained multi-coloured light onto the climbers. She pointed toward a young girl suspended in an acrobatic pose beneath a gnarly overhang. "We won't be doing that, will we?"

"Not today," Rob said. "Maybe save it for next time, eh?"

The corner he escorted her around deadened the worst of the noise, and he stopped in front of a bright orange slab, its rumpled surface stretching to about fifteen feet, liberally dotted with plastic holds and fixed metal loops. Jem felt queasy just looking at its summit ledge. Although she loved the mountains, she had no head for heights.

"I don't think I can do this, either," she whispered. "I'm not very strong."

Rob sat her on a bench at the base of the wall. "I think you can. A lot of people have the wrong idea about climbing. They assume it's all about arm strength and dangling off ledges by your fingertips, but your legs are the key to making progress. You need your quads not your biceps for this, which means women instinctively climb better than blokes, because they're less inclined to act like knobs and try to pose."

Jem laughed in spite of herself. "I doubt you'll ever have a student less inclined to pose."

He gave her his hand and pulled her up. "Smashing. Right, let's crack on."

His introduction to the basics was thorough and punctuated by practical examples. "Use your feet, put your weight over your feet, put your waist over your feet," he told her, hopping on and off the wall with enviable poise. "Okay, come and have a go."

Snug in a harness far more orthodox than the one she'd hashed together on Barton Bridge, and belayed by Rob's colleague, she took her first tentative step on the wall. Rob joined her on a parallel hold.

"Don't look up, look down," he said. "Plan where you're putting your feet, not your hands."

It was sound advice, and she plotted her next couple of moves with relative ease, advancing halfway up before she made the mistake of glancing beyond her shoes to the crash mat below.

"Jesus," she hissed. Perspiration slicked her palm, and her right hand slipped from its hold, flailing in midair until she found an alternative grip. Her knuckles blanched, and she thought she might be sick.

"Take a minute, Jem," Rob commanded, pulling her attention away from the floor. She nodded in fitful jerks, reminding herself that even if she fell, the top rope would catch her. But what if it didn't?

"Sorry," she said. "Me and heights, we don't really get along."

He barked a laugh. "Now you bloody tell me." He moved across to her, close enough that he could speak without his colleague overhearing. "Do you want to stop?"

"No." She didn't want to give in. She wanted to get to the sodding top.

He considered her carefully for a moment and then waved her onward. "Okay, good. Where are you going next?"

"There, I think." She sidestepped onto a conveniently placed hold and gained another foot.

"You're a natural," he said, ignoring his mobile phone as it chirped.

She stared at him and dried her forehead on her sleeve. Her shirt was soaked and clinging to her, and her legs felt like wet spaghetti. "Bugger off," she said, forcing the words out between mild bouts of wheezing. "And shift your arse off that spot. I need it."

He hopped obligingly to one side, slowing his own progress to let her reach the summit alone. Her fingers clawed for purchase, and one final push allowed her to collapse her top half over the ledge. She stayed there for a few seconds, panting and smiling like an idiot, and then allowed her belaying buddy to gently guide her descent. Back on the crash mat, bouncing foot to foot, she pulled Rob into a hug and kissed his cheek when he offered her his hand.

"Thank you," she said, feeling simultaneously lighter than air and fit to burst.

"My pleasure." He sounded like he meant it, and his face was flushed with pride. "I'm very glad my one o'clock cancelled."

She stopped untying the knot at her waist, the alarm he'd muted suddenly making sense. "What time is it?" She'd been scheduled to meet Sylvie at one.

"Twenty to two."

"Really? Are you sure? Shit, I have to run." She handed him her gear. "Thanks again for everything. I'll pay the extra at the desk."

"Don't worry about that. My cancellation will have covered it."

"I'll leave you a big tip, then," she called over her shoulder, already halfway to the changing room.

She showered in five minutes and applied generous amounts of deodorant, throwing on fresh clothes before chucking a couple of clips into her hair and hoping for the best. A gang of kids directed her to the Beast, but Sylvie wasn't on the wall, and a chap swinging nine feet above Jem told her that Sylvie had soloed her chosen route in less than an hour.

At a loss, Jem returned to the front desk, where Kel met her with a round of applause.

"Congratulations," Kel said, giving her a drumstick lolly. "To commemorate your first ascent."

"I'll treasure it." Jem pocketed her prize. "I don't suppose you've seen Sylvie?"

Kel's nose crinkled in discomfiture, and she fished a slip of paper from a pile of messages. "I have, actually. She left this for you."

The message was short and succinct. *Met a couple of friends here, and we've gone to the Butterbean Cafe. Get a taxi and join us if you want. S.*

"They do the most revolting omelette," Kel said. "You'd be better off eating that piece of paper."

Jem was too thrilled with her afternoon's adventure to feel slighted. "I don't think she was really my type," she said.

Kel took the message back, screwed it up, and tossed it over her shoulder. "Naw, Sylvie's a strutter. She brings women here all the time, but she's happier if you just stand on the mat and admire her. You had fun anyway, didn't you?"

"Very much so." Jem gave her thirty quid. "Can you pass that on to Rob?"

"Will do, but he won't want it. His cancellation paid for your extra time."

"Tell him to pay it forward for someone else, then."

Jem paused at the exit to shoulder her rucksack and zip her coat. She'd have to phone for a taxi, but she preferred to wait outside, where the air was cooler and didn't smell of body odour and soggy chips. Perched on the car park wall, she fished out her mobile as it vibrated with a text. Before she'd even read the message, her excuses were piling up on each other: I twisted my ankle and I think it needs an X-ray, chickpeas make me sneeze, my cat's stuck up a tree…

The last one set her off laughing, and she opened WhatsApp fully prepared to deal with Sylvie having a strop. Instead, she found a message from Rosie. *In Manchester, but I can still fabricate feline shenanigans if you need me to.*

Jem hovered over the reply pane, her heels thrumming against the bricks. The main bus route into Manchester was only a five-minute walk away, she had a few quid left in change, and she really didn't want to waste her good mood by going home with her tail between her legs.

My date ditched me for a vegan omelette, she typed. *Fancy meeting for a brew in town?*

The gap that ensued seemed to stretch for hours. A flock of seagulls cackled their disdain overhead, and she was busy googling local taxi firms when a message flashed up. *How the fuck do you make a vegan omelette?*

She snorted, scaring one of the gulls. *I don't think I ever want to find out.*

Rosie didn't leave her hanging again. *How's about Northern Soul for a fry up?*

The suggestion made Jem's mouth water. She hadn't realised how hungry she was until then.

Sounds fabulous. Save me a seat, and I'll be as quick as I can.

CHAPTER NINE

The lunchtime rush had long since passed, emptying Northern Soul's small cafe and giving Rosie a choice of tables. She slid into a corner booth, stowing a bag of second-hand books and a Gabbotts Farm ham shank she'd picked up for her mam. She'd been coming to the cafe for years, in and out of uniform, and the waiter put a latte in front of her without prompting.

"Kash not with you?" he asked.

"Not today. I'm waiting for a friend."

"Oh aye." He waggled his eyebrows. "Do you want me to dim the lights?"

She raised her mug and her middle finger, quickly lowering the latter when Jem walked in and hesitated on the welcome mat. The lights were moody enough already, and she was obviously struggling to pick Rosie out of the gloom. Having tracked Rosie's gaze, the waiter hurried over and returned with Jem on his arm.

"Can I get you a drink, love?" he said, his flat Manc accent somewhat undermining his genteel welcome.

"Tea, please." Jem shoved her bum into the booth and leaned back against the tatty leather. She looked tuckered out but elated, as if she'd spent the morning having really great sex, which didn't seem to tally with her being abandoned mid-date. "God, my arse will never be the same again," she said.

Rosie almost choked on her latte froth. "Why? What the hell have you been doing?"

Jem held up a finger, pausing for dramatic effect as the waiter arranged a teapot and related paraphernalia in front of her.

"Sugar?" he asked, as if sensing Rosie's impatience.

"No, thank you." Jem poured the tea and added milk, prolonging the agony as she took a dainty sip.

"Jemima Pardon," Rosie said. "Behave yourself."

Jem spluttered over the rim of her cup, no longer able to keep her face straight. "Okay, okay. Sylvie would have given the Amazons a run for their money. She had a passion for protein shakes, her driving was even worse than yours, and she took me climbing. Climbing! Can you imagine? On a huge wall about yo big." Jem waved a hand in the vague direction of the ceiling and then paused to consider its height. "Only bigger. But this bloke helped me, and I made it to the top, and when I got down again, Sylvie had got fed up of waiting and buggered off for butterbeans or something."

"Wow," Rosie said. "We'll come back to the slight on my driving. How high was this wall, really?"

Jem shrugged, but even in the dull light Rosie could see the glimmer of satisfaction in her eyes. "About fifteen feet."

"And you'd never climbed before?"

"No. Never. I don't even like heights. They scare the pants off me."

Rosie clinked her mug against Jem's cup. "This calls for a celebration. Grab a napkin and wipe the grease off that menu. Dinner's on me."

Northern Soul might have been a dingy little fleapit, but Jem's all-day breakfast ticked the right boxes, and judging by the satisfied murmurs coming from Rosie at regular intervals, its meat pie, chips, and mushy peas were also a hit.

Jem dipped a piece of black pudding in runny yolk, added a dollop of brown sauce, and chased the mouthful with a bite of toast. "I have thighs of steel," she announced, apropos of nothing, and Rosie dropped all the peas off her fork.

"Explain," Rosie said, giving up on the peas and attacking her pie.

"That's what Rob, the climbing bloke, told me. I think he was just being nice, though, because every time I lift my leg higher than kerb height now I almost fall over."

"They got you to the top of that wall, Jem." Rosie nibbled her pastry thoughtfully. "How the heck did you end up going climbing, anyway?"

"Long story short? Ferg mentioned my love of mountains and climbing, but neglected to mention that I only hike in the former and read about the latter. Or Sylvie neglected to take that on board, which I suspect was more the case. Apparently, she has a habit of dragging dates to the climbing centre in the hope that they'll chicken out and just watch her perform."

"You proper pissed on her chips, then," Rosie said with glee.

Jem hadn't thought about it like that. She had wanted to prove something to herself, not push Sylvie's nose out of joint. "That might explain her buggering off to Hulme without me."

"Are you bothered?" Rosie dabbed her lips with a napkin, her expression sombre.

"Not really." Jem smeared butter on a fresh piece of toast. She took her time, spreading it right to the edges and cutting the piece into triangles. It helped her to qualify her statement with a degree of detachment. "I have form."

"Form?" Rosie repeated, and then frowned as she caught the gist. "What? With dates dumping you?"

Jem chewed her toast. It had gone cold, but she didn't want to waste it. "Not just a date, a girlfriend of six and a half months. At Milton Keynes, of all bloody places."

"Wha—how?" Rosie screwed up her napkin, her meal forgotten. Jem pinched one of her chips.

"We were on the train, coming back from a weekend in London. Hayley spotted someone on the platform, some random woman she fancied more than me, so she got off and I never saw her again."

"Jesus wept. What did you do?"

"What could I do? The train was leaving. She yelled at me not to follow her and disappeared into the crowd. All I had left of her was half a crap buffet car butty and her copy of *Wuthering Heights*." Jem swirled another chip in Rosie's ketchup and gravy. She hadn't told this story in years, and she was heartened by how little it was affecting her. At the time, she'd gone home to sob on her dad's shoulder, and the humiliation had lingered for months.

"Miserable cow," Rosie said fiercely. "You're better off without that one."

Right up until this week, Jem had thought she was better off without anyone. Her most enduring relationship since Hayley had been a fling with a Polish paramedic who had fled back to Poland after a month because the damp Manchester climate made her hair too frizzy.

"Yep," she said, keeping the latter point to herself. "Ferg got curious and Facebook-stalked her a while back. She got married to a very pale performance poet. In a yurt." Jem finished her chip and blew her fringe from her eyes, and then snarled and clapped a hand on it. Enough was enough, she decided. She'd succeeded in one new venture today, so why not double or nothing? "Is Thornton's still open?"

Rosie checked her watch. "Should be. Why?"

"Original or treacle toffee, wasn't it? If you can fit me in for a restyle this evening, I'll buy you a box of each."

"Not what you imagined, eh?" Rosie said, unlocking the door of a tiny whitewashed cottage.

"Not at all," Jem admitted. "I had you in a city centre flat, all polished laminate and mod cons and service charges."

She knew Stanny Brook well. She occasionally went there with the dogs, wandering along the footpaths that zigzagged across the surrounding fields and dipped down to the river, where she'd seen kingfishers and the glint of brown trout in the deeper pools. Wild garlic and bluebells filled the woods in spring, and the town seemed miles away, despite only being a ten-minute drive. The secluded patch of countryside fell within the boundary of Darnton Station, but she was rarely called to emergencies there, and she'd never imagined it as somewhere Rosie might live. She stepped back to admire the cottage's mullioned windows and original stonework. Tucked away off the main road, with a view out toward Stanny Pike, it seemed like an ideal refuge for someone raised in a large, chaotic family, and Jem could only covet it.

Rosie kicked her boots off on the step. "It was love at first sight. I'd say 'come in out of the cold,' but it'll be bloody freezing till I put the heating on."

Jem stood on the doormat, wrestling with her trainers, while Rosie disappeared to tinker in the kitchen. After the hyperactive stress of the morning, the cottage felt like a haven. The lamps Rosie had switched on in passing cast the living room in mellow amber, and it smelled of fresh baking and woodsmoke.

"Make yourself at home," Rosie called over the splash of a tap. "I'll give you a tour when I've put the kettle on."

Not quite ready to dispense with her coat, Jem sat on a worn, brown leather sofa and ran her fingers across the multicoloured blanket tossed over its back. The blanket was one of many dashes of brightness scattered about the room; all the cushions on the suite clashed, and what appeared to be an ongoing crocheting project was spread over the arm of the lone chair. A cast iron log burner took centre stage in the fireplace, and a modest television seemed little more than an afterthought, squeezed into the far corner with a basket of wool almost hiding it from view. Keepsakes and family photos lined the mantelpiece: Rosie's mum and stepdad slicing a three-tier wedding cake, and a boy and two girls at various stages of growing up. Jem stood and picked up a picture that had drawn her eye: a daft-looking dog captured on a faded Polaroid, rolling around on a tatty back lawn with a far younger version of Rosie.

"That was Annabelle," Rosie said, peeking over Jem's shoulder. "She was a mutt with a bit of sheepdog in her. Herded everything, and I really do mean everything. We took her to Blackpool once, and she made all the donkeys stand in some poor bugger's windbreak."

"Was he in it at the time?" Jem asked, tickled pink by the idea.

"No. He'd gone to get himself an ice cream. Had a hell of a surprise when he came back." Rosie set down a tray of tea and cake on the coffee table and crouched by the burner to stack kindling on screwed-up balls of newspaper. The fire caught slowly, egged on by a lot of creative swearing, and she blew on the stuttering flames to encourage their spread. "Grab a brew. Your toes should start to thaw in about half an hour."

"How long have you lived here?" Jem cradled her mug in both hands, stifling a yawn. She wanted to shove her feet beneath her, snuggle under the blanket, and not move again till morning.

Rosie balanced two larger logs on top of the blaze she'd nurtured. Seeming satisfied with her efforts, she shut the burner's door and sat beside Jem. "Three years. I'd been renting in Levenshulme, and I just got sick of the noise and the traffic and being broken into every other week. The bastards even nicked my knitting. Can you believe that? What kind of lowlife scrote pinches someone's half-finished cardigan? Anyway, that was the last straw. I bought this as a fixer-upper. I've done bits of it myself, and I'm still chipping away at it."

Jem inched her toes toward the fire, craving the warmth it had started to emit. "Crafty and handy, eh? I'm impressed."

Rosie took a short bow. "I learned most of it from my mam. She does all the DIY at hers, because my stepdad's bleedin' useless at it."

"You're going to tell me you made this cake as well, aren't you?" Jem said. It was a good cake, coffee and walnut, with a feather-light sponge and rich buttercream.

Rosie waved a hand, dismissing the compliment, although she looked rather smug. "I'm not one to brag, but I could certainly give you the recipe, should you want it. Bring that with you, and I'll show you around. We can do your hair in the spare bedroom. The upstairs always warms up first."

She led the way into a compact galley kitchen, flicking on an outside light that shone silver over a small sunken garden. Winter had left the beds Spartan, but the light caught blood-red branches of dogwood, wisps of ornamental grass, and the bowed white petals of a hellebore. A stone patio provided an elevated vantage point, and Jem pictured Rosie out there in the height of summer, shaking off the stress of a long day with a glass of wine she'd probably grown the grapes for.

"It's beautiful." Jem went up on her tiptoes to better admire the plot. She had crammed her own backyard with pots and planters, and she occasionally sunbathed on the air raid shelter, but it was a poor substitute for a proper garden.

Rosie stood shoulder to shoulder with her. "It's piddly, but it's big enough for me, and the patio's a right suntrap. I can get tomatoes and cucumbers to grow there, no problem." She knocked the back of her hand against the tap dripping persistently over the sink. "As you can see, the kitchen is a work in progress."

"I rent with a bloke who conjures up a dozen new pie recipes a month," Jem said. "It's a miracle if I can get into our kitchen."

Rosie whistled her appreciation, not at all sympathetic to Jem's plight. "Really? Does he use you as his guinea pig?"

"All the time, hence—" Jem used both hands to slap her arse. "I was a size eight when I moved in."

Rosie belly-laughed and linked Jem's arm. "Super skinny girls always look bloody miserable, Jemima. No cheese, no chip butties, no chocolate. Ugh."

"Two protein shakes a day and a superfood salad, if you please," Jem said, managing a fair approximation of Sylvie's infomercial pitch.

"Bloody hellfire. Was that your muscle-bound date? I'd rather eat my own toenails." Rosie led Jem up the stairs, pushing open a door and stopping on the threshold. "Welcome to Salon Chez whatever the hell name I made up the other day. Grab that chair and get comfy while I find some towels."

Jem did as instructed, parking herself in front of a tall mirror and trying not to let nerves get the better of her. If it all went to shit, as expected, she would go home and give herself a crew cut.

Rosie came up behind her and caught her eye in the mirror. "Don't look so worried. Here, Fluffy wanted to say hello." Without further ceremony, she plonked the bearded dragon onto Jem's lap. "He likes having his head massaged."

Jem cooed and stroked Fluffy on the spot Rosie indicated. He raised each front leg in turn, looking like a kitten kneading a blanket, and Jem was so entertained that she barely noticed the spray of warm water on her hair.

"Bold pixie, then," Rosie said. "Still okay with that? And I'll colour it later, if you don't react to the patch test."

"Yep." Jem put out a finger for Fluffy to catch hold of. "Yep, that's fine." She was still playing pat-a-cake with her new pal when Rosie scooped him up.

"He'll get a fur coat if I don't shift him," Rosie said, carrying him past Jem and out of the room. Startled, Jem put a hand to the nape of her neck, feeling the draught there.

"Oh!" She looked in the mirror. Most of her hair was now lying on the floor, and it seemed Rosie was about to start fine-tuning what remained. "How long—did I fall asleep?"

"No, but you do seem quite easy to distract," Rosie called back. Her voice quietened as she returned. "Sorry for pulling a Fluffy-assisted fast one, but I didn't want you legging it after the first snip."

"You're forgiven." Jem allowed Rosie to gently position her head, soothed by the touch and the rhythmic snick of the scissors. "The nurses would do that to me all the time when I was a kid. Distract me, I mean. I was in and out of the hospital every other month, and all they needed to do was wave a rubber glove balloon at me and I'd let the docs stick their needles wherever they wanted."

Rosie hummed, the sound low and contemplative. "Was it an attention thing?"

Jem started to nod but aborted the gesture in case Rosie took her ear off. "Probably. Foster kids are all starved for it, I suppose. I'd get moved around a lot: a group home for a few months, then maybe a family would want to try me out for size. I had what they called 'complex needs,' so my family placements tended to be short-lived. I didn't find out till years later, but Social Services warned my parents I had developmental delay."

Rosie stopped cutting, her scissors poised but unmoving. "Did anyone ever set the record straight?"

"Yeah, my dad. He played a long game, sent my assigned social worker a copy of my GCSE results. I got fives As, an A star, and two Bs."

"Swotty sod," Rosie said without malice. "I scraped through mine and had to resit a couple. All that stuff with my stepdad—" She waved the scissors, dismissing the subject. "Anyway, I only knuckled down properly at college, when I turned over the proverbial fresh leaf."

Jem smiled at her in the mirror. "My dad would say, 'it doesn't matter how you get there as long as you get there.' Course, he'd usually roll that one out whenever he'd gone the wrong way and was too stubborn to ask for directions, but the sentiment is sound."

"I think I'd like your dad."

Jem shut her eyes as strands of hair cascaded in front of them. "You would, without a doubt. You're both as daft as each other."

"I take no offence. Now, just keep your eyes closed for ten while I perm what's left of your fringe."

Jem laughed. "You wouldn't do that to me."

"No, I wouldn't, but keep them closed anyway. I do like a big reveal."

The big reveal came mere moments before curiosity could bust a hole in Jem's gut. She heard Rosie put the scissors down and then a triumphant "ta-da!" as Rosie clasped her shoulders. Braced for impact, she squinted through one eye to get the measure of things. She knew Rosie would see through a lie, but she planned to moderate her reaction if she hated the result.

"Blimey." Abandoning any attempt at subterfuge, she gaped at her reflection. Rosie hadn't been kidding when she'd said "bold." She had cut Jem's hair shorter than it had ever been, gathering it in close at the back and sweeping it over at the fringe. It was classy yet low maintenance, and it made Jem burst into tears.

"Shit!" Rosie gave her a handful of tissues from a nearby box. "It'll grow back, I promise. It won't take long, and you can wear a hat or something. Maybe a snood. I'll knit you a snood."

Jem blew her nose. "I love it."

"Bleedin' Nora, you almost gave me a heart attack. Do you really like it?"

"I do. It's ace. It looks dead swanky."

"Well, thank fuck for that." Rosie ruffled Jem's fringe, feathering it with her fingertips. "Bit of styling gel through here in a morning, Ms. Pardon, and you'll be fabulous all day."

Jem caught Rosie's hand and pressed a quick kiss to the back of it. "Thank you. I'm not sure a box of toffee really covers this."

Blushing flame red, Rosie began to brush the hair from Jem's shoulders. "It's been a pleasure," she said quietly. "You don't owe me a thing."

CHAPTER TEN

Nice easy one to start the morning," Jem's dispatcher had said. He was new to the RRV desk and at the end of his night shift, so she couldn't fault his optimism. "Fifty-eight-year-old male, back pain. Clammy and short of breath, but aren't they all?"

They generally were, because back pain hurt like the devil, but on this occasion Jem's swift assessment suggested her patient's symptoms were being caused by an aneurysm leaking blood into his abdomen. His face was the colour of cold porridge, his blood pressure was in his boots, and his heart was racing. If the aneurysm ruptured, it would kill him within minutes.

She checked her fob watch, one eye on the monitor as it recalculated his blood pressure. She had been given an ETA of ten minutes for the ambulance three and a half minutes ago, and she was starting to sweat through her shirt.

"Easy, Ian," she said. "I know it hurts, but try to keep still."

His blood pressure had dipped again. She adjusted the flow of his IV and gave him a further small dose of morphine, trying to keep him comfortable and calm while balancing his pressure on a knife edge: too low and he'd die, too high and he'd die even faster. She unzipped the side of the defib, making the pads easier to grab. She didn't want to stress him further by sticking them on his chest.

"Will he be all right?" his wife asked. She was still in her nightie, looking pale and scared, and oblivious to her bedhead.

"He needs surgery," Jem said. His odds of surviving a rupture repair were about one in five, but she kept that to herself. "We'll tell the hospital that we're coming in with him, so they'll be ready. Do you want to get dressed? The ambulance should be here soon."

"Yes, okay." The woman grabbed whatever clothing was to hand and disappeared with it into the bathroom, leaving Jem alone with Ian. As soon as he heard the bathroom door click, he pulled his oxygen mask down.

"How serious is this?" His voice was weak and tremulous, but he'd found Jem's hand and was holding it tightly.

"Pretty serious." There was no point sugarcoating her answer; she could see from the fear in his expression that he'd worked it out for himself. She took a shaky breath. His prognosis might have been less bleak had anyone else been sent to him.

"Shit." He grimaced, his free hand clawing at his abdomen. "Don't tell Margaret. She'll only panic."

"I won't."

He stared at the ceiling for a long moment. "Should someone call the kids?"

She put his mask back into place. "That might not be a bad idea."

He nodded, his eyes closing. "Take my phone. It's in my jacket—Ally and Jake."

Jem did as he asked, pocketing the mobile as she caught the first wail of a siren. The crew didn't wait to be let in; she heard their boots on the stairs shortly after the ambulance doors slammed.

"Hey, Bob," she said, relieved to see familiar faces.

"How do." Bob immediately stooped to disconnect the monitor. "Did you request the dream team or did you just get lucky?"

She took the ECG leads from him. "I'm always lucky. You know that."

Dougie had followed him in, toting the track chair she'd advised them to bring. Careful not to jolt Ian, they extricated him as she packed her kit away. She met Dougie at the back of the ambulance and gave him Ian's phone.

"Will you get someone to call his son and daughter? Someone who's not his wife, that is."

"Will do." Dougie paused at the driver's door, keys readied. "There's an AP waiting on station for you. Looks about twelve, stupid moustache?"

"Great." She slung her bag into the RRV. "Let me know how you get on with Ian, won't you?"

"Of course." He started the engine and then wound his window down. "Jem?"

"Yeah?"

He blew her a kiss. "Your hair looks bloody marvellous, flower."

Expecting a summons back to station, Jem put her "clear" through and rummaged around for her banana as she waited for the verdict. Breakfast had been a hurried bowl of cereal at five thirty, and the last thing she wanted was a rumbling belly interrupting her debrief. She was chewing her first bite when the radio buzzed.

"Hey, Jem," Ryan said. "There's a Darren Baxter waiting at Darnton for you, if you can make your way—actually, scratch that: choking baby coming through."

"Bloody hell," she said, off the air. Then, "Anyone else running?"

"Crofton, but they're eighteen out, and you're four."

Cursing the satnav for buggering about, she lobbed her banana onto the passenger seat and turned off the side road, hitting her sirens at the first set of traffic lights. The baby had probably just coughed on a feed, scaring its parents half to death, but Jem of all people couldn't afford to be complacent, so she put her foot down, dodging early-morning commuters still bleary-eyed and caffeine deprived, and pissing off a bus driver who was disinclined to pull in for her. The RRVs were nippy little beasts, though, and a straight run down the main road allowed her to beat her ETA by forty seconds. The front door of the address was wide open, often an indicator of a bad job, but the wail of a newborn audible above the *Teletubbies* theme tune suggested the crisis had passed. Occluded airways didn't allow for shrieking.

"Hello? Ambulance." She gave a perfunctory knock and walked into the living room, where a toddler wearing only a nappy sat eating Coco Pops on the sofa. The toddler grinned and waved her spoon, splattering the filthy fake leather with chocolate milk.

"Hey, sweetie. Where's your mum?" Jem said. Beyond a connecting door, the cries had softened to a series of hiccupping sobs. She pushed the door open. "Ambulance. Are you in here?"

"Yeah, hiya." The young woman at the kitchen table blew a plume of e-cig smoke toward the ceiling and nodded at the baby strapped into a bouncer. "She went all red in the face for a couple of minutes, but I think it were wind."

Jem slowly set her response bag, her defib, and her advanced life support bag onto the kitchen laminate and unclipped her radio. "Tell the crew not to rush," she told Ryan. "And if you need them for anything else, use them." She crouched by the baby. "May I?"

The woman used her e-cig to make a "be my guest" gesture and scratched her belly through her onesie.

Cradling the baby, Jem took her into the living room, away from the smoke. The woman stopped in the doorway, leaning on the jamb.

"What exactly happened?" Jem asked.

"I were feeding her, and when she were done she puked up a bit and coughed and went bright red, but by the time I'd finished phoning the ambulance she were fine."

There wasn't much Jem could say to that, so she gave the baby a thorough once-over and cancelled the ambulance when the mum declined a trip to the hospital.

"What's her name?" Jem asked, starting her paperwork.

The mum slotted the baby into another bouncer two feet away from a widescreen television and sat her own arse in the puddle of milk on the sofa. "It's Polly."

"Surname?"

"Jolley. With an e."

Jem blinked. "Polly Jolley?"

"Yeah." The mum puffed on her cig again. "Cute, isn't it?"

"Mm." Jem felt an instinctive kinship with the poor child as she signed her own stupid name on the form. "Any further problems, call one-one-one for advice, okay?"

"Yep, fine. No worries." The mum tickled the toddler's belly and stole a spoonful of soggy cereal. "Is that everything? Only I have to get Holly ready for playgroup."

Not sure whether to laugh or cry, Jem opted for a diplomatic retreat. She squeezed her kit through the door and paused at the front gate to let a gang of schoolchildren go past. Starting work so early was always a brain bender, with everyone else's rush hour occurring three hours into her shift, when she was busy plotting her first brew and toilet break.

"Is the AP still waiting for me?" she asked Ryan as she shoved her bags into their cubbyholes.

Ryan did nothing to hide his irritation. "He is, and he's been pecking my head every ten minutes for the last hour. I'd give you a job if there was anything in the stack besides a nineteen-year-old with a blood blister, and Mary Kirkholt."

Jem fastened her seat belt, her foot idling on the accelerator. "How many is this for Mary today?"

"Three. She got herself wrapped up in loo paper this morning. Then, ten minutes after a crew had untangled her, she called again to say they'd knocked her moisturiser beyond her reach."

"The silly sod." Jem had been to Mary more times than she could count. She knew the key-safe number by heart, how many sugars Mary took in her coffee, and the names of all her cats. Regular callers to 999 were a bit like weeds; when one died, another two sprang up in their place, though Mary was more hygienic and harmless than most. "What's up with her now?"

"She's stuck on her commode."

"You know she won't be. She's like a whippet, transferring off that thing."

Ryan's sigh was the epitome of long-suffering. "I know that, you know that, the well-meaning but sadly ineffectual Frequent Caller Team know that, but when Mary calls…"

Jem finished the thought for him. "Mary deprives someone else of an ambulance for half an hour."

"Exactly."

"Never mind, she has loads of decent biccies." Mary kept a stash especially for crews, and her mugs were clean enough to have a drink out of. She was lonely and mildly demented, although that didn't excuse her for being a royal pain in the arse.

"Alpha Six One Three are going to her, if they can heroically limp there with their rattling suspension and wonky side door," Ryan said.

Jem smothered a laugh. Bob and Dougie were notorious for wrecking buses and would be more than willing to sit with their feet up at Mary's for an hour. "I'm sure they'll manage. Am I heading to station, then?"

"Yes, please. Call clear when you're done."

Schools traffic and commuters slowed Jem's progress to walking pace. She whacked the radio on full belt, singing along to the songs she recognised and flicking channels to avoid the ads. For once, the BBC weather forecast was spot on, and the predicted rain began to fall as she finished her banana at a pedestrian crossing. Ignoring the advice of the lollypop lady, the children in the road sprinted for cover, their bags held over their heads as they tussled with each other for pole position.

The downpour persisted, but the traffic petered out the farther Jem got from the town centre, and she pulled into the car park at Darnton before she could be diverted to another emergency. Having entered the station unnoticed, she dabbed her hair dry in front of the loo's tiny mirror and then ran her fingers through its cropped strands, still inclined to do a double-take when her fringe fell just so without requiring a twenty-minute resuscitation effort and half a ton of clips.

"Right," she said, not exactly brimming with confidence but not about to hide in the cubicle either. "Let's get this over with."

She found Baxter in the office, playing on a phone he quickly shoved into a drawer. He looked even younger by daylight, the over-keen central heating giving his cheeks a rosy apple gleam.

"Morning." She stayed by the door, anxious to start things off on the right foot. "You wanted to see me?"

He stared at her for a couple of seconds as if trying to place her face, and then hid his discomfiture in a flurry of paper straightening and file opening.

"Yes," he said, his voice cracking. He cleared his throat and tried again. "Yes, I need to go through a clinical debrief for the Abbey Vale job. There's been a lot of media interest, and it's likely to go to Coroner's, so I want to make sure we've crossed all our t's."

This was new. Jem was no stranger to Coroner's Court, but she'd never had any official preparation beside a copy of her Patient Report Form and Kev tagging along for moral support. Baxter was also new to his role, though, so she supposed she couldn't fault him for being thorough.

"Do you want a brew?" she asked. Once the meeting finished, she was unlikely to hit station again before midday, and there was no way she was raking over the details of that night without a mug of tea in her hand.

"No, thank you."

Pre-empting any dissent on his part, she went to the kitchen and made her drink, collecting a packet of shortbread from her locker on her way back. He'd covered the desk in case-related paperwork during her absence; she could see copies of her police statement, her Patient Report Form, and the forms Harriet had completed after terminating the resus.

"Talk me through the job, step by step." He clicked his pen three times to get its recalcitrant nib out and turned to a fresh page in his notepad. "I'll stop you when I have a question."

She sipped her tea and pulled her PRF toward her. She had completed it in retrospect, recording her actions in clinical terms and abbreviations—BLS commenced immediately, IV access gained, left external jugular, Airway secured, 7.0 ETT—and she fell back on that same tactic now, distancing herself from the emotions she'd felt, and not mentioning how close the physical strain had come to overwhelming her. Baxter filled his pad with an illegible scrawl as she spoke, and she paused in expectation when he rattled his pen against his thumb. She had just described the moment that Kyle had stopped breathing, and her mouth was so dry she had difficulty swallowing her tea.

"Why didn't you call for backup?" he asked. "When Parker went into cardiac arrest, why didn't you request immediate assistance?"

She indicated a line in the middle of her PRF. This wasn't her first rodeo; she knew how likely these jobs were to come back and bite her on the arse, and she had documented absolutely everything, no matter how trivial.

"I'd informed my dispatcher of Kyle's deterioration. I think my exact words were, 'I need help out here. This lad's about to arrest.' Once he actually had arrested, I was a little too preoccupied to repeat the request." Trying to rein in her temper, she gripped her mug until her fingers began to tingle. She was usually far more diplomatic when dealing with management, but Baxter's question was a ridiculous one, and it had hit a nerve. Later newspaper reports had seized on the lack of an appropriate ambulance response that night, raking the service over the coals for inadequate staffing and sketchy emergency provision, and she wasn't about to take the fall for NHS budget cuts and the resultant organisational chaos.

"Have you listened to the tape?" she asked. It was the first thing he should have done—all radio exchanges were recorded for posterity—but she wasn't surprised when he shook his head. "Ask for a copy of it," she said. "I run alongside this dispatcher for most of my shifts, and he's on the ball. If he'd had backup to send that night, he would have sent it."

Baxter's answering grunt was as opaque as his handwriting, so she considered her point made and moved on to describe her actions and interventions prior to Rosie and Kash arriving on the scene.

"Did you decompress his chest?" he said, interrupting her mid-sentence.

In lieu of an immediate answer, she bit into a piece of shortbread, took her time chewing it, and finished the last of her tea. It stopped her from walking out of the room and returning with Kev and a union representative.

"No, I didn't," she said.

He sat up straighter, everything about him more animated as he seized on a potential mistake. "Bilateral needle decompression is indicated in cases of traumatic cardiac arrest."

Jem clasped her hands in her lap. While she lacked confidence in most social circumstances, she had no such qualms when it came to the technicalities of her profession. "I'm aware of that. In this particular case, however, the patient's lungs were functioning just fine, and the portion of grey matter I found on the riverbank strongly implied that the arrest was due to cerebral trauma. The last thing he needed was me giving him a double pneumothorax because I'd blindly followed the guidelines."

"So you decided to go against protocol," Baxter snapped.

"I used my common sense," she said quietly. "Have you seen a copy of the post-mortem?"

He folded his arms like a petulant child. "No. Have you?"

She hadn't, but thanks to Rosie she knew what had been on it. "Kyle Parker died of a diffuse axonal injury secondary to a massive basilar skull fracture. He had multiple minor injuries consistent with an assault, and his tox screen was positive for a whole cocktail of crap. Other than the head injury, his gross anatomy was intact." She didn't spell the rest out for him. She just said a silent "thank you" to Rosie and watched his face turn even redder.

"You get a lot of jobs like this, don't you?" he said, taking hold of a pile of PRFs—her PRFs, she realised—and leafing through them. "You're averaging about three arrests per shift: suicides jumping off buildings in front of you, chokings, hangings, stabbings, a couple of shootings, cot deaths. You've had six partners come off your line in the past eighteen months, citing stress as the reason, and an unusual percentage of calls that turn out to be far more serious than their initial triage code would suggest."

Unsure where he was going, she didn't respond. It wasn't as if she was unaware of the facts he had just reeled off, nor could she deny them.

"Kyle Parker will be your fourth Coroner's Court appearance this year," he continued, "and we're only in the middle of March. Some paramedics never get to go there in the entire course of their careers."

Something in his tone made her ears prick up. She studied him with more care, noting how tightly he held her paperwork, and the undisguised resentment in his expression. He wasn't angry with her, he was jealous that she had dealt with jobs he would probably give his eyeteeth to experience. To a certain extent she understood his envy. She had felt the same way when she first started, craving the excitement of major traumas and the critically ill, calls that would put all of her training to good use, but no one wanted to deal with a near-constant deluge of such jobs, and she would be content to see out the remainder of her career working shifts with a regular mate, managing falls and innocuous bellyaches and idiots who should know better.

"I don't self-allocate," she said, reminding him that his role as an Advanced Paramedic allowed him to do just that. "I go to the jobs I'm sent to, and I can't help what they turn out to be."

He scoffed as if to dispute that, but it was a kneejerk reaction he took no further. "The court will require a statement from you," he said, drawing a line beneath the discussion but seeming satisfied he'd won some kind of victory.

She collected her mug and biscuits, her patience worn to the point of snapping. "I'll email it to Legal as soon as they formally request one."

"I'd like to see a copy before then."

"Fine." She stood and opened the door, letting in a blast of diesel fumes that still smelled better than his office. "I'm going to tell control I'm clear."

She walked out without waiting for permission and sank into a crew room chair between Bob and Dougie, who were sitting with their feet up, watching *Homes Under the Hammer*.

Dougie muted the television. "You all right, flower?"

"Yeah, thanks."

Bob looked sceptical but didn't comment. He collected their mugs and went into the kitchen. Seconds later, she heard water pouring and the creak of the toaster's lever.

Dougie picked a crumb out of his beard. "We saw Spence at West Penn. He reckons Baxter's after a transfer to this group."

"Terrific. We're already firm friends." Too stressed to dwell on the possibility, she changed the subject. "How was Mary Kirkholt?"

Bob returned in time to catch the tail end of her question. He arranged brews and toast on a low table and helped himself before answering. "She was fine, very chirpy, and absolutely not stuck on the loo. KitKats and Jammie Dodgers today, and we're now off the road until someone comes out to fix our side door, so it's all coming up roses."

"I should call clear." Jem unclipped her radio, but Dougie put his hand on hers.

"Have five minutes. If they really need you, they know where you are."

She relented and picked up her mug, shocked when her hand trembled hard enough to slosh tea over its rim. She hadn't realised how badly Baxter had unsettled her. "Okay, five minutes."

Bob passed her the toast. "Good girl. Oh, by the way, we asked our dispatcher to follow up on that bloke from this morning. Ian with the aneurysm."

She nodded, braced for the worst. "And?"

"Stable and heading to High Dependency, and his children are sitting with his missus."

Jem dropped her toast onto her plate. "Get out. *Really?*"

"Yep, really. Apparently, his wife wanted all our names for a thank-you card." He cackled with his mouth full. "Tell Baxter to put that in his pipe and smoke it."

CHAPTER ELEVEN

The lad emptied a packet of prawn cocktail crisps into his mouth, wiped his greasy fingers on his jeans, and opened a Mars Bar. Despite his penchant for snacks, he was tall and wiry, and his low-riding jeans revealed a pair of once-white Calvin Kleins. Acne bloomed pink on his nose and chin, and although his clothes were all label brands, they didn't appear to have been washed this side of Christmas.

"Four, maybe five weeks," he said through a mouthful of chocolate, turning to his mate for confirmation, but the other lad shrugged and continued to type on his phone. "What we in now?"

Rosie stepped out of the small pool gathering by her boot. The canal bridge offered shelter from the elements, but the rain hadn't stopped all day, and water was running in a thin line to widen already well-established puddles.

"It's March the fifteenth," she said. "Which would mean you last saw Kyle around Valentine's Day?"

The crisp-eater clicked his fingers. "Yeah, yeah, that's right. He got Tahlia one of those massive cards and a load of chocolate so she'd shag him, but then he fucked her off, so she started shagging Demi-Lee, which is kinda cool."

Rosie recorded the comment verbatim, amused by the prospect of typing everything up for Steph, who had hand-picked her for house-to-house that morning and then sent her chasing after a gang of Kyle's latchkey kid mates.

"Do you have an address or contact details for Tahlia?" she asked.

The lad chugged from an energy drink and burped close-mouthed. The stink of fish and artificial fruit flavour hit her as he exhaled.

"Her dad chucked her out cos she's a lezzer. She was crashing with Demi-Lee for a while, but Woody reckons he's seen her down the old mill."

Rosie grimaced. "The one on Bennett Street? Looks like something out of a horror film?"

"Yeah. Second floor's dodgy as shit. Mickey Foss fell through it a few months back, and he's been a cabbage ever since."

"Thanks for the heads up. Can you describe Tahlia for me?"

Still busy working on his Mars, the lad raised one finger as if loath to spoil his final bite. He swallowed and immediately began to pick his teeth. "She's half-Paki," he said around a grubby digit.

Rosie gave him a look that made him bite down on his knuckle. "Can we phrase that any better?"

"Sorry, miss," he said, his cheeks reddening. "She's small and, um, light brown, and she has long dark curly hair, and she doesn't wear one of them scarf things. I think she's about fourteen."

"Thank you. I'm sure that'll be very useful." Rosie tucked her notepad into a pocket on her stab vest and looked around at the group: two lads and two girls, all of them skinny and shivering, and none of them older than fifteen. "Does everyone have somewhere to stay tonight?"

They nodded en masse, offering up addresses that were probably false and a shelter known only as "Olly's." She handed the lad her card. "If you think of anything else that might help, or you need help yourselves, give me a call, okay?"

He shoved the card into his pocket without glancing at it. She knew that none of them would ever contact her, but still, she had to try. She updated her status with comms as she slogged along the waterlogged towpath, avoiding dog shit and the odd needle discarded by the smack rats who congregated beneath the next bridge down. Surrounded by abandoned mills and factories, this part of the canal had long since been claimed by Manchester's cast-offs: the drunks and the addicts, the homeless and the destitute. Only someone with a death wish or a very strong belief in a higher being would venture there after dark. She passed a pair of the latter by the lock, their matching red coats identifying them as volunteers from the neighbourhood church. The elder of the two tipped his hat at her.

"How do, Officer. All quiet on the western front?"

"For once. I think the rain's keeping them in. Even the geese look cheesed off."

He chuckled. "It carries on like this and the town centre will go under again. Sandbags are already out down Hearts Cross."

That came as no surprise. The small village of Hearts Cross bordered Stanny Brook, but it sat squarely in a flood zone and its residents were still counting the cost from the last time the river burst its banks. With government austerity policies biting hard, the council had little in the pot for essential services, let alone flood defences, and they had employed a head-in-sand approach to future breaches in the hope that the sun might finally shine on their patch and negate the need for expensive works. Such blind optimism with regard to the region's climate confirmed long-held suspicions that most of the councillors were morons.

"Have either of you met a lass called Tahlia on your travels?" she asked. "About fourteen years old? Possibly sleeping rough?"

"No," the younger chap said. "There are kids dotted about in a few of the mills, but the buildings are death traps, so we stay out of them."

"That's understandable." She gave them her card, issuing the usual request should they cross paths with Tahlia before she did. The church ran youth groups and a food bank and took a mobile soup kitchen into the town centre at night. No one seemed to mind listening to a sermon if they were hungry enough. "Right then, I'd best let you get going," she said.

They performed an awkward shuffle on the narrow path, Rosie stepping aside and slipping on a muddy verge. Rain was seeping beneath her shirt, and her trousers clung to her thighs as if they'd been spray-painted on. She stamped sticky lumps of mud from her boots as she walked on, her foul mood exacerbated by a WhatsApp message from Kash showing nothing but a Big Mac and a large fries.

I hope it gives you heartburn, she replied, and swore at the central locking on her patrol car when it flashed the indicators but failed to open the doors.

In no rush to get to Bennett Street, she took a roundabout route that weaved through the back streets of east Manchester. She beeped her horn and waved at the owner of the Manc Muffin, who always piled extra bacon on her breakfast barm. Then she circled around the back of the massive gas holders, slowing to admire their Scalextric-like structure, their framework bleak but bold against the washed-out sky. The regeneration triggered by the building of the Etihad Stadium hadn't reached this far, but the redbrick terraced streets felt like home to her, and she hoped any eventual attempts to gentrify the area wouldn't drive its soul from it.

She didn't bother stopping at the front of the old mill. Every man and his dog knew that was where the padlocked gates and security warnings were. Instead, she drove slowly around the block toward the straight section that ran alongside the river. She and Kash had crawled through a gap in the fence there one night, on a mission to disrupt a medium-sized rave that hadn't let a lack of electricity dampen its spirits.

Recognising the bright red slab of hoarding that marked the illicit entrance, she parked the car and tried to summon the energy to get out. The mill dominated the neighbourhood, towering above the tightly packed houses and spoiling the view from every backyard. It got set on fire once or twice a year, but it seemed impervious to serious harm, and no one would accept responsibility for its demolition. She snapped a photo, focusing on a broken window and bricks burned black and splintered at the edges, and then attached the image to a message for Jem. *I'm going in. If you don't hear from me in an hour, send help.*

Jem must have been between emergencies, because a reply came quickly. *Send help where, you pillock?*

Bennett Street, Ardwick.

Christ, is that the old mill? Jem punctuated her question with horrified emojis. *Are you on your own? Please don't go upstairs. I went to a lad not long back who'd fallen through the second floor and mashed his brains.*

Small world, Rosie thought. *I'll be fine*, she typed, unsure why she had chosen to contact Jem and not Kash. *Don't worry, I'll let you know when I'm out.*

Please do, and be careful. There are rats in there bigger than Alsatians.

No, there aren't. Rosie sent the text and then tagged on an addendum. *Shit. ARE there?*

No, but they're well organised and toothy. Crap, got a job. TEXT ME.

I will, I promise, Rosie replied, and got out of the car.

As if to add insult to injury, the mill was tall enough to create a wind tunnel, funnelling gusts that tore at her uniform and hair and hurled rain against her.

"Fucking hell," she spat, but the wind whipped the curse away as well, following it with a prolonged barrage that rattled loose panels of fencing and sent howls echoing off the brickwork. Her access route took her across a minefield of wooden planks, shattered bricks, and litter of every imaginable kind. The locals had turned the perimeter into a makeshift tip, dragging out their unwanted sofas and white goods to dump them amongst the nettles and brambles. The last time the river had burst its banks, it swept most of the crap away, but people had wasted no time refilling the gaps.

Rosie took her time navigating the obstacle course, wary of falling and ending up with her hands full of glass or contaminated sharps. The building cast a long shadow, exacerbating the weather's overbearing gloom, and she switched on her torch as she approached a pile of wooden crates stacked to boost trespassers through an empty window. The crates rocked beneath her weight, and she scrambled through quickly before she tempted fate, grateful to land on a solid concrete floor that was covered in charred remnants and rat droppings but not liable to collapse without warning.

A slow pan of her torch revealed hefty floor-to-ceiling pillars and a series of low brick walls that had formed partitions back when the mill was operational. Any remaining machinery had been removed by the owners or looted for scrap metal, and the expansive space was now strewn with cider bottles and beer cans, junk food wrappers, and the odd condom. The closest corner, where two of the windows still had glass, showed signs of more prolonged inhabitation: a circle of ash from a small fire, tattered blankets, and a pair of soiled trousers, but no one seemed to have been there recently and the clothing wasn't that of a teenage girl.

Using that corner as a starting point, Rosie zigzagged across the floor, trying to cover as much of it as possible whilst keeping a close eye on where she was putting her feet. Several sections of the concrete had traps cut into it, covered only by rotting wooden doors and almost impossible to spot, even in daylight. Someone had splattered a couple with yellow paint, but a large hole in the centre of another implied Mickey Foss wasn't the only one to have come a cropper in here. Kneeling by the gap, she directed her torch through it and leaned low, straining to pick out objects in the murk. Dank air hit her face, bringing with it a stagnant tang, and she could see floodwater several metres below, its ink-black surface rippling in the draught. She shivered, pushing away from the edge and then dusting off her knees as she stood. A quick check of her watch told her she had twenty-five minutes left before Jem might raise the alarm, but there was only the very back of the room still left for her to explore.

Following the rear wall brought her to a recess housing a flight of stairs. Happy to heed Jem's warning about the upper levels, she was about to call it a day when a sudden smash of glass and a stifled laugh sounded clearly from the floor above.

"Shit." She kicked the dusty bottom step, glaring at its fresh footprints. The prints were smaller than hers and overlapping, suggesting more than one person was up there.

The first step creaked but held as she put her foot on it. She set her jaw, resigned to her fate and somewhat comforted by the prospect of Jem being sent to her should she break her neck. Jem would no doubt be less than impressed, however, so she crept upward at a snail's pace, avoiding any obvious weak spots in the wood and holding the handrail in the few places it was securely fixed. Still hidden in the alcove at the top of the flight, she mulled over her options. The last thing she wanted was to spook anyone and have to chase after the buggers, so she tiptoed to the door and pushed it open a crack. She could hear three distinct and distinctly young voices: two girls and one lad. The kids were close by and to her left, and judging by the smell that hit her, they were all stoned.

"Yeah, but it's not unpossible is it?" the lad said. "They've got a horn."

One of the girls laughed. "They've got *antlers*, y'thick twat, not horns, and they'd never shag a horse."

"So where do they come from, then?" he asked, after a prolonged spell of inhalation that ended with a violent fit of coughing and another wave of dope smoke wafting over Rosie.

"Africa, I think. It were on ITV," the second girl said. "But they got one in Chester Zoo, Woody, I seen it."

Rosie's ears pricked up at the mention of the lad's name. She walked across to them, her presence completely ignored until she stopped a couple of feet away from their smouldering disposable barbecue and cleared her throat. The trio were slouching on the floor in a nest of blankets and sleeping bags. The girl with her back to Rosie craned her neck, grinning as she viewed Rosie upside down. Her lank hair—blond, streaked through with bright green—fell about her face, and her tongue piercing flashed gold in the torchlight.

"Hiya. You're dead pretty. D'ya want a burger?" She rolled over clumsily, scrabbling about on the floor to retrieve a dirt-speckled barmcake housing a disc of grey meat.

"Uh, no. Cheers, though," Rosie said. With none of the kids showing any inclination to do a runner, she sat on a spare crate at Woody's side.

Woody sucked on his joint and then seemed to realise he'd made a grave mistake, not in smoking a Class B substance in front of a police officer, but in not offering her a toke. "It's really good shit," he said, turning the spliff's soggy side toward her.

"It's tempting, but I'll pass, thanks."

He shrugged at her refusal and unscrewed a half-empty bottle of cider. "Have you ever been to Chester Zoo?" he asked, regarding her with red-rimmed eyes and scratching at a scab on his cheek.

Rosie crossed her legs at the ankles, settling in for the long run. "Yeah, once, I think. Why?"

"Did you see the unicorn?"

The blond girl laughed so hard that her alcopop shot out of her nose.

"Ah," Rosie said as their earlier exchange began to make sense. "I don't believe it was there at the time, so no."

"I've never been to a zoo," he said. "I shot a squirrel with an airgun once, but it's not the same as seeing a real-life unicorn."

Rosie nodded, doing her utmost to remain professional. "Maybe you should do a bit of googling when you get home."

The second girl—ghostly pale and Goth to the nth degree, with self-harm scars running the length of both forearms—held out a tube of Smarties and tipped a few into Rosie's palm. "We'll tell him later," she whispered.

Rosie colour-ordered her Smarties on her knee and started with a purple one. "Break it gently," she said. "It'll be like finding out about Father Christmas all over again."

The Goth girl giggled. "He still spends half of Christmas Eve hanging out of the window with a pair of binoculars he won on a tombola." Her brow suddenly furrowed as she noticed Rosie's uniform for the first time. "Shit. Are you going to arrest us for the weed?"

Rosie pondered that while she sucked her sweets. "No. But I might have to wag my finger sternly and tell you to behave in future."

Woody spilled cider down his chin, the four-litre bottle too heavy for him to keep raised. He was smaller than Kyle, and a familial resemblance to the Goth suggested they were siblings. "You're nice," he said. "I like you."

"I like you too, so let's do a bit of a deal." Rosie took out her notepad. "I'm looking for a young lass called Tahlia, and I was speaking to a mate of yours down by the canal who said you'd seen her in here."

Woody's mouth twisted, drawing his lips to one side and making his nose twitch like an inquisitive rabbit. Rosie assumed he was puzzling out how she knew his name or why she was looking for Tahlia, or perhaps he still hadn't moved beyond the unicorn conundrum.

"Tahlia," she prompted him, stopping just short of clicking her fingers. "Fourteen years old, mixed race, long curly hair, had a fling with Kyle Parker? You tell me where I can find her, and I'll forget all about the weed."

The penny dropped in slow, clearly signposted intervals. Rosie had finished her Smarties and arranged another batch by the time he answered.

"Demi-Lee's bird!" he said. "I fancied her for a bit, but Kyle said he'd knock me head off if I tried owt."

"When did you last see her?"

"'Bout two weeks ago. Her and Demi-Lee had a barney and split up, and she had nowhere to stay. She crashed in here for a couple of nights, then she took all her stuff and never came back."

"Did she say where she was going? Might she have gone home?"

"Naw, her dad's dead strict, and he'd have killed her for being a lez. She said she'd got a really nice place, but she wouldn't say where, so she was probably bullshitting."

"Do you know where her parents live?"

"North Curzon. Tarrick Street, I think, but I don't know what number."

The girls were nodding along as he spoke, making no attempt to contradict him or elaborate on the details, and they shook their heads when Rosie asked if they had anything to add.

Satisfied they were telling the truth, she pushed to her feet and folded her arms. "Right, come on."

They gawped at her.

"You promised you wasn't going to arrest us," the blonde said.

"I'm not, but I can't leave you in here trespassing willy-nilly, drinking underage, and smoking dope. Do you have homes to go to?"

She got a couple of shrugs and a "yeah."

"Are your parents or guardians there?"

"Our mam's at work," Woody said. He pointed at the blonde. "Her big sister will be in."

"And how do we feel about her big sister?"

"She's all right," the blonde said. "She'll make us pizza and won't tell on us."

That was good enough for Rosie. In a perfect world, she'd have delivered the children safely into the arms of their frantic yet forgiving parents, but the world was far from perfect, and a big sister who gave a damn and supplied pizza was better than nothing. She collected the cider bottle and stamped out the barbecue. "Mind how you go on the stairs," she said. "If you get down them in one piece and don't try to scarper at the bottom, I'll buy you all a McFlurry."

The woman put an arm around her boyfriend and laid her head on his shoulder. "At least the old sod went peacefully," she said, and Jem almost spat her chewing gum into the bucket of bloody vomit at her feet.

The protracted and grisly demise of Stanley Brown had been anything but peaceful. A chronic alcoholic with a gastric ulcer, he had decorated every room of his flat with bright red sprays of gore before collapsing in the corner behind his telly. Rigor mortis had frozen his face in an agonised grimace, and his outstretched limbs were contorted, as if he'd spent his last seconds warding off a wild animal.

The woman made an elaborate sign of the cross, only in reverse and enhanced by a knock-kneed curtsy, and then gave her boyfriend a chirpy thumbs-up when he came back into the room carrying a six-pack and a large plastic bag. Busy with her paperwork, Jem hadn't noticed him leave, but he'd evidently been raiding Stanley's kitchen.

"Stan would want us to have these," he said. He handed the woman a pilfered can of super-strength lager and toasted the body with his own. "Cheers, pal. You were the very best of us." Dabbing his dry eyes with a ragged handkerchief, he turned to Jem. "You need owt else from us, love?"

"No, thank you. You've been very helpful. I'll just wait for the police to arrive." She raised an eyebrow at the plastic bag. He was struggling to lift it, and glass clinked every time he moved. Pre-empting any enquiry on her part, he gave her a brisk nod and sidled toward the front door.

"Come on, Yvonne. I'm sure the paramedic is very busy."

Although far from sober, Yvonne got the message and tottered across to join him on the threshold. "We'll be in the Red Lion if anyone needs us," she said.

"Grieving," he added, and stumbled in his haste to get out of the door.

Jem waited until the lift silenced the irregular clack of Yvonne's high heels. Then she went into the kitchen, where the smell of sweet copper and decomposition wasn't quite so eye-watering. The soles of her boots stuck to the lino as she walked to the cleanest countertop, and flies were gorging themselves on the unwashed dishes that filled the sink. She scratched her arm and then her head, setting off a chain reaction of furious itching that only abated when her mobile buzzed with a message from Rosie. *Safe and sound and on my way to MaccieD's. Fancy a Flurry?*

Love one, Jem typed. *But I'm stuck babysitting a body until your lot arrive.* She was about to send the text when someone knocked on the door.

"Hello? Police!" a man shouted.

"In the kitchen," she called back. "Watch where you're putting your feet."

The officer swore every couple of steps, making it easy for her to gauge his approach. With his presence guaranteeing she'd be able to leave the scene, she erased all but the first two words of her message and added, *Meet me in the B&Q car park in fifteen.*

She rendezvoused with Rosie at the far end of the B&Q car park, well beyond the steady stream of baby boomers laden with gardening supplies and buckets of grout. For the sake of convenience and staying dry, she took a leaf from every police series she'd ever watched and lined her driver's window up with Rosie's. Rosie—who apparently also watched too much telly—made a show of checking for witnesses before she passed Jem the ice cream, still wrapped in its brown paper bag. For extra effect, she'd donned her sunglasses despite the pouring rain.

"Very incognito," Jem said. "I'm sure no one's spotted us, sitting here in our subtly marked cars." She hit her blues for the benefit of a woman who'd stopped to stare, and the woman flounced off, steering her trolley-load of magnolia Dulux into a bollard.

"Nothing to see here," Rosie announced loudly. "We're allowed to take a break, no matter what the *Daily Mail* might say." She waggled a finger toward Jem's paper bag. "You struck me as an extra sauce kind of lass. So to speak."

Jem said nothing, but she felt her ears go hot. Ducking her head to hide the telltale flush, she delved into her bag, popping the lid off her Flurry and then gaping at it. The tub was full to overflowing and covered in liberal dollops of raspberry, with half a ton of chocolate embedded in the ice cream. She sat up straight again, her pink ears forgotten. "How the hell did you wangle this? I've never been able to wangle this, even when I'm in uniform."

"I batted my eyelashes at the cute lad behind the till," Rosie said, and displayed another bag from the passenger side. "He gave me a free apple pie and a burger with extra gherkins."

"You have a real gift." Jem settled back in the seat and entered her rest request on the RRV's data terminal. She'd told Ryan she was happy to take her break off-base, which gave her twenty minutes to catch up on all Rosie's gossip. "So, what do you know? What were you doing in the old mill?"

Rosie caught a drip of ice cream with her finger and wiped it off on a napkin already dirt-smudged and crumpled. She'd obviously given herself a cat lick, but she'd missed a grey streak on her cheek and the cobwebs stuck to her hair.

"Trying to find Kyle's mates," she said. "I found a few by the canal who knew him in passing, but I failed to track down Tahlia, who may have been his girlfriend for a short spell before she joined us on the Dark Side by dating Demi-Lee."

"The plot thickens," Jem said.

"Indeed it does. Tahlia had been crashing in the mill, but by all accounts she's moved to somewhere splendid." Rosie tapped her teeth with her spoon, deep in thought. "Which seems unlikely."

Jem had only been to the mill once, but the prospect of spending a night there gave her the collywobbles. "Where the hell are Tahlia's family in all of this? Does she have any, or is she in care?"

"They live on North Curzon. I think Steph will be paying them a visit in the not too distant. According to a very stoned lad, Tahlia's dad kicked her out after her dalliance with Demi-Lee."

"Poor kid," Jem said. Not for the first time in her career, the phrase "there but by the grace" sprang to mind. She had responded to numerous 999 calls for looked-after children, most in their early teens, running away from their care homes, taking drugs, self-harming, or getting drunk. Sometimes they got into the wrong car with the wrong man. Oftentimes they did the same thing all over again, and she came to know the children by name. She turned up the car's heating as goose pimples rose on her arms. "What about the local shelters and hostels? Is someone checking those?"

"As we speak." Rosie flicked through her notebook. "Have you heard of one called Olly's? A lad mentioned it, and I assumed I'd be able to get the address from comms, but they haven't been able to find it."

"Doesn't ring a bell. I'll ask around, though."

"Cheers. I'll probably be on that tomorrow, unless Steph finds me another plum gig involving towpaths and dilapidated buildings."

Jem busied herself making patterns in her ice cream, concentrating on the swirl of sauce so she wouldn't blurt out the question teetering on the tip of her tongue. Whatever was going on between Rosie and Steph, it was none of her business. If Rosie wanted to tell her, she would tell her.

"Two years and three months," Rosie said, her voice barely audible above the rain drumming on the cars. "That's how long we were together. We split up last September."

"Oh." Jem put her tub down. "Sorry, Rosie, I didn't mean to pry."

"You didn't pry."

Jem regarded her carefully, trying to catch signs of anger or regret, but Rosie was nibbling a piece of Flake she'd dipped in raspberry, and she seemed quite cheerful.

"I wanted to, though," Jem admitted.

"Well, yes, I could see that." Rosie bit her chocolate. "But in contrast to my bull-in-a-china-shop approach, you are far too polite to be nosy."

Jem checked the clock on the dash. She had eight minutes left on her break, which didn't seem anywhere near long enough for this conversation. It would be cowardly to change the subject, though.

"It must be hard to see her all the time at work," she said. "I know people who've had to move stations or groups after a break-up with a colleague."

Rosie reached a hand out of her window, letting rain collect on her mucky palm. She watched it drip through her fingers for a few seconds before answering. "It helps that she's Major Crimes and not a bog-standard plod, which is ironic, because that was half the problem in the first place. She wanted me to follow in her footsteps, work on her team, but I was happy doing what I'm doing. I'd like to take my National Investigators' Examination—that's the first step to qualifying as a detective—but I'll do it when I'm ready, not to please whoever I'm sleeping with."

"Sounds fair enough."

"Not to Steph," Rosie said, and for the first time Jem heard the bitterness and hurt beneath her words. "Steph is Type A to the core, and I'm…well, I'm not sure what the hell I am. It wasn't all bad, of course. We got on fine at first, had a great social life, lots of nights out and weekends away. I don't really know at what point it stopped being fun. I can't remember it being a major light-bulb moment or anything; I just realised she was whittling away at me bit by bit. Every decision we made together was actually her decision, and I was constantly making compromises to keep her on side. It was exhausting, and I was miserable, so I ended it."

She was back to staring at her palm again. Jem took hold of her fingers and gave them a squeeze.

"Did she just let you?" she asked. "End it, I mean."

"No, not really," Rosie said quietly. "We're not a couple, not by a long shot, but she pesters me to go on dates with her and makes sure I'm assigned to her cases, and every so often she'll get me drunk enough that I'll sleep with her." She withdrew her hand from Jem's and tucked it between her thighs, her embarrassment evident in every stilted movement.

"Hey," Jem said. She waited until Rosie looked at her. "I can fabricate feline shenanigans just as well as you can, so phone me if you ever need me, okay?"

"Steph knows I don't have a cat," Rosie said. Her face was pale, but she was starting to smile.

Jem shook her spoon at Rosie, splashing ice cream down the side of the car. "I'll use my imagination. I'm very creative when I set my mind to it. Do we have a deal?"

"Okay, yes, we have a deal." When they shook on it, Rosie kept a tight hold of Jem's hand. "On a scale of one to ten, how pathetic do you think I am?"

"Zero. Minus one. Don't be bloody stupid," Jem said. "Nobody's perfect. We all fuck up, get stuff wrong, and do things we'd want to change if we had the chance." She held Rosie's gaze, making sure she'd got her point across, and then jumped as the RRV's data terminal began to bleep and her radio blared in synch with it. She scrolled down to the job information and sighed. "I rest my case," she said, turning the monitor so Rosie could read it. *Male, nineteen. Head stuck in a gate.*

"For fuck's sake." Rosie could barely swear for laughing. "That scale I just mentioned? He's getting an eleven."

CHAPTER TWELVE

Jem straightened Ferg's bowtie and steered him in front of her bedroom mirror. "They're not going to know what's hit them," she said, brushing a crumb from his kilt. "Damn, Ferg, you have better legs than me."

"Hairier legs," he corrected her. "And ginger hair at that."

"Shush, it's all part of your charm. You'll have them queuing out of the marquee again."

They walked downstairs together. She was ready for work and scheduled to drop him at the train station half an hour before the start of her shift.

"How ever are you going to manage without me?" he asked. He'd always been as much a big brother as a best friend, and there was genuine concern in his expression, despite his lightness of tone.

She handed him his laptop case. "It's only five days, Ferg. I just need to drag my poor aching bones to the end of this shift, and then I'm planning a long weekend of lounging about with my feet up. I might walk the dogs if I'm feeling energetic, which, I have to admit, is unlikely."

"You could always ask Officer Rosie to lend a hand," he said, and reacted with exaggerated innocence when she walloped him. "What? You speak very highly of her, and you've already been on a couple of dates."

"We have never—those weren't *dates!*" Jem folded her arms, the poster child for indignation and denial, though she knew she was playing right into his hands. As predicted, he paid no heed to her protest.

"There are few things more romantic than sharing a McFlurry at B&Q, Jemima."

"I can think of plenty of things." She wrapped his scarf around his neck, pulling it tighter than was strictly necessary. "Stop being an arse and grab your suitcase, or you'll be catching the bus to Piccadilly."

The station's drop-off was half empty, and Jem risked the ire of the taxi drivers by getting out to hug Ferg.

"There's a chicken and mushroom pie in the fridge for your tea tonight," he said. "And I made a lasagne as well." He winked at her. "It's big enough to share."

Unable to be cross with him when he'd gone to so much trouble, she kissed his cheek and gave him a bottle of Lucozade, a box of paracetamol, and a hip flask full of whiskey. "Hangover cures," she said. "The choice is yours. I'll see you Tuesday."

He laughed, tucking the hip flask beneath his kilt. "See you Tuesday, hen."

She waited until he reached the main entrance, where a growing throng of impatient commuters assimilated him. The traffic heading away from Manchester was starting to pick up, most of the cars heading to the flyover that would take them out of the city and into Trafford Park. After almost being sideswiped by a speeding VW at the Apollo roundabout, Jem drove up Hyde Road as if everything was out to get her, a tactic that had kept her collision-free for the years she'd lived within the city limits. The main strip of shops in Gorton was stirring to life, with shutters clattering open on its newsagents and cafes, while white van men made a beeline for the twenty-four-hour supermarket. She overtook a street sweeper, and, forgetting she was in her own car, waved at an ambulance, whose driver waved back regardless. She laughed and cranked the radio up a notch. She loved the city, loved its eclectic neighbourhoods and its fierce sense of pride. Like any sprawling multicultural metropolis, it had its problems, but it usually faced them cheerfully and head on, with a pint in its hand.

Through Gorton and out the other side, she hopped on the ring road for a junction, arriving at Darnton with ten minutes to spare. She made a quick brew and breakfast and had only eaten half her cereal when Caitlin came into the crew room.

"Hey. How did you get on?" Jem asked. The previous night had been Caitlin's first shift on the RRV, and she'd looked scared to death when Jem gave her the keys at handover. Jem might not have liked her, but she knew how nerve-wracking it was to work solo, and Caitlin barely had a year's experience as a paramedic.

"It was fine." The flatness of Caitlin's answer made it clear that was all she had to say on the subject. "Darren wants to see you in the office."

Jem pushed her cornflakes away. "Now?"

"Yes. Now."

Rather than leave her pots for someone else, Jem washed and dried her dish and mug first. Then she knocked on the office door at dead on six, ensuring any possible bollocking would at least be on the clock. She entered the room to find Baxter and Caitlin both seated and waiting for her.

"Is there a problem?" she asked, genuinely perplexed. She'd assumed the summons would pertain to Kyle Parker, but Caitlin was an unexpected spanner in the works.

In lieu of an answer, Baxter tossed the controlled drugs book for the RRV onto the desk. Every ambulance carried an identical book, locked away in a safe with the boxes of morphine and diazepam. It was the paramedic's responsibility to complete a check each shift to confirm that the numbers recorded tallied with the physical stock. Jem picked the book up, still unsure what the issue was. The count had been correct at the start and end of her shift, and she had handed the safe key directly to Caitlin.

"Caitlin contacted me to report a discrepancy with the morphine at the start of her shift last night," Baxter said. "There are three missing, and no one witnessed either of your entries."

"The car hadn't been manned when I took it over yesterday morning, and there was no one else on station," Jem said, staring at the damning red ink, all-caps scrawl occupying the three lines below her signature. She had logged eighteen vials, Caitlin only fifteen, and Baxter had confirmed Caitlin's count. She shook her head. "This can't be right. I remember putting them all away." She faltered, her protest losing conviction almost immediately as she began to doubt herself. She had finished late and checked the drugs whilst waiting on scene for a doctor to return her call. By the time she got back to station, she'd been fuming and exhausted, and she hadn't thought to ask Caitlin to countersign the book.

"We searched the RRV thoroughly," Baxter said. In contrast to Jem, his voice was gaining confidence as he sensed her uncertainty and warmed to his theme. "My best guess is you left the vials on the roof of the car when you counted them, and they're smashed on a roadside somewhere."

"I don't do that," she said. Several other paramedics had made that mistake, but she had never been one of them. "There was a memo."

He took the book back, setting it in front of Caitlin, who placed her hand on its cover. "In which case, the police may have to be informed. They might want to search your house and your car, and I need to speak to Kevin regarding disciplinary proceedings."

"Fine, that's fine. I'll contact my union rep," Jem said, too bewildered to offer any kind of defence. She knew for sure she hadn't stolen them. "Am I okay to sign on now?"

"Yes. Someone will be in touch in due course." He unlocked his computer screen and began to type an email, effectively dismissing her.

Caitlin unclipped the radio from her belt and looped the RRV's keys over its antenna. "I haven't used anything, and you've got half a tank of fuel," she said, passing everything to Jem and showing all her teeth when she smiled.

"Thanks." Jem closed the office door behind her and leaned against the corridor wall, fumbling for her inhaler. The spray worked quickly to alleviate her wheezing but ramped up her sense of panic. "Bloody hell," she whispered. Ordinarily, a slip like this would result in an appendix being placed in her file, a time-limited warning that would progress to a disciplinary should she transgress again before it expired. With Baxter involved, however, she had no idea what might happen to her, or in which direction he might try to push Kev.

She walked slowly to the RRV and sat in the driver's seat. She needed to sort her kit out and speak to a rep and try to pinpoint every potential place she could have mislaid three glass vials of a Class A, Schedule 2 drug. The lad on dispatch sounded knackered, running through the usual short list of questions and acknowledging her request to complete a vehicle check with a distracted "yeah, that's fine. G'night, then."

She managed to put a brave face on things as she changed a defib battery and looked through the response bag, but it crumpled as she switched on the suction. Common sense told her to leave a message for her union rep, and that nothing could be done to help her until she'd informed him of the accusation. She didn't want to be sensible, though. She wanted an unaffiliated-with-the-ambulance-service shoulder to cry on, and then she might be able to buckle down and get on with things.

She toyed with her mobile, scrolling through the directory, past Ferg, who would be well on his way to London by now, and past her dad, who had enough on his plate and would likely still be in bed. Those were her top two choices, she told herself as she hunted in vain for a tissue. Those were the people she would have called first, had they not been unavailable or hurtling below the Watford Gap. Her third option was merely a fallback in their stead, someone she knew would be awake, because they too started work at stupid o'clock. The triangular bandage she shook out billowed like a white flag as the draught from the heater caught it. Ignoring its gratuitous symbolism, she used it to blow her nose and then called Rosie.

❖

Preferring to enjoy a leisurely breakfast and then hare around getting everything sorted at the last minute, Rosie was still in her pyjamas and sharing an apple with Fluffy when her mobile rang.

Taking advantage of the distraction, Fluffy pinched the last chunk and scurried under the sofa with it.

"You better run, you little sod," she said, flipping the cover back on her phone just in time to see Jem's name but not fast enough to answer the call. "Huh."

Jem had disconnected after only three rings, suggesting she'd either bum-dialled or had second thoughts. Rosie peeled a banana, keeping one eye on the phone to see whether an explanatory text or another call might be forthcoming. It was ten past six, so Jem would have started her shift. Given their dual tendency to attract shit luck, if Rosie disturbed her as she drove to a job it would probably result in a multi-vehicle pile-up. The phone rang again as Rosie took her first bite of banana. She swallowed and answered simultaneously, producing a sound reminiscent of a choking frog.

"Hello?" Jem said. "Rosie, is that you?"

Rosie hacked a cough and started again. "How do. It's me. Sorry, I had a gobful of banana."

Jem chuckled and then took a long breath, as if the air around her had suddenly cleared. "Am I okay calling this early? Only, I thought you'd be up, and I didn't know who else—"

"You're fine," Rosie said, cutting across her rambling. "I'm up, dressed, raring to go—one of those is a fib—so what's wrong? And don't tell me 'nothing,' because you'd be crap at lying even over the phone."

"It's not nothing," Jem said. "That Advanced Paramedic from the Kyle Parker job? Baxter? He's accused me of losing some morphine, and I don't think I did but I can't prove I didn't." She relayed the facts without inflection, as if she'd already admitted defeat. "And I'm not sure how far he'll take it. He's threatened to have the police search my house."

Rosie used a knife to chop the end off the banana, the blade hitting the table with a cathartic thump. She fed the piece to Fluffy as he slinked over the laminate. "Are you running an illegal drug den, Jemima? Fuelled with the spoils of your day job?"

"Definitely not. Christ, I feel guilty if I've got a headache and I take a couple of Brufen from the bag."

"I wouldn't lose any sleep about the search, then. Knowing how overstretched our lot are, I can see them getting around to it about a week on Wednesday. Have you spoken to a union rep?"

"Not yet. But I'm going to," Jem added hurriedly, as if afraid Rosie might scold her for neglecting the priorities. The thin rasp of her irregular wheezing was transmitted clearly, despite the patchy mobile reception.

Rosie left her chair and paced across the kitchen, battening down the urge to go to Darnton and have this conversation in person, perhaps calling in on Baxter if she had a minute or two to spare. "It'll be okay," she said once she could keep the agitation from her voice. The last thing Jem needed was Rosie feeding her anxiety. "I'm assuming this isn't the first time that drugs have gone missing."

"Hardly. There was a spate of paramedics leaving them on the roofs of the RRV when they checked the safe and then forgetting they were up there."

Rosie gave a disbelieving laugh. "What happened to those dozy buggers?"

"Slapped wrist, warning on file," Jem said, sounding a little brighter. "The powers that be issued an angry memo."

Rosie whacked her palm on the countertop. "Right then, that's your precedent set. Any union rep worth their salt will make mincemeat of that little tosser if he tries to go down a different path with you, so don't be fretting."

"Okay, okay, no fretting, I promise. I'm sorry to bug you with all this, it's just that my dad's chasing around after a traumatised eight-month-old, and Ferg's gone to Lollapielooza for a long weekend, and—"

"Excuse me?" Rosie said. "Lollapie what now?"

Jem stifled a giggle. "Lollapielooza. Seriously, that's what it's called. It's the UK's only pie expo. 'Showcasing the best in British pies,'" she added, as if reading from the brochure. "He'll be back and very hung-over on Tuesday."

"Hmm." Rosie scratched Fluffy, who raised a foot in appreciation. "Does this mean you'll be home alone and dwelling on all this morphine business?"

"Yeah, it might," Jem conceded. She coughed, but it didn't sound like an asthma-type cough, more a placeholder as she debated what to say next. "Are you working this weekend?" she finally asked.

"Nope. As of seven o'clock tonight, I am off till Monday morning." Rosie watched Fluffy knead the countertop, which seemed appropriate given the amount of dancing around that she and Jem were doing. "Do you fancy going out somewhere?" she asked, just as Jem said, "Maybe we could meet up?"

"Okay, then, that's sorted," Rosie said, overriding any potential second-guessing on Jem's part. "I need to scoot or I'll be late for work. Text me a time and a location of your choosing."

"I will. I have lasagne." Jem hesitated, as if despairing of her non sequitur, and seconds later Rosie heard a soft thud.

"Was that your head?" Rosie asked.

"Yes."

"On the steering wheel?"

"Yes. I didn't have a desk, so I made do."

Rosie laughed. "Is this what happens when an introvert and an idiot try to arrange a date?"

"Quite possibly," Jem said. Then, quieter, "Is that what we're doing?"

"I'm not sure." Rosie wondered whether she'd overstepped a mark, but she'd always been an in-for-a-penny type. "Just out of curiosity, would you swipe left or right on me?"

"Which one's no?" Jem asked.

Rosie winced. "Uh, left, I think."

She heard Jem swear softly as a now-familiar beeping set off in the background. "Damn, I've got a job. I have to go."

"Oh, okay, no worries," Rosie said, chewing on her lip.

"Rosie?" Jem raised her voice above the rattle and creak of the garage doors.

"Yeah?"

"I'd swipe right, you pillock," she said, and ended the call.

❖

Gregory Evans clattered his fist against the wall he'd stalked toward. A mounted light fitting sent up a cloud of dust and dead moths, and he left a thin smear of blood on the nicotine-stained Anaglypta. Well acquainted with his behaviour, Jem kept her distance, ensuring there were plenty of obstacles for him to fall over if he decided to go for her throat. Not that she was overly concerned about his temper tantrum; she'd been coming to Greg for years, and the worst he'd ever done was throw up on her response bag.

He snarled at her, baring wet gums. "I wanna die, you stupid bitch. That's why I took 'em."

"And you took six of these?" She displayed the box of ibuprofen. "Is that right?"

"Yeah, and I cut meself. See?" He held out wrists covered in superficial scratches, none of which would prove fatal. Upon Jem's arrival, he had immediately surrendered the razor blade he'd used to inflict the damage. It might have cut through butter if he'd pressed hard enough, and the amount of rust and muck on it suggested the greatest risk to his well-being was infection.

"How much have you had to drink?" she asked.

"Nothin'," he snapped, and then seemed to remember who he was talking to. "Two cans."

It was always "two cans." No matter how drunk the patient or how chronic their alcoholism, they'd never had more than two cans. He smelled so strongly of booze that he was making Jem's eyes water, and every now and again he would sway as if the carpet was attempting to pitch him off it.

She wrote "patient appears to be intoxicated" on her paperwork and moved on. "When were you last in A&E?"

"Dunno. What's today?"

"Thursday."

"Tuesday?" he said.

She scribbled a note. "Same again?"

"No." He glared at her. "I took paracetamol that time."

"Right. Are you going to let me take your obs? Blood pressure, pulse, the usual?"

There were a number of typical Greg scenarios. His favourite was telling the crew to fuck off. That was a crew favourite as well, because it got them out of the address within minutes. Less common was compliance, and on odd occasions he would fake a seizure. He had apparently exhausted his cooperation quotient for the week, because he looked Jem right in the eye and fell back on option one.

She held up her hands. "Fine. I'll wait outside for the crew. If you need me in the meantime, you know where to find me."

He popped the top off a fresh can. "They can fuck off 'n' all. I'm not going nowhere."

Relieved that she wouldn't be stuck on scene playing Greg's refusal game for the next few hours, Jem returned her response bag to its slot and sat on the back ledge of the RRV. A new message from her union rep confirmed a preliminary fact-finding meeting first thing Monday morning and asked her to forward any pertinent details. Taking advantage of the lull, she typed an email on her phone, managing to wrestle with the autocorrect and get the thing finished before she heard sirens. The din ceased a good distance from the address, the crew clearly in no rush, and she'd pocketed her phone and plastered on a welcoming smile by the time they parked behind her.

"Is he for coming or not?" the paramedic asked.

"Or not," Jem said, and continued over his groan, "Six Brufen with a shitload of lager, no vomiting, no apparent plan, minor scratches to both wrists from a manky razor blade." She displayed the blade as Exhibit A.

"I hope he gets fucking tetanus," the EMT said.

Jem dropped the blade into her sharps bin. "Looking at his house, I think he'd be immune." She handed the tech her paperwork. "Do you want me to stick around?"

"No," the paramedic said. "No point in all of us being bloody trapped here."

"Cheers." She took her keys from the carabiner on her fleece. "He's gone for Arsehole setting today, so you might need the police."

"With a bit of luck it'll do us for a finish," the tech said.

"What time are you off?"

"Three," he said, absolutely deadpan.

She checked her fob watch and laughed. It was only ten o'clock.

"PC Jones!"

Rosie stopped so abruptly that her boots skidded on the loose gravel of the car park, her hand still outstretched with the key fob pointed and ready to zap. Kash had brought coffee and chocolate muffins, and they'd been looking forward to a good day of responding to whatever emergencies the folk of east Manchester might throw their way.

"So close," she muttered. "We were so damn close, Kash."

They waited for Steph to catch them up, her heels a terse drumbeat accompanying the start of another downpour. She was trying to shield her hair from the elements, but the wind was having none of it, and she swore at the mess it was making of her French twist. Rosie squinted at the storm clouds massing overhead, vast swirls of grey with white foaming at the edges like furious breakers. If someone had asked her to paint her mood, she'd have pointed upward.

"Did you not get my message?" Steph yelled, still a few feet away. "I told your sarge to hold you at the briefing."

"Must've slipped his mind," Rosie said. Steph was close enough now that Rosie didn't have to shout. "A batch of new flood warnings came in at the last minute, and he had to reorganise everyone."

"Well, I need you." Steph gave her a printout. "That's Tahlia Mansoor's home address. Check if she's there, and if she's not, get as much information about her possible whereabouts as you can."

"Are we both going?" Kash asked.

"No. Your sarge said he couldn't spare you." Steph held up a hand, pre-empting any dissent. "You're to run solo for the shift."

The colour rose in his face, but he said nothing. He balanced a muffin on top of Rosie's coffee and passed them to her before striding back toward the station for a fresh set of keys.

"It's your lead," Steph said to Rosie. "I thought you'd be happy to follow up on it."

"I'm ecstatic." Rosie clicked the fob. "I'll let you know what I find out."

Steph caught her arm. "We could meet for lunch if you like. Your sarge doesn't need to know. I can log it as a debrief."

Rosie didn't shake her off, but it was an effort not to. "Are you suggesting we bend the rules to suit ourselves, Detective?"

Steph's tinkling laugh bore no humour in it. "Touché."

Rosie folded the printout and slipped it into her stab vest. "I'll phone you later."

She was trembling when she got into the car, an insidious jittery sensation that made her drop her key and then over-rev the engine. She gripped the wheel, letting spots of rain blur the windscreen until Steph disappeared from view. Kash messaged her within minutes. *You okay?*

Yes, she replied. *Sorry.*

Not your fault. I'll see you later. Be careful out there.

She took heart from the traditional sign-off, replying in kind and then allowing herself a moment to sip her coffee and share half her muffin with the fat pigeon waiting hopefully at the side of the car. She opened the window fully, bringing in clean, rain-scented air that cleared the steam and made her think of Jem. It always seemed to be raining whenever they met up. She wasn't sure she'd even recognise her in the sunshine. She flicked another chunk of cake at the pigeon.

"Good thing it's always pissing down here, eh?" she said, and set off toward the exit.

Twenty-four Tarrick Street, North Curzon, sat at the far end of a neat terraced row. Its garden was well tended, with a raised bed recently dug over ready for planting, and a basket of winter pansies adding a welcome splash of colour to the doorstep. A Toyota Yaris occupied most of the small driveway, and the flickering of a television in the front room confirmed someone was home. Rosie used the knocker to rap on the door and readied her ID as a figure appeared in the hallway. The door opened on the security chain. The street might have been spick and span, but South Curzon was less than a hundred yards away.

"Mrs. Mansoor?" Rosie said.

"Yes, I'm Melissa Mansoor. Can I help you?" On recognising Rosie's uniform, the woman opened the door wider. She was in her early forties and dressed in a traditional salwar kameez, with her blond hair tucked beneath a colour-coordinated hijab. She dried her hands on a tea towel, but soap suds still clung to her forearms.

"Sorry to disturb you," Rosie said. "I'm PC Jones, and I'm based at Clayton. We're investigating the Kyle Parker case. I'm not sure if you've seen it on the news?"

Melissa nodded, her eyes flitting to the street, where curtains were beginning to twitch. "We saw it. Would you like to come in?"

"Yes, thank you." Rosie followed her into a rear living room that was evidently used for guests. Small dishes of sweets and mints were laid out on a polished black glass coffee table, and the two long sofas were in pristine condition, as if bought for show, not actual sitting. She balanced on the edge of one, trying not to leave an indentation, and took out her notepad and pen.

"Can I get you something to drink?" Melissa asked.

"No, thank you."

Melissa remained standing, forcing Rosie to look up at her. "So, this boy's death. What does it have to do with my family?"

"I'm looking for Tahlia," Rosie said, keeping things simple. The last time she'd inadvertently interviewed a witness, Steph hadn't taken kindly to it. "According to Kyle's friends, she dated him for a short while, but then she and her father had an altercation about a relationship with a girl. Is that right?"

Melissa had wrung the tea towel into a tight line, her knuckles blanching around the cloth. She glanced at the mantelpiece, where a matched set of family photographs took up most of its length. Without waiting for permission, Rosie stood and went over to pick up a photo of a young girl in a smart school uniform. She was holding a *One Hundred Percent Attendance* certificate and grinning ear to ear.

"Is this Tahlia?" Rosie asked.

Melissa nodded, her eyes brimming with tears. "She's just a baby," she whispered. "And we can't find her anywhere."

Rosie took the photo back to the sofa, propping it on the coffee table where Melissa couldn't avoid it. She'd assumed this would be a five-minute "Tahlia's not here and good riddance to her" type of house call, but Melissa's statement had set alarm bells ringing.

"What do you mean, you can't find her?" she asked. "Have you been looking for her?"

Melissa pulled a tissue from an ornate metal box. "Day and night. My husband is a taxi driver, and he's been searching for her between fares. He was so angry with her over that girl, but he didn't mean for this. He would never—" She began to sob, hiding her face in her hands.

"How long has she been missing?"

"Today is the seventeenth day." A terrible hollowness to Melissa's voice gave Rosie an idea of the toll those days had taken. "We know she stayed with Demi-Lee for a while. We spoke to Demi-Lee's mum, and we thought she'd come home of her own accord, but she never did."

"Why haven't you reported her missing, Mrs. Mansoor? She's only fourteen."

The question prompted a fresh bout of tears. "I know! I know that!" Melissa grabbed the photo and held it to her chest. "Faisal said he would find her, that you would blame him if we told you, and our other children would be taken away as well. We kept hoping she would walk through the front door and we could pretend this had never happened."

Rosie bullet-pointed the answer, careful now with her record of the visit. If Tahlia's disappearance ended as badly as Kyle's, she didn't want to be the weak link in the evidence chain.

"What did you tell her school?" she asked. Any prolonged, unexplained absence would have been investigated, had some kind of reason not been given.

"That she was visiting family in Pakistan." Melissa looked sickened, as if she was only now envisioning the pit she and her husband had dug for themselves. In addition to the potentially permanent loss of their daughter, the family would be assessed by social workers and safeguarding teams, who would decide whether Tahlia's siblings were also at risk. "What will happen now?" she asked. "Will you help us look for her?"

"Yes." Rosie was certain of that at least. "She'll be formally reported as a missing child, and the teams working the case will continue to search for her. You and your husband will probably be interviewed by the lead detective, and you have to be prepared for the involvement of Social Services."

"Just find Tahlia," Melissa said. "Whatever else happens, happens. Please, just find our daughter."

CHAPTER THIRTEEN

Flashes of blue and red reflected off the waterlogged road, where two fire engines, a couple of police traffic units, and a standard patrol unit were lighting up the junction like Blackpool Illuminations and acting as a lure for a crowd of bloodthirsty but ultimately disappointed onlookers.

Zipping up her high-vis jacket, Jem picked a route across to the closest traffic officer. Cubes of safety glass crunched beneath her boots as she surveyed the scene, judging the damage to the vehicles and the likely speed of impact. The two cars sat at angles to each other, one tiny and crumpled beyond repair, the other built like a tank and slightly dented at the front.

"Four in the Range Rover," the traffic officer said as Jem raised a gloved hand in greeting. "Dad reckons they're all fine, though, and the driver of the Picasso legged it."

"I'm so glad we haven't risked life and limb to rush here," Jem said, deadpan. A newly forming habit had her checking the scene for Rosie, just in case, but she couldn't see her amongst the rabble. "Do we know who dropped the nines for it?"

"That stupid sod over there." The officer pointed to a slouching lad wearing a tatty Man United cap and a knockoff Adidas tracksuit. He was snapping selfies, using the cars as a backdrop. "He swears there was a fire at first, but—and I quote—'the rain done put it out.'"

The job had been passed to Jem as *Multi-vehicle collision, one car on fire, four people trapped*, which explained the large number of resources deployed. She blinked droplets from her eyelashes, ruing her decision to cut the hood off her coat because it flapped and looked stupid and because drunk patients liked grabbing hold of it.

"Suppose it didn't occur to him that those *trapped* victims might simply have wanted to stay dry," she said.

"Suppose not." The officer opened a packet of toffees and offered Jem one. "I'd arrest him for wasting everyone's time if I could be arsed filling in the paperwork."

"Fair enough. I'll make sure no one's suddenly developed whipcash. Is my car all right where it is?"

"It's fine. We'll be clearing up for a while yet."

The Range Rover's tinted glass concealed its occupants until the driver lowered his window. He gave Jem a thin smile, obviously tolerating the fuss under duress and keen to be on his way. The woman beside him continued to speak into her mobile and didn't deign to acknowledge Jem was there. With a new headlight and a dab of superglue on the vanity plate, no one would suspect their car had been in a collision.

"Hello, sir," she said. "My name's Jem, and I'm with the ambulance service. The police officer said no one in your car is injured. Is that correct?"

"Yes, that's correct." He tapped an impatient beat on the handbrake, striking a chunky gold ring against the lever. "Did the officer say when we might be able to get going?" The civility of his tone couldn't disguise his broad Mancunian accent, and angry streaks of red coloured the black tribal tattoo on his neck when Jem shook her head.

"Sorry, no, he didn't. I'm sure it won't be long, though." She moved closer until she could see the back seat passengers: a lad and a girl in their mid-teens. "Hey," she said, making eye contact with the lad as the girl played on an iPhone with a bejewelled case. "Are either of you hurt?"

"Naw," the lad said. "I thought he'd hit a speed bump."

The girl sniggered and twirled the stud in her nose. "You're such a dick," she told the lad.

Soaked through and also feeling narky, Jem ripped off her nitrile gloves and shoved them into her pocket. "Right, then. I'll leave you in peace."

"Hey, it's easy money," the traffic officer said, when she told him she was clearing. "We get paid for this shit regardless."

It was true, and she dealt with enough bad jobs to appreciate those that turned out to be false alarms. She hung her jacket over the RRV's passenger seat and started the engine. Rosie had sent a WhatsApp while Jem had been on scene, a stock photo of a Twix next to a cup of coffee, with the caption, *Do you have time for a tutorial?*

Hold that thought, Jem replied. *I'll let you know where I am in a couple of hours.*

Rosie tore onto the street, her blues and siren still blaring, the Clayton van less than thirty yards behind her and making just as much noise. An elderly man grabbed his poodle, cradling it to his chest as if the vehicles might snatch it away, while a postie stamped out his fag and crossed himself. Rosie counted the numbers down, screaming to a halt in front of thirty-nine, her seat belt already off and her Taser unbuckled.

"This one!" she yelled to the officers scrambling from the van. "Wife said they were round the back."

Guided by the sound of raised voices, they moved en masse, no plan or formation, just five uniformed officers itching for a scrap after a shift spent dragging cars out of floodwater and supervising sandbag distribution. Rosie pushed the side gate with the hand that wasn't holding her baton. She lived for calls like this, pelting full-tilt into the gods only knew what, with an assortment of crappy weapons at her disposal and a team of her best mates backing her up.

The commotion became louder and more distinct as she jogged between two garages: a woman's voice, high-pitched and hysterical, and two men shouting over each other.

"Help!" the woman shrieked. "Someone please help us!"

Rosie bolted around the corner expecting carnage—an ongoing fight to the death, blood spraying, bones breaking, perhaps a severed limb or two—and found a housewife whacking at her neighbour over a neatly trimmed privet hedge, as her husband waved a pair of loppers like the spoils of battle.

"What the actual fuck?" one of the officers said, almost going arse-over-tits on a tub of slug pellets.

"Help!" the woman screeched again, still brandishing what appeared to be a rolled-up apron. "Help!"

"Oi!" Rosie's bellow was loud and low enough to cut through the melee. "Police! What the hell is going on here?"

The three potential perps froze in unison and looked across at their audience. Confronted by a wall of solid blue, they swiftly surrendered their garden implements and raised their empty hands.

"He stabbed him," the woman wailed, fanning herself with a hanky. "Oh, my heart can't stand this. I might faint, or have my angina."

"Shall I zap the buggers anyway?" the officer asked.

Tempting though the suggestion was, Rosie holstered her baton and breached no man's land by stepping onto the lawn. "Who exactly stabbed whom, ma'am?"

"He"—the woman flapped her hands at the neighbour— "stabbed my Malcolm. Show them, Malcolm."

Now looking sheepish, Malcolm lifted his shirt to reveal a taut beer belly with a smudge of green on it. "Here," he said, indicating the smudge.

Rosie touched the mark. It was a piece of privet leaf, which fell off onto her palm. "I think you'll live," she said. "What did he use? A garden cane?"

The man toe-poked the loppers. "He was cutting our side of it. We've asked him not to umpteen times, but he's sneaky. He'll wait till we've gone out or the weather's like this and we're not watching for him."

"Sir?" Rosie turned to the neighbour. "Do you have anything to add to this?"

"He threatened to break my loppers," he mumbled. "And I only bought 'em on Saturday."

Rosie had heard enough. "Do any of you think it's appropriate to drag five very busy members of the local police force into your privet dispute?"

The men shook their bowed heads. The woman continued to waft her hanky about but had the sense not to remonstrate.

"In which case, we'll leave you to reach some sort of resolution that does not result in any further ructions," Rosie said. "If we have to come back here, we'll arrest the lot of you. Is that understood?"

Taking their silence as acquiescence, she rejoined her colleagues.

Smiffy, the eldest on the van, clapped an arm around her shoulders. "'Privet dispute,'" he said. "I liked that part the best, PC Jones."

"I can't help it, Smiffy. I am naturally punny." Rosie checked her phone and extricated herself from his grip. "Now, if you'll excuse me, gents, I have to rendezvous with a lovely young paramedic who's got a nifty trick to teach me."

"There you go, sweetheart. And you can put that bloody money away."

Jem knew better than to argue with Paula. She dropped a couple of quid into the cafe's charity box and shoved the chocolate into her pockets to leave her hands free for the drinks. Reminded of her B&Q conversation with Rosie, she tapped the box, the proceeds of which were being donated to a city-centre homeless charity.

"You ever hear of a shelter called Olly's, Paula?"

Paula's vigorous wiping of the counter became slow, contemplative circles. "No, I haven't. Is it local?"

"I think so, but I've never heard of it either." Making a snap decision, Jem wrote "Tahlia Mansoor" on a blank section of the takeaway menu. All sorts of gossip passed through the small cafe, and Paula was perfectly placed to eavesdrop. What she didn't know about local affairs probably wasn't worth knowing. Jem slid the menu across the countertop. "Police are looking for this lass, and that shelter was mentioned as a possible place of safety for her. She's fourteen, mixed race, been missing from home for a couple of weeks. Can you keep your ear to the ground for me?"

"Of course I can, love." Paula folded her dishcloth into a neat square. She had mild OCD when it came to cleanliness and tidiness. "Was that you, out on your own with the lad by the river the other night?"

"Aye. Did one of the papers give my name?"

"No, I just bloody knew it. I told Dan as much. 'That'll have been our Jem,' I said, and he bet me fifty pence I was talking shite."

"He owes you fifty pence," Jem said. "Make sure he pays up, as well. He's tighter than a duck's arse." She collected the drinks and waited until Paula came round to get the door for her. Paula shimmied in front of the counter and then rolled up her left trouser leg to reveal a newfangled prosthesis.

"What do you think of this? Swanky, eh?"

"Hey, check you out!" Jem said. "That's fab."

"I'm jogging again." Paula did a little jig on the spot to demonstrate. "Not far, just around the lake, but it's a start, right?"

"Absolutely. It's bloody brilliant." Jem gave her a brew-restricted but heartfelt hug. It was less than eighteen months since a truck had mounted the pavement and hit Paula while she'd been out running. Jem had crawled beneath the chassis and clamped her fingers around Paula's exposed femoral artery. It had taken over an hour to extricate them, and a further half-hour until the surgeons at A&E had allowed Jem to let go. As bonding experiences went, it was certainly a unique one.

"Are you on a bus today?" Paula asked, indicating the two cups.

"No, the car. One of these is for a friend."

"Is it, now?" Paula elbowed her. "A 'friend' you're meeting mid-shift?"

"She's a police officer, Paula. We did the Kyle Parker job together and got talking, that's all."

"Mm-hm," Paula said, scepticism radiating from every inch of her. "Your hair looks gorgeous, by the way."

"Thanks." Jem took a nonchalant sip of her tea. "She cut it for me."

Paula hooted, her hands flying up as if she'd just scored the winner in added time. "Name," she demanded. "So I can tell Dan all about her."

Jem kissed her on the cheek. "Her name is Rosie, and she's very sweet, but do feel free to make something more salacious up for Dan."

"I most certainly will." Paula held the door open. "Take a sneaky pic and send it to me."

"I most certainly will not," Jem said, and walked out into the rain.

Her radio buzzed as she put the key into the RRV's ignition. "Hey, Ryan. What's up?" She punched her pin into the data screen and winced. She would go out of the system for her break at four o'clock, which meant he had one hundred and fifty seconds to pass her a job before he lost her for twenty minutes.

"Sorry, Jem. I know you're heading in for your rest, but would you mind checking out a possible Joey on your way? There's no one else available, and we need to get it out of the stack."

She relaxed into her seat. Hoax calls were easy to deal with: drive past the telephone box, have a look whether anyone was there, and confirm with control that the time-wasting little shitbags had scarpered.

"Put it through," she said. "And think kindly of me at home time."

"I always think kindly of you. We've got a mobile number for this one. Young lass shouted for help and gave a garbled address, then hung up. You're about six minutes from the street we've pinned the call to."

"Right-o, thanks. Speak to you in a bit." She acknowledged the job as the screen started to bleep, and then used hands-free to call Rosie.

"How do," Rosie said, sounding uncharacteristically harried. "If this dopey pillock in front of me slams on to read another road sign, I'm having him for reckless endangerment. Where are you? Because at this rate I might miss you."

"Worry not, I'm going to be late anyway," Jem said, rather touched by how stressed Rosie was. "I'm making a detour to an abandoned call first. It's only on Mansfield Street, so I shouldn't be too long."

"Mansfield Street? Is that off Dunnock?"

Jem adjusted the satnav to widen the view. "Yes, it's the one with the big detacheds on it. There's a nursing home at the bottom end."

"And a beautiful patch of wasteland opposite," Rosie added. "It's very scenic after dark or in a pea-soup fog."

Jem laughed and turned onto Dunnock, muting her sirens as she decelerated for a speed bump. Dusk was well established, helped along by the ever-present rain and a thin shrouding of mist. "In which case, we have the perfect conditions. And it's got to be prettier than the B&Q car park."

"Not to mention closer." Rosie swore, and there was a distinct squeal of brakes in the background. Jem tensed, waiting for the crunch of metal on metal, but all she heard was Rosie slap something hard and mutter something very impolite.

"Ooh, are you going to arrest him?" Jem asked.

"No, I am not," Rosie said through teeth that were audibly gritted. "I am going to sit calmly at this red light and tell my lot that I'm coming to help you with access or something. I shall see you in three."

"Okay, great," Jem said, delighted to have her company. "Bit of luck, we'll be done before the brews go cold."

She disconnected and drove slowly past number five Mansfield Street, craning her neck to examine it for signs of life. The large, three-storey Edwardian sat in darkness, its driveway empty and all its curtains drawn. The lower two floors had ornate wrought iron bars across their windows, although in this area they were unlikely to be there for decoration. The same style of metalwork had been used to construct the balcony jutting from the top floor, as if the view at some point might have been worth sitting out for. From the safety of her seat, Jem looked at the cracked driveways and unkempt front gardens. Originally built for the local mill owners, the houses would once have been desirable properties, but half of them were boarded and derelict and the remainder had been split into bedsits and hostels, the grandeur of their architecture lost on the drunks and no-fixed-abodes who passed through them now.

A sudden flare of white behind Jem made her snap upright and then feel stupid as the headlights from Rosie's patrol car became more distinct. She met Rosie on the kerb, her arms folded against the chill and the street's eerie stillness.

"Chuffing hell." Rosie shuddered, a frown creasing lines into her forehead. "Were you going to go in on your own?"

Jem took her response bag from the back, preferring to err on the side of caution, even if the job did turn out to be a hoax. "My dispatcher messaged me to say they had no previous calls from the address, so yeah, I'd have gone in on my own. Or knocked, at any rate. I don't think anyone's home."

"They better not be." Rosie aimed the beam of her torch at the ground-floor windows. "My goose pimples have got goose pimples."

Feeling braver for having Rosie there, Jem led the way along a path that curved through an overgrown lawn and up the steps to a covered porch. "There was no answer when the call-taker tried ringing the mobile number back," she said, using a solid brass knocker to thump the front door. "It went straight through to voice mail."

"I hope he left a nowty message."

Jem peered through the letterbox. "Can't see a damn thing, and it smells..." she paused, grappling for the right word, "very unwashed."

Rosie squatted at her side and nudged her over. "Police!" she shouted, pitching her voice a notch lower to lend it an impressive authority. "Open the door or lose it!"

Jem looked at her askance. "Are you going to kick it in?"

"Am I 'eck as like, but they don't know that." Rosie stood and assessed the doorframe, pressing down its length. "It's locked, and I think it's bolted top and bottom. I'd break my bloody foot."

"Ambulance!" Jem called. "Is anyone there?" She counted to ten and then lowered the flap and shrugged at Rosie. She was unhooking her radio from her belt when a sharp bang made them both jump.

"Whoa!" Rosie said. "Where the hell did that come from?"

"I'm not sure." Jem reopened the letterbox. "Hello? Can you hear me?"

Another bang prompted them to look down, and they scoured the undergrowth with their torches.

"Cellar," Rosie said, circling the lowest point of the wall with her light. Before Jem could voice a caution, Rosie was off the steps and tearing at the weeds, clearing a space large enough to reveal a tiny barred window. She tapped the pane and then gasped, falling onto her arse as something hit the glass from the inside. "Jesus wept!" She redirected the torch she'd dropped, but nothing else appeared. With one hand splayed across her heart, she flopped back, her legs outstretched. Her breath misted in front of her as she panted. "The little bastard. That's taken years off my life, that has."

Jem giggled nervously and jumped down to help Rosie brush wet grass from her trousers. "Can we get in anywhere?" she asked.

Despite the rust coating the bars, they held firm when Rosie shook them. "I'll have a scoot around the back. If there's no access, I'll call up for an enforcer ram. Are you all right here for a minute?"

"Yep." Jem pulled a piece of dandelion from Rosie's hair. "How's your ticker?"

"Still going like the clappers. I won't be long."

Jem gave her a few seconds to scramble clear and then returned to the letterbox. "Okay, love, we saw you there. Bang once for yes and twice for no. Can you get to the front door?"

Her skin prickled as a rapid couple of thumps sounded.

"Are you hurt?"

A single thump.

"Are you on your own?"

A pause, followed by two thumps.

"How many are there of you?"

Two deliberate thumps.

Jem nodded, somewhat reassured by that. "Hold on, we're getting help. Try not to be scared."

That earned her a frantic series of bangs. She closed the flap and voiced Ryan. "This isn't a hoax," she said. "I'm with a police officer, and we're going to force entry. I'll need a bus. We have a person injured, condition unknown, but they're conscious and breathing."

"Aw, hell," he said, and she knew what was coming. "I've got nothing at the moment. There's six crews stuck on the corridor at West Penn."

"No worries. Just bear us in mind." There was no point stressing him out if they were going to have to wait for police backup regardless.

A triumphant yell from Rosie cut across his acknowledgement, and Jem ran to find her, following the fresh boot-prints through the undergrowth. She stopped at a tall metal gate that barricaded the side of the house. Rosie was already on the other side, poking her fingers through the thick bars like an inmate in an old-fashioned jail.

Jem leaned forward, winded by the exertion and the stress. "There are two people in the cellar," she said. "One of them is hurt, and they can't get out. It's probably kids who've broken in and come a cropper."

"I should've bloody seen this coming," Rosie said. "We could have been at B&Q slurping up coffee through a Twix, but no…" Her protest lacked any genuine rancour, and she waggled her fingers until Jem touched their tips. "Can you get over? There's a window round the back we should be able to break and squeeze through. My lot have okayed it, because anyone who might be able to help us is buggering about in the floods."

"Of course I can get over." Jem hoisted the bag above her head, standing on tiptoe so Rosie could reach it. "I climbed a fifteen-foot wall on Tuesday."

"Good point." Rosie stood clear, giving Jem space to kick off from the top and land on the narrow path. Jem's boots skidded on the lichen-slickened stone, and Rosie grabbed her arm to stop her from falling.

"Thanks." Jem clung on for a moment and then stepped cautiously across the most treacherous slab. "Lead the way."

Rosie had set a wheelie bin and a hefty stone in readiness beneath the window, and she shinned onto the bin as if she'd been born to break and enter. Jem found herself admiring the easy athleticism and the flattering cut of Rosie's uniform.

"What are you smiling at?" Rosie asked.

Caught red-handed, Jem shrugged. "You," she said, and Rosie laughed, striking a pose on the lid.

"Is it the Taser? All the girls love the Taser."

"Amongst other things." Jem handed her the stone, and Rosie accepted it without question, refocusing on the business at hand. "I've got the oxygen cylinder if you prefer a battering ram," Jem added.

"This'll do." Rosie rolled the stone in her gloved palm, assessing its shape, before bashing its sharpest edge against the glass. The outer layer of the double glazing splintered but held, so she tried again, knocking out the pieces as they fell loose. She finished the remainder with her feet, sitting on the bin and booting the stubborn shards into submission. Then she was gone, shimmying through the gap and disappearing into the gloom on the other side. She reappeared just as swiftly. "What a shithole," she said, lighting the way for Jem.

They paused to get their bearings in a poky kitchen apparently fitted sometime in the 1960s. Every shelf was bare, and the fridge was open, its only contents an ancient carton of sterilised milk. The air smelled fusty, as if this was the first time in years that the room's seal had been breached.

"It doesn't look like anyone lives here," Rosie said, running her finger through a thick layer of greasy dust.

"Not for a good while," Jem said. She could see the front door at the far end of a dingy hallway and a flight of stairs at the midpoint. The house had been elegant in its heyday, and the staircase swept upward to a broad landing. "Hello?" she shouted from the kitchen door. "Can you hear me?"

The familiar thud sounded in response, close by and beneath her feet.

"Where's the hatch?" Rosie asked.

Jem went to the stairs. "I don't know. These only go up."

Rosie knelt, aiming her next question at the floorboards and pressing her ear against them to catch any reply. "How do we get to you?"

"Ladder," a tremulous voice called back. It was a girl, her words only just audible. "Through a cupboard."

"A cupboard?" Rosie looked at Jem for clarification. "Where the hell are they? Narnia? Can I arrest her for taking the piss? That's reasonable, isn't it?"

Jem shook her head, deciphering the directions with ease. "Didn't you ever have an under-the-stairs cubbyhole? For coats, shoes, Hoovers, general junk? It must have a trap or something." She led Rosie to a small door cut into the side of the flight. Everything in the hall was covered in psychedelic floral wallpaper, and the door had been all but camouflaged in the darkness. Its hinges creaked, the sound as grating as fingernails on a chalkboard, and a cloud of dust flew up when she knelt in the narrow space. She covered her nose and mouth with one hand as she crawled beyond the threshold, her torchlight bouncing off wellies and moth-eaten anoraks. Toward the back, a square of carpet had been tossed on the floor. It came away easily when she pulled at it, and she froze, her torch slipping from her fingers. "Shit. Rosie?" She scrabbled for the light, hoping she'd been mistaken.

"What is it? What's up?" Rosie pushed her way in just as Jem managed to refocus her torch. "Oh hell, you're fucking kidding me."

Jem touched the padlock, shifting it from side to side. It was heavy duty, brand new, and firmly locked. She leaned low, her ear almost touching the wood, and knocked on the hatch. "Can you hear me?" she called.

"Yes!" The girl sounded terrified, and sobs broke her words apart. "Yes, we're down here! *Please* get us out!"

Jem had a thousand questions, but Rosie was up and moving, speaking urgently into her radio as she ran back to the kitchen. She returned within seconds, carrying a dilapidated knife block and the stone.

"We need to jemmy it," she said, flinging out a carving knife and a long, thin sharpener. She fitted the latter into the loop of the padlock and used it like a lever, changing her angle of approach repeatedly as she felt for a weak spot. Jem took the stone instead and bashed it into the slats. The shock of the blow reverberated up her arms, but she'd sheared off a chunk of wood that flew past Rosie into the hall.

"Right. Brute force and ignorance it is," Rosie said. She adjusted her grip on the knife sharpener so she was holding it like a spear and aimed it between the slats. "Get clear of the hatch!" she yelled, stabbing the sharpener into the crease as Jem resumed her indiscriminate hammering. The boards began to bow beneath the combined onslaught, cracks appearing at random, before one entire length snapped cleanly in the middle. Rosie joined Jem to stomp on the weakened planks, until their boots smashed a hole large enough for them to climb through.

"There's a fixed ladder," Jem said, tapping the top rung with her toe and then pressing harder to test its integrity. The ladder squeaked and juddered beneath the pressure, but it seemed robust enough.

"Do you want me to go first?" Rosie asked.

Jem shook her head and grabbed her response bag. "I'll see you down there."

The smell was the first thing to hit her, a foetid cocktail of human waste and wet rot, undercut with a trace of vomit. She breathed through her nose, acclimatising to the stink, and panned her torch around as she reached the bottom of the ladder. The light picked out an empty water bottle, the wrapper from a loaf of white bread, crisp packets, and a roll of toilet paper. She found the children in the farthest corner: two girls huddled beneath a blanket, their hands raised to shield their eyes. They were filthy and shivering and obviously traumatised.

"Please don't hurt us," one of them said. Her voice was hoarse, as if she'd been screaming for days. Wincing, she licked her chapped lips and tightened her hold on her friend. "We didn't do nothing wrong."

"We're not going to hurt you," Jem said. She took a cautious step, aware of Rosie a couple of paces behind her. "I promise we're not going to hurt you. My name's Jem and I'm a paramedic, and Rosie here is a police officer. You're safe now, okay?"

"Okay," the girl said. She was the elder of the two, perhaps fifteen, and Jem could see streaks of blood on her fingers as she stroked the younger girl's hair. Dark shadows encircled her eyes, and she looked half-starved, her cheekbones too prominent in her muck-streaked face.

"What's your name?" Jem asked, still slowly approaching them.

"Ava," the girl said, sitting up straighter, her confidence growing. Her hair was dyed bright pink beneath the grime, and both ears sported multiple piercings, as if she'd been the class rebel before someone shoved her in a cellar and knocked all the fight from her. "I think Chloe's broke her ankle. She fell off the crates, and I heard it snap. We were trying to get her phone to work."

Jem looked at the shattered wooden boxes Ava indicated. Although the girls had managed to improve the phone's signal, the collapse of the stack explained why no one from ambulance control had been able to contact them again. Jem set her bag at the girls' feet and unzipped it, ignoring the trickle of cold sweat between her shoulder blades, and trying not to think how easily the call might have been dismissed outright by an overburdened dispatcher, or how many times she had given up after a cursory knock at a probable hoax.

"You did a great job," she said, forcing brightness into her voice. "Don't worry, I'll sort Chloe's leg for her. Which one is it, Chloe?"

Chloe stared at her for a long moment, her nostrils flaring and her good leg scuffing the floor. Tears had bled mascara down her cheeks, and little remained of her crimson nail varnish. Jem had grown up with girls like Chloe, all attitude and aggression until someone bothered to scratch the surface.

"He said he'd come back for us," Chloe whispered. "But he never. He just left us in here for days and days." She started to cry. "I want to go home."

Rosie knelt beside Jem and put a hand on Chloe's thigh. Jem could sense the tension radiating off every inch of her, the urge to pepper the girls with questions, to get them to name names and provide descriptions and a full account, but all she did was pass Chloe a tissue.

"Let Jem take a look at your ankle," she said. "She's dead gentle, and as soon as she's done, I'll give you a piggyback out of here. What do you reckon? Does that sound like a plan?"

Chloe's head bobbed. She'd cried herself out within seconds. "I'm hungry," she said.

Jem patted her pockets and pulled a Twix from each. She was happy to take the blame for not keeping Chloe nil by mouth, if it turned out she needed an anaesthetic.

"Don't stuff it all in at once," she said as wrappers went flying. "Rosie won't be impressed if you puke down her neck."

Chloe sniggered through a mouthful and tapped her left leg. "It's this one."

Jem raised the blanket, finding Chloe's shoe and sock already removed and a black-and-blue ankle swollen to the size of a grapefruit. "Can you wiggle your toes for me? Good girl. Feel me touching you here? How about here?"

Chloe nodded, her cheeks bulging. "Is it broke?"

"I'm not sure," Jem said, delving into her bag for ibuprofen. "Ankles tend to swell a lot even if they're not broken, but it'll definitely be sore for a while. How old are you?"

"Thirteen and a half."

"Any allergies to medicines?"

"Nope."

"Excellent. Get these down your neck." Jem handed her the tablets and turned to Rosie. "All my splints are in the ambulance. Grab some of that wood, and I'll improvise."

"Wilco." Rosie moved with alacrity, returning with numerous pieces of wood she'd kicked off the crates. Jem selected a matched pair and set them either side of Chloe's ankle.

"Hold these for me?" she asked Rosie. She began to wind a bandage around the makeshift splint, her face close to Rosie's as she worked. "What the hell is going on?" she murmured.

"I don't have a fucking clue," Rosie said. "Let's get them out and worry about the rest of it once they're safe. Will your radio work down here?"

"No."

"Mine neither." Rosie took an uneven breath. "But backup should be on the way. We can put them on a priority as soon as we get a signal."

"All right." Jem felt calmer for having a plan. She added a final piece of tape to the bandage. "How's that?" she asked Chloe. "Can you still wiggle your toes?"

"Yep," Chloe said, demonstrating.

"Fab. Are either of you hurt anywhere else?" Although Jem kept her question nonspecific, she shared a relieved glance with Rosie when the girls shook their heads. "We're all set then," she said, shrugging into the straps on her response bag so she could wear it like a rucksack. "Chloe, loop your arms around Rosie's neck. Ava, you stand up with me and get your sea legs."

They did as she instructed, Ava swaying as a head rush hit her but staying on her feet. Rosie lifted Chloe with ease, settling her in place, and then led the way to the ladder at a pace that suited Jem and Ava. Her foot was on the bottom step, her hands poised to pull herself up, when she froze and peered toward the hatch. Even in the torchlight, Jem saw the colour drain from her face.

"Shit," Rosie hissed. "Can you smell smoke?"

"No," Jem said, still supporting Ava and a few feet shy of the ladder. "What? From upstairs?"

"Yeah, I think so. Shit." Rosie turned in a full circle, searching for another way out, her light exploring every inch of the barred window.

"Has someone set the house on fire?" Ava whispered. Her fingers dug into Jem's arm with bruising force.

"I don't know," Jem said, but she could smell the smoke now, an insidious hint drifting down and getting stronger by the second. "We'll have to go up," she said to Rosie. "We don't have a choice. Go on, *go!*"

Rosie didn't argue. Jem followed on her heels, crawling into the cubbyhole and practically dragging Ava off the top rung. The tiny room was full of smoke, the violent crackle of the fire close by and growing in intensity. Still on her hands and knees, Jem could barely see Rosie, but she could hear Chloe crying. She reached out, finding Rosie's ankle and squeezing it. "Right behind you," she said.

It was worse in the hallway, the smoke thick and noxious, with eager flames eating along the carpet and the front door. A small explosion in the kitchen confirmed both exits were blocked.

"Up," Jem said between bouts of coughing. "Top floor. There's a balcony."

"All together," Rosie said. "Stay as low as you can."

Jem did her best to keep up, forcing one foot in front of the other, one arm tucked around Ava, and the weight of the bag almost dragging her back to the bottom. Her lungs ached, and she felt dizzy and sick and more scared than she had ever been. She heard Rosie yelling into her comms, but she didn't have the breath to do likewise.

There was less smoke on the first floor, and they spent a moment gulping in the cleaner air before Rosie forced them on again like a drill sergeant. Six steps, seven, eight. Jem took to counting them: fifteen between each floor, then a further two as the landing split.

"Left," she gasped at the top of the second flight. "There were patio doors."

Rosie took her word for it, ushering them all inside the first bedroom. She set Chloe down and used her jacket to plug the gap at the bottom of the door before trying to open the patio. It was locked. Jem threw off the bag and dragged the oxygen cylinder out.

"For the window," she said, but when she tried to raise it, she found it too heavy. Rosie plucked it from her hands.

"Should be using this for you," she said.

"Yeah, maybe later," Jem conceded. Her lungs felt like stone, dull and unresponsive, and it was getting harder to make them work. "Just get us out of here."

Rosie nodded and battered the cylinder against the glass. A fine pattern of cracks appeared in the first pane, and she grunted with the effort, hefting the cylinder for another attempt. She had taken in smoke as well; her chest was heaving, and her eyes were red-raw and streaming.

"Ava, help me move Chloe into the corner," Jem said. Wisps of smoke were beginning to eddy around the doorframe, and the carpet seemed to undulate as something collapsed on a lower storey. She didn't want the girls in the middle of the room. She had been in several burned-out buildings where the centre of the floor had been the first thing to fall.

"Almost there," Rosie yelled, as Jem sat Chloe by the wall and ripped her radio from her belt. Ignoring the priority button, she hit the open channel and shouted over the din of Rosie smacking the cylinder into the glass again.

"I need urgent backup to five Mansfield Street, Stamford. House fire with four trapped on the top floor." She had to stop to get her breathing back under control. "We're trying to break a window—"

Ryan's voice cut across her. "*Jem?* Are *you* trapped?"

"Yes," she said, surprised by her own composure. "Send whatever you've got, mate."

"Fucking shit," he said, and pandemonium erupted on the channel as crews began to call up with their locations and availability.

She listened for a few seconds, reassured by how close some of the vehicles were, but let the radio drop when she heard Rosie cry out in pain.

"Rosie?" It was difficult to see clearly; the smoke was distorting the finer details, like a cobweb caught on her retina. She inched across to the lighter part of the room, her hands outstretched for obstacles.

"It's nothing, stay put," Rosie said, but she didn't resume her hammering. Instead, Jem heard the cylinder drop to the floor and a whispered "damn it."

She found the cylinder first, stubbing her toe on the metal and staring in horror at the blood coating its length. "What the hell have you done?" she said, yanking Rosie's shirt to pull her around.

"Nothing." Rosie stooped for the cylinder, but her fingers were bloody and she couldn't grip it. "I cut my arm on the glass. Wrap it with something, Jem. Quickly, come on!"

"Put some pressure on it and keep it elevated," Jem said, using her scissors to hack a strip from the closest curtain. Rosie's "cut" was a deep laceration extending from her wrist to mid-forearm, and it was bleeding heavily. Jem bound the cloth around the gash, pulling it tight and knotting the ends. "Here, I can—" She went to pick up the cylinder, but Rosie took it from her.

"Fetch the girls. I just need to knock a couple more pieces out," she told Jem. Then, softer, "Go on. I'm fine."

Jem did as she asked, hopping Chloe across the floor to the window in time to feel the first rush of cold air on her face. Rosie was waiting on the balcony, while a dishevelled crowd gawped up at her from the pavement. Three of them had brought buckets of water.

"I think it'll hold us all," she said, but it wasn't as if they had another option, so Jem boosted the girls through the empty frame. As Ava dropped clear on the other side, Jem sagged onto her knees, coughing and choking and only vaguely aware of someone shaking her shoulders. Then she was standing, Rosie's arms around her, the smell of blood and smoke and sweat all over her, and Rosie was pushing her and cajoling her and pleading with her to "fucking *move*, right fucking *now*!"

Jem reacted more to the stark panic than the command, landing in a heap on the metal. She could feel Rosie slapping and tearing at her pockets, though she wasn't sure why. Below them, the road was a sea of blue lights, their intensity dazzling after so long in the dark, and everyone around her seemed to be yelling.

"Here," Rosie said, not yelling, just insistent. She pressed the inhaler against Jem's lips, lifted Jem's hand, and closed her fingers around the plastic. "Come on, Jem. I don't know what I'm doing with it."

Jem pushed the spray three, four times, doing her best to synchronise her breathing with it but mostly failing.

"Someone fucking help us!" Rosie screamed over the side of the balcony. Smoke billowed from the ruined window, and something disintegrated with enough force to rattle the foundations. The girls cried out, clinging to the railings and each other. Jem heard the mechanised whir of a ladder platform and a man barking instructions she couldn't understand.

"Ava, get Chloe up," Rosie said, and knelt beside Jem. "Can you stand with me?"

Jem nodded but then slumped to the side when she tried to get her legs under her. "Sorry," she whispered. Nothing was working properly, and her vision was failing too; Rosie's face kept disappearing at the edges. The balcony rocked again, banging her into its bars as a firefighter hurried over to crouch by them.

"She's asthmatic," Rosie said. "I don't think I can carry her on my own."

"I've got her, love," the man said, hauling Jem into a sitting position. "You go on ahead. The lift won't take all of us at once."

Rosie seemed on the verge of refusing, before her common sense kicked in. She touched Jem's cheek. "I'll see you in a minute," she said, and bolted to the ladder.

An alarm blared as the lift began to descend. Jem listened to its progress, her view blocked by the man in front of her. "Are we…we waiting for…the next ride out?" she asked.

"Yes, but I got us a FastPass, so we'll be able to jump the queue."

She couldn't reply for coughing, but she managed to give him a thumbs up that made him smile.

"Stick your arm around my neck," he told her, when the alarm began to sound again. He cradled her against his chest and lifted her as if she weighed nothing at all. What little she could see suddenly pitched and rolled, and the sky, bright with fire and blue neon, swapped places with the balcony and the drunks holding their vigil on the road. She squeezed her eyes shut, blocking out the nausea and the noise and the relentless ache in her ribs, and let the man carry her down.

CHAPTER FOURTEEN

O fficer, you need—"
Rosie shook off the paramedic's hand. "I'm fine. See to the girls."

"*They're* fine," he said, clearly exasperated. "*You're* bleeding."

"Where's Jem?" She paced away from the ambulance, almost in tears. She'd been rational and efficient since she got off the lift, taking the time to arrange a police escort for Ava and Chloe and providing a very brief overview for her sarge. Her arm wasn't bleeding that badly, and she no longer felt like coughing her spleen up, but she'd lost Jem in the melee and couldn't see her anywhere.

The paramedic took one look at her face and relented. "I think she's with Bob and Dougie."

"Which vehicle?"

He pointed past the first two fire engines. "That one."

"Thanks. I don't mean to be an arse."

He pulled off his gloves and balled them up. "Tell her Spence sends his love."

She ran to the ambulance, dodging fire crews and hoses and the occasional belligerent rubbernecker, and banged on its back door.

"Give us a minute!" a man shouted.

"Is Jem in there?" She tried to sound imposing, but she could barely speak for crying.

The door opened, and a grey-haired man, sweating and obviously stressed to fuck, looked out. "I'm guessing you're Rosie," he said. "I'm Bob."

She dried her eyes on the scrap of curtain binding her wrist. "Is she okay?"

He shook his head, and she followed him inside, shutting the door behind her and staying in the corner, out of the way. She heard Jem before she saw her: the rapid gasp of every snatched breath, and the drawn-out wheeze that marred each exhalation.

"Look who I found," Bob said to Jem, cupping her chin and supporting her head so she could see Rosie. "Will you behave yourself now and keep that mask on?"

Jem sobbed once, and Rosie sat on the floor beside her stretcher, taking hold of the hand that wasn't tangled in an IV line and monitoring leads.

Bob didn't bother trying to get her into a seat. He grabbed his paperwork and slapped the bulkhead. "Stick your foot down, Dougie. Put them on standby. Her sats are only eighty-six, and she's knackered."

The vehicle moved off, its sirens blaring to clear a path through the chaos. Rosie squeezed Jem's clammy fingers. "Hey," she said. "I know you're tired, but no slacking on the breathing, okay? I'm not doing all the bloody paperwork for this."

Jem managed a weak smile and then set off coughing, until she retched and yanked her oxygen mask down.

"Help me...I can't..." She slapped at Bob's arm as he tried to resecure the mask. "I can't breathe."

"Jem, you need the medicine," he said. The liquid-filled chamber beneath the mask created a thin mist as the oxygen hit it, but none of the mist was going anywhere near her. On the monitor, eighty-six percent dropped to eighty-five and then eighty-three.

Rosie knelt up properly, wrapping her arm around the head of the stretcher so she wouldn't go flying. "Here, let me hold it for you." She placed the mask close to Jem's face, though not so close it made her claustrophobic. "How's that? Any easier?"

"Yes," Jem whispered.

"We'll have you there in no time," Bob said. "You know what Dougie's driving is like." His eyes were fixed on the sats reading, and he'd set a ventilation bag in readiness by his feet. He mopped his brow with a paper towel when the figure climbed to eighty-eight.

"That's the best they've been," he said to Rosie. "She'll go straight into Resus at A&E, and they'll be ready for her, so don't worry."

"Easier said than done," Rosie said, watching Jem's eyes roll as she fought to stay conscious.

Bob was watching her as well, missing nothing, his foot tapping an uneasy beat on the ventilation bag. "Yeah, isn't it just?"

"On my count." Bob's curt instruction brought a semblance of order to the staff gathered in the Resus bay, most of whom obviously recognised Jem.

Rosie found a spot on the periphery, her attempts to feign authority undermined by the blood and soot covering her, and ignored by a team who had far greater concerns. Jem wasn't ignoring her; her eyes had tracked Rosie's position since their arrival in the bay, but as the team slid her onto the bed her gaze fell away, as if she was humiliated by her own weakness.

"Jem Pardon, thirty-two years old," Bob said, once she'd been settled and a nurse was hooking up the monitors. "Mild indications of smoke inhalation after a house fire, but severe exacerbation of chronic asthma. Initial sats were eighty-one, now ninety after back-to-back nebulisers and hydrocortisone IV. Resps are up at twenty-four, tachy at one-thirty plus. I know she's been vented at least twice, and she has a specialist care plan here."

"We've fast-bleeped Respiratory," a doctor said. "Cheers, Bob."

Bob threw his paperwork onto his empty stretcher and put his hands on Rosie's shoulders. "This is Rosie. She also needs checking over at some point, but she appears spry enough for now." He ushered her into a chair and wrapped a blanket around her shoulders. "I'll be back to see you both in a bit."

Rosie nodded, overwhelmed by the cacophony of monitor alarms and the press of too many bodies in too close a space. She was out of her depth here, unfamiliar with the equipment, the terminology, and the staff, and she couldn't simply show her warrant card and demand answers in an environment where her uniform held little sway. She had rarely been ill as a child—the usual bouts of chicken pox and snotty noses were the only things she remembered—and her good health had followed her into adulthood. She couldn't imagine herself in Jem's position, managing an illness that could put her in Resus at the drop of a hat, joking about chocolate at B&Q one minute and fighting for her life the next.

From where Rosie was sitting, she could only catch glimpses of Jem, but nothing she was hearing sounded good. She stood up and chanced a couple of steps to her right, keeping her back to the cubicle's curtain. Everyone remained engrossed in their respective tasks, and no one scolded her or sent her back to the chair. No one even seemed to notice, aside from Jem, who waited until a doctor had drawn a blood sample from her wrist, and then beckoned Rosie over.

"Do you want me to phone your dad?" Rosie asked.

Jem shook her head. "He'll worry."

"Is this not worth worrying about?" Every number on the screen was red and flashing, and Jem's sats were back to hovering in the high eighties.

"Been worse," Jem said, with grim pragmatism. A rapid clack of heels sounded outside the curtain, and she looked past Rosie with obvious trepidation. The curtain was whipped aside without ceremony, and Rosie clamped her mouth shut, aware that she was staring.

"What the bloody hell have you two been up to this time?" Harriet Lacey said, scanning the notes on Jem's chart. "Has she had the mag sulf yet?" she called over her shoulder.

"Just drawing it up," a nurse replied.

"Good. Fast as you can, please. Her gases are crap, and she usually responds well to that." Harriet's expression gave nothing away as she listened to Jem's chest and cast an eye over the monitors.

"Please don't..." Jem kicked with her feet, trying to sit up properly. "Don't—I'm okay." She started to cough, collapsing back against the pillow as sweat beaded on her hairline.

"Last resort, Jem," Harriet said. "And we're not there yet. Let's see how you are after the magnesium and an hour or two on CPAP. Does that sound all right?"

Although Rosie had no idea what bargain had just been struck, some of the tension eased from Jem's posture. The nurse connected a small IV bag to one of the lines and adjusted its flow.

"Lovely, thank you," Harriet said. She slung her steth around her neck. "Goodness, Jem, you're making my eyes water. Shall we get you into a gown while we set the CPAP up? Officer Jones?"

Rosie all but snapped to attention, supporting Jem as the nurse dispensed with preliminaries and cut Jem's uniform away. The gown went on before her boots and trousers came off. Rosie tucked a blanket over Jem's bare legs, mortified on her behalf, though Jem seemed resigned, or perhaps accustomed, to the indignity. The mild effort of moving knocked her sats again, and Harriet wasted no time placing a large plastic mask over her face, securing it with two thick straps, and activating the machine its hose was attached to.

"I'll check your gases again in an hour and we'll go from there," she said as the machine began to work in synch with Jem's breathing. "I think CPAP warrants a call to your parents, don't you?"

The mask precluded any debate on the subject, but Jem showed no sign of dissent. Harriet pulled her mobile from her pocket, checking the monitors again as she did so. "Your sats are already ninety-one. Why don't you shut your eyes for a while so you don't scare the pants off your dad when he gets here?" She wrote a note on Jem's chart, waiting until Jem had slipped into a doze before she went over to Rosie. "Sit down before you fall down, and stick your tongue out for me," she told her, attaching a probe to Rosie's finger.

The adrenaline rush that had seen Rosie through the last couple of hours seemed to abandon her abruptly. Too bewildered to protest, she followed the instructions, her backside hitting the chair hard as her legs folded beneath her.

"Lower your head." Harriet placed a hand between Rosie's shoulder blades. "It'll pass."

"Will she be okay?" Rosie mumbled, studying her boots as they blurred and sharpened again. "And what's CPAP?" She felt like an infant, full of questions but only capable of articulating them in the simplest terms.

Harriet squatted at Rosie's side, no mean feat in the heels she was wearing. "I think she'll be fine. She tends to bounce back quite quickly, even when she's come in this poorly. Knowing her, she'll probably get a HDU bed for the night and be well enough to go home in another day or so."

"Really?" Rosie pushed upright, struggling to reconcile Harriet's optimism with Jem's current condition. "What does the mask do?"

"It stops her from getting exhausted, and it prevents her airways collapsing as she breathes."

"In a nutshell?" Rosie said, suspecting there was a lot more to it than that.

Harriet smiled, graciously conceding the point. "Yes, in a nutshell. Now"—she pulled a small trolley closer and uncapped a nasty little needle—"I'm going to run your blood gases. Once I'm sure you don't need to be in the cubicle next door, I'll get someone to examine whatever you're hiding beneath that rather grim scrag of carpet."

"It's curtain," Rosie said, still eyeing the needle. "And it's just a scratch."

"Mm-hm. Am I correct in assuming you'd like to stay in here with Jem?"

"Yes."

Harriet turned Rosie's uninjured wrist, evidently preparing to draw the blood sample, but instead of jabbing it she held it in her hand. "Let us do what we need to do, then. She'll probably be asleep for an hour or so. You can have a shower and get changed and still be here when she wakes up. How does that sound?"

"It sounds good," Rosie admitted.

"Excellent." Harriet shifted her fingers, feeling for the pulse at Rosie's wrist and readying the needle. "Brace yourself, Officer Jones. I've been told this stings quite a bit."

In Rosie's experience, the best police partnerships were formed around the basic mandate of always having your mate's back. When she'd messaged Kash to ask for clean clothes, he'd gone beyond the call and brought her fresh underwear and a flask of his mum's curry as well.

"The foil has chapattis in it," he said. "Take it home if you don't feel like it now."

"I will. Thanks, Kash."

"How is she?" Never comfortable around the ill, injured, or dead, he had retreated to the foot of Jem's bed.

Rosie stroked her thumb across the back of Jem's hand. She didn't think they were at the hand-holding stage yet—hell, they hadn't even arranged their date—but the last time Jem had woken, she'd wrapped her fingers around Rosie's and promptly fallen back to sleep. Rosie hadn't dared to move since.

"Stable at the last count," she said, refocusing on Kash's question. "Her doc said her gases have improved, whatever that means, and they've started to wean her off that mask. Her dad's got his hands full with a new pair of foster children, but he's going to come as soon as he can."

Kash plucked up the courage to sit in the cubicle's spare chair. "What about you?" he said, giving her a pointed look.

"I think I'm okay." She knew better than to tell him she was fine—he would skewer that lie in a heartbeat—but she couldn't describe the terror of hearing the flames creep closer, of feeling the heat on her skin and the quaking of the building, and she had no words for the helplessness she'd felt as she'd watched Jem slowly suffocate. Aiming for nonchalance, she swallowed a mouthful of tepid coffee, but the cup clipped the edge of the overbed table as she put it down. Kash handed her a wad of paper towels and said nothing.

"Have you heard anything about the girls?" she asked. "The sarge popped his head in a while back, but he didn't have much of an update."

"Only that they're on the children's ward with their families, and they won't be interviewed until tomorrow morning at the earliest. Smoke inhalation, dehydration, and a badly sprained ankle. The elder one—Ava?—reckoned they'd been down there for about four days, but she refused to give any other specifics, and no one's going to push them until Psych have completed an assessment."

Rosie rubbed her sore eyes. She was so tired that the room kept spinning, but she was scared of what she might see if she went to sleep. "Were they runaways?"

"Yes." He paused to check a note he'd written. "Twenty-three days listed as missing and vulnerable. They'd fallen off the radar completely, not a sight nor sound of them reported to the Misper team. Detective Merritt has been informed because of the circumstantial similarities, but there's nothing concrete to link them to the Kyle Parker case."

Rosie nodded, mulling the information over. In the house there had been no time to connect the dots, but she could see a pattern taking shape now, and it kicked her lethargy into touch. "Someone's tempting these kids off the street, aren't they?" she said. "Promising them the world, until they step out of line and end up locked in a cellar."

"It's one possible theory," he said, always the more circumspect member of their duo. "Has Detective Merritt been in touch?"

"Numerous times." Rosie's mobile vibrated whenever she moved it, reminding her she had yet another message from Steph. She'd spoken to her briefly and emphasised the lack of mobile reception in Resus.

Kash didn't press the topic. "You're a popular lass. Everyone's been asking after you. I think Smiffy might've shed a couple of tears."

"Fuck off. It was probably wind." She wafted her free hand at him. "Get back home before Makeenah reports *you* as a misper."

He stood and knuckled her cheek. "Don't be a stranger."

"I won't. I'll text you. Tell your mum thanks for the curry."

He was almost to the edge of the bay when she called him back. "What's up?" he said.

"The fire—" She shook her head at her own stupidity. She was so addled, she hadn't even thought to ask. "Do they know how it started?"

His expression hardened. She'd seen him punch a wall once, and he'd looked more placid then than he did now. "Early indications suggest petrol," he said as if reading from a formal report. "Poured through the letterbox at the front and thrown through the window you'd smashed in the kitchen. Major Crimes are treating it as arson and attempted murder."

"Jesus." She'd known that, somewhere at the back of her battered brain, but it was appalling to have her suspicions confirmed. Perhaps that was why she hadn't asked.

"We'll get the fuckers," he said. "Most of Major Crimes are working it, and loads of our lot volunteered for the overtime."

"Is that why I'm so popular?" she said. It was easier to make a joke than stew over what she'd just been told. "Everyone's getting double bubble because of me."

He laughed. "You might be on to something there. Give Jem some of that curry when she wakes up. It'll clear her sinuses right out."

"I have no doubt of that." Rosie had encountered his mum's curries on numerous occasions, and none of them had stinted on the spice. "But I'm not sure her doc will approve. I'll see you soon, mate."

Jem stirred as he left, lifting her head and rubbing at a crick in her neck. It would have been such a normal gesture, had her hand not been trailing a couple of IV lines. She mimicked writing something, and Rosie gave her the pad and pen Harriet had provided.

You look worn out, Jem scrawled in a wavering script. *You don't have to stay.*

"I know I don't," Rosie said. "But you're no trouble, so I thought I'd keep an eye on you until your dad gets here."

I'm sorry, Rosie. For all of this, Jem wrote slowly, her hand trembling.

"Hey," Rosie said. "There's nothing you need to apologise for."

Jem tapped the pad with the pen as if about to disagree, but then touched the bandage covering Rosie's forearm instead. *How many stitches?*

"Thirteen." Rosie chuckled as Jem drew a shocked face. "Yeah, I think she added an extra one for irony's sake."

Jem took too deep a breath and started coughing, setting off a chain reaction of pressure sensors on the CPAP. *Bloody thing*, she wrote. *How're my sats?*

The monitor was out of sight behind her. Rosie spent a couple of seconds pretending to analyse it so Jem wouldn't guess how closely she'd been keeping tabs. By this stage, she could have provided a detailed graph broken down into half-minute increments and featuring all the occasions where Jem had got lazy, dipped below eighty-five percent, and given Rosie a bout of palpitations.

"Hovering around ninety-four, occasionally peaking at ninety-five," she said. "You're officially cooking on gas, Ms. Pardon."

Jem made an okay sign. *I could murder a brew.*

"I bet you could. Shall I see if your doc—" Rosie broke off when she saw Harriet approaching the cubicle. "Holy shit. Did I *summon* her?" she whispered, and Jem spluttered a laugh.

OW, she scribbled, her hand splinting her overworked ribs.

"Sorry." Rosie pulled at her scrubs top until its creases disappeared, and hid her filthy socks beneath a blanket. Harriet had extended her shift to oversee Jem's treatment, but she didn't have a hair out of place, and every time she walked in she brought with her the scent of fresh strawberries.

"You look perkier," she said, setting her steth on Jem's chest. "Try not to cough. I like having eardrums." She sat on the bed when she'd finished and read through the latest obs. "You're still tight on your left side, but I want to try you on nasal O2 and nebs and see if we can keep your sats where they are. Do you feel up to that?"

Jem wrote *YES* and underlined it.

"Good," Harriet said. "Give me ten minutes to get everything written up."

She was back in five, armed with a lidded beaker of tea and a packet of biscuits.

"You know it'll feel weird, so don't panic," she said, uncoupling the straps and easing the mask from Jem's face. She placed a thin plastic tube below Jem's nose and adjusted its flow of oxygen, her eyes never leaving Jem as she did so. Rosie inched forward in her seat, waiting for something terrible to happen, for Jem to turn blue or start gasping or lose consciousness, but Jem took a few deliberate breaths and then held out her hand for the brew.

"It's as if we've done this before," Harriet said, tilting the beaker for Jem to take a sip.

"Uncanny, isn't it?" Jem's reply was rough and scratchy, as if someone had sandpapered her vocal cords. "Thanks, Harriet."

"My pleasure. You're doing really well. There's no HDU bed for you at the moment, but at this rate we'll be able to admit you onto Respiratory instead."

"Sounds like a plan."

Harriet smiled. "I thought so. Keep up the good work, and I'll see you in half an hour."

Jem waited for Harriet to leave and then drank more of the tea unaided. She frowned at the layer of soot she was smearing on the plastic. "Do I look like a chimney sweep?" she asked.

"You are slightly smudged in places," Rosie admitted. "Do you want me to cadge some soap and a flannel?"

"You're not giving me a bloody bed-bath, Rosie Jones."

Rosie laughed, a proper carefree laugh that rolled in her belly and made her feel seven feet tall. "Would you rather that agency nurse with the mad moustache and the twitch did it?"

"Good Lord, no." Jem closed her eyes. "All right. Go and find the stuff before I change my mind."

The staff on the respiratory ward greeted Jem like a family friend, assigning her to a side room and turning a blind eye to the hoodie-wearing, barefoot bobby who'd accompanied her from A&E. Katya, her named nurse, found tomato soup and picnic boxes from somewhere, and then returned halfway through their supper with Jem's dad.

Jem dropped her sandwich as he entered the room. She thought she'd stuck a reasonably firm lid on the evening's events, until she burst into tears and fell forward into his arms.

"Shush now, Jemima. Shush," he murmured against her cheek, but his hold on her was fierce, and she knew he was crying as well. She wrapped her fists in his rain-damp jacket and listened as the thrum of his heartbeat became slower and more regular. He pulled away at length and dabbed her eyes with his hanky. "There you go. No more tears, love."

"I didn't mean to scare you, Dad. I'm really sorry. We found these girls, and someone set the house on fire…" She paused to let her lungs catch up. "And this is Rosie. She broke a window and got us all out."

If her dad recognised Rosie's name, he didn't let on. He stood to shake her hand in both of his. "Pete Pardon. It's a pleasure to meet you. Jem was lucky to have you there today."

"I think we were all lucky," Rosie said. She didn't elaborate. Earlier she'd used Kash's update to fill in the blanks for Jem, but with the trauma still so recent and raw, neither of them had wanted to dwell on the details.

Jem's dad had never liked making anyone feel uncomfortable. He returned to his seat and pulled a tin from a plastic bag, flipping the lid and displaying the contents like a pirate with a chest full of treasure. Even with the stream of oxygen beneath her nose, Jem caught the scent of chocolate and butter.

"Your mum baked these for you," he said.

"Aztec biscuits?" Jem's guess was confirmed when she spied the pieces of cornflakes. She offered Rosie first pick. "I've not had these in ages. Mum would make them for me whenever I landed in the hospital."

Her dad chuckled. "I should've bought shares in Kellogg's. Jem was single-handedly keeping the buggers in business."

"They're really good," Rosie said through a mouthful, her hand catching crumbs. "Can I leave my butty and have these instead? That's okay, isn't it? We've had a very stressful day."

"Just this once," Jem's dad said. "Ferg was all for hopping on the next train when I spoke to him, but I persuaded him to stay put and give his presentation."

"Thank you," Jem said. Knowing how much preparation Ferg had put in for the event, she hadn't wanted to tell him what had happened, but neither had she wanted him to read about it in the paper. "I'll text him later and make sure he's not on the sleeper express."

Her dad put his half-eaten biscuit down. "Did the news get it right? They said the fire was started deliberately."

"We think so," Jem said. She could see he was furious, but she couldn't be angry or vengeful or anything much at all when just staying awake was demanding everything from her.

"Bloody bastards," he said. He rarely swore unless severely provoked. He sniffed in deference to Rosie; if he'd been wearing his cap, he would probably have tipped it. "Sorry, love."

Rosie bit into another biscuit. "No need to apologise. I swear like a sailor."

"It's true," Jem said. "She's a terrible influence."

Her dad was watching them both, his expression inscrutable, and she saw him relax in subtle increments. His jaw unclenched, and he stopped picking at the dry skin on his fingers. His mobile had chimed with her mum's ringtone twice since he'd arrived, but he hadn't looked at the messages. He'd always been the one to stay with Jem in the children's ward, making dens out of the camp bed he was supposed to be sleeping on, and bringing in enough sweets to share around. The habit had died hard, although these days he tended to keep her company only if she was admitted to the HDU or the ITU.

"Get going if you need to," she said. "I'm all right, really."

"No, no, it's fine. I've only just arrived." He sighed as his phone rang again. "We got twins on an emergency placement this morning. The lad's autistic and a real handful. He helped to make those biscuits, but ten minutes later he smashed the kitchen up."

Jem turned over to face him properly. It left her winded, but she persevered. "Dad, please go home, or I'll be worrying about Mum."

"I don't want you to be on your own, not after everything that's happened today. I know you're not a child anymore, but I'd rest easier if someone was with you. And don't give me that look, Jemima Pardon."

She *was* giving him a look, but not for the reason he assumed. She'd lived with him long enough to know how he operated, and she was a dab hand at spotting an ulterior motive.

"I'll stay with her," Rosie said, completely oblivious. "These chairs aren't too bad once you get used to them."

He beamed at her. "Would you mind?"

"Not at all."

"Don't I get a say?" Jem asked, though it was hard to be indignant and wheezy at the same time.

"Apparently not," Rosie said, and accepted the tin of biscuits from Jem's dad.

He ruffled Jem's hair. "I'm sure this would look terrific without the soot."

"Kiss Mum from me," she said.

He took his cap from his pocket and pulled it on. "Keep us updated, Rosie."

"Of course I will."

The door clicked behind him as he left. Rosie let his footsteps fade before she turned back to Jem, drumming her fingers on the lid of the tin. Jem knew what was coming, and she was already laughing.

"Did he just set us up?" Rosie asked.

Jem bit into another biscuit. "Yep."

Rosie looked at the closed door and then back at Jem. "The crafty old sod," she said.

❖

When Jem had asked her nurse to leave the light on, Katya had swapped the overheads for the angle-poise lamp attached to the bed frame. It cast a soothing glow, ideal for lulling susceptible patients to sleep, but Jem was restless and uncomfortable after hours spent in the same position, and the last time she'd catnapped, she'd dreamt of the fire.

"Rosie? Are you awake?" she whispered.

"Yes, but you shouldn't be."

Jem was too preoccupied by fidgeting to react to Rosie's schoolma'am impersonation. "Can you help me? I need to get up."

"Not a problem." Rosie readied the bed's remote. "Say when."

"No, not sit up. Stand up," Jem said. The room felt too small: stuffy and airless despite her oxygen. She pulled at the neck of her gown, though it sat loose and nowhere near her throat.

"Hey, easy." Rosie untangled Jem's fingers, freeing the material and straightening the gown. "Shall I call Katya?"

"No." Jem kicked at the sheets, twisting them around her legs. "Help me to the window. Please."

"What? Jem, I can't."

"I'll do it by myself," Jem said, managing to get a foot out.

Rosie glowered, but whatever she saw in Jem's eyes made her blink first. "Okay, okay, you stubborn bugger. Let me get a chair ready."

She drew back the bedding, allowing Jem to manoeuvre herself to the edge of the mattress, a task of Herculean proportions, given that she was toting various attachments and still as weak as a kitten. Had Rosie called her bluff and left her to it, she would have ended up flat on her face.

"Is Katya going to kick my arse for this?" Rosie asked, wheeling a drip stand into position.

"No." Jem clung to Rosie's arm and lowered her feet to the tiles. "She was in your shoes last time."

"I'm not wearing any bloody shoes." Rosie wiggled her toes. "SOCO confiscated my boots, and Kash brought me a bra but no trainers."

"Don't…don't make me laugh," Jem said, already flagging with half the distance remaining.

Rosie tightened her hold. "We're doing great. I can probably drag you from here if you peg out."

"Sod off." Jem dropped into the chair with an audible thud and leaned her head back, her chest heaving.

Alerted by the clang of a monitor, Katya rushed in seconds later, muting the alarm and standing with her hands on her hips. "Again?" she said, but her stance softened as Jem nodded. She opened the window a crack and wrapped a blanket around Jem's shoulders. "Half an hour and then back to bed with a neb. Yes?"

"Absolutely," Jem said. The air smelled of fresh rain and spices from the local kebab shops, and it felt wonderful, as if it was rushing to fill her lungs. It was a fallacy, she knew, but there was a reason so many of her respiratory patients were sitting on their doorsteps when she arrived in the RRV.

Rosie pushed her own chair alongside Jem's. "Are you warm enough?" she asked.

"Mm-hm." Jem nudged her foot against Rosie's. "Stop fretting."

"Your dad left me here to fret! He thought I was responsible and well behaved, and instead I'm marching you over to the window and parking you in a draught." Rosie tucked her hair behind her ears and then curled one strand forward again, undecided. "Sorry, I'm not very good at this," she muttered.

"At what?"

Rosie gestured around herself. "All this. Any of it. It's like everyone's talking in a foreign language, and I haven't the foggiest idea what's going on, and you're in the middle of it, taking it all in and coping."

"I don't cope very well," Jem said. She'd been hanging on by a thread for hours now, tolerating the needles and the side effects of the drugs, and telling herself they were a small price to pay for being alive. In truth she was sore and cranky, and she wanted to go home to her own bed and sleep for a week. "I hate being in the hospital, and I hate my fucking crappy lungs. They're rubbish at the best of times, but when they're bad they…It feels…" She faltered; she hadn't tried to put this into words before. "It feels like there's a brick wall sat in my chest, and I have to force every breath over that wall, and sometimes I get to the point where I can't do it on my own." She started to cough and took a gulp from the glass of water Rosie handed her, swallowing convulsively until the irritation subsided.

"I think you're dead brave," Rosie said.

"I'm just used to it." It was a fact, not a play for pity. "And you saw me in Resus, Rosie. I'm anything but brave."

"Bollocks," Rosie said, and she sounded like she meant it, despite Jem's scepticism and lingering embarrassment. "I was scared to death watching you. You, meanwhile, were busy cutting deals with Dr. Lacey. I bet there aren't many people she does that for."

It took Jem a minute to catch Rosie's reference. She couldn't remember the specifics of that conversation with Harriet, only the all-encompassing fear and the sheer relief brought about by the outcome. Given the circumstances, Harriet probably hadn't decoded any of it for Rosie, and Jem thought she should at least try to.

"I didn't want to be tubed," she said. "When they put you to sleep and stick you on a ventilator. I'm terrified of it." The admission cost her nothing; Rosie had already seen her at her worst.

"Right." Rosie's eyes widened. "Christ. Was that on the cards?"

"Yeah, it wasn't far off. If the CPAP hadn't worked, it would've been the next option." Jem stretched her palm on the windowpane, letting it cool before placing it against her sticky forehead. "My dad's always been there when they've done it, and his face is the last thing I see before the drugs hit me. He'll smile at me and tell me he'll see me when I wake up, but he gets this tic at the corner of his eye when he's worried, and I don't know whether I'll be able to wake up again, and he obviously doesn't know either." Her voice and her courage wavered. She had never said this to anyone. Not to her dad, not to Ferg, not to anyone. "Perhaps one day I won't."

"God, Jem." Rosie used the heel of her hand to wipe her eyes. "I thought kids grew out of asthma. Shouldn't you be growing out of it by now?"

Her indignation made Jem smile. "My birth mother smoked pretty much everything she could get her hands on while she was pregnant with me. Crack, heroin, you name it. She shot me out eight weeks early and basically buggered up my lungs."

"That was good of her," Rosie said with admirable diplomacy.

"Yeah. Needless to say, I've never tried to track her down. On the bright side, Harriet's kept me stable for about ten years now. Tonight was a blip, but there were extenuating circumstances, so I'm hoping a blip is all it was."

"Ten years, eh?" Rosie nibbled on a smoke-blackened thumbnail. "And she's your respiratory specialist?"

"Yes," Jem said, busy working the sums out in her head. "It's more than ten. Blimey, thirteen, I think. I was referred to her just before I started as an ambulance tech." She stopped counting on her fingers and looked at Rosie, who seemed to have developed a series of nervous twitches, chewing a nail one moment and twisting her hair into a knot the next. Jem buried a laugh behind her blanket. "She's lovely, isn't she?" she said, adding a wistful sigh for maximum effect.

"Aye," Rosie said, her hair so snarled around her pinkie that it had whitened the tip.

"She's also very straight," Jem added.

"Really?" Rosie frowned and slowly unravelled her little finger. "But I thought you and her had had a thing." She folded her arms, obviously stumped. "Have you never had a thing?"

"Nope. She's married to an orthopaedic surgeon called David, and they have two precocious children. What the hell is wrong with your gaydar?"

Rosie shook her head in dismay, but she was starting to laugh. "Clearly it's defective. You just…you finish each other's sentences, for fuck's sake. If you were on the telly, I'd definitely ship you."

Jem covered her face with her hands. "Bloody Nora. Please don't ever repeat this conversation in front of her."

Rosie waited until Jem peeked out, and then gave her a Scout's honour salute, looking delighted. She had probably been worrying about Harriet since that night in the wood with Kyle Parker. "My lips are sealed," she said, and checked her watch. "Your thirty minutes are up. Are you ready for the return trek?"

"As I'll ever be." Clutching her drip on one side, Jem took Rosie's hand and managed to stand. "Nothing to it," she said, tottering through a head rush that almost knocked her back onto her arse. Three steps across, she stopped to cough and felt Rosie slip an arm around her.

"Easy, I've got you," Rosie said.

Jem leaned into her. "Do you think people would ship us?" she asked, and felt the low rumble of Rosie's answering chuckle.

"The plucky paramedic and the wayward but debonair copper?" Rosie set them off walking again, slow and steady, each step perfectly coordinated. "I reckon we'd be a shoo-in."

Chapter Fifteen

Rosie's newspaper rustled as she licked her finger and flicked to the rest of the article. "'The investigation is ongoing,' blah blah, 'Manchester Metropolitan Police are appealing for witnesses.' Oh, and apparently we spent 'a comfortable night at West Pennine Med.'" Scoffing, she rapped the arm of her chair. "Whoever wrote this piece has never tried kipping in one of these." She closed the paper, her concentration waning as she watched Jem attempt to pass a comb through her hair. Despite the reporter's claims, neither of them had slept well. A post-breakfast physio session had seen Jem walk to the nurses' station, with the promise of a shower dangled in front of her like a carrot. She had managed both, but she had nodded off twice with the comb still in her hand, and she was on the verge of making it a hat trick.

"C'mere." Abandoning the paper, Rosie sat on the bed and held out her hand for the comb. Jem relinquished it without a protest. Her cheeks had lost all the colour they'd gained from the warm water, and her chest sounded like it needed oiling. On the sats monitor, ninety-three percent flickered in amber figures. Rosie put her hands on Jem's shoulders. "Can you lean forward? That's enough, that's fine."

Jem gave a satisfied sigh as Rosie began to ease the tangles from her hair. Katya had replaced the manky hospital soap with proper body wash, and the stink of smoke had at last disappeared beneath the scent of vanilla and honey.

"Thank you," Jem said. "Y'know, for last night. For everything."

Rosie fussed with Jem's fringe, uneasy with the gratitude. She didn't want Jem to feel indebted to her; that wasn't why she'd stayed. "Not quite what I had in mind for a first date, Jemima," she said.

"No?" Jem smiled. "We did get fireworks, of a sort."

"This is true." Rosie guided Jem back to the pillows. "The travel arrangements were also exclusive and very efficient."

"Free accommodation," Jem added.

"And your dad made sure we spent the night together," Rosie said.

Jem spluttered and set off coughing. "Well, this just got very weird."

"It did rather." Rosie retrieved the paper and snapped it open. "Moving right along, apparently too much cauliflower might give you tinnitus."

Jem's cough tapered into a yawn. "What a load of twaddle. They'd print anything."

Rosie lowered the paper again. "You're welcome, by the way. And I'm really glad you're okay."

It was quiet for a moment, and the room darkened as the morning's persistent drizzle became a downpour that splashed off the windowsill. Beyond the door, someone's off-key whistling competed with the drone of a floor cleaner.

"Can our second date just be dinner and a movie?" Jem asked as the cleaner moved on and the whistling faded.

"That sounds perfect." The words left Rosie in a rush of unguarded happiness. Last night had been hell, but they'd got each other through it in one piece, Jem was on the mend, and a proper date was still on the cards. Rosie felt weightless somehow, as if she too had had a brick wall in her chest and it had suddenly fallen. She ran her fingers across the back of Jem's hand, tracing the livid bruise left behind by an IV. "How's about I cook and we sprawl on the sofa to watch something daft?"

"Mm," Jem murmured, half-drowsing. The hand Rosie was still stroking was splayed on the sheets. "Can we have popcorn?"

"I think that can be arranged. Now go to sleep, or Harriet won't be letting you out on Sunday."

"She bloody will," Jem said, but her vehemence was undermined somewhat when she began to snore.

Rosie's search for the paper's sudoku was interrupted by a nurse coming in to start Jem on a neb. Inured to being mauled about with, Jem didn't stir, and the nurse nodded his approval as her sats improved.

"Brew?" he whispered to Rosie.

"Yes, please."

Shortly after he had left, the door opened again. Rosie turned in anticipation, but her smile vanished as Steph hurried over to her. She crouched by Rosie's chair and pulled her into an embrace, then cupped her face and kissed her. Rosie froze, caught completely off-guard, though every fibre of her wanted to smack Steph's hands away and wipe the taste of Steph's gloss from her lips.

"Just—no." She shoved back hard in the chair, sending its legs squealing across the tiles and waking Jem, whose eyes widened as she yanked at the nebuliser. Rosie went to Jem's side, evading Steph's attempt to intercept her. "Hey. Sorry, it's okay," she said, perching on the bed and righting the mask. She had done this so many times in the night that it felt like second nature. "You're okay."

Jem glanced beyond Rosie, and there was an uncommon ferocity in her expression when she looked back. She laid a hand on Rosie's thigh, despite Rosie's reassuring nod, and didn't move it even when Steph's lips thinned into a bitter line.

"I was worried about you," Steph said before Rosie could speak. "You didn't answer my calls." She stood, forcing Rosie to look up at her, and folded her arms. Rosie recognised the stance and the tone, but neither had any impact.

"I told you the reception is bad in here," she said. She didn't add, "And I had more important things going on," but Steph obviously got the gist, because she gave Jem a look that would have curdled butter. She took a file from her briefcase and threw it onto Rosie's chair.

"A team of psychologists and social workers tried to interview Ava Reynolds and Chloe Harrison this morning. Neither girl would cooperate, and they're demanding to speak to you."

"To me? Why?"

"To both of you, and I don't care why. I just need answers to the questions on the front sheet of that file." Steph snapped the latches on her briefcase. "They'll be down to see you in the next half hour. I've spoken to your doctor, Ms. Pardon, and she's given her permission, albeit reluctantly."

Rosie wished she'd been a fly on the wall for that conversation. Harriet had stayed late into the night, and she'd been back on the ward at shift changeover.

Rosie managed to retrieve the file without leaving the bed and found a bullet-pointed list of questions. "Am I recording the interview?"

"Audio only." Steph set a small Dictaphone on the overbed table. "Ring me when you're done. If you can find somewhere with reception, that is." Evidently satisfied with her parting shot, she strode to the door, almost colliding with the nurse as he returned with a tray of brews and mid-morning medicines.

"Who pissed on her chips?" he asked as the door closed behind her.

"No one. That's her default setting." Rosie passed Jem her tea and a small cup of tablets.

"I like it better when *you* call me 'Ms. Pardon,'" Jem muttered, and Rosie laughed over the rim of her mug.

"Down the hatch," the nurse told Jem. "Then you're getting a couple of visitors, so chair or bed?"

"Chair." Jem reached behind her head to untie her gown. "And do I have any clothes that don't come with 'West Penn' stamped on them?"

"Not as such," Rosie said. "But I've got a spare T-shirt and a pair of tracky bottoms, if the price is right."

Jem's payment options were limited to a malted milk biscuit and a cache of small red tablets. She shrugged and offered both.

"I'll stick to the biscuit, thanks," Rosie said.

"Wise choice," Jem said, and necked the tablets in one.

Resting her hands on the sink, Jem studied her reflection in the bathroom mirror. Her complexion sat somewhere between catastrophic hypovolaemic shock and day-old corpse, while her eyes were encircled by blue-black shadows. The nebs had left her lips dry and cracked, and she'd caught her chin on something, probably the balcony, tearing an uneven laceration through its centre.

"Bloody hell," she said, scratching her nose where the oxygen tubing was chafing it.

A knock on the door preceded Rosie's singsong, "Are you decent?"

Jem spat mouthwash down the plughole and slumped on the toilet seat. "No." She hid her face in a towel. "I'm a monster."

Rosie came in regardless and sat on the clinical waste bin. She tugged the towel away. "Don't be a daft ha'p'orth. You've been ill, Jem." She tapped the IV line in Jem's wrist. "You're still ill. You're allowed to look like death warmed over." She scrutinised herself in the mirror and wiped sleep from her eye. "I, on the other hand, have no such excuse."

"I think you look gorgeous," Jem said. "But then I'm biased, because I fancy you." She laughed at Rosie's stunned reaction and double-checked her O2 cylinder, wondering if she was hypoxic. She hadn't meant to say that out loud.

Rosie fake-swooned, almost upending the bin. "That's the most romantic thing anyone's ever said to me, and in this"—she gestured expansively at the pile of incontinence pads, the boxes of examination gloves, and the shower cubicle with its emergency alarm—"most idyllic of settings." Within seconds, she'd fashioned a couple of pieces of loo roll into a flower. "Jemima Pardon, I fancy the pants off you as well."

Jem took the flower, though she stopped short of sniffing it. "Is it sleep deprivation?" she asked, linking Rosie's arm and walking with her to the door. "Making us act like twerps?"

"It's sheer joie de vivre, Jem!" Rosie said, and then paused to reconsider. "And possibly sleep deprivation and PTSD as well."

She sat Jem in the closest chair and propped the door open in readiness. A social worker in his mid-forties came in first, taking an unobtrusive seat in the corner as Ava steered Chloe's wheelchair straight into the bathroom wall.

"These things are fucking shite," she said over Chloe's yelp, and caused further ructions by attempting a three-sixty. Outrage and effort made her face as pink as her hair, giving her the look of a pissed-off imp, albeit one wearing slipper socks and Minion pyjamas.

"Sit your arse down," Rosie told her, no stranger to dealing with moody teens. "There are cans of pop and all kinds of crap on Jem's bed. Help yourself."

Placated by the vending machine stash, Ava sat cross-legged on the chair next to Jem. She opened a packet of crisps but then scrunched the bag closed again and placed a careful finger on the dressing securing Jem's cannula.

"Don't worry," she said in a confidential undertone. "It doesn't hurt when they take 'em out." She displayed the bandage on her own wrist and offered Jem a Quaver.

"Thank you," Jem said, crunching a crisp so she wouldn't start sniffling.

"We brought these for you, Jem!" Finally facing forward, Chloe held up a bag of Haribo. "We got two, but Fat Face ate one for breakfast."

"I've been there myself," Rosie said. "It can't be helped." She'd already set the recorder going, but she propped her feet on Jem's chair, letting everyone relax and eat their snacks. The girls appeared to have rediscovered their mettle overnight. They were still pale and undernourished, but the beaten-down kids Jem had found cowering in a corner had been replaced by scrappy teenagers who swore like sailors and thought nothing of stealing chocolate from a police officer.

"I'm going to my nan's," Ava said through a mouthful of Crunchie. "Tonight, instead of going home."

"Is that a good thing?" Rosie asked.

"Yeah, cos that prick Davey won't be there. He's my mam's boyfriend. He's already got four kids, but he knocked up my mam six weeks after moving in."

Rosie took a swig of her Pepsi Max. "Was he the reason you ran away?"

Ava shrugged. "I bet they didn't even notice I was gone. My nan's ace, though. She stayed with us last night."

"What about you, Chloe?" Jem asked. "Are you going home?"

Chloe nodded. "I told our Kirsty I was sorry for nicking her iPad, and she says she won't set the coppers on me." Her hand flew to her mouth as she stared at Rosie. "Shit. Fucking shit."

Ava dropped her crisps and went to kneel by the wheelchair. "Rosie won't tell, will you, Rosie?"

"Absolutely not," Rosie said.

Jem's eyes flicked from Ava to Chloe as she gauged their exchange, trying to work out their relationship. They were obviously close but seemed more akin to siblings than best friends.

"How long have you two known each other?" she asked, and wasn't surprised when Chloe took Ava's hand in lieu of providing an answer.

"About three weeks," Ava ventured. "We got picked together."

Rosie leaned forward slightly, the detail catching her attention. "Who picked you to do what?"

Chloe had started to tremble, her slippered feet clattering the wheelchair's footplate. Ava squeezed onto the chair and pulled her close.

"We met down by the canal," Ava said quietly. "All the kids go there after school, and you can crash in the mills if the smack rats aren't around."

"Ava was there before me," Chloe said. She cupped her hands over Ava's ear and whispered something inaudible.

Ava whispered a reply and then jutted out her chin and folded her arms. "If we tell you what we did, are you going to arrest us?" she asked Rosie.

"Did you murder anyone?" Rosie said, copying Ava's pose as she threw the challenge back.

"No!" Ava looked horrified. "But we stole loads of things."

"Do you promise to renounce your life of crime and become upstanding citizens?"

"Huh?" Chloe said.

Rosie pared things down to the essentials. "Will you be good from now on?"

Both girls nodded.

"Excellent. No, I won't arrest you." Rosie made a rolling gesture. "Carry on."

Chloe started on a bag of M&Ms, sorting the colours into order on her thigh and making Rosie smile. "Ava taught me how to shoplift," she said, still arranging the sweets. "Just things we needed, like butties and pop, or things we could sell, like razors. Nance said we were dead good at it."

"Who's Nance?"

Chloe nudged an orange M&M into line, her eye contact nonexistent. "She's just Nance."

"She came to one of the mills and offered us a job," Ava said. "There was a lad with her, all decked out in gear. He said she'd given him all kinds of stuff, and we were sick of eating Pot Noodles, so we went with them, and it was fine for the first few days."

"We got nice clothes," Chloe said, "and Converse. And Bill showed us a trick to do in the street, where I fell down and pretended like I was unconscious, and Ava pinched purses and phones from everyone who came to help."

Jem's monitor suddenly registered a pulse rate of one-twenty. She whacked the alarm to silence it and shook her head, warning Rosie not to intervene. "Ava, did Nance take you to a shelter called Olly's?" she asked.

Ava stared at her. "How did you know?"

"Bill and Nancy," Rosie said, the light evidently dawning. "Their surname didn't happen to be Sykes, by any chance?"

"Dunno," Ava said. "They were just Bill and Nance."

"Could you tell us where the shelter is?" Jem asked, her enthusiasm for the new lead making her forget she wasn't actually a police officer.

Ava filched one of Chloe's sweets, careful not to disrupt the order. "They took us in one of those big cars, but the windows were black so we couldn't see much, and Chloe fell asleep."

"How far from the canal, at a guess?" Rosie asked.

"Half an hour? Maybe. I'm not sure." Ava chewed her bottom lip with teeth dyed blue by the sweets. "I'm sorry."

"It's okay, love. You're doing really well. The shelter must've been great after roughing it at the mill, eh?"

"I suppose," Ava said. "But we never got to keep any of the cash, and Nance locked us in at night, so we got fed up and tried to do a runner."

"Who caught you?" Jem asked.

Ava slipped an arm around Chloe's shoulders. "Bill. He called us 'ungrateful little twats' and said we needed to be taught a lesson. Then he locked us in the cellar and left us there."

Chloe was staring at the wall behind Jem, her expression blank. Tears were running unheeded down her cheeks.

"I think that might be enough for now," the social worker said.

Rosie held up a hand, taking out her mobile with the other. "One minute," she said, and clicked on a photo of Kyle Parker. "Ava, did you see this lad at the shelter?"

Ava took the phone but barely needed to look at the image. "He was the one with Nance at the mill. Strutting about like he owned it or summat. We were shifted around a lot, though. No one really stayed at the shelter after the first couple of nights. They took us to a few different houses."

Rosie crouched by the chair and swiped the screen to bring up another photo. "What about this lass? Do you recognise her? Her name's Tahlia."

Ava shook her head. "I'm not sure. I might have seen her in the old mill or by the canal, but I got drunk most nights." She nudged Chloe, who shut her eyes and refused to look.

"Okay, love." Rosie retrieved her phone. "It's okay, we're finished now."

"I want my mum," Chloe whispered, the plea so emphatic it made Jem ache with homesickness. She watched the social worker wheel the chair to the door, Ava following closely behind him.

"Hey, wait a sec," she said, realising there was a puzzle piece missing. "Were Bill and Nance in charge at the shelter?"

"No," Ava said. "I heard them talk about a boss, but we never met him. He had a weird name. Fage, Fage-in?" She shoved a handful of M&Ms into her mouth and licked her palm clean. "Or summat daft like that."

CHAPTER SIXTEEN

Jem's nightmare was different this time. The fire hadn't changed; the smoke still choked and blinded her, and the air was hot enough to burn her throat, but Rosie wasn't there to pull her out of the window, and when Jem collapsed on the balcony there were screams echoing from the room she'd just escaped.

She awoke feeling sick and utterly lost. The unfamiliar surroundings, the clothes she was wearing: none of it made any sense until she saw Rosie sparked out on the camp bed beside her hospital bed and everything slotted back into place.

"God," she whispered. The dream continued to claw at her, forcing her to go to Rosie's side, to kneel and double-check Rosie was really there, safe and sound and still breathing. "You're okay," Jem whispered, feeling the soft puff of Rosie's breath on her palm. "You'll be okay, I promise."

She tiptoed to the bathroom and splashed cold water on her face. Then she cupped her hands beneath the tap, letting them fill. The water was stale, but its chill eased the dryness in her mouth and settled her stomach. She sat on the closed toilet lid and pulled up her knees, wrapping her arms around them to try to hold them still. Her chin juddered when she lowered it, knocking against her shaking legs and making her bite her tongue. The tang of blood mingled with the chemical taste of the water. She wiped her lips with a handful of toilet paper and stayed where she was, waiting for the shivering to stop.

Rosie still hadn't stirred when Jem went back into the room. Curled on her side beneath a pile of blankets, she looked content, as if she was satisfied she'd done everything asked of her and she was finally letting herself rest. Jem returned to her bed, but she couldn't settle, and the sight of Rosie peacefully blowing spit bubbles whilst scrunching her nose just made everything worse. Moving slowly so she wouldn't start coughing, Jem hooked her oxygen tubing onto a portable cylinder and wheeled it out into the corridor, closing the door behind her. One of the nurses stopped her by the linen cupboard and told her there was a chap at the desk attempting to blag his way past the ward sister.

"Is it my dad?" she asked. He'd spoken to her last night, but he hadn't mentioned a visit.

"No, a younger bloke in an ambulance uniform. Looks like something was sick all over his shoulder before he came out."

That narrowed things down slightly, and Jem relaxed, ruling out Baxter as her potential visitor. "It'll be Kev, my manager. He's got more kids than sense."

Kev waylaid her halfway to the nurses' station, hugging her and then stepping back to appraise her. "I expected worse," he said. "Bob and Dougie were in bits when they got to station the other night."

"I can imagine." Taking his arm, she led him into the day room, where she muted the telly and dropped onto the sofa. "They popped in for a few minutes this morning. Bob ate most of my grapes, once he'd stopped blubbing."

Kev hefted a gift bag. "The group had a quick whip-round. Everyone sends their best."

She arched an eyebrow. "*Everyone?*"

"Baxter and Caitlin were on mandatory training," he said, easily catching her drift. "And you're not to worry about the morphine business. It'll all come out in the wash."

"That's apt, given how much he'd love to hang me out to dry." She coughed against the stress clamping around her ribs. With everything else that had happened, the threat of the disciplinary had understandably slipped her mind. "I was supposed to have a meeting with a rep about it on Monday. My doc's promised to discharge me tomorrow, so I might be able to come in for it. Maybe I can resume on light duties or—"

"Jem." Kev put a hand on her arm. "Take a breath."

She took several. "Am I going to get sacked, Kev?" she asked quietly.

"I very much doubt that, love, no matter how hard Baxter might push. Besides which, his timing is terrible." Kev fished in his pockets and pulled out a handful of newspaper clippings. "The fire has been quite the story. The *MEN* ran it on the front cover. So did the *Guardian,* the *Indie,* and the *Tameside Chron.* One of the *Daily Mail* hacks turned up on station, but Dougie told him to piss off. We've had a couple of requests for an interview, but I asked the media department to handle them."

"I don't want any fuss," she said, glad for once to have been isolated in the hospital. "I just want to get home and get back to work."

"Better not rush things, then. How's Officer Rosie?"

Jem smiled. She never had told him Rosie's surname. "She's fast asleep. Well, I hope she is, or she'll be wondering where I am."

"I might have a word with her sarge, see if we can get you on opposing shifts. You don't half get into trouble when you're together." He chuckled, obviously meaning nothing by it, but the unease that had lingered since her nightmare ramped right back up. He walked her to her room, and she stood on the threshold, watching Rosie blink blearily at her.

"What did I miss?" Rosie asked.

"Nothing," Jem said, but the kneejerk denial seemed to stick in her throat, and she knew now what she had to do. She smiled to soften the bluntness of her tone, though she felt like curling into Rosie's arms and sobbing her heart out. "Go back to sleep."

Rosie slapped the parking ticket onto her windscreen and collected her rucksack from the back seat. At Jem's insistence, she had gone home for the night, but although she felt better for having had a bath, a meal cooked from scratch, and eight hours in her own bed, she had spent half the evening texting Jem and the other half of it wondering how Jem was getting on. She stumbled on the kerb that marked the car park boundary, flummoxed by a relationship that had sneaked under her defences and blossomed into something that was making her trip over her own feet. It had never been like this with Steph, who clicked her fingers to see how fast Rosie would come running and left her with a bitter taste in her mouth. In all honesty, it had never been like this with anyone.

Re-shouldering the bag, Rosie took an exaggerated step onto the pavement and walked toward the hospital entrance. With outpatient appointments and elective surgeries on hold for the weekend, the main corridors were quiet, allowing her to steer well clear of the night shift workers dead set on getting home and willing to take out anyone who got in their way.

She found Jem sitting on the edge of the bed. Her hair was still wet from the shower, and she'd cobbled together an outfit comprising a pair of overlong pyjama bottoms and a pink scrubs top. Someone had already stripped her bedding, and a wad of gauze had replaced the cannula on her wrist. She smiled at Rosie, but she seemed tired and distracted, her reddened eyes meeting but unable to hold Rosie's gaze.

"Everything okay?" Rosie asked.

"Fine," Jem said. "Harriet's just gone to get my prescription. She shouldn't be long."

"No worries. We're not in a rush, are we?" Rosie dropped the rucksack on the bed and began to unpack it. Not wanting to bother her dad, Jem had given Rosie a house key and sent her on a mission to retrieve clean clothes. "I think I found everything. And I binned a piece of cheddar that had gone a very strange shade of green."

Jem collected the clothes in one hand and hitched up her trousers with the other. "Thanks. I'll go and get changed. They'll have someone else in this room before the bed goes cold."

Rosie nodded, although she wasn't sure that was true. Harriet had wanted to keep Jem in the hospital over the weekend, and she'd only relented when Jem had agreed to let Rosie stay with her.

Rosie waited until the bathroom door clicked shut, and then sagged into the closest chair. She had fairly bounced out of bed that morning, eager to get Jem home and spoil her rotten. She had assumed Jem would share her enthusiasm, never considering Jem might be trying to come to terms with everything that had happened over the last few days.

"You're a bloody idiot," she muttered, lowering her head into her hands. She looked up again when Harriet walked in, but she couldn't muster anything beyond a perfunctory greeting. "Hey, Doc. Jem's just getting dressed."

Harriet sat on the adjacent chair and gave her a bag full of medicines and a slip of paper with two phone numbers on it. "My mobile and home number. If there's a problem, call me. Whatever time, I don't mind. Jem's not daft, but she doesn't like being in here, either, so she'll try to get by even when she shouldn't."

Rosie slid the paper into her wallet, glad of the security it offered, although less comfortable with the role of minder. "She seems quiet this morning," she said.

"I noticed. It's not uncommon after a trauma like this. You may find yourself struggling as well. Don't be too proud to ask for counselling if you need it."

"I won't." She might have said more, had Jem not come back into the room. Swaddled in an oversized fleece, Jem hid her hands in its sleeves and folded her arms, though the hospital was stifling.

"Ready for the off?" Harriet asked.

"Yes," Jem said. She seemed far less certain now that she had permission to leave. "Thanks, Harriet." For a moment, she hesitated. Then she hugged her tightly, hiding her face against Harriet's chest.

"My pleasure." Harriet kissed the top of her head. "You're both to stay out of mischief for a while, is that understood?"

"Loud and clear," Rosie said.

"We'll try," Jem added.

Leaving Harriet at the nurses' station, they walked toward the main entrance, dodging porters wheeling elderly patients from one ward to the next, and domestic staff making the most of the Sunday morning lull. With Jem clearly not in the mood for small talk, Rosie cast the odd surreptitious glance at her, mindful that this was the farthest she had walked since her admission, and keenly attuned to signs that she was starting to struggle.

"I'm *fine*, Rosie," Jem said, catching one of Rosie's split-second appraisals.

Rosie raised her hands in surrender and said nothing.

The ride to Jem's house passed in a similar fashion, with Jem staring at her breath fogging on the passenger window, and Rosie doing her damnedest to concentrate on the roads. She wanted to ask what was wrong, to offer help or a shoulder to cry on, but she no longer shared Harriet's conviction that the fire lay behind Jem's sudden reticence, and she was scared she wouldn't like the answer if she asked. It seemed to take forever and no time at all before she was turning onto Jem's street, creeping through the double-parked cars, and pulling into the driveway. Jem unfastened her seat belt as Rosie switched off the engine. She leaned forward, her hands clasped in front of her, her hair concealing her face, and Rosie waited, braced as if for a punch.

"I don't want you to come in," Jem said, the words dropping like a stone into the silence.

"Jem—" Rosie lowered her hands from the wheel, leaving damp prints on the plastic. She'd seen this coming, but she still didn't feel prepared, still didn't know what to say, and every option she came up with—reminding Jem of her promise to Harriet, playing on her physical vulnerability—seemed more underhand than the last. In the end, there was only one question she really wanted the answer to.

"Did I do something wrong?" she asked.

Jem shook her head, splashing tears onto her knees. "No, no, no," she said quickly, almost chanting the denial. "It's me. I don't want this. Any of this, and I should have told you, but I couldn't. I'm sorry." She grabbed her hospital bag, shoved the car door hard against the wind, and scrambled out onto the driveway. Rain soaked her within seconds, but Rosie could see that she was still crying. "I'm sorry," she said again, and let the wind slam the door for her.

"Jem? Hang on a minute. *Jem?*" Rosie grappled for her seat belt, fumbling with its latch and getting the strap tangled as she shoved it out of the way. Jem was on the front step, turning a key, pushing the door with her foot, and she'd gone inside before Rosie could get out of the car. Even from a distance, Rosie heard the jangle of the security chain as it slid into place.

"Fucking hell," she whispered. She sat back in the car, hoping for a reprieve that wasn't going to come. A minute ticked by, then another. She waited until her hands had stopped shaking. Then she started the engine and drove away.

❖

Crouched behind the front door, Jem listened to the car turn in a slow circle on the gravel. Its tyres hit the pothole Ferg had been promising to fill for the last four months, the front tyre bouncing through and then the rear. The engine idled at the gate, as if Rosie was giving her the opportunity to come out again and make this right, but the car didn't pause for long. Jem heard the rev of acceleration, and within seconds, there was nothing but the sound of the clock ticking in the living room and the fast, irregular wheeze of her breathing.

"It's for the best," she whispered. "It's for the best. You'll be safe now."

The more she thought about it, the more convinced she became that she and Rosie had never stood a chance. They had barely taken the first steps in their relationship, and she had almost got Rosie killed. Her luck hadn't been this extreme with anyone else, but then she had never met anyone quite like Rosie, who had barged into her life, shaken everything up, and given her a glimpse of what she could have. Before Rosie, she hadn't realised how lonely she had been or how happy it was possible to be, and none of her previous breakups had ever felt like this. They had been difficult and miserable and occasionally downright bizarre, but they had never felt so cruel.

She flipped the cap off her inhaler and took two puffs. The medicine worked quickly, allowing her to stagger upstairs to the bathroom, where she knelt by the toilet and vomited what little she had eaten for her breakfast.

She groaned, coughing bile and phlegm into the bowl. Her stomach and chest ached, and she felt dizzy enough to lean her forehead against the toilet seat. Closing her eyes, she pulled a towel from the radiator and used it to cushion her head as she curled onto the floor.

She wasn't sure how long she lay there. Long enough to wake with goose-pimpled arms and chattering teeth. She could practically see Rosie standing in front of her, full of righteous indignation and warnings of pneumonia. It would have been worth the scolding just to have her there, but Jem couldn't undo the damage she had wrought, and she left her mobile where it was, burning a metaphorical hole in her coat pocket.

She flushed the toilet and dragged herself up, clinging to the towel rail until she was certain she wouldn't faint. Then she returned to the front door to collect her bag of meds. A quick check of the living room clock told her she was overdue a dose of steroids, so she counted the pills as she walked to the kitchen: seven to start off with, reducing on a daily basis. She would be back at work before she got to five. Back to normal, doing her job and keeping her head down, trying not to bump into Rosie, not to call her or text her or think about her or—

She stopped short in the kitchen doorway, her hand poised to switch on the light. The sun played its part perfectly, though, choosing that instant to shine on the large bunch of flowers in the middle of the table. Rosie obviously hadn't been able to find a vase, so she'd co-opted an orange B&Q bucket, no doubt tickled by the serendipity. Beside the flowers, she'd arranged boxes of microwave popcorn and a selection of DVDs. Venturing beyond the threshold, Jem found a veg rack full of fresh produce and a fridge newly stocked with essentials. A rolled pork loin beside the lasagne on the bottom shelf suggested a roast had been on the evening's menu.

"Shit."

She filled a glass with water, swallowing the tablets one by one in an effort to keep them down. Her mobile buzzed, and she knocked the glass against her lips, spilling water on her chin. It took her three attempts to enter her passcode, but the message was from her dad, not Rosie.

Hallo, sweetheart. Home safe and sound?

Her bottom lip began to tremble. She wanted to tell him everything, to sit by his knee and explain why she'd done what she'd done and how broken it had made her feel. He would only try to fix it, though. He was her dad, after all. He wouldn't want to admit this was something beyond repair.

Home safe, she typed. *All well.*

It was a long time before she hit send.

CHAPTER SEVENTEEN

I don't bloody know." Rosie stabbed at a cherry tomato, sending it spiralling across the table. "I haven't got a bloody clue. One minute we're planning a day of crap films and popcorn, and the next she's slamming the damn door on me."

Kash carefully set the tomato back onto a lettuce leaf. He must have known there was more to come, because he stayed quiet, letting her continue.

Rosie dropped her fork onto her plate. She'd ordered the first thing on the menu, but she'd hardly touched her pasta, and the dressing on the side salad was turning her stomach. "I even bought the films and left them on her kitchen table. I'm so fucking stupid," she said, burying her face in her napkin. "But it felt like we were just getting something started."

He pulled at her hand, untangling the cloth and wrapping his fingers around hers. "Why don't you go and see her?" he asked.

"I can't," she whispered. "She sent me away."

"Don't you think you deserve to know why?" He made it sound so reasonable, as if Jem was the one at fault, but he hadn't seen how devastated she'd looked standing in the rain on the driveway.

"I don't want to push her," Rosie said. "I don't want to make things worse."

He squeezed her hand. "Worse than this?"

She shook her head, her throat prickly with grief. "I miss her, Kash. I really fell for her. Fluffy was smitten as well, and he's a capricious little demon."

"I could tell," Kash said. "Not about the damn dragon, but I could tell with you. Things didn't bother you like they usually do: late finishes, that scrote grabbing your arse, Smiffy smearing Bovril all over the kitchen. Even Steph couldn't get a rise out of you."

She frowned. "I whacked that scrote with my baton."

"Yeah, but you didn't break anything, and you got him a brew once he'd apologised." Kash stole a piece of her garlic bread. "Bottom line is: Jem's good for you, and you'd be an idiot to just walk away from this mess."

"I *am* an idiot, Kash. You know that better than anyone." She tried to laugh it off, but she knew he was right.

He picked up the fork she'd abandoned and pushed it back into her hand. "Eat your lunch and get a decent night's sleep."

"Then what?"

He crunched into the bread, smearing grease and garlic all over his chin. "Then pull on your big-girl knickers and phone her."

❖

The voice mail Steph had left for Rosie was curt and succinct. "I need to go over your interview and statement. Call me."

Rosie slapped her keys onto the kitchen counter. Her lunch with Kash had killed a couple of hours, but if Steph was working the Sunday on overtime, she would be dragging the shift out till the death, and she would expect Rosie to heed her request. The girls' positive identification of Kyle Parker had made a more detailed debrief inevitable, and, as usual, Steph's timing was impeccable.

Rosie looked at her messages again. The slightest word from Jem would usurp Steph in the running order, but there was nothing beside a text from her mam, so she curled under the blanket on the sofa to return Steph's call.

Steph was still aloof when she answered, clearly irritated that Rosie hadn't jumped to it and rearranged her weekend.

"Did you have your phone switched off?" she said. "I've tried calling you umpteen times."

"It was on." Rosie didn't attempt an explanation. She'd checked her mobile whenever it had buzzed, and let it go to voice mail on seeing Steph's name.

"Are you still with Jem?"

"No, I'm at home." Rosie somehow managed to keep her voice level. The last thing she wanted was Steph smelling blood in the water. "I'll meet you at Clayton in half an hour."

Her eyes strayed unbidden to the phone's screen as she hung up: no messages, no missed calls. She debated texting Steph to cancel their meeting and then drawing the curtains and locking the front door. She could put her jammies on and drown her sorrows in something strong enough to let her sleep; it wasn't as if a hangover would make her feel any worse. Instead, she retrieved her keys and walked out into the rain.

The Clayton car park was unusually busy for a Sunday, suggesting plenty of staff were taking advantage of the open season on overtime. Unable to face a mob of concerned colleagues, Rosie nosed into a space in the far corner and waited out the shift changeover. She would undoubtedly run into people who knew her, but at least their numbers would be fewer. Turning up in plain clothes got her past the locker room unscathed, and she was halfway along the main corridor when Smiffy came out of the kitchen and almost collided with her. His delighted yelp brought out most of his van, their brews and butties in hand.

"Good to see you, love," he said, his customary gruffness tempered by genuine warmth. He squeezed her biceps, the closest he would ever come to giving anyone a hug, and pressed a KitKat into her hand. "You look peaky, PC Jones. Get this down your neck."

"I will. Thanks, Smiffy." She leaned against a motivational poster featuring a line of shiny-faced bobbies all ready to go out and do their best. Most of them sported Biro fangs and moustaches. "Are you helping investigate the fire?" she asked. Smiffy ran her shift pattern, so it was a fair assumption, given that he was here on his day off.

"Aye. We've been on the house-to-house all weekend, and we're fingertip-searching this afternoon. It's taken a while to shore up the foundations and make the building safe."

"Did anyone see anything that night?" She would rather get an update from him than attempt to wheedle one from Steph. She never knew what Steph might want in exchange.

He took a swig of his cup-a-soup, crunching a crouton as he considered. "Not much. A vague description of a stocky white man running from the rear of the house. He had either"—Smiffy began to check the options off on his fingers—"a cap pulled low, a woolly hat on, or a hood up, and he might've had a beard or possibly a scarf. It was dark and already smoky by then, and our best witness was smacked off his tits. The house next door but one, allegedly home to a law-abiding family of excellent repute, has CCTV fixed to every other brick, and it caught a dark SUV driving away at speed. No make, model, or plate visible." He blew on his soup, sending steam twirling toward the ceiling. "Sorry it's not better news, love."

"It's not your fault, mate. Cheers, though."

She walked toward the Major Crimes office with all the enthusiasm of a condemned woman, clutching her KitKat as a lacklustre final meal. Steph had propped the door open, and she met Rosie on the threshold, barring the way as if Rosie hadn't earned the right to access the inner sanctum.

"I've booked Interview Three," Steph said. The small room, especially designed to host victim or relative interviews, was cosy and welcoming, and, more to the point as far as Rosie was concerned, came with its own brewing facilities.

She put the kettle on as Steph arranged her paperwork and opened a laptop. No one had ever fathomed how to turn the radiator off, and it was blasting out heat. Already sweaty with apprehension, Rosie slung her coat over the closest chair and opened the window wide. The scent of kebab spices and chippy drifted in, so reminiscent of that night in the hospital with Jem that she stabbed her teabag with a spoon, wretched all over again.

"When are you resuming work?" Steph asked, gesturing at the bandage around Rosie's forearm.

Rosie set the mugs beside the laptop. Its screen was locked and password-protected. "I never called in sick," she said. She had planned to, before everything had gone to shit with Jem. She sat a full sofa cushion away from Steph. "I'll be in as usual tomorrow."

Steph tasted her coffee and got up to add more milk. "Forgotten how I like it already?" she said. A pout curled her bottom lip, but she ran a hand across the nape of Rosie's neck before she sat next to her. "You scared me the other night. I don't know what I'd do if anything happened to you." The close confines gave her voice an uncomfortable intimacy, and she shifted until they were thigh to thigh.

Rosie hadn't come here for a tête-à-tête. She leaned forward, sorting through the paperwork and re-establishing the gap between Steph's body and her own. Ignoring Steph's indignant snatch of breath, she focused on the transcribed pages in her hand. "Do you want to start with the interview?"

"Okay, fine, I get it," Steph said. "Have it your own way."

Rosie leafed through the papers, searching for a particular quote. Ava had said, "There was a lad with her, all decked out in gear." Rosie could see Ava's grin, her teeth stained bright blue from the M&Ms.

"Are you speaking to the runaways dossing around the canal?" she asked. "This couple, Bill and Nance, they're using those mills as a hunting ground and taking kids with them to act as lures."

"We tried," Steph said, "but we've only managed to catch a handful. Two, maybe three at best. They've either disappeared of their own volition or they've been cleared out."

Rosie clasped her mug to ease the ache from her fingers. She'd gone from too hot to freezing cold in a matter of minutes. "My money would be on the latter," she said. "These people are probably responsible for Kyle Parker's death, directly or indirectly, and they didn't bat an eyelid at attempting to murder us. God, they came so fucking close to killing Jem." She paused, unable to continue, and swallowed a mouthful of tea that burned a line straight to her stomach. The pain helped to sharpen her focus. "Smiffy said you got a dark SUV on CCTV. Could the girls have been taken from the mill in the same car?"

"It's possible. I've got a couple of lads from B-shift sifting through footage from local cameras, but it's like looking for a needle in a haystack without a reg plate to pinpoint." Steph toyed with the laptop, awakening its log-on screen but not entering any details. "We did get something on CCTV, though."

Rosie looked at her, intrigued but on guard. "What?"

Steph's eyes glinted in the low light. She was obviously pleased to have stirred Rosie's interest. "Footage of Kyle Parker on the night he died," she said.

"Christ. Where from?"

"A petrol station on the main road, approximately two miles from Ellery Lane. Time stamp puts it about ninety minutes before his body was found."

"Is he on his own?"

"Nope." Steph swirled her index finger on the laptop's mouse, bringing the screen to life again. "I don't have the authority to share this with you, Roz. It's for Major Crime eyes only."

Rosie frowned. "Then why mention it?"

Steph's smile reminded her of a predator toying with its prey. "Because I've missed seeing that spark in you. The one that makes you sit up and pay attention."

"Pay *you* attention," Rosie said, the light beginning to dawn.

Steph shrugged. "Dinner at mine, and you can watch the tape to your heart's content."

Rosie was so gobsmacked she actually laughed. "No," she said. "Thanks, but no."

The laptop slammed closed as Steph hit the back of its screen. "What? Why not? Have you got a hot date with Jemima?"

"No, I haven't. I just don't want one with you."

Steph turned so sharply that she sent a thick waft of scent into Rosie's face. Rosie had loved that particular fragrance once, but now it just made her queasy.

"I don't get it," Steph said. "I don't get what you see in her. How has she managed to turn you into her fucking lapdog?"

Rosie picked up her coat and slid her bad arm into its sleeve, her actions calm and deliberate and a direct contrast to Steph's foot-stamping tantrum. "I'm going home," she said. She stood too abruptly and had to grab the sofa to steady herself. "Was this the reason you brought me here? To bribe me into having dinner with you?"

"Would you have agreed to see me if I'd just asked nicely?" Steph snapped. She came to stand directly in front of Rosie. Although they were matched in height, the spite radiating off her made her seem taller.

Rosie let her coat fall, one shoulder in, the other out. She didn't have the energy for any of this. "What do you think?" she said.

"I think you and Jem deserve each other."

Rosie nodded, not insulted in the slightest. "I really hope so."

Steph arched an eyebrow, clearly wrong-footed. "Don't come crawling to me when it all goes to shit, Roz."

"Wouldn't dream of it." Rosie busied herself sorting out her coat. Her bad arm was stiff and clumsy, making the zip a challenge. "Let my sarge know when you've sorted out the permissions on the CCTV."

"When did you grow a fucking backbone?" Steph asked, incredulous.

"Thursday," Rosie said. She didn't react as Steph stepped toward her, but Steph merely returned to the sofa and logged on to the laptop. She moved a video file into the centre of the screen and then walked to the door.

"I'm not going to apologise," she said.

That was the least of Rosie's concerns. "I'm not going to ask you to."

"Lock up when you're done," Steph said, and shut the door behind her.

For a couple of minutes, Rosie stayed where she was, unsure what had just happened and almost certain that watching the video footage would bring Steph back into the room, flushed with triumph and ready to collect her dues.

"Fuck it," Rosie whispered, as yet another minute passed and the corridor beyond the door remained deserted. She resumed her seat and opened the video file, then pushed the table farther away to put some distance between herself and whatever the CCTV might have captured.

For the first forty seconds, she watched a static shot of the shop's front counter as a disembodied hand arranged special-offer protein bars and restocked a turning display of vaping liquids. At forty-seven seconds, a middle-aged man approached. Balding, with a taut beer belly and a smart-casual dress sense, he was average height and average in general, the sort of bloke no one would bat an eyelid at in the street. He'd pulled up the collar of his jacket against the rain, and his wedding ring caught the light as he placed three bars of chocolate on the counter and pointed to whatever he wanted the cashier to fetch for him. As a packet of cigarettes and a litre bottle of vodka were placed beside the chocolate, the man slipped his debit card into the reader and turned to address someone behind him.

Even though Rosie had prepared herself for seeing Kyle on the tape, his appearance was still unsettling. He slouched by the counter, twirling the vape display and pointedly ignoring anything the man said to him. His Superdry T-shirt and skinny jeans accentuated his slight build, the designer outfit at odds with his greasy hair and grimy face, as if someone had increased his clothing budget but hadn't attended to his personal hygiene. He swiped the chocolate and the cigarettes, chewing one of the bars open-mouthed and shrugging off the hand the man laid on his shoulder. Seconds later, he flicked the wrapper to the floor and stalked out of shot. Evidently flustered, the man grabbed the vodka, with one eye on Kyle and the other on the card reader. He didn't wait for his receipt. The paper fluttered to the counter, and Rosie jumped as a blast of static marked the end of the recording.

Too intrigued to worry about Steph barging in, she made another brew and rewatched the file several times. She jotted notes in bullet-point form, shaping theories and raising questions she had no one to discuss with. She closed the laptop when her eyes started to blur and the twinges in her arm grew into something with sharp needles for teeth. She felt dirty, as if the footage and all it implied had tainted her. They would find the man; the CCTV would provide excellent screen captures, and a public appeal featuring his image was bound to be successful. He probably had a family, perhaps a son of Kyle's age who would have to go to school and explain to his mates exactly why his dad had been arrested. Within ninety minutes of eating that chocolate, Kyle had been dead: drugged and drunk, with his brain in bits. Rosie could still feel the flex of his ribs beneath the heel of her hand and see the utter hopelessness in Jem's eyes.

She took her mug to the sink, running the water until it steamed and then scrubbing her hands before she started on the pots. The water left her fingers red and swollen, and it didn't make her feel any cleaner.

CHAPTER EIGHTEEN

"Whoa!" Janelle blew a pink bubble of admiration and popped it on her nose. "That's proper manky."

Sam poked a cautious finger at one of Rosie's sutures. "Did a shark bite you?"

"No, love." Rosie began to re-bandage her arm. "I cut it on a broken window."

When he held out the Curly Wurly he'd promised as payment for a look at the wound, she snapped it into three and shared it between them. The beanbag crinkled as she inched lower, and she yawned, getting comfortable. She'd lost count of the recent nights of broken sleep, or no sleep, or sleep plagued by nightmares.

"Rosie was in a fire, you twerp," Janelle said around a mouthful of caramel and melting chocolate. "Mam's kept all the cuttings from the papers."

Sam sniffed and then wiped his nose on his school shirt, already distracted by something on his tablet. "I wish it'd been a shark."

Janelle bum-shuffled across the carpet until she was sitting between Rosie's legs. Resting her head on Rosie's chest, she patted Rosie's bad hand.

"Does it hurt?" she asked.

Rosie kissed her dark curls. "No, not really."

"Only, you look dead sad."

"I do?" Rosie had called at her mam's for breakfast before her shift, unsure whether she wanted company but resolved to get on with things. Her determined bonhomie had fooled her mam, but Janelle had always been the one to see through Rosie's bullshit. As a child, she'd spotted medicine concealed in yoghurt, refused to believe that the tune on the ice cream van meant it had run out of ice cream, and lain in wait for "Father Christmas" with a torch and an ancient Instamatic. The photo of Rosie drunkenly sorting presents into stockings was still pinned above Janelle's bed.

"Yeah, your eyes aren't smiling," Janelle said. "And you didn't eat your sausages, so I know something's up."

"Nothing gets past you, Sherlock, does it?" Rosie sighed. "Okay, okay. You know Jem, the paramedic who was in the fire with me?"

"Yup. Mam said you stayed with her in the hospital."

"I did." Rosie hesitated, unsure how to phrase this. "Well, we were getting to be really good friends, but then she decided she didn't want to be friends any more."

Janelle turned onto her front, propping her chin on both hands and studying Rosie with a mildly unnerving intensity. "When you say 'good friends,' do you mean girlfriends?" she asked.

Rosie nodded, refusing to look away. "Yes, I mean girlfriends."

"Ooh, have you got a girlfriend, Rosie?" Sam yelled from across the room.

"Oi! Shut it!" Janelle yelled back. "We're having an intervention."

"An inter—where the blazes do you learn these things?" Rosie asked.

"Telly, mostly," Janelle said. "Is Jem off work today?"

"I think so, but I'm not."

Janelle made a point of checking her watch. "You've got plenty of time to drop by her house on the way in."

Her nonchalance made Rosie laugh. "You make it sound so easy."

Janelle punched Rosie's thigh, a sign of affection that had endured since toddlerhood. "Text me and let me know how you get on," she said, and proceeded to roll Rosie off the beanbag.

Rosie's mam waylaid her before she could open the front door, pressing a tinfoil parcel into her hands and kissing her cheek.

"Have that for your lunch," she said. The subtle arch of her eyebrow told Rosie she hadn't been fooled after all. "Make up for the breakfast you hardly touched."

"Thanks, Mam."

Rosie didn't say anything else. She couldn't. She gave her mam a hug and hurried through the rain toward her car. Convinced the last thing Jem needed was a predawn wake-up call, she defied Janelle's edict and drove straight to work, where she walked into a mess room abuzz with anticipation. Kash grabbed her by the shoulders as soon as he saw her, spinning her around and marching her to her locker.

"Come on, come on, we're going in five minutes," he said.

She started to change into her uniform, heedless of the crowd. "Going where?"

"Major Crimes got an ID on a bloke spotted with Kyle Parker not long before the kid turned up dead. He was caught on CCTV. A clip was shown on the news this morning, but they put it up on the Facebook page overnight and hit the jackpot within a couple of hours."

"Crikey," she said. She hadn't told him about the footage Steph had shown her, but she assumed this was the same bloke. The tape obviously hadn't remained a Major Crimes exclusive for very long. "What's our part in it all?"

Kash held his nose with one hand and set her boots by her feet with the other. "Tactical Aid are making the arrest. Steph wants us there for crowd control and fingertip once the dust has settled."

"Where are we heading?"

"Cedar Road, Heaton Chapel. Looking on Street View, it's proper leafy suburbia, all tree-lined pavements and double-parked cars. By the time we get there, the school run will be in full swing, hence the crowd control."

She paused halfway through fastening her laces. "Is Steph sure he'll be in?"

"An unmarked car parked by the address says yes. If he leaves for work in the meantime, Tactical Aid will grab him on the fly."

"Excellent," she said, thrilled with the break in the case and at having a task to keep her busy.

Kash fell in step with her as they walked to the door. "It certainly has potential. Speaking of which, did you get in touch with Jem?"

"No, not yet." She raised a hand, forestalling any rebuke. "Don't frown, it doesn't become you. I'm going to phone her later. She won't be in work today, and I don't want to wake her, that's all."

"Fair enough," he said. They had worked together for almost three years, and he had sound instincts when it came to subjects best left alone. "Come on, Smiffy promised to save us a seat."

The trip across Manchester to Stockport was a white-knuckle ride, dodging buses, half-asleep commuters, and suicidal cyclists. Rosie tracked the van's progress on her phone, following a stuttering red arrow through Longsight and Levenshulme as shops began to open and locals with jobs in the city crammed into bus shelters to avoid the unpredictable downpours. The driver extinguished the lights and sirens as he left the main road and began to weave through residential streets, the outlying scruffy redbrick terraces giving way to semi-detacheds with well-tended gardens and fancier cars.

"Next right," Rosie told Kash, and seconds later, the van slowed to make the turn. The Tactical Aid Unit were already waiting, their presence at the arrest probably overkill but intended to send a message to the perps who hadn't yet been found, to Bill and Nancy and Fagin, but primarily to the person who had set fire to a house, trapping four people inside it.

"You okay?" Kash asked in an undertone, as the van pulled into a parking spot at the far end of Cedar and their sarge began his briefing.

"Yeah," she said. She'd fastened her stab vest too tight, and the shirt below was damp and clinging to her. "I'm fine."

"Smiffy, Topper, and Jonas, block off from number nine," their sarge was saying at the front of the van. "I don't want anyone getting past you until this bloke's out. Rosie, Kash, and Lem, block from one. That's the school end, so you might have your hands full."

"Bollocks," Kash said, and Rosie widened the view on her phone to show the academy two streets away.

"Cheer up, mate. Where's your sense of adventure?" she said, very much in the mood to brawl with a bunch of gobby schoolkids.

He flipped her the bird and then grabbed his seat as the van doors slammed behind Smiffy and his crew, and the driver made a hasty U-turn to drop off the remaining officers without driving past the perp's house. When the van stopped again, Rosie jumped out first, gauging the progress of the TAU and bagging a prime spot from where she could watch the action and head off any potential troublemakers. Their presence was instantly noted by a group of uniformed teens toting rucksacks and cans of energy drinks. The lads crowded forward en masse, prompting Rosie to unbuckle her baton.

"That's as far as you go," she said.

The tallest of them—acne-riddled and stinking of weed—placed a deliberate boot over her imaginary line. "Free country, innit?" he said.

"It will be in approximately…" she checked her watch. There was no set timetable for the arrest, but it made her look official. "… ten minutes. Until then, you don't come past this point."

He took another step, egged on by three sniggering mates, two of whom had their mobiles out.

"You're being recorded," she said.

"Yeah, I know." He grinned and gave a little wave to the phones.

She tapped the camera on her vest. "This one's admissible in court, pal."

He shrugged, but the gesture lacked his earlier bravado. "Be a load of shite anyway. Five-O arresting some poor fuck who's done nowt wrong, as usual." He shoved the smallest lad, causing him to stumble, and then glared at Rosie. "What? You gonna do me for assault?"

"Not today," she said, her tone leaving him in no doubt as to what she saw in his future.

"Yeah, whatever. Fuck off," he said, and led his posse back the way they'd come.

Kash watched them wander out of earshot. "I'm so glad my three are still nonverbal or at the 'daddy, need go wee-wee' stage," he said, opening a packet of gum and offering one to Rosie.

She chuckled but then sobered as she heard the sound of boots pounding toward them. "Aye up. Here we go."

Three houses down, the TAU lead hammered on the front door, his team poised around him. "Police! Open up!" he yelled, and Rosie saw a succession of nearby curtains start to twitch. The neighbour at number one came out in his dressing gown, his legs bare and a copy of the *Daily Telegraph* clutched beneath his arm.

"What on earth is going on?" he demanded.

"Sir, please go back inside," Kash said.

"Is that Adrian's house? Why are you at Adrian's house?"

"Sir, please go back inside," Kash repeated, emphasising his request by barricading the garden gate and unfastening his CS gas.

The TAU had charged into number five, their shouts of "Clear!" muffled by a woman yelling and the cries of children.

"Shit," Rosie said. "He's got kids."

"He's got two," the neighbour said. "Eleven and fifteen. You can't seriously be arresting him."

As if to prove the neighbour wrong, the TAU sarge marched down the garden path with the man Rosie had last seen buying vodka and chocolate for a fourteen-year-old boy. Apparently dressed for work, he was wearing a smart grey suit, but his head was bowed and his hands were cuffed behind him. A woman ran after him, her slippers slapping the paving stones and her nightie flying up around her thighs.

"He didn't do it!" she shrieked. "He didn't do anything wrong! That boy asked him for sweets, that's all!"

Rosie snapped around to look at Kash, who seemed just as appalled. "Did she fucking *know*?" she said.

Kash shook his head, stunned. "Perhaps she saw it on the BBC."

"And what, they decided to sit there and wait for the knock on the door?"

"Maybe not," he said as a TAU officer carried a holdall through the porch and handed his sarge what appeared to be a passport.

"Bloody hell." Rosie absently yanked a schoolkid to a standstill by the scruff of his neck. "I guess that's just pissed all over his chances of getting bail."

CHAPTER NINETEEN

Jem woke with a thick head and a cough reminiscent of a cat hacking up a fur ball. She was already upright, propped on a pile of pillows, but she leaned forward to rest her hands on the mattress, assuming the tripod position of the chronically oxygen deficient. A couple of blasts from her inhaler kicked the worst of it into touch, and she relaxed back, watching shadows cross the ceiling as the sun shimmied in and out of the clouds. It was late by her standards, almost eight thirty, but she had lain awake until three and then clocked every subsequent hour, on the hour. If there was a bright side, what little sleep she'd managed had been too meagre for nightmares.

Her phone buzzed as she was mustering the energy for a shower: Ferg video-calling her on WhatsApp.

"Shit." She dipped her fingers in her glass of water and damped down her hair, then straightened her T-shirt. She couldn't pretend she was up and dressed, but she hoped she'd look a little less lamentable. Plastering on a smile, she accepted the call.

"Good morning," she said, all bright and breezy and trying not to cry.

Ferg made a show of peering into the screen. "You look terrible, hen. Did I wake you?"

"No," she said, abandoning her attempts to pull the wool. He knew her too well to be fooled, in any case. "Waking me would imply I actually slept."

He clucked his tongue. "Should you have stayed in the hospital?"

"I don't think so. My inhalers and the steroids seem to be doing the trick. Harriet gave me so many pills I'm rattling."

"Is Rosie not taking care of you, then?" He wagged a remonstrative finger. "You'd be getting breakfast in bed if I was there. Has she not done you a nice bacon butty?"

For a split second, Jem debated the merits of lying, coming clean, or feigning a broken connection. She wasn't quick enough for Ferg, however.

"Jem, what did you do?" he said, his lovely Scots burr now more of a growl.

"Nothing." She held the phone farther away, lessening the impact of his glare. "Everything's fine."

"She's not there, is she?"

Jem shook her head, unable to answer.

"And you're not fine at all, are you?"

"No," she whispered.

"Do you want to tell me about it?"

"No." She couldn't. He might understand, but she wouldn't be able to put it into words.

"Do you want me to come home?"

She managed a smile, grateful to have him on her side no matter what. "Thanks, but no. I might go and see my mum and dad later. I'll be all right, really."

"You will, will you?" He gulped from a mug of what looked like diluted tar. His eyes were heavy-lidded and bloodshot, and whenever he turned his head she swore she could see pigtails.

"How hung-over are you, Ferg?"

"Scale of one to ten?" He grimaced. "Twelve. The Wiganers were in last night, and they can down ale like you wouldn't believe."

"I can imagine." A couple of the lads on her paramedic course had been from Wigan. Pies and pints had been the loves of their lives. "What time did you get to bed?"

He had the grace to look guilty. "Ask me if I've been to bed."

"Fergus McClellan! You're an absolute disgrace."

He snorted into his brew. "You're only jealous."

"I am. You definitely had a better night than I did." She blew him a kiss. "Thanks for phoning."

"My pleasure. Want my advice?" He held the phone in both hands, keeping it steady and focused, and he didn't wait for her to answer. "Sort this thing out with Rosie. Every time you mentioned her, your face lit up like a wee bairn on Christmas morning."

She did her damnedest to ignore an analogy so perfect it broke her heart all over again. "I don't think it's sortable," she said.

"You'll never know if you don't try," he said, and the screen went blank.

She stayed where she was and pulled her quilt up to her chin. His closing comment had hit home, burrowing beneath her skin like a thorn she couldn't get a needle to. Yesterday morning, when she'd been sleep-deprived and poorly and floundering out of her depth, she'd thought that destroying any chance of a relationship with Rosie was best done brutally. Let Rosie hate her and be relieved to walk away. With the benefit of hindsight, however, though Jem still agreed with her reasoning, she cared too much for Rosie to leave her without an explanation. No matter what she'd said to assure Rosie, she knew Rosie would be blaming herself, and that was the last thing she wanted.

Snarling in frustration, she threw off the quilt and stomped into the bathroom. She would have a shower and something to eat, and take her meds. She really should phone her dad and text Harriet, and then, when she had run out of ways to procrastinate, *then* she might feel brave enough to speak to Rosie. Sitting on the side of the bath with the shower running as hot as it would go, she waited for the room to warm and let the first tendrils of steam dismantle the wall in her chest.

The house on Cedar Road had fallen quiet, its hush broken only by the creak of floorboards and the rap of cupboards closing. It always seemed strange to Rosie that she was allowed to enter someone else's home and search its most private places, leafing through diaries and opening bedroom drawers, tossing out underwear to ensure nothing had been concealed beneath the faded, well-worn knickers and the lacy matching sets reserved for special occasions.

The house hadn't been quiet when she first walked in. The TAU had escorted Adrian Peel's wife back into the living room, where she'd sat in the centre of the sofa, her arms around her children, and continued to protest her husband's innocence. The daughter, dressed for school and wide-eyed with bewilderment, had still been clutching half a crumpet, while the son typed on his mobile phone and scowled at anyone who came near him. They were all on their way to Clayton now, to be interviewed once lawyers and social workers had been arranged.

"I wonder if the lad was the one who caught the footage online," Rosie said to Kash as they each chose a side of the master bedroom and began to process it. "The only time he showed any emotion was when Steph confiscated his phone."

Kash crouched by the mirrored dresser, out of sight apart from his dark hair bobbing in the reflection. "We'll find out soon enough," he said. "It'll all be on his internet history. Going off his reaction, I don't think he was convinced by his dad's 'I was just buying a poor waif some chocolate' cover story."

"No one in their right mind would be." Rosie laid three jackets out on the bed. "Have you still got the clip on your mobile?"

"Yeah, here." He opened the file and tossed his phone into the middle of the bed. Thanks to a friend on the TAU, he'd acquired the unexpurgated CCTV footage shortly after the arrest.

"That jacket's missing," she said, comparing Peel's outfit in the video to the clothing she had taken from his wardrobe. "And he wasn't wearing it this morning."

Kash peered over her shoulder to examine a freeze-framed image. "Might be hung up downstairs, or in the wash."

"I'll double-check with Smiffy. The jeans are too nondescript for me to tell, but that shirt's not here either."

"That raises a big red flag."

"Aye." She keyed Smiffy's point-to-point code into her radio. "Doesn't it just?"

Twenty minutes later, as Rosie helped Kash upend the mattress, Smiffy radioed to confirm that neither the jacket nor the shirt had been found in any of the obvious places.

"I've spoken to DS Merritt, and she'll mention it in the interviews," he said. "But Peel has already started playing silly buggers. When the custody sarge asked him to confirm his name, he said 'no comment.'"

"I bet you a fiver he cracks," Rosie said. "Give him a couple of hours in a windowless cell, wearing manky custody-issue sweat pants, without a phone, not knowing when someone will look in and catch him on the loo. He'll be singing like a canary as soon as Merritt offers him a brew and a butty."

"A fiver, eh?" Smiffy said. "You're on. I'll come up and shake on it when we're done in the kitchen."

"I'd have gone for a tenner," Kash said, hooking his thumbs beneath the fitted sheet and stripping it from the mattress. "Peel won't last half an hour with Steph."

"Smiffy never bloody pays up anyway. He still owes me from that…" The thought went nowhere as the edge of the mattress hit the overhead light and set it swinging, the bulb's beam playing over an irregular bump in the mattress's base that she hadn't previously noticed. "Just lower this again, gently," she said, and Kash did as she asked, bringing the bump into reach. She slid her fingers over it until she found a small tear she could fit her hand into. She reached inside and pulled out a mobile phone and a leather wallet.

"Would you look at that," Kash said as she held them up. "He had his mobile on him when he was arrested."

"Not this one," she said. The phone was fully charged and locked, and the wallet was stuffed with twenty-pound notes. "What's Mr. Two-point-four-kids doing with a burner?"

"Renting another kid," Kash said with rare hostility.

She sealed the phone and wallet in evidence bags and stripped off her gloves. The bedroom was full of smells that were just too personal, and the warm ripeness of body odour from the sheets seemed thick enough to coat her tongue. "Are you okay here for a few minutes?" she asked. "I need a bit of fresh air."

The air outside was very fresh, with hail bouncing amongst the raindrops and crunching underfoot. She found an isolated spot down a small ginnel, away from the house and the prying eyes of its neighbours, and somewhat sheltered by a conifer's overhanging branches. She took her phone from her pocket with chilled fingers and fluffed her passcode twice. Even when she'd managed to access the main screen, she wasn't sure of her intentions. Although she was no longer afraid of waking Jem, she didn't know whether it would be better to text her and try to arrange a face-to-face meeting, or phone her and see whether she would actually answer.

A half-melted hailstone dripped from a branch and slithered down her neck, as if goading her into making a decision.

"All right! All right!" she said, and dialled Jem's number.

Jem answered her phone without looking at the caller ID. Forewarned might be forearmed, but it also allowed her to be a gutless wonder.

"Hello?"

"Jem?" The voice sounded strange, its features distorted by pain and panic.

"Paula? Is that you?" Jem did check the caller ID then, almost sure but still needing confirmation. "Are you all right?"

"No." Paula started to cry. "Can you come to the cafe? I can't get hold of Dan, and the police say they'll be half an hour."

"Of course I can," Jem said, rummaging in the drawer for her car keys. "What's happened?"

"They burned me," Paula whispered. "I couldn't stop them." Jem heard her retch and then vomit, and the call cut off.

"Paula? Shit!"

Jem didn't waste time trying to redial. She kicked off her slippers on the way to the door and snatched her coat from the end of the banister.

Despite the mid-morning dawdlers clogging up the roads and the surface water playing havoc with visibility, Jem made it to the cafe in less than ten minutes, thanks to her knowledge of the back streets and speed cameras. She grabbed the first aid kit she'd thrown onto the passenger seat and rattled the handle on the cafe's front door. The door was locked, its sign turned to "closed" in spite of the early hour, and the blinds were drawn. The hair stood up on the back of her neck, and she clutched the first aid kit like a shield. Almost afraid to look behind herself, she turned slowly to check the street for anything out of the ordinary. There was nothing. Hers was the only car parked in the vicinity, and a stray cat skulking along the pavement was the sole sign of life.

"Paula?" she shouted through the letterbox. "Paula, it's me." A key rattled and two bolts slid back, but the door didn't open until Jem pushed it. "Paula?"

The cafe was dark, and a clatter off to her left made her jump. She coughed, whirling toward the sound and then stumbling back when Paula lurched into her arms.

"Hey. Hey, you're okay. I've got you." She held on to Paula tightly, but Paula's bad leg gave way, taking them both to the floor.

"I'm sorry," Paula whispered, sobs hiccupping through the words. "Dan's in a meeting, so he'll have his phone off, and I didn't know who else to call. I know you've not been well."

"I'm fine, all mended. What the hell happened?" Even in the dull light, Jem could see the cafe had been ransacked. Tables and chairs were overturned, and the counter was in pieces. "Where are you hurt? Were you robbed?"

Taking a breath, she forced herself to stop firing out questions. She was accustomed to dealing with other people's crises—she'd been doing that for years—but emergencies were far easier to cope with when the patient was a complete stranger. She hugged Paula close, stroking the tangles from her hair, until the tremors wracking her slowly subsided. It gave Jem the chance to gather her wits and view the scene with necessary detachment.

"Paula, where are you hurt?" she asked again.

"Hands," Paula gasped. "He burned my hands." She was holding them out in front of her, her elbows on her knees. The sun flitting between the blinds' slats illuminated raw patches on her fingers and palms, the skin glistening and blistered.

"Jesus," Jem said. She took off her coat and tucked it around Paula. "Give me a minute, okay?"

As Paula nodded, Jem scrambled up and hit a light switch. Nothing happened, and she squinted upward, swearing at the shattered bulbs and ruined shades. Shards of glass and crockery covered the floor, splintering beneath her trainers as she ran to each window in turn and opened the blinds. She locked and bolted the door on the way past, and then knelt by Paula and retrieved the first aid kit. The astringent smell of tea tree oil overwhelmed that of fried breakfasts as she tore open a packet of burns dressings.

"There were two of them, two men," Paula said. "Waited until the morning rush finished, then came in with metal bars." She groaned as Jem carefully turned her hands over.

"How much did they take?" Jem asked, aiming to distract her while she wrapped the pads over the burns.

"They didn't take anything."

Jem paused in the middle of bandaging the first pad into place. "Then *why*? What the hell were they doing?"

"Warning me," Paula said quietly. "They were warning me not to ask questions. They smashed everything and pushed my hands on the grill, and then they just walked out."

"Oh *shit*," Jem whispered. "Is this because of me? Because I told you about Tahlia and the shelter?"

Paula nodded with obvious reluctance. "I can't think of anything else, love. I've been asking my regulars if they've heard of a place called Olly's or seen that missing lass." She winced and repositioned her unbandaged hand. "Word must have got back."

Jem resumed dressing the wounds, her actions slow and deliberate. If she stopped to consider, even for a moment, the chain of events she had set in motion here, she wouldn't be able to help Paula.

"Did you see their faces?" she asked.

Paula shook her head. "They both wore balaclavas. After they—when they left, I couldn't get to the door. I couldn't see their car, but I heard them drive away."

Jem tied off a second bandage and found a box of paracetamol. "Here, take these," she said, popping out a couple of the pills and fishing a bottle of water from under a chair. The men had wrenched the drinks fridge off the wall and sent its contents flying. "I wish I had something stronger with me, but they'll do till I get you to the hospital."

"I need to wait for the police. I need to tell them…" Paula paused to swallow the tablet Jem set against her lips, choking slightly when Jem tilted the water too far.

"Tell them what?" Jem asked, blotting up the spillage with a piece of gauze.

"One of the men, he had a tattoo. It was really distinctive. One of those black, angry-looking things on his throat. They might be able to identify him from it or something. I don't know how it works, but it could help."

Jem put the water down as a sudden rush of adrenaline made her giddy. "A tribal design?" She pointed to her own neck. "Here?"

"Yeah. It went right up to his ear."

"Fucking hell. God, I'm such a fucking idiot." Jem stood and paced away, pulling out her mobile and scrolling through its call register. Rosie's number was on top of the list, a missed call logged within seconds of Paula's. Jem hovered over the link, desperate to tell Rosie about this, to use it as an easy way back to her. She didn't, though. She knew Rosie was the wrong person to contact, and she refused to resort to a coward's tactic. She found the right person much farther down the register and hit the number before she lost her nerve.

The call was answered promptly.

"Detective Merritt, Major Crimes."

Rosie signed the evidence label on the bag she'd just sealed, shimmying her torso from side to side as she did so. Her legs and bum were numb and tingling, and she'd lost most of the feeling in her left foot.

"Kash!" she yelled from her spot on the study floor. "Is it lunchtime yet?" She rolled onto her hands and knees and used Peel's desk as leverage to stand. "Kash? Come on, my stomach thinks my throat's been cut."

"Just finishing the bathroom," he yelled back.

She limped across the landing and bobbed her head around the door. "Holy shite," she said, taking in the rows of tablet boxes arranged on the bathmat. "His or hers?"

"Hers, mostly. According to the advice leaflets, she's a depressed insomniac with chronic pain and a vitamin B deficiency."

Rosie sat on the loo seat. "And a husband who likes young boys."

Kash completed his line-up with a box of lorazepam. "That may well be a causative factor."

"Aye," Rosie said, but she had lost all interest in the mini-pharmacy. Using her foot, she slid the mat away from the side of the Jacuzzi bath, toppling the tablets like a row of dominoes. Kash scowled at the mess she'd made, but one look at her expression curtailed any remonstration.

"What is it?" he asked.

She dropped off the loo and knelt beside him. "That panel's been moved." She ran her finger along a faint line of grime ingrained on the lino. "This marks where it was, but they've pushed it farther back when they replaced it."

He caught on at once. "I wonder when and why."

"Who knows?" She began to scout around for anything she could use to unscrew the fixings. "Could have been a leaky tap, but it would be remiss of us not to double-check. Hang on a tick, I think there was a toolbox in the hallway."

She was back before he could destroy the nail file he'd co-opted in lieu of a screwdriver.

"Here, try this, you daft bugger." She handed him a Phillips, and he worked the panel free, setting the screws in her waiting palm and then easing the top edge away from the lip of the bath. She directed her torch into the void and gave a low whistle as its beam caught a plastic bag tucked in the farthest corner. "Okay, I'm going to go out on a limb and say it wasn't a leaky tap." Aware of his aversion to creepy crawlies, she shoved her gloved hand into the gap and gasped as something multi-legged scurried over her wrist.

"Is it gone? What was it?" he asked from the safety of the doorway.

"Yes, it is, and I'd rather not know. Lay that towel out." She snatched at the bag, feeling the plastic snag and tear on the bare floorboards. The bag was knotted at the top and stuffed to the brim. She could see fabric through the gaps and knew before they'd opened it what they were about to find. "I'll buzz Steph," she said, unravelling the sleeve of a pale blue shirt. "Leave everything in situ and tag it as a job lot."

Radio in hand, she went onto the landing but took an unconscious step back as she saw Steph striding up the stairs. There was a gleam in Steph's eyes that automatically put her on guard.

"I was just about to call you," she said. "We've found the clothes Peel was wearing the night of Kyle's death."

"Bag them and prioritise them for the labs," Steph said, dismissing the discovery with a flick of her hand. "When did you last speak to Jem?"

Rosie felt for the wall behind her, letting its cool weight ground her. She hated the way Steph said Jem's name.

"Why?" she hedged.

"Not today, then." Steph smiled, evidently regarding that as some kind of victory. "I just got off the phone with her."

"Right." Rosie waited for the punch line. If Steph played true to form, it would come before long, and it would almost certainly hurt.

"She's at West Pennine A&E," Steph said, and everything else seemed to disappear beneath the boom of Rosie's pulse in her ears.

"Is she okay?" she snapped, cutting off whatever Steph was saying.

"What?" Steph paused, looking puzzled. "Jem? Yes, she's fine. She's there with a friend."

"God." The thudding in Rosie's head slowed and began to fade. Had she not still felt so off-kilter, she would have been humiliated by her reaction. "Steph, what's going on?"

Steph took out her notepad and flicked to a page full of neat handwriting. "A couple of hours ago, a woman called Paula was assaulted at the cafe she owns. Jem had told her about Olly's, and it seems someone didn't take too kindly to Paula asking questions of her customers. When she described the perps, Jem recognised one of them from a car crash she'd attended."

Rosie raised an eyebrow at the coincidence. "Small world."

"He has a rather conspicuous tattoo and, fortunately for us, an equally conspicuous vanity plate on his Range Rover. Jem remembered it because it was about the only thing damaged in the accident." Steph turned her notepad and tapped a line written in all caps: "FGN1."

"Fuck off." Rosie let out an astonished laugh. "Did we just find our Fagin?"

Steph smiled back. "It would seem so. His full name is Frank Galpin, so I'm sure he finds the pseudonym ingenious. I've got the TAU heading to his address. If you're done bagging and tagging here, do you fancy an afternoon doing likewise out in Droylsden?"

Rosie nodded and then caught hold of Steph's arm. "Was Jem really okay?" she asked quietly.

"She was fine," Steph said, for once choosing not to be an arsehole. "Ray's with them now, taking statements. She said she was going back to work tomorrow."

"That sounds about right. Thanks, Steph."

Steph shrugged. "We'll be leaving in ten. Get that clothing to SOCO and meet us outside."

At the soft sound of approaching footsteps, Rosie closed the drawer she'd been rooting through and went to stand by the bedroom window. Mrs. Galpin, Frank Galpin's elderly and very accommodating mother, had been plying the search team with brews since their arrival in her house, her generosity undiminished by the abrupt invasion of her privacy. According to the TAU sarge, she had requested that Galpin be allowed to put on a shirt and tie before they arrested him.

"Here you go, dear." Mrs. Galpin placed a tray laden with coffee and fondant fancies on the dresser.

"Thank you," Rosie said. "But please don't feel you have to go to any trouble for us."

Mrs. Galpin waved away her protest. "Nonsense, I know how hard you all work, and I'm sure we'll have this misunderstanding cleared up in no time."

Rosie busied herself adding milk to her coffee, stirring it for longer than necessary in the hope Mrs. Galpin would sense her discomfiture and leave her to squirm in peace.

"He's never been in bother of any kind, you know," Mrs. Galpin continued, as Rosie added a spoonful of sugar she didn't even want. "He's a good lad. He looks after me and holds down a full-time job."

Giving up on the idea of Mrs. Galpin making a diplomatic exit, Rosie perched on the corner of the bed with a fondant fancy. "What does he do?" she asked.

"He's self-employed. He renovates properties for the buy-to-let market." Mrs. Galpin brushed a couple of crumbs into her palm. The four-bed detached house was well appointed and spotless, and her air of general fastidiousness suggested she would still do her own cleaning were she physically able.

"Must be a handy person to have around the house," Rosie said, mentally noting the information and drawing a big flashing asterisk beside it. Galpin's property portfolio would make for interesting reading, though she suspected a three-storey Edwardian might recently have been struck from his list.

"He is." Mrs. Galpin beamed, obviously proud of her multi-faceted son. "Did you see the wet room? He put that in himself, and he did our conservatory." She sniffled suddenly and dabbed her moist eyes with a lace-edged handkerchief. "Is he going to be home soon?"

Rosie put down her cake, the token bite she had taken sticking in her throat. A hurriedly arranged computerised identity parade had seen Jem pinpoint Galpin, while Paula had matched his tattoo but not his face. Jem was still at A&E, going through the misper files in an attempt to pick out the children she had seen in the back of the Range Rover. About his adult female passenger, she could recall little other than dark hair that had possibly been cut into a bob. As yet, there were insufficient grounds to charge Galpin, but he would probably be in custody for forty-eight hours.

"I'm not sure," Rosie hedged. "Will you be all right here on your own?"

Mrs. Galpin nodded and jutted out her chin. "I'm only seventy-four, dear. Of course I'll be all right."

Although Rosie was wary of turning a casual chat into an interview, she decided to risk Steph's wrath and make hay while Mrs. Galpin was being forthcoming. It was too late to turn her body cam off, so she left it recording. "Do you have any other family or friends?" she asked. "Someone who might be able to help out with the bits and pieces Frank would usually do? Maybe a daughter-in-law or grandchildren?"

"I have no one but Frank," Mrs. Galpin said. "And he never married. He never needed to."

It was such a strange turn of phrase that Rosie's coffee went down the wrong way and made her cough. As Mrs. Galpin handed her a glass of water and a tissue, Rosie took advantage of their proximity, noting the confidence with which Mrs. Galpin moved, her deft grip and unflinching eye contact. Beguiled by her hospitality, Rosie hadn't paid her much attention, a cursory first impression dismissing her as a sweet, obliging old dear, but perhaps that had been Mrs. Galpin's intention all along.

"Sorry," Rosie said, continuing to splutter a little for effect. "I was in hospital with smoke inhalation over the weekend." She watched Mrs. Galpin's reaction, but there wasn't the slightest flicker of recognition, no indication that Mrs. Galpin had put two and two together and linked Rosie to the fire at Mansfield Street. All she did was tut and take Rosie's glass from her.

"You poor thing. What on earth are you doing back at work?"

"I can't afford to go on the sick," Rosie said, still thinking on her feet. "I have a younger brother and sister depending on me." She dug out her mobile and flicked to her photo gallery. "This is Sam. He's a bright little chap, but he's dead cheeky."

Mrs. Galpin smiled and lowered her glasses onto her nose. "Bonny lad. Look at that grin."

"Yeah, he gets away with murder," Rosie said without inflection. She took the phone back and found another photo. "Here you go, this is Janelle."

Rosie had to give Mrs. Galpin credit, she was very good at this, but Rosie was equal to the challenge, and she caught the split-second look of confusion that was immediately swallowed by something altogether darker as Mrs. Galpin realised what Rosie had done.

"What a sweetheart," Mrs. Galpin said, picking up the tea tray.

Rosie closed down the image of Tahlia Mansoor and slipped the phone back into her pocket. "This shouldn't take much longer," she said, and reopened the drawer.

The final page of the file loaded another gallery of lost children. A few glared out from young offender mug shots, but most of the submissions were random snaps: school photos mingling with candids taken on the beach or at birthday parties. One of the youngest girls grinned and stuck her tongue out for the camera, the shot inappropriate for identification purposes but perhaps chosen by a parent desperate to prove they had raised her in a loving home.

Jem considered each image in turn, maximising the child's profile on the laptop's screen so she could give it her undivided attention. She had found the lad from Galpin's car six pages in, but the girl didn't feature in any of the photographs. She pushed the overbed table aside as Paula shook off another dose of morphine and reached for a glass of water with her bandaged hand.

"Hey, easy. Let me get that." Jem helped her to drink and used a damp paper towel to wipe the sweat from her face. "Dan should be here in about half an hour," she said, pre-empting Paula's repeated enquiry. "You might have a bed over at Wythenshawe by then, so he'll be able to travel with you."

"Wythenshawe? Why am I going there?"

"You're being transferred to the burns unit." Jem spoke slowly, but this wasn't the first time they'd had this conversation, and it wouldn't be the last. "Your burns aren't too severe, but anything involving hands tends to make the A&E docs a bit twitchy."

"Okay." Paula's eyes were already closing. "And Dan's coming, right?"

Jem tucked the sheet around her. "Half an hour. I'm going to stay till then."

"Thank you," Paula said. She didn't stir as the curtain around her bed opened and Steph Merritt walked in. Raising a peremptory finger to her lips, Jem led Steph into a corner away from the general hubbub of Majors.

"Anything from the last file?" Steph asked without preamble. She sounded frazzled, and the latest downpour to hit the region appeared to have caught her unawares; her coat was dripping, and her hair was beginning to curl at the edges. She probably wouldn't have put in a personal appearance had she not entrusted Jem with a Major Crimes laptop.

"No, nothing." Jem sidestepped a nurse carrying a bedpan to the sluice and waited until the sluice door closed. "Did you speak to Ava and Chloe?"

"Yes, but they've thrown a bloody spanner in the works."

"How?" Jem asked. Steph seemed in the mood to offload her frustrations on someone, and Jem wasn't above taking advantage of that.

"They've both identified Galpin from his mug shot, but they identified him as Bill not Fagin. Galpin will most likely claim the reg plate is a coincidence when we question him."

"Shit. Where does that leave you?"

"Back to square one," Steph said. "Roz has come up with some harebrained theory about Galpin's mother, but she has absolutely nothing to base it on, and I can't go around arresting grannies on supposition alone."

It took Jem a moment to work out who "Roz" was, and she placed the nickname more by Steph's air of contempt than anything else. She smiled, glad that Rosie was still out there, pushing all of Steph's buttons and driving her to distraction.

"His mum, eh?" Jem mulled the idea over. "Some men do have that weird Freudian thing going on. He lives with her, doesn't he?"

"Yes, but she's eighty if she's a day, and highly unlikely to be the kingpin of an underage forced labour ring." Steph's mobile buzzed, and she answered it, asking the caller to hold. "Are you finished with the laptop?" she asked Jem.

"Yep."

"Good. I'll phone you if I need anything else from you."

Jem checked her watch as Steph headed for Paula's cubicle: 7.35 p.m. Rosie should be home by now, if she had managed to bypass the myriad flooded roads around Hearts Cross, and Jem had a stack of missed calls to return. Reluctant to bump into Steph again, she pulled up the hood on her sweater and slipped out of the department via the ambulance entrance.

For once, the ambulance bay stood empty. Rain dripped from its canopy, washing away a thick pool of blood and swirling the fag ends into the gutter. Jem found a sheltered spot by the oxygen store and bit her thumbnail as Rosie's phone flirted her straight to voice mail. She didn't want to leave another message, and she was vacillating between trying again or giving up and going back to Paula when Rosie returned her call.

"Hello? Jem?" Rosie sounded as if she'd been running, and a door slammed, silencing the roar of the weather. "God, sorry, the wind caught it. I've only just got in. I thought I was going to miss you again."

"It's okay," Jem said, the chaos of Rosie's life wrapping around her like a comfort blanket. "I'm still at A&E with Paula, and I can't get reception in her bay."

"I heard, Steph told me the basics. Is Paula all right?"

"She will be. Her husband was in Newcastle on business, but he should be here before too long."

"Good. You'll need an early night."

"Ah," Jem said. "Steph told you I'd resumed for work, did she?"

"She did. You are thoroughly rumbled, Jemima."

Jem closed her eyes. She had expected the call to be tense and awkward, not this sweet, instant familiarity that made her want to drive over to Rosie's and pretend the last couple of days had never happened.

"I need to speak to you properly. To explain everything," she said, determined to get the conversation back on track. She couldn't indulge herself. It wasn't fair to Rosie. "Will you be in tomorrow night?"

"Yes, around this time," Rosie said, her tone matching the formality of Jem's. "Do you want to come here?"

"That might be better. Ferg will be home around eight."

"Okay." Rosie hesitated. "Jem, take it easy tomorrow."

"I will."

"I *mean* it."

"I know." Jem looked up at the rain flashing in white lines across the security light. "Be careful out there."

"You too," Rosie said, and cut off the call.

CHAPTER TWENTY

Nothing ever changed at Darnton Station. The tap over the kitchen sink was still dripping, there was still no loo paper in the ladies' toilet, and chronic understaffing meant Jem was on the RRV again. She took its keys from the safe and dumped her helmet bag and high-vis jacket on its front seat. Unsure of the state of the roads, she had set off early that morning, and she had another half-hour to kill before she needed to sign on. She relocked the car and rested her hands on the car's cold bonnet, listening to the loose panel flapping on the roof and a fox yapping on a nearby street. She had been nervous about work since waking, her stomach too unsettled to tolerate her mug of tea, and her fingers mucking up the buttons on her shirt as she tried to fasten it. While she had always subscribed to the "getting back on the horse that threw you" theory, she wondered whether she might have been better leaving the damn thing in the stable for the rest of the week, although fretting about her shift was at least taking her mind off what she might say to Rosie that evening.

"Too bloody late to change anything now," she said, and shoved herself off the RRV.

The scent of frying bacon greeted her as she entered the main station, which was odd, given the absence of ambulances in the garage. She followed her nose regardless, taking a single step across the crew room threshold before Dougie swept her up in a bear hug.

"Morning, flower," he said as Bob wandered out of the kitchen brandishing a spatula. "We thought you might like some company, so we swapped onto the sixes."

"And brought breakfast," Bob added.

She kissed Dougie's cheek. "Thank you. Have I ever told you that I love you both?"

Bob blushed, and Dougie linked arms with her, ushering her to a table set with mismatched plates and mugs. Neighbouring Crofton Station had lost its stove after a near miss involving an absentminded crew, a forgotten pizza, and rather a lot of smoke alarms going off, but the management had never followed up on their threat to replace Darnton's with microwaves. As Dougie brought in tea and toast, Bob filled Jem's plate with bacon and eggs and tucked a paper towel into the neck of her shirt.

"In case you're as messy an eater as Dougie is," he said.

She smiled, her collywobbles kicked into touch by her first mouthful of smoky bacon. Almost everyone on the service complained about the job; about the late finishes, the overwhelming volume of calls, the morons and frequent fliers, the verbal and physical abuse, and the fleet of knackered vehicles, but those who stuck it out became a part of the best kind of family.

"Did I miss anything?" she asked, slapping together an egg white and tomato sauce butty and laughing at Bob's appalled reaction. She took a bite and spoke around it. "Hey, don't knock it if you've never tried it."

"I never want to try it, and no, I don't think so," he said.

"Broke-Back Brenda's dead," Dougie offered.

Jem put down her sandwich. "Get out! Really?" Brenda had been one of their most persistent and unpleasant morphine chasers. "What got her in the end?"

"She choked to death on an egg white and ketchup butty," Bob said.

Jem flicked a piece of crust at him. "Poor Brenda. I'll sort of miss her. She had a very creative vocabulary."

"And a nice cat," Dougie said.

Bob raised his mug. "To Brenda and Mr. Bigglesworth."

Dougie grinned and knuckled Jem's chin. "Bet you're glad to be back, aren't you?"

They signed on together, checking through the updated road closures and flood warnings as the banks of yet another local river capitulated to the rain.

"They'll have to issue us with bloody scuba gear if this carries on," Bob said. "Oh, here we go." Their terminal began to bleep, and he read the job details aloud for Jem's benefit. "Male, twenty-two. Car stalled in flood. Shivering and feels faint."

"Go save a life, boys," Jem said and opened the garage door for them.

The daily briefing broke apart in dribs and drabs, a handful of officers sticking around to compare assignments or attempt swaps, while the majority went straight out to bagsy the cars least likely to smell of stale kebabs. Rosie stayed in her seat, her notepad blank aside from a doodle of a rowing boat with a flashing beacon on it. When the sarge had thrown the briefing open for questions, Smiffy had asked whether there were any plans to provide officers with Jet Skis. Everyone except his van was running solo, and a third of the shift hadn't yet made it to the station.

"You okay?" Kash said from somewhere behind her. He had started to leave with the crowd and then noticed she hadn't moved.

"Yeah." Even to her own ears she sounded unconvincing.

"Worried about meeting Jem?"

"Yep," she said without equivocating. She desperately wanted to sit down and speak to Jem properly, to have a chance to state her case and try to sort out whatever had gone awry between them. The three-in-the-morning terrors had got to her, though, planting an insidious little niggle that kept telling her Jem's mind was made up and this would probably be the last time she would see her. No matter what she did, she couldn't shake it off, and it was making her feel sick.

Kash retook his seat. They had never had a very tactile partnership, but he put his hand on her arm. "How about I buy you a brew later?"

"Definitely. Text me in a few hours and let me know where you're at."

Left alone, she took out her phone, reminded of something else that had kept her tossing and turning through the early hours. Tahlia Mansoor's photo was still open in her gallery, the phone's screen smudged by her repeated efforts to enlarge or zoom in on the image, as if a clearer view of the school badge or the stitching on Tahlia's blazer might somehow tell her where Tahlia was. As the screen timed out and locked itself, she pushed back her chair and headed for Major Crimes.

She found Ray first, sitting in his customary spot by the open window and blowing vape smoke through the crack.

"She's in the loo," he said, sending a sweet smell of cherries towards her. "You better get a wriggle on, though. She's interviewing Galpin in ten."

Knowing how long Steph could take touching up her makeup, Rosie went straight into the ladies' toilet. As predicted, Steph was leaning over the sink, reapplying mascara in the cleaner section of the mirror. She spotted Rosie immediately, but the twirl of her brush never faltered.

"Admit it," she said, setting the brush aside and uncapping a lipstick. "Your memories of this countertop are as fond as mine."

Rosie followed her gaze to the space beside the sink, but that night alone with Steph in the office might as well have been a lifetime ago, and the mention of it evoked the emotional equivalent of a shrug.

"I need to speak to you about Tahlia Mansoor," she said.

Steph rolled her lips together, evening the spread of dark red. "What about her?"

"I think there's a possibility she might be able to identify Frank Galpin's mother." Rosie phrased the statement carefully, couching it in uncertainty in an attempt to placate Steph, but Steph slammed down her lipstick and turned to face her.

"I'm not having this discussion again, Roz."

"Did you even bother to watch the video?" Rosie snapped, her mood as brittle as Steph's. "That woman recognised Tahlia. You can see it clear as day in her reaction, which means there's a chance they met face-to-face. We know what these arseholes are capable of, Steph. We need to find this kid before they do."

"Who do you mean by *we*?" Steph asked. "There is no *we*. It's *my* team working this case, and we'll be spending the day interviewing Frank Galpin and Adrian Peel, not chasing after a girl who may have no connection whatsoever to the investigation." She threw her makeup into its pouch and yanked the zip closed. "Shouldn't you be out with the rest of your mob, filling sandbags or something?"

Rosie didn't waste her breath on an answer. She walked out of the room and shut the door behind her.

The Entonox mouthpiece made an obscene farting sound as the child sucked on it, the noise and the hit of pain-relieving gas sending him into a fit of giggles.

"You're doing brilliantly," Jem said, rechecking the splint around his fractured leg. "That's it, pretend you're sucking up a really thick milkshake. What's your favourite flavour?"

"Chicken nuggets and chips," he said and took a puff that made him reel like a first-time drunk.

"The ambulance is here," his teacher told Jem. "And his mum is going straight to the hospital."

"Great, thanks." Jem waved at the approaching crew, both of whom were wearing hooded coats and wellies. "How bad is it out there?" she asked, meeting them halfway. She had been waiting for backup for over an hour, and three of the school's playing fields had been under water on her arrival.

"If you've got a couple of oars, a rudder, and a tiller stashed in your car, you'll be fine," the paramedic said. "Half the Crofton crews are stranded at home, and Pud brought a lilo and floated it around the car park."

She laughed. "Outstanding. Right, let me tell you about our chap with the midshaft tib fib."

She was wading through the car park, cursing herself for not remembering to pack her own wellies, when her radio buzzed.

"Kev wants to see you on station," Ryan said. "Something about missing morphine."

"Crap," she whispered, off the channel. That was the last thing she needed. She hadn't spoken to a union rep, she hadn't prepared anything in her defence, and, to be frank, she had enough on her plate today. She thumbed her talk button. "I'll be there as soon as I can."

"Don't be rushing in this weather," he said, obviously reading between the lines. "And if a cardiac arrest comes in, it's yours."

In keeping with Jem's general run of fortune, no emergency dire enough to warrant her attendance prevented her getting to Darnton, even with the roads snared up and traffic moving at a snail's pace. Her boots squelched on the carpet as she walked toward Kev's office, announcing her presence to all and sundry, and stopping her from hiding in the loo until Ryan managed to find her a job. She knocked on Kev's door, listening for his customary "How do!" before she pushed it open.

"Oh." She hesitated on the threshold. She had assumed he would be with Baxter, but Amira was the only other person in the office. "Sorry. Do you want me to wait in the crew room?"

"No, come on in." Kev indicated the empty chair beside Amira. "How are you feeling?"

Scared shitless, she thought, and then realised he was asking after her health.

"Fine, thanks. I'm on a course of steroids, so I'm permanently starving, but I feel fine, thanks." Giving up on coherence, she sank into the chair. "Do I need a union rep for this, Kev?"

"No, love." He gestured to Amira, who twiddled with her mobile phone and then passed it to Jem. It was strange seeing her without Caitlin. All trace of the cocksure bully she had been in Caitlin's company had vanished, and she couldn't look Jem in the eye.

"I'm really sorry I didn't tell anyone sooner," she said. "But Cait can be—well, we're supposed to be best mates, and you know what she can be like."

Jem frowned, still attempting to make head or tail of the proceedings. A WhatsApp message from Caitlin filled the phone's screen, the text almost lost in a sea of horrified emoticons: *Fuck fuck fuck. Help!*

"Scroll down," Amira said, noting Jem's confusion. "It's all on there."

Jem did as instructed, reading through the next handful of messages. "Blimey. This explains a lot."

Amira shook her head. "She panicked, but that doesn't excuse what any of us did."

According to the texts, Caitlin had started her first shift on the RRV by losing the three vials of morphine in question when she'd fallen for the oldest trick in the book: driving off with them on the car's roof after getting a job in the middle of completing her vehicle checks. Shunning Amira's advice to come clean and tell a manager, she had instead schemed with Baxter to shift the blame on to Jem.

"Why the hell would Baxter agree to put himself in the middle of this?" Jem asked, but even as she hit the question mark, she had a light-bulb moment. "Ah. They're a couple, aren't they?"

"They met on a training day, and they've been seeing each other for about six months," Amira confirmed. "He didn't know Cait had sent the texts, and she didn't know I'd kept them. I only found out what she'd done after you'd been dragged into the office, and she swore me to secrecy. I don't have any excuses, though. I should have told you or Kev."

Kev rustled the paperwork in front of him, looking even more worn out than usual. As a manager, he was happiest when the crews simply got on with things: started their shift on time, worked to the end of it without mucking anything up, and went home. While he'd had plenty of chats in his office with Jem, they had primarily been welfare checks after potentially traumatic jobs, rather than untangling her from some arse-backwards conspiracy.

"I've spoken to Caitlin and Baxter this morning," he said. "Baxter admitted to falsifying the entry in the controlled drugs book, and Caitlin owned up to everything else. They've both gone off sick with stress, and they'll face a proper disciplinary hearing, if or when they come back."

"What a bloody mess," Jem said. If it was up to her, they'd all shake hands and have done with it, but these things were never up to her.

Kev crammed his papers into a file and lobbed the file in a drawer. "It is, but it's my mess to sort, and it's a load off your mind. Caitlin was supposed to be on the car tonight, so you'll have no one relieving you."

Jem slapped her hands on the arms of her chair. "No worries," she said. Water dripped from the cushion when she stood; she had been so stressed that she had forgotten to take her coat off. "Shit, sorry about that."

Somewhat overlooked in the corner, Amira sniffed and cleared her throat. Tears had ruined her mascara, trailing black lines down her cheeks. "What'll happen to me, Kev?"

Kev glanced at Jem, as if expecting her to turn her thumb up or down. She raised an eyebrow at him and then reached a decision in his stead. "Nowt," she said. She didn't need her pound of flesh. She was just relieved to have the issue resolved. "I'll make a brew, and that'll be the end of it. Is that all right with everyone?"

Evidently satisfied with her verdict, Kev passed her his mug. "Stick a couple of sugars in mine, love," he said, and ripped open a packet of Jammie Dodgers.

Even if Rosie had neglected all her local knowledge and followed her phone's wonky satnav, she still wouldn't have been able to justify passing the old mill en route to yet another sandbag distribution assignment. After holding a brief, one-sided debate upon the matter and concluding that her sarge probably had better things to do than track her whereabouts, she decided to take the risk. Fifteen minutes later, she turned onto Bennett Street and almost collided with a wheelie bin floating down the road. The river at the back of the houses was well on its way to providing the neighbourhood with a spontaneous spring clean, and most of the local residents had piled their belongings on the upper floors and taken refuge in the closest secondary school.

The lack of parked cars made Rosie's job easier, allowing her to circumnavigate the mill's perimeter and confirm with near certainty that no suspicious vehicle was loitering in the vicinity. There were no dark-coloured SUVs with personalised plates or cars expensive enough to stick out like a sore thumb. The few vehicles she did pass were unoccupied scrap heap contenders, and at no point did she spot any signs of life beyond the security fence.

She stopped by the hoarding she had sneaked through five, or was it six days ago? So much had happened since her run-in with the spliff-smoking, unicorn-discussing trio that it was hard to conceive less than a week had passed. She itched to go inside the mill, to search for any indication that Tahlia might have been using it as a refuge, but her unauthorised detour had already taken too long and she couldn't justify entering on foot. Intent on providing a visual deterrent for anyone who might be lurking, biding their time for their own illicit reconnoitre, she drove around the block once more before reluctantly rejoining the main road and the slow crawl of early commuters attempting to get home.

Water sloshed over the top of Jem's boots as she waded up the avenue, counting the house numbers and trying not to drop any of her kit into the lively flow tugging at her legs. She had abandoned the RRV two streets away and asked Ryan to put HART on standby for a possible extrication. HART, equipped for water rescue, was in high demand, so pre-emptively adding her call to their list seemed prudent.

A high-pitched series of yells guided her to the right address, and she opened the front door after a perfunctory knock, walking into a living room ankle-deep in filthy water.

"Hello? Ambulance," she called into the murk. The power had gone out across the area over an hour ago.

"Upstairs," a woman replied. "Through the kitchen. Hurry!"

The beam of Jem's torch guided her between a corner sofa and a coffee table bedecked with sodden leather placemats. Pumpkins and onions glided by as she entered the kitchen, and she almost skidded on a submerged potato.

"Shit," she said, hefting her response bag back onto her shoulder and starting up the stairs. "Which room, love?" she shouted.

"Second—" the woman's voice broke off to pant, "left."

Multiple candles flickered as Jem pushed the door, the light dimming and then flaring to reveal a twenty-something Pakistani woman kneeling by the side of the bed. Heavily pregnant and clearly in the latter stages of labour, she murmured a grateful string of Urdu on seeing Jem.

"Hey, my name's Jem." The mattress springs creaked beneath the weight of the bags she threw onto it. "How many weeks along are you?"

"I'm Madina." The woman managed a small wave. "Thirty-six plus five. He's my first. My mum says boys are always impatient."

Jem began to lay out the contents of her maternity pack. It didn't take an obstetrician to see that Madina was on the verge of a home delivery; within a minute of one contraction ending, she began to pant through the next.

"Allah!" She lowered her forehead to the mattress, her fingers clawing at the bedding. "Hospital, now. Quick!"

Aware that nothing aside from the birth would be happening quickly, Jem pushed the Entonox mouthpiece to Madina's lips. "Here, here, breathe on this. It's for the pain. Big deep breaths, good, perfect." She keyed her radio. "Hey, Ryan. Birth imminent. Backup and a midwife would be great, if you've got anything."

"I have a paramedic solo on the way to you, ETA six, but ETA on HART is upward of an hour. I'll give Maternity at West Penn a ring now."

"That's fine. Tell the solo to leave the bus next to my RRV, grab a torch, and wade down."

"Will do. Good luck."

She rolled her eyes and tossed the radio next to a pile of knitted baby clothes. Madina had sagged back against the wall, her brightly coloured salwar hobbling her at the ankles.

"How's about we get you untangled from these, eh?" Jem said, unhooking one foot and then the other. She felt surprisingly sanguine for someone tasked with delivering a baby in a power cut, with flash floods crippling the region. Being on the RRV, she had seen an exponential rise in her tally of home births, and she usually enjoyed the experience, provided it was complication-free.

"I need the hospital," Madina said. "He's breech."

Jem stopped shoving an incontinence sheet beneath Madina's bottom. "Of course he is," she said, grabbing the maternity notes and finding the date for a planned caesarean and an entry detailing a failed attempt to turn the baby. Fuck. She squeezed Madina's hand. "We'll manage, I promise."

Anything else she might have said was lost beneath Madina's screech of pain as a sudden gush of black-stained fluid saturated the sheet.

"Not here," Madina cried. "Not here."

"Hands and knees," Jem said, almost dragging her into position. "That's it, good girl. He's going to need space to come out."

"Hallo? Jem?" The hail preceded a pounding of boots up the stairs, and Jem smiled as Amira stuck her head around the door. "Holy shit," Amira whispered as, right on cue, a tiny pair of legs presented themselves.

"My sentiments exactly," Jem said, gauging the baby's progress. "Grab the oxygen and the neonate bag and mask, and switch the pads on the defib. Just…just get everything ready, okay?" Using her forearm, she supported the baby's torso, preparing to deliver his head. "You're doing really well," she said to Madina. "You've definitely got a boy."

Madina managed a short gasp of laughter and then yelped and pushed the baby's arms out. Jem swapped her hold, taking the baby by his feet and lifting them in an attempt to deliver the head. It had sounded so simple in the practice guidelines. In reality, it was akin to wrestling a slimy fish with its upper third stuck in a vice, and the head was not for shifting. She threw Amira a "what the fuck now?" glance, and Amira knelt beside them, obviously none the wiser but welcome moral support.

"Shit. Uh, give me a little push?" Jem said, and felt the head slip as Madina bore down. "Go on, go on, that's it. I've almost got him." Employing a few manoeuvres that certainly weren't in the manual, she managed to manipulate the baby free, lowering him onto the dry towel Amira held out and then rubbing him vigorously. She rocked back on her heels, shaking her head in amazement as the baby wailed and punched the air.

"Is he okay?" Madina asked. Tethered in position by the umbilical cord, she couldn't yet turn to see him.

"There's nothing wrong with his lungs, that's for sure," Jem said. She handed Amira a pair of scissors for the cord. "Are you doing the honours?"

Nodding, Amira picked up a couple of clamps, but then seemed to have second thoughts. "Will you show me?" she whispered. "I've never done it before."

Jem sat by her side and took one of the clamps. "Course I will. It's dead easy."

Madina was watching everything over her shoulder, her gaze constantly coming to rest on her son as Amira cut the cord and swaddled him in a warm blanket. Finally able to move, she shuffled around until she was propped against the bed, and took hold of him. "He's beautiful," she said, busy counting fingers and toes.

"He is." Jem stroked a tiny thumb and then started to laugh. "That's the first water birth I've ever done."

The song blasting from Rosie's car radio almost overwhelmed the ring of her phone, until the Bluetooth kicked in and sent it through to hands-free. Spotting Jem's name on the screen, she stopped singing mid-lyric.

"So much for taking my mind off things," she said, and accepted the call.

"Hallo? Rosie?" Jem said, raising her voice above a rhythmic slosh of movement and her own laboured breaths.

Rosie pulled into a side street that wasn't yet awash. "Hey, it's me. Are you swimming?"

Jem huffed a wheezy chuckle. "Paddling, more like. I got stuck in Hearts Cross on a home birth. HART have just come out with a dinghy, but I need to get the RRV back to Darnton, so I'll be late getting to yours. Is that okay?"

"It's fine. I'm on my way home now." Rosie checked the clock on her dash, calculating the time as a plan started to form. "Come whenever you can. I'll be a while yet as well. The roads are carnage."

The splashing stopped as Jem paused, gasping quietly. "Yeah, tell me about it," she said, once she had the energy to reply. "I'm knee-deep on one at the moment."

Rosie closed her eyes, reluctant to overstep the boundaries Jem had established, even if she didn't understand them. "Just take your time," she said. "And I'll see you soon."

She restarted her engine and made a U-turn, pausing to see whether common sense might kick her notion into a cocked hat. A bus went by at ten miles an hour, its passage sending waves onto the submerged pavement. It was heading toward Stanny Brook. She waited for it to pass and turned in the opposite direction.

In the hours since she had last driven down Bennett Street, most of its inhabitants seemed to have fled for higher ground. Here and there candles threw silhouettes against drawn curtains, but the majority of the houses were unlit, and the street itself was black as pitch. To her left, the old mill seemed even darker, a huge beast hunkered in her periphery, chucking out the occasional fridge or mangy armchair as the overflowing river freed the rubbish abandoned around it. She parked in the driest spot she could find and swapped her trainers for the wellies stashed in her boot. Raising her coat's hood provided little protection, but she felt safer somehow with her face concealed, as if the monsters lurking in the mill might not be able to see her coming.

She made it to the hoarding before she conceded defeat and announced her presence to monsters real or imaginary by switching her torch on. Its beam cut a stark line above the multiple streams winding through the wasteland. The relentless pound of the river was too close for comfort, but she chose her route with care, traversing no man's land without snapping anything, and locating the window she had previously used for access. A couple of the stacked crates had succumbed to the rising water, but she clamped her torch between her teeth and managed to hoist herself through.

"Now what?" she said, more to dispel the creeping fear than out of hope of inspiration. Her tendency to barrel straight in and ask questions later had brought her to the mill, but she couldn't very well scour five storeys of dubious integrity on her own in the dark.

Aiming her torch at her wellies, she began to inspect the floor for fresh footprints, finding a track made by a heavyset pair of boots that had recently scuffed grip marks into the accumulated muck. For want of a better idea, she followed their path, skirting the perimeter to the farthest side, where something seemed to have caught the person's interest; the prints circled a small section of a sheltered corner, the marks deepening at several points as if the person had crouched for a closer look. Whatever they might have found had since been removed, however, and Rosie kicked at the dirt, her frustration boiling over. As avoidance strategies went, this current escapade was an extreme one, even by her standards. She should be at home, putting the heating on, lighting a fire, and drinking inadvisable amounts of caffeine. She made an abrupt about-turn, resolved on going back and chewing off a couple of fingernails while she waited for Jem.

She was midway across the rear wall, almost to the opening for the stairwell, when she saw the light. It vanished in a heartbeat, as if someone had switched on a torch but then extinguished it immediately. Without making a sound, Rosie panned her own torch in the same direction, finding nothing at first and then glancing the beam off a small scurrying figure. The figure froze in the light, bent low in an effort to remain concealed, before springing up and starting to run. The motion made the hood on his jacket fall back, but she couldn't see his face, just short dark hair sticking out beneath a baseball cap.

"Hey! Stop!" Rosie yelled. "Stop! Police!" She set off after him, leaving the relative safety of the walls to sprint toward him in a direct line. Her torch beam jolted as she ran, giving her flashes of wooden planks and splintered glass. She heard a scuffle and a cry of distress, and paused to get her bearings before spotting her quarry picking himself up after a fall no more than twenty yards ahead.

"I'm not going to hurt you," she called, well within earshot. "I'm a police officer. I'm looking for Tahlia Mansoor."

Her appeal fell on deaf ears; he was already moving, heading left, away from the access window. She chased after him, so close now that she could hear panicked gasps and the creak of the flooring beneath him. He dodged right and jumped clear, legs stretching and feet skidding, and she stopped dead, surrounded by streaks of worn yellow paint, and realising too late exactly where he had led her.

"Fuck! Fucking shit."

The wood covering the trap cracked and then shattered beneath her weight, plunging her into the void. She cried out, her limbs flailing and then tensing for the impact, but she hit water rather than concrete, the air knocked from her as she was spun forward in a tumult of debris. Unable to see anything, she gasped, saturating her lungs, and reached for a surface that wasn't there. She felt a cold draught and snatched a breath, only to have it punched out of her as the current tossed her around again.

Colliding with a solid wall slowed her progress, and she grappled for purchase, her fingers scraping the abrasive concrete. She righted herself, feet down, head above the water, and took huge hungry mouthfuls of air, but she quickly lost her hold, the flood reclaiming her and hurtling her along the wall in a relentless drive. She stopped suddenly, without warning or apparent reason, her right leg held static as her body twisted. Three seconds of grace was all she got before the pain hit her, a blast of agony in her right thigh that made her cry out and then vomit into the water.

"Oh God," she whispered. Using one hand to steady herself, she pawed at the wall with the other, trying to find what was hurting her so badly. Her fingers closed around a length of rebar jutting from the concrete, and she tracked it to the point where it disappeared into the middle of her thigh. She could feel the warmth of her blood joining the current that was wrenching at her, and she bit through her lip as the motion repeatedly jarred the metal against her femur.

For an untold amount of time, all she could do was grip the wall and breathe through the pain. She began to shiver as the water lapped at her chest, sending ripples through her damaged muscles, and she sobbed quietly, unable to move yet unable to stay still.

"Please help me, please." She kept her entreaty to a whisper, afraid to make anything worse by raising her voice, before an abrupt return to clarity overrode the shock. "Hey! Hey! *Help!*" she yelled. "Are you still up there? Can you hear me? My name's Rosie, and I'm a police officer. I need your help, *please!*"

Daring to let go with one hand, she found the inner pocket where she'd stashed her mobile to keep it dry. She tapped its newly smashed screen, yelping in relief when it lit up, but its signal was nonexistent, denying her even the "emergency calls only" option.

"Shit. *Shit.*" Thrown into a blind panic, she tried to free her leg, managing to move it a fraction. When the pain came, it seemed to come from a distance. She dimly heard herself scream and saw the water twist and roil in the light from her phone. Then her forehead bounced off the concrete, and everything faded out.

CHAPTER TWENTY-ONE

The whoop and wail of sirens had become the city's soundtrack, a raucous orchestra of emergency services, their resources stretched to breaking point and getting nowhere fast. Well off the clock and still only halfway to Darnton, Jem hadn't gone anywhere for fifteen minutes, and brake lights stretched ahead as far as she could see. The traffic jam was giving her far too much time to agonise over what she might say to Rosie, should they actually get to meet up that night, although that was looking ever more unlikely. When her phone rang, she answered it without thinking, sending the call through to hands-free and smiling at the name on the display.

"I thought it might be you," she said. "Are you stuck too? I haven't moved for ages."

"Is that Jem?" The girl sounded young and uncertain, and she immediately started to cry. "I tried to call nine-nine-nine, but there was a queue, and your name is top of her list."

"What the—?" Jem rechecked the screen, but she hadn't been mistaken. "What are you doing with Rosie's phone? Where is she? Is she okay?"

"No."

"Jesus," Jem whispered. "What happened?"

"She fell through the floor. I made her fall." The girl sniffled and then blew her nose on something. "I came back to help her, but she wasn't really awake."

"Fucking hell." Jem checked the distance between the RRV and the surrounding cars. "Where are you?"

"The old mill off Bennett Street. Can you help her?"

"Yes, I'm a paramedic." Jem whacked her blues on and hit the sirens, shifting into the central gap that formed as the cars parted for her. "How badly is she hurt?"

"I don't know. She's in the water."

On some level, Jem was processing the information, even as she accelerated and hit her priority button, yelled at Ryan for backup, and then yelled at the fuckwit in front of her who pulled into the middle instead of pulling right.

"Okay," she said, fighting to breathe through the stress compressing her chest. "Okay. Are you with her?"

"No. There's no signal down there."

"Can you take me to her?"

"Yes, yes I can," the girl said. "I'll meet you by the gap in the fence on Bennett."

"Ten minutes." Jem swerved around a van. "It'll be all right. She'll be all right. What's your name?"

"Tahlia," the girl said, and disconnected the call.

The RRV fishtailed as Jem threw it around the corner of Bennett Street. She tried not to look at its data screen, tried not to think what might have happened to Rosie in the last seven minutes and twenty-three seconds. She didn't need to search for the fence; she stopped behind Rosie's car, her legs shaking so violently that she stalled the engine and sent the RRV lurching into Rosie's bumper.

"Shit."

She didn't know whether to laugh or cry, and ended up doing a messy combination of both as she ran to the boot and began to stack her kit on the pavement. Unable to carry everything, she ransacked her bags, amalgamating them into one and throwing vials of drugs into her pockets. A girl approached Jem as she was settling the response bag and defib on her shoulders.

"Tahlia?"

The girl nodded, squinting against the blues Jem had left on to guide others in. She was filthy and gaunt, and her clothes were wet through. Her hair, almost hidden by her cap, looked as if it had been hacked off with a penknife. "Rosie's been talking to me," she said. "But the water's getting deeper."

"Bloody hell." Jem tapped her pocket, checking for her inhaler. "Come on, let's go."

They weaved across the wasteland at a near jog, taking a route Tahlia was obviously familiar with, despite the fresh hazards of near-darkness and unpredictable flotsam. Using a stack of rickety crates like a staircase, she scrambled through a broken ground-floor window.

"Hurry." She beckoned to Jem, heedless of Jem's burden or the rattle of her breathing.

Jem ignored them as well, launching herself over the sill and keeping up with Tahlia. From a distance, she saw the gaping hole in the floor, the splintered wood splattered with streaks of paint that hadn't been enough to alert Rosie.

"Is she down there?" Jem knelt at the edge, straining to catch sight of anything but whirls of brown water in her torchlight.

"She's this way," Tahlia said, hauling on Jem's sleeve. "She got pulled farther along." Choosing her path with care, she guided Jem to a smaller opening seemingly designed for people rather than goods or waste, with a concrete lining and a metal access ladder. "Do I have to go down?" she asked, crouching at the top.

"No." Jem took off her high-vis jacket and wrapped it around Tahlia's shoulders. "You stay close by and yell as soon as you hear people coming. Show them where we are."

"What if it's not them?" Tahlia said. She was rocking gently, back and forth. "Men keep coming to find me."

Jem set a foot on the ladder and swung into the gap. "Look for the uniforms. Yellow jackets like mine, helmets, big boots. There'll be loads of them, and they won't be quiet."

Tahlia studied the fluorescent material of Jem's jacket. "The other men all wear black."

"You won't be able to miss this bunch, I promise," Jem said, already on the move. "They won't be long. Just be brave."

Taking her own advice to heart, she persevered on the ladder, her feet slipping on the slick metal as a cold layer of slime coated her hands. With her torch in her pocket for safekeeping, she descended into complete darkness, tapping each rung with her boot before she trusted her weight to it, and eventually stepping off onto a narrow concrete ledge. She took out her torch and panned it around a vast expanse of turbulent water enclosed by lichen-covered walls. She couldn't see Rosie anywhere.

"*Rosie?*" The rank air made her cough until she doubled over. She took her inhaler and tried again. "*Rosie!*"

Gauging the direction of the current, she set off along the ledge, keeping one hand in contact with the wall for balance and using her other to aim the torch.

"*Rosie!*"

At regular intervals, she paused to shout and listen for a response, though it was difficult to isolate anything beside the constant white noise of the flood. She heard sporadic thumps as rubble ricocheted off the walls, the slosh and slide of her own laborious progress, and then finally, faint and wavering and not too far ahead, the incongruous sound of singing.

"Keep going, Rosie," she whispered. "Pick another verse. I'm almost there."

She couldn't run—she could barely increase her pace beyond the tentative steps she was taking—but she could see Rosie's hair now, and make out a tuneless but determined refrain from "Amarillo." The lyrics stopped as Rosie spotted the light, and her hand appeared above the ledge, waving frantically.

"Down here," she yelled, her voice hoarse and broken. "Here. I'm down here."

Jem shoved her kit against the wall, and then knelt and clasped Rosie's hand in both of hers. "Hey, I've got you. I've got you."

"*Jem?*" Rosie's head shot up, but she was blinking, blinded by the glare of the torch after so long in the dark. Her bottom lip quivered. "Are you really here, or did I die?"

Jem stroked Rosie's forehead, avoiding a jagged laceration. "You haven't died, you silly sod, but you've got yourself in a bit of a pickle."

"I didn't mean to." Rosie's face crumpled, and she started to cry. "I can't get out. I tried, but there's metal in my leg and I can't pull it, it's proper stuck, and the water's coming up. You should go, Jem. I don't want you to watch. Please don't watch."

"Hey, hey. Shh." Jem squeezed her hand. "HART and Fire and your lot are all on their way. Just hold on a little while longer for me, okay?" Refusing to panic, Jem focused on the basics, shining the torch around Rosie to establish her position and general condition. Trapped at a slight angle, her head twelve inches below the ledge, Rosie had jammed her right hand into a gap between two bricks to keep herself steady. The water had covered her chest, but she wasn't shivering, and her skin was mottled and clammy. Jem hit *priority* on her radio, her fingers pressed to the rapid pulse at Rosie's wrist. "ETA, Ryan. I need water rescue and enclosed space capability and someone with bolt cutters ASAP."

"Twenty to twenty-five," he said. "Half the available resources are en route to you."

"Thank fuck for that. Keep me updated." She pulled out her IV pouch. "Score the pain out of ten for me," she told Rosie, sticking the pulse oximeter on her finger and then attaching the defib's blood pressure cuff and setting it to calculate. "Let's say one is a paper cut, ten is stepping barefoot onto Lego."

"Four?" Rosie hedged, busy staring at the cuff.

"Four, eh?" Jem made no attempt to disguise her scepticism. Tight lines were etched across Rosie's forehead, and her jaw was clenched. At some point she had bitten her lip so hard it was still bleeding. "Try again without fibbing."

Rosie sighed, obviously embarrassed. "It keeps making me throw up."

"Don't worry, I can fix that." Jem fastened her tourniquet around Rosie's wrist and slapped the back of her hand. "Are you allergic to anything?"

"Ferrets."

"Drugs, Rosie. I'm not going to launch a bloody ferret at you."

"Oh. No, no drugs."

"Good. Bear with me, your veins have gone to shit." Despite her misgivings, Jem managed to slide the cannula into place at the second attempt and secured it with a bandage. Rosie's blood pressure was low, her pulse was racing, and her temperature wouldn't even register, so Jem hung a bag of warm saline from a section of pipework and set the infusion running. "I can't give you too much of this," she said, injecting a cautious dose of morphine. "I don't want you falling off your perch. It should help, though."

"Mm." Rosie took a deep, relieved breath as Jem continued to work. "That's better than a pint with a whiskey chaser."

Jem smiled and snapped the tops off her last couple of vials. "Smashing. I'm nearly finished. The nausea should ease, and this is to stop you from bleeding too much. Then all we have to do is sit tight and wait for the cavalry, okay?"

"Okay," Rosie said. "Is Tahlia all right? I didn't realise it was her. I chased her. Probably scared her half to death, but I think she came back for me, didn't she?"

"She did. She's up by the ladder—"

A sudden crack cut Jem off, and she spun the torch around, searching for the source of the noise. The water seemed to boil, white foam cresting on the ripples, and a mass of wooden planks and bricks whipped past. When she turned back, the water was touching Rosie's chin.

"Fucking hell," she whispered.

Rosie had to angle her head to keep the water away from her mouth. "It's doing that more often," she said. "I think there's a barrier or something that's breaking down. If it goes…" She shook her head. "Jem, you need to get out of here. If it goes, it'll take both of us with it."

"I'm not leaving you," Jem said without hesitation. "I'm not going anywhere." She felt different as soon as she had made her decision, peaceful somehow, as if something unfathomable had slackened its hold on her. She had never been able to define it or give it a name, but it had tainted her life for as long as she could remember, and this—this seemed like the end game, one way or another. "You're going to be fine," she continued, sticking an imaginary middle finger up at their probable fate. "We're going to be fine."

"Are we?" Rosie asked quietly. There was a palpable weight to the question, and Jem leaned low, brushing the tears from Rosie's cheeks.

"I'm so sorry," she said, abandoning everything she had planned and rehearsed, because it all seemed insignificant now. "I didn't mean to hurt you. I would never—" She faltered, already lost. She still didn't have the words for this.

Rosie reached up and tugged at Jem's sleeve. "You would never what?" she said, and yanked harder when Jem didn't answer. "For fuck's sake, just *tell* me, Jem. We might not get another chance to have this out, and I want to know what the hell is going on with us." She spluttered on a mouthful of water and arched an eyebrow. "Seriously, how much worse could it get?"

"That's the point, Rosie. I didn't think it could get any worse. I thought I'd stopped it. I thought leaving you would stop it, but it hasn't." Jem coughed, unable to regulate her breathing as despair overwhelmed her again, but even in the throes of wheezing and rasping she saw the moment the penny dropped for Rosie.

"You think the fire was your fault. That you actually caused it to happen." Rosie spoke slowly, as if still working things through. "Jem, that wasn't *you*. That was some arsehole with a couple of litres of petrol and a match."

"I know." Jem drew up her knees and wrapped her arms around them. "Logically, I *know* that, but you were there because of me, and this stuff happens to me all the time. Jesus, look what's happening to us now. I don't have any luck, none at all. Girlfriends disappear on me, and dates ditch me, and I get bad job after bad job at work. Even the calls that sound simple turn out to be something awful." She held Rosie's gaze, willing her to take this seriously. "It's exhausting. Every time I sign on, I know what's coming. I should probably just resign. Maybe then it would stop, and all the patients I might have been sent to would be okay."

"Do you really believe that?" Rosie asked. She shifted slightly, grimacing at the discomfort. "That it would stop if you weren't there?"

Jem wasn't able to answer that, not with any degree of assurance. She had gone so far as to write her resignation letter, though. It was saved on her computer desktop for the day she finally snapped.

"I'm not sure what I believe," she said, although that wasn't strictly true. She had a theory, at least. She'd just never had the guts to voice it. "I think I used all my luck up when I was little."

"What? You mean when you were adopted?" Rosie said, easily following her logic.

"Yes." Jem wiped her eyes, bringing Rosie back into focus. "Perhaps you only get so much, and all of mine has gone."

Rosie held out her hand until Jem took it. "What if I said that meeting you in that puddle on Barton was the luckiest thing that's ever happened to me?"

"It can't be," Jem sobbed. "You can't say that, Rosie. It isn't fair."

"It's the truth. I'm not scared of you."

Jem shook her head, utterly undone. "You should be. *I'm* scared of me."

Rosie adjusted her grip, interlacing their fingers. "You give yourself too much credit, Jemima Pardon. I'm quite capable of getting in a shitload of trouble regardless of your influence. You don't get to claim ownership of this particular fuck-up." She smiled, warming to her theme when Jem made no attempt to contradict her. "Hey, my stupid dumb luck might cancel out yours and reset the clock, or rejig the scales or whatever. You delivered a baby today, didn't you?"

"Little boy," Jem said. "He was breech."

"And?" Rosie squeezed Jem's hand.

"He came out kicking and screaming," Jem admitted, but she was starting to smile as well. "Actually, now you mention it, I had a chap survive an aneurysm last week, and the missing drugs thing all got sorted, too."

"See?" Rosie said. "We're already on a roll. What did we call that thingummy on the bridge? A talisman? We're lucky talismans for each other."

Jem made a show of tilting the morphine syringe in the torchlight. "How much of this did I give you?"

Rosie snorted. "Not nearly enough."

Jem set the blood pressure cuff going again. She stared at the numbers as the cuff inflated, but she was miles away, considering what Rosie had just said and daring to imagine a possible future.

"Jem?" Rosie said in an undertone, as if afraid of startling her.

"What?"

"I think we should chuck caution to the wind and give us a chance. What do you reckon?"

"I reckon you might be right," Jem said, and saw the delight slowly spread across Rosie's face.

"Really?"

"Yes." Nothing more coherent seemed to be forthcoming, so Jem answered in kind, dangling half over the ledge to cup Rosie's face for an inverted kiss. Their chapped lips met and parted a fraction, enough for a hint of warmth to ease the persistent chill, and Jem closed her eyes, giving in to the sensation, until a wave smacked into the wall and drenched them both.

"Perfect," Rosie said, peeling a strand of weed from her cheek. "I've had a few kisses in my time, but that was my absolute favourite."

"We certainly pick our moments." Loath to sit up again, Jem checked her watch. "They shouldn't be too much longer. How's the pain?"

"About a five." Rosie wrapped her free hand around Jem's arm, pulling her into a vague semblance of an embrace. "How's the chest?"

"Middling. But let's not be borrowing trouble."

Rosie considered that for a moment, and her shoulders shook as she tried to suppress a laugh.

"Harriet's going to fucking kill us," she said, a split second before all hell broke loose and she disappeared beneath a deluge that peppered the wall with pieces of brick and surged over the ledge.

"Rosie!" Jem lurched forward, catching hold of Rosie's coat and hanging on through the worst of the onslaught. She didn't have the strength to lift her, but Rosie managed to break the surface, spluttering and gagging on the water she'd swallowed.

"Oh God." She retched, sank again, and re-emerged to vomit. "*Jem?* I can't—" She couldn't keep her head up, the water was too high, and Jem instinctively tried to pull, stopping only when Rosie screamed and slapped at her arm.

"I'm sorry, I'm sorry." Jem loosened her hold and reached for her response bag, rifling through it until she found the largest endotracheal tube in her resus pouch. "Rosie!"

Rosie's head jerked, her face flashing white above the flow and vanishing just as quickly. Her hand slipped from the wall, and the defib wailed as her sats plummeted.

"Shit!" In desperation, Jem swung herself off the ledge and into the water. Gasping against the sudden shock of the cold, she wrapped a fist in Rosie's hood and pressed the tube to Rosie's mouth. "Breathe through it," she yelled, but there was no sign of Rosie complying, and the alarm on the defib kicked up a pitch. Jem fumbled blindly, finding Rosie's mouth again and ramming the tube against her lips. "Rosie! Fucking breathe through the fucking tube!"

That got the message through. Rosie pursed her lips, missed her target, and then snagged the base of the tube, almost taking Jem's finger with it.

"That's it, love," Jem said as water shot from the plastic opening. She found a hollow in the wall and shoved her free hand into it, stabilising them both. "That's it, just breathe." She saw Rosie take an experimental breath and then another with more confidence, and the defib fell silent. "You're doing really well," Jem said, her entire body shaking with relief and excess adrenaline. "They'll be here any minute."

She didn't know whether Rosie could hear her, but she felt Rosie's head rest against her chest as Rosie put an arm around her and drew her close. The tube, sturdy enough to keep itself clear of the water, bobbed gently with every inhalation, and Jem fixated on it in the dim light, reassured by the strength of Rosie's hold on her and by the defib's continued quiescence. Huddled over Rosie, she was able to shield her from the worst of the passing wreckage, barely registering the frequent hits she took to her back and shoulders. Her breaths wheezed out far more slowly than Rosie's, and when at last she heard the first distant call of the rescue team, she wasn't able to respond to them.

"They're coming," she whispered through chattering teeth. "We'll be out of here in no time."

Powerful lights slashed across the water as multiple voices shouted their names.

"Here!" She didn't manage a yell, but someone must have heard her, because an excited clamour rose up and boots stomped in their direction.

"*Jem!*"

"Over here!"

Letting go of Rosie's hood for a second, she lobbed a chunk of brick onto the ledge. That did the trick, and bedlam erupted above them as a team of five threw down their kit and tools and spoke at once. Spence was the only paramedic amongst them, and Jem realised the remainder were uniformed police officers.

"Fucking hell," Spence said. "Is she breathing?"

"Yes." Jem was still watching the tube. "Someone will have to—" she coughed, rocking them both, "have to brace her right thigh and cut the metal. Don't try to pull it. It's stuck fast near her femur."

Two of the officers had climbed from the ledge, and they ducked beneath the water, their torch beams circling and shifting as they assessed their task.

"Her sats are fine," Spence said. He set his own probe on Jem's finger. "Yours are shite."

Jem ignored him. "There's morphine in that ten-mil syringe. She needs it before they cut. I don't want her hyperventilating."

"Okay. The rest of HART are five minutes out, but we'll get it done if Smiffy's happy."

"I'm happy," Smiffy said, treading water and taking the bolt cutters from his colleague. "Tell me when."

Jem injected a generous dose of morphine into Rosie's IV. She knew the instant it hit home; Rosie slumped against her, and the motion of the tube lessened. "Now," she said to Smiffy. "Quick as you can."

He and his mate plunged out of sight again, and she felt one of them move Rosie slightly, repositioning her leg. There was no caution or indecision. Jem heard the crunch and snap of the metal and Rosie's weak cry of protest. The tube floated free, snatched away by the current, and the men resurfaced, bringing Rosie with them. Hands reached down, grabbing her coat, her belt, anything they could get a grip on, and she was dragged from Jem's arms to the relative safety of the ledge.

"Get her on her side," Spence said. "Easy, mind her leg."

Left behind and beginning to drift from the wall, Jem jumped when Smiffy clasped her arm, her fists punching the water.

"I'm going to boost you, and Topper's going to pull you up," he told her.

She did her best to help them, scrabbling her feet on the bricks as they hoisted her, and managing to sit unaided once they'd deposited her on the ledge. She choked out a lungful of water, took her inhaler as a stopgap, and crawled across to Rosie.

"She's being a pain in the arse," Spence said, by way of a greeting.

"Is she now?" Jem smoothed sodden strands of mucky hair from Rosie's face and kissed her cheek. "Are you misbehaving, Rosie Jones?"

Rosie's eyes fluttered open, and she pawed at her oxygen mask, stretching its elastic band until Jem relented and lowered it.

"You're all right?" Rosie asked, her words rolling together like warm toffee.

"I'm fine." Jem huffed at Rosie's cross-eyed look of disbelief. "I'll *be* fine." She turned to Spence. "What in the blazes have you given her?"

"Ketamine." He shrugged. "She kept trying to get up."

They looked round at the sound of approaching footsteps: HART and Fire, storming in en masse about ten minutes too late.

Spence went to meet them, and Jem settled in his spot by Rosie's side.

"Jem?" Rosie said.

"What?"

"Do I get to keep my metal?"

"Your what?" Jem followed Rosie's gaze to the chunk of rebar still protruding from her thigh. "This? What the hell for?"

Rosie smiled. "Memento."

"Of the day you almost drowned?"

Jem assumed it was the ketamine talking, but Rosie shook her head, her expression clear and adamant.

"Of the day we took our chance," she said.

Chapter Twenty-two

"O w."

Even smacked off her head on a concoction of general anaesthesia and morphine and who knew what else, Rosie regretted trying to roll onto her back.

"Stay on your side, Rosie." Jem's flat instruction suggested she'd been saying this a lot. "You had five inches of metal stuck up your—oh, hello." Her tone brightened as she realised Rosie was actually focusing on her.

"Hiya." Rosie pulled a face at the reediness of her voice and was relieved to be offered a sip of fruit juice rather than water.

"Not too much, you've been puking all morning," Jem said, easing the straw from Rosie's lips.

"I have? What time is it?"

"Almost ten."

Rosie scrubbed at her cheek with fingers still pruney on one side and battered on the other. Her addled brain was sluggish at joining the dots, but when it had, she narrowed her eyes. "Jem?"

"What?" Jem said, all Bambi-like innocence. She was dressed in multiple layers of normal clothing rather than pyjamas, but the oxygen tubing beneath her nose somewhat gave the game away.

"Why aren't you in bloody bed, that's what?"

Jem pushed her chair back. "I've been in bed." She gestured to the adjacent bay and the bed with its rumpled sheets. "Then I asked nicely, and Katya let me get up."

"Katya? Your nurse from last time?" Rosie frowned; she was apparently still missing a few dots. "Okay, fill me in from the top."

Jem pinched a handful of grapes from a stash beyond Rosie's limited field of vision and popped the largest into her mouth. "What's the last thing you remember?" she asked around it.

Rosie stared at a blank bit of wall, filling it with images of rising water and darkness and Jem, clearly terrified but trying not to show it.

"Hey." The soft word came with the gentlest of kisses, pulling her back to the hospital room. Jem stayed almost nose to nose with her, cradling her face with warm hands. "Sorry, that was a stupid question."

"No, it wasn't." Rosie's mood improved as everything else suddenly slotted into place. "I remember you kissing me upside down."

Jem laughed. "Okay, well, that's the most important thing. The rest of it isn't quite so exciting. You had an op to sort your leg out, I spent a few hours in Resus, and we were both admitted onto Respiratory because they need to monitor you for secondary drowning, although you're not showing any signs of that."

"Good," Rosie said. "That sounds very unpleasant. What about the case? And Tahlia?"

"I can't shed any light on the case," Jem said. "No one has been in with an update, and I've not seen anything on the news. Kash told me that Tahlia is settling in at home, and he thinks they're interviewing her today, so we might know more later." She wheeled an overbed table crammed with tins and bags into view. "On a happier note, my dad brought more Aztec biscuits, and your mum cooked us a roast dinner. Kash collected clean clothes *and* trainers for you, and Ferg popped round about an hour ago with hot toddies he swears are medicinal." She patted a tall silver flask and then glanced at the vomit bowls stacked in readiness. "Maybe wait till the morphine wears off, eh?"

"Yeah." Rosie experimented with bending her leg but didn't get very far. "Shit. I'm not sure I want it to wear off."

"I'm not surprised." Jem handed her a sealed plastic bag. "That's your culprit. The bottom bit did most of the damage by digging itself in around your thigh bone."

The rebar rolled lazily as Rosie held the bag to the light. One end of the metal was snapped clean where Smiffy had cut it, the other twisted almost into a hook.

"You've got quite a few stitches," Jem continued. "But your surgeon said you'll be right as rain after a course of antibiotics and some physio."

"Don't mention the bloody rain," Rosie said.

"Puddles and sore hands." Jem displayed fingers as shredded as Rosie's. "Isn't that our theme?"

Rosie chucked the bag out of sight and tapped Jem's knee until she got the message and kissed Rosie full on the lips. Rosie tasted cinnamon and whiskey on the tip of Jem's tongue, and felt her sway sideways as her breathing went haywire. When they parted, Rosie traced Jem's smile with her finger.

"I think this is a much better theme for us," she said.

Rosie used her crutch to tag the wall and shimmied around to face her bed again. The abused muscles in her thigh didn't appreciate her efforts, but she swung her crutches onward regardless. Jem was sitting with her feet up in her usual spot, and she peered over her reading glasses to watch the next lap. Far more accustomed to hospital admissions than Rosie was, she had tolerated their two-day incarceration with enviable fortitude.

"If I tell them I smoke, will they let me go outside?" Rosie asked.

Jem turned the page in her well-thumbed novel. "No, they'll slap a nicotine patch on your arse."

"So much for that brilliant idea," Rosie said, and tripped over a crack in the flooring. "What time is it?"

"What time was it when you last asked?"

"Eleven twenty-eight."

"It's eleven thirty-eight, then," Jem said without looking at her watch.

Rosie's arms were beginning to tire. She wobbled another couple of feet, passing the bottom of Jem's bed and the pair of slippers she'd designated as her midway marker. "Have you chosen your lunch?"

"Cornish pasty. And no, you can't steal half of it." Giving up on her book, Jem pushed her glasses to the top of her head and stretched her arms out. She was only wearing a thin T-shirt, and as the fabric pulled taut across her chest, Rosie overbalanced, colliding with a bedside cabinet.

"You okay there?" Jem sounded amused, and she didn't lower her arms.

"Yep, I am definitely okay." Rosie righted herself. "I meant to do that."

Jem laughed and came to stand in front of her. The heat of the room had dashed pink across her cheeks, and her eyes were bright with mischief. "You should sit down before you fall down," she said, going up on tiptoes to nibble the end of Rosie's nose.

Rosie groaned, lowering herself carefully into one of the chairs they'd set by the window. Her legs felt like jelly, and it wasn't wholly due to exertion. "I want to go home," she said. "I want to watch crap films with you and Fluffy, and mix my painkillers with alcohol, and fall asleep in your arms."

Jem perched on the side of the chair and ran her fingers through Rosie's hair, separating the tangled strands. "We'll have a serious chat about option B later," she said. "But we can pencil the other two in for tonight. If Harriet said early evening, she meant early evening, so we have"—she did the sums on her fingers—"about four more hours to kill."

The knock on the door would have been a welcome distraction, had Steph's outline not shown clearly through the glass.

"Just when I thought the day couldn't get any worse," Rosie said.

"Come in," Jem called. Then, quieter, "You're not allowed to weaponise your crutches unless severely provoked." She stayed where she was, casually parked at Rosie's side as if daring Steph to make an issue of it, but Steph sank into the chair opposite, looking so weary that Rosie would have offered her a brew had it not involved getting up again.

"Sorry to come unannounced," Steph said. She fiddled with her bag, drawing a file out of it and then a box of Special Toffee. She set the box on the windowsill, tapping its top with one finger. "For you to share."

"Thanks," Rosie said. She wasn't sure what to do with this sombre, non-combative version of Steph. It wasn't one she had ever encountered. Jem must have been similarly wrong-footed, because she cleared her throat and shifted to the edge of the chair's arm.

"Can I get you a coffee?" she asked.

"No, no. I won't be long." Steph draped her coat over her lap and opened the file. "I was in the neighbourhood and thought you'd appreciate an update."

"We would," Rosie said. She and Jem had given statements to a detective from Major Crimes, but his visit had been brief, and he hadn't divulged much information. "Being in here is like being stuck in a vacuum. Have you been keeping things out of the media?"

Steered back onto safer ground, Steph seemed to relax. "Yes, which has been relatively easy with the flooding dominating the news. We've worked around the clock with the TAU to round up the last of Fagin's crew, and we think we've finally got them all."

Rosie heard Jem catch her breath and took her hand without thinking. "How many were involved?"

"As of three a.m. this morning, we've arrested and charged seven adults," Steph said, which went some way toward explaining her dishevelled state. "And you were right, Rosie."

"I was?" Rosie bum-shuffled; the constant ache in her thigh was making it difficult for her to concentrate. "About what?"

"About Mrs. Galpin." Steph took a photo from the file and passed it over. It was a custody suite mug shot of Frank Galpin's mother, and if looks could kill, the photographer would have been six feet under by now. Gone was the fondant-fancies-toting old dear, replaced by a glowering, five-foot-three battleaxe.

"Wow, really?" Rosie peeked again at the image. "Fucking hell, she's giving me the willies. Was she running the whole shebang, then?"

"It would appear so. Mrs. Fiona Galpin was identified by Tahlia Mansoor, who had seen her ordering Frank about at the main shelter, Olly's. Only one of the other children we've spoken to was able to ID her. It seems her involvement was very much of a behind-the-scenes nature."

"How many children have you found?" Jem asked. Her hand felt damp against Rosie's, and her posture was as rigid as a board.

Steph checked her notes. "Eighteen at the last count. About half have been reunited with their families, and the remainder have been taken into care. They were scattered around five of Frank Galpin's renovated houses, and I use the term 'renovated' very lightly. Olly's was refurbished to a high standard, to lull the kids into a false sense of security, but the others were barely habitable and seem to have been selected for either their isolation or their lack of sober neighbours."

"It's easier to pimp kids out to respectable husbands and fathers when there's no one around to witness it," Rosie said. She had been clenching her jaw so hard it was beginning to hurt. For the first time, she was almost grateful to have been sequestered away in the hospital, kept away from the perps being processed through the custody suite, from the fingertip searches, and from sifting through the devastation the Galpins had caused.

"Were all the kids being used like Kyle?" Jem asked quietly.

"No, not all of them," Steph said. "Preliminary interviews suggest the children tended to start out stealing, a few using tricks similar to those described by Ava and Chloe, but most just performing common or garden shoplifting or burglaries. Once they were recruited and trained, they were kept compliant by rewards, punishments, and recreational drugs. The longer they remained involved, the more likely they were to end up addicted and dependent, and that's when they were moved on to the prostitution side of things." She sighed and rested her hands across her notes. "A handful of the kids have been pissed off at us for interfering. Frank Galpin painted himself as a good mate; a big brother or a father figure, which is obviously something these children have been missing. They were paid for their work and had a roof over their heads, even if it was a crappy one. It was only those who stepped out of line who really suffered, and many of these kids had suffered far worse in the care system."

Jem nodded, but she didn't seem capable of replying. Rosie could only imagine what she was thinking. It was little wonder she had been so obsessed with the luck surrounding her adoption, given the alternatives that might have awaited her.

"How the hell did Tahlia get away?" Rosie said. "I'm assuming she was one of their kids at some point."

"She was, briefly," Steph said. "But she cottoned on to the downsides almost immediately and did a runner. There was no real urgency for them to find her until you showed Mrs. Galpin her photograph."

"Shit," Rosie whispered. "I could have got her killed."

"Hey," Jem said in a tone sharp enough to make Rosie look at her. "Tahlia would still be fending for herself in the old mill if it weren't for you."

"I suppose."

"Jem's right," Steph said, shocking the hell out of Rosie. "The Mansoors are pushing for some kind of commendation."

"Oh God, really?" Rosie had never been one for ceremony, especially if it involved rubbing shoulders with the top brass. "Can we nip that in the bud?"

"We can try. But you know how starved our lot are for positive media attention."

"Aye." Rosie wasn't going to argue with that one. "Did Frank own the house on Mansfield Street?" She didn't think the Galpins would have been stupid enough to torch a property with their name on it, though, and she wasn't surprised when Steph shook her head.

"It belonged to the deceased mother of one of their associates. Fiona Galpin didn't just prey on vulnerable children, she used her own social care package as a trawling ground." Steph's voice had hardened, and her lips were pressed into a thin line. "She had three local council-subsidised care calls a day, ostensibly to help her dress and prepare her meals, et cetera, and all the adults we've arrested had links to her care agencies. She would take her time, get to know them, and suss out their susceptibility. Those she deemed desperate enough or easy enough to manipulate, she would offer jobs to. The woman the kids knew as Nancy was one of her first: twenty-five years old, with two toddlers, debts, and a deadbeat baby daddy. She swapped a minimum wage, zero-hours contract for a supervisory role in Galpin's operation."

"It'd be easier to sympathise had a child not died because of them," Rosie said.

Steph hadn't been making much eye contact with Rosie until then, but it was rock solid as she nodded her agreement. "I know. At the moment, we're not sure how deep anyone's involvement went. The Galpins were up to their eyes in it, but the other adults are all claiming their input was minimal, and three of them have pinned the fire on Frank. Number plate analysis from ANPR cameras has placed the FGN1 Range Rover close to Mansfield Street that same night. It's not definitive proof by any means, but it'll help us to build a case against him."

"Will Ava and Chloe have to testify?" Jem asked.

"We've discussed the possibility of them testifying via a video link." Steph's dour expression altered to one of admiration. "Ava is definitely up for it; she's a proper little spitfire, but Chloe's struggling, and they'll both be seeing a counsellor on a weekly basis." She closed her file, as if to signal that her unofficial briefing was drawing to an end. Rosie felt Jem tighten her grip, readying them both for whatever was to come.

"I interviewed Adrian Peel on Tuesday," Steph continued. "He no-commented the first hour, before going to pieces when I presented him with the burner and the bag of clothes you found."

"Should've bet Smiffy a bloody tenner," Rosie muttered.

"He never pays up anyway," Steph said. Her expression was reminiscent of a cat full of cream, and Rosie knew the interview had gone precisely to plan.

"How much did Peel cop to?" Rosie asked.

"He admitted to taking Kyle Parker out to Abbey Vale that night. Unbeknownst to him, Kyle had filched his wallet and got hold of his name and address. When Kyle tried to extort money, there was a struggle, during which Peel 'lost the plot'—his words—and punched him. Just the one punch, he says, but Kyle landed badly, hitting his head. According to Peel, Kyle got up and staggered off toward the river, at which point Peel panicked, abandoned him, and ran."

"Fucking arsehole," Rosie said.

Jem put an arm around her shoulders. "We'll never know what really happened, will we? For all we know, Peel threw him into the water, or he could have stood there, watched him fall in, and then walked away and left him."

"Without an independent witness, Peel's word is all we have to go on," Steph said. "Crown Prosecution are edging toward manslaughter rather than murder. We're almost certain to get a conviction on the former charge, but whether he'll pay a fitting price for his crime…" She opened her hands helplessly. "We can only do what we can do, and the law often falls short in these cases."

"Not your fault, Steph," Rosie said. "This was a shitty case from day one."

Steph slid the file into her bag. "It was, and it didn't half snowball. My boss is pleased as Punch with the way everything has turned out, though, so at least someone's happy."

"The Mansoors will be happy," Rosie said. "Maybe this will make them realise there's worse things than having a queer kid."

"Ava and Chloe are doing okay as well," Jem added. "And we made it out the other side, so it could've been worse."

Rosie gave a shocked laugh, leaning back to appraise her. "Who the hell are you, and what have you done with Jemima Pardon?"

"I'm turning over a new, optimistic leaf," Jem said. "I think it's about time."

Steph's self-conscious cough broke the moment. At some point she had stood and put her coat on.

"I should get going. I'm glad you're both safe." She paused by Rosie's side and rested a hand on her shoulder. "I'll see you when you get back."

"Yep," Rosie said, the prospect not as alarming as she might have expected. She waited until the door closed, blocking out the hum of noise from the corridor. "You all right?" she asked Jem.

"Aye. Are you?"

"Yeah, I think so."

Rosie picked up the box of toffee and gave it a shake. "Do you want a piece, or are you saving yourself for your Cornish pasty?"

Jem laughed. "What do you reckon? Get the bloody box open and stop being a berk."

Epilogue

Jem's breath puffed out in white bursts as she stopped on the doorstep to watch the moon gliding from behind a thin layer of cloud. There wasn't much light pollution in Stanny Brook, and she could see countless pinpricks of stars in the clear patches of sky. Perhaps her next read would be a book on astronomy, so she might be able to name what she was looking at.

"Ye gods and little fishes. Put wood in t'hole!" Rosie bellowed from the depths of the cottage. Not quite as enamoured of the night sky, she had already levered her boots off and disappeared into the kitchen to whack the thermostat up.

A week after the last flood warning had been lifted, Greater Manchester was a solid block of ice, with plummeting temperatures freezing the waterlogged fields and parks and gardens. It made walking anywhere tricky, but Jem had befriended a neighbouring Jack Russell, and Rosie was full of beans following the removal of her stitches, so a picnic at the monument on the Pike had been the order of the day.

Jem bolted the door and stacked her boots next to Rosie's. Rubbing her chilled hands together, she wandered into the living room, where Fluffy blinked at her from his climate-controlled vivarium, showing no inclination to leave his branch and be sociable.

"I don't blame you," she said, crouching to arrange kindling and paper on the log burner. The match flickered in the chimney's draught, the paper catching quickly and the kindling as usual being a complete bugger.

"Kettle's on," Rosie said. She knelt beside Jem and pinched a match from the box, lighting a piece of paper at random. "I wish I could tell you I had a knack for this, but mainly I just cross my fingers and hope for the best."

The embers flared en masse and then snuffed out just as rapidly. Jem sighed and pulled more kindling from the stack. "Back to the drawing board."

Rosie scrambled up again as the kettle whistled. "Back to the kitchen for me. Good luck with all that," she said, and cackled when Jem lobbed a ball of newspaper at her.

Jem smiled as she listened to her pottering about the kitchen, opening drawers, sliding the kettle off the burner, and playing a tune on the mugs with a teaspoon. She pictured where Rosie was as she moved: hopping with impatience by the hob as the tea steeped, or leaning on the counter that overlooked the garden. Jem had spent so long at the cottage since their discharge from the hospital that its layout was as familiar to her as the house she rented, and it was starting to feel like home in a way that the rental never had, although she suspected Rosie was a very large part of that.

The kindling finally succumbed, and she shut the burner's door as Rosie returned with steaming mugs.

"You have a precious gift, Jemima," Rosie said, placing the mugs on the coffee table. "I think that means you need to stay here forever."

"Does it now?" Jem plonked herself onto the sofa and hooked her arm through Rosie's. It was still early days in their relationship, and even with her new tendency toward optimism, a tiny part of her was battening down the hatches for disaster and disappointment.

Rosie regarded her in the glow of the fire. "No, there's no rush," she said. "And we could sit here like mature adults and discuss our potential future and promise each other the world. Or"—she reached into the pocket of her hoodie—"you can teach me how to suck this brew up through a Twix."

Jem laughed, raising Rosie's hand and kissing her fingers before taking the bar of chocolate from her. "I'm not sure we'll ever be mature adults." She tore open the wrapper and handed Rosie one half of the Twix. "Right, here goes, and it's very technical, so pay close attention."

Rosie nodded, her expression rapt. She was holding the Twix exactly as Jem was, as if that made a difference.

"Step one," Jem said. "Bite the top end off your Twix." She demonstrated for good measure, chewing and swallowing as Rosie followed suit. "Step two: bite the bottom end off."

Rosie giggled around a chunk of shortbread. "I think I see where you're going with this."

"You never know." Jem positioned their mugs at the edge of the table. "There might be a shock twist." She paused for dramatic effect. "And the final step: stick one end into your brew and suck the other end really hard."

"On three." Rosie dunked her bar and readied herself. "Okay, three." She lowered her head and took a prodigious slurp. She was grinning when she came back up. "Hey, it works!"

"Did you doubt me?" Jem touched her thumb to the chocolate coating Rosie's lips. "You missed a bit."

"Yeah?" Rosie flicked her tongue out, but she didn't seem to be trying very hard. "Whereabouts?"

"Everywhere," Jem said, and did a far more thorough job with her tongue than Rosie had. She heard Rosie moan and felt her turn her head a fraction, and then they were kissing like teenagers: no finesse and little coordination, their teeth and tongues clashing and their hands roaming. A mess of sensations shot through Jem, giving her a head rush that almost tipped her onto the cushions.

"Here or upstairs?" Rosie asked. Her hands skimmed over Jem's bra as she kissed the faint scars below Jem's eye.

"Here." Jem didn't think she was capable of stairs, but she caught hold of Rosie's wrists, trying to be practical. "What about your leg?" They had been patient, waiting for Rosie to heal, and they had never let things get this far.

Rosie brushed her thumbs across Jem's nipples. "Do you want me to stop?" she murmured against Jem's cheek.

"Oh God, no. Please don't stop," Jem said, and Rosie's mouth closed on hers again.

The house was still cold, and goose pimples covered Jem's torso when Rosie began to tug at her shirt.

"Shit, hang on. Give me a minute." Rosie tucked Jem in again and dashed around the room, collecting throw rugs and blankets. She arranged them into a multicoloured nest on top of the hearth rug and beckoned Jem to join her in the middle of it. "Better?"

Jem nodded, tongue-tied and nervous and more turned on than she could ever remember being. "Take your sweater off," she told Rosie, and Rosie obeyed without question, pulling her hoodie and T-shirt off in one go and wriggling out of her bra. Her bare skin reflected the firelight, and Jem followed the patterns with her lips until Rosie was squirming beneath her. "Lie back," Jem whispered, dispensing with her own shirt and bra as Rosie lay down and held out her arms. Jem straddled her and put her mouth to Rosie's ear. "Tell me what you want."

Rosie swallowed and licked her lips. "You," she said. "I just want you."

Jem trailed her fingers across Rosie's breasts. "That can be arranged." She shifted lower, kissing Rosie's navel and the heated skin just above the button on her jeans.

"Off as well?" Rosie asked, clearly trying to be helpful but fumbling with the fastenings and getting everything wrong. Jem clasped her hands and moved them away.

"Let me." She popped the buttons one by one, widening the fly and then lying down beside Rosie and working her fingers beneath Rosie's underwear.

"Fucking hell," Rosie whispered. Her legs fell open as Jem dipped her hand, parting the slick folds and then stroking upward. "Fucking hellfire."

It was easy to find a rhythm that Rosie liked. She wasn't shy or quiet, and she moved in synch with Jem, gasping when Jem circled her clit and rising to meet Jem as she entered her.

"God, yes, that, there," Rosie chanted. Her body suddenly stiffened, her legs rigid but trembling as she came around Jem's fingers. Jem rode the contractions out, kissing the warm swell of Rosie's breast as Rosie began to relax.

"Whoa," Rosie said. She sounded dazed. "The bloody ceiling's spinning."

Jem laughed and eased her hand to the top of Rosie's knickers, teasing the curls of hair. "Fabulous. That's the effect I was after."

It took Rosie a couple of attempts, but she managed to roll over and face Jem. "I thought you were all quiet and unassuming." She took Jem's hand and played her tongue across Jem's damp fingers. "And really you're quite naughty."

"Am I?" Jem bit her lip as Rosie sucked her index finger right down to the knuckle. She wriggled, shameless and desperate to be touched. "Please, Rosie. *Please*," she whispered.

Rosie didn't muck about. She had Jem naked within seconds, kissing her fiercely and then spreading her legs and settling between them. "Remember to breathe," she said an instant before she ran her tongue across Jem's clit.

"Shit, aw shit." Jem closed her eyes, her head falling back as Rosie's mouth covered her. Rosie kept the touch feather-light at first, sending Jem into a frenzy of pleading and writhing, before gradually increasing the pressure. Jem panted, twisting the blankets into knots, and then cried out when Rosie's fingers thrust into her.

"Don't stop," she begged, wondering vaguely if this would be her new favourite phrase. "Please don't stop."

Rosie obliged with enthusiasm, her fingers working Jem as her tongue continued to glide over Jem's clit. Jem opened her eyes, saw Rosie half naked and beautiful, framed by the firelight, and came so hard that Rosie eventually stopped everything she was doing and simply leaned back to watch her.

"Bloody hell." Jem's hand flew out, clutching the top of the coffee table. She felt as if she was falling, though she had nowhere to go. "*Rosie?*"

Rosie kissed her clit, sending more sparks dancing across her vision, and then curled up beside her. Jem stayed still for a long moment, her chest heaving and her legs quaking. Rosie was murmuring something to her, but she couldn't distinguish actual words. She felt a tap on her hand and looked down to see Rosie proffering her inhaler.

"I don't need it," she said.

"No?"

"No." She kissed Rosie's sticky lips. "This is the good sort of breathless."

"Excellent." Rosie launched the inhaler over her shoulder and then winced as it clattered off something. "I'll find it later, I promise."

"I'm sure it's not gone far," Jem said, yawning. Really good sex always made her sleepy, not to mention thirsty. She took Rosie's hand, turned her wrist, and kissed the bee inked onto her skin. "Think those brews are still warm?"

"Probably not." Rosie said. "And mine was a write-off anyway. I dropped my bloody Twix into it. Do you want me to make you a fresh one?"

Jem tightened her hold, keeping Rosie from moving while she tucked blankets over and around them. "No. I want you to stay right here with me."

Rosie rested her palm on Jem's cheek. "You are lovely," she said, and the gentle fondness in her voice brought tears to Jem's eyes. "Shh, now, Jemima Pardon. No crying."

"I'm not crying, love," Jem said, blinking the tears away. "I just never thought I'd find someone like you."

Rosie's chuckle vibrated beneath Jem's ear. "Were you hoping you'd end up with someone sensible?"

"I didn't dare hope I'd end up with anyone. I wouldn't *ever* have dared hope I'd end up with you."

"Must've been fate," Rosie said, "you and me in that puddle. Whatever will we do now it's stopped raining?"

Jem covered Rosie's hand with her own, entwining their fingers. She felt Rosie kiss her forehead, and she took a deep, steadying breath that filled her lungs and made her smile. "I think we'll manage just fine," she said. "I can't wait to see what we'll get up to in the sunshine."

The End

About the Author

Cari Hunter lives in the northwest of England with her wife, their cat, and a field full of sheep. She works full-time as a paramedic and dreams up stories in her spare time.

Cari enjoys long, windswept, muddy walks in her beloved Peak District. In the summer she can usually be found sitting in the garden with her feet up, scribbling in her writing pad. Although she doesn't like to boast, she will admit that she makes a very fine Bakewell tart.

Her first novel, *Snowbound*, received an Alice B. Lavender Certificate for outstanding debut. *No Good Reason*, the first in the Dark Peak series, won a 2015 Rainbow Award for Best Mystery and was a finalist in the 2016 Lambda and Goldie Awards. Its sequel, *Cold to the Touch*, won a Goldie and a Rainbow Award for Best Mystery. *A Quiet Death*, the final book in the series, was a finalist in the 2018 Lambda and Goldie Awards, and won the 2017 Rainbow Award for Best Mystery.

Cari can be contacted at: carihunter@rocketmail.com

Books Available from Bold Strokes Books

All She Wants by Larkin Rose. Marci Jones and Tessa Dalton get more than they bargained for when their plans for a one-night stand turn into an opportunity for love. (978-1-63555-476-2)

Beautiful Accidents by Erin Zak. Stevie Adams and Bernadette Thompson discover that sometimes the best things in life happen purely by accident. (978-1-63555-497-7)

Before Now by Joy Argento. Can Delany and Jade overcome the betrayal that spans the centuries to reignite a love that can't be broken? (978-1-63555-525-7)

Breathe by Cari Hunter. Paramedic Jemima Pardon's chronic bad luck seems to be improving when she meets police officer Rosie Jones. But they face a battle to survive before they can find love. (978-1-63555-523-3)

Double-Crossed by Ali Vali. Hired thief and killer Reed Gable finds something in her scope that will change her life forever when she gets a contract to end casino accountant Brinley Myers's life. (978-1-63555-302-4)

False Horizons by CJ Birch. Jordan and Ash struggle with different views on the alien agenda and must find their way back to each other before they're swallowed up by a centuries-old war. (978-1-63555-519-6)

Legacy by Charlotte Greene. When five women hike to a remote cabin deep inside a national park, unsettling events suggest that they should have stayed home. (978-1-63555-490-8)

Royal Street Reveillon by Greg Herren. Someone is killing the stars of a reality show, and it's up to Scotty Bradley and the boys to find out who. (978-1-63555-545-5)

Somewhere Along the Way by Kathleen Knowles. When Maxine Cooper moves to San Francisco during the summer of 1981, she learns that wherever you run, you cannot escape yourself. (978-1-63555-383-3)

Blood of the Pack by Jenny Frame. When Alpha of the Scottish pack Kenrick Wulver visits the Wolfgangs, she falls for Zaria Lupa, a wolf on the run. (978-1-63555-431-1)

Cause of Death by Sheri Lewis Wohl. Medical student Vi Akiak and K9 Search and Rescue officer Kate Renard must work together to find a killer before they end up the next targets. In the race for survival, they discover that love may be the biggest risk of all. (978-1-63555-441-0)

Chasing Sunset by Missouri Vaun. Hijinks and mishaps ensue as Iris and Finn set off on a road trip adventure, chasing the sunset, and falling in love along the way. (978-1-63555-454-0)

Double Down by MB Austin. When an unlikely friendship with Spanish pop star Erlea turns deeper, Celeste, in-house physician for the hotel hosting Erlea's show, has a choice to make—run or double down on love. (978-1-63555-423-6)

Party of Three by Sandy Lowe. Three friends are in for a wild night at billionaire heiress Eleanor McGregor's twenty-fifth birthday party. Love, lust, and doing the right thing, even when it hurts, turn the evening into one that will change their lives forever. (978-1-63555-246-1)

Sit. Stay. Love. by Karis Walsh. City girl Alana Brendt and country vet Tegan Evans both know they don't belong together. Only problem is, they're falling in love. (978-1-63555-439-7)

Where the Lies Hide by Renee Roman. As P.I. Camdyn Stark gets closer to solving the case, will her dark secrets and the lies she's buried jeopardize her future with the quietly beautiful Sarah Peters? (978-1-63555-371-0)

Beautiful Dreamer by Melissa Brayden. With love on the line, can Devyn Winters find it in her heart to stay in the small town of Dreamer's Bay, the one place she swore she'd never remain? (978-1-63555-305-5)

Create a Life to Love by Erin Zak. When sixteen-year-old Beth shows up at her birth mother's door, three lives will change forever. (978-1-63555-425-0)

Deadeye by Meredith Doench. Stranded while hunting the serial predator Deadeye, Special Agent Luce Hansen fights for survival while her lover, forensic pathologist Harper Bennett, hunts for clues to Hansen's disappearance along the killer's trail. (978-1-63555-253-9)

Death Takes a Bow by David S. Pederson. Alan Keys takes part in a local stage production, but when the leading man is murdered, his partner Detective Heath Barrington is thrust into the limelight to find the killer. (978-1-63555-472-4)

Endangered by Michelle Larkin. Shapeshifters Officer Aspen Wolfe and Dr. Tora Madigan fight their growing attraction as they work together to destroy a secret government agency that exterminates their kind. (978-1-63555-377-2)

Incognito by VK Powell. The only thing Evan Spears is focused on is capturing a fleeing murder suspect until wild card Frankie Strong is added to her team and causes chaos on and off the job. (978-1-63555-389-5)

Insult to Injury by Gun Brooke. After losing everything, Gail Owen withdraws to her old farmhouse and finds a destitute young woman, Romi Shepherd, living in a secret room. (978-1-63555-323-9)

Just One Moment by Dena Blake. If you were given the chance to have the love of your life back, could you ignore everything that went wrong and start over again? (978-1-63555-387-1)

Scene of the Crime by MJ Williamz. Cullen Mathew finds herself caught between the woman she thinks she loves but can no longer trust and a beautiful detective she can't stop thinking about who will stop at nothing to find the truth. (978-1-63555-405-2)

Accidental Prophet by Bud Gundy. Days after his grandmother dies, Drew Morten learns his true identity and finds himself racing against time to save civilization from the apocalypse. (978-1-63555-452-6)

Daughter of No One by Sam Ledel. When their worlds are threatened, a princess and a village outcast must overcome their differences and embrace a budding attraction if they want to survive. (978-1-63555-427-4)

Fear of Falling by Georgia Beers. Singer Sophie James is ready to shake up her career, but her new manager, the gorgeous Dana Landon, has other ideas. (978-1-63555-443-4)

In Case You Forgot by Fredrick Smith and Chaz Lamar. Zaire and Kenny, two newly single, Black, queer, and socially aware men, start again—in love, career, and life—in the West Hollywood neighborhood of LA. (978-1-63555-493-9)

Playing with Fire by Lesley Davis. When Takira Lathan and Dante Groves meet at Takira's restaurant, love may find its way onto the menu. (978-1-63555-433-5)

Practice Makes Perfect by Carsen Taite. Meet law school friends Campbell, Abby, and Grace, law partners at Austin's premier boutique legal firm for young, hip entrepreneurs. Legal Affairs: one law firm, three best friends, three chances to fall in love. (978-1-63555-357-4)

The Last Seduction by Ronica Black. When you allow true love to elude you once and you desperately regret it, are you brave enough to grab it when it comes around again? (978-1-63555-211-9)

Wavering Convictions by Erin Dutton. After a traumatic event, Maggie has vowed to regain her strength and independence. So how can Ally be both the woman who makes her feel safe and a constant reminder of the person who took her security away? (978-1-63555-403-8)

A Bird of Sorrow by Shea Godfrey. As Darrius and her lover, Princess Jessa, gather their strength for the coming war, a mysterious spell will reveal the truth of an ancient love. (978-1-63555-009-2)

All the Worlds Between Us by Morgan Lee Miller. High school senior Quinn Hughes discovers that a broken friendship is actually a door propped open for an unexpected romance. (978-1-63555-457-1)

An Intimate Deception by CJ Birch. Flynn County Sheriff Elle Ashley has spent her adult life atoning for her wild youth, but when she finds her ex, Jessie, murdered two weeks before the small town's biggest social event, she comes face-to-face with her past and all her well-kept secrets. (978-1-63555-417-5)

Cash and the Sorority Girl by Ashley Bartlett. Cash Braddock doesn't want to deal with morality, drugs, or people. Unfortunately, she's going to have to. (978-1-63555-310-9)

Counting for Thunder by Phillip Irwin Cooper. A struggling actor returns to the Deep South to manage a family crisis, finds love, and ultimately his own voice as his mother is regaining hers for possibly the last time. (978-1-63555-450-2)

Falling by Kris Bryant. Falling in love isn't part of the plan, but will Shaylie Beck put her heart first and stick around, or tell the damaging truth? (978-1-63555-373-4)

Secrets in a Small Town by Nicole Stiling. Deputy Chief Mackenzie Blake has one mission: find the person harassing Savannah Castillo and her daughter before they cause real harm. (978-1-63555-436-6)

Stormy Seas by Ali Vali. The high-octane follow-up to the best-selling action-romance, *Blue Skies*. (978-1-63555-299-7)

The Road to Madison by Elle Spencer. Can two women who fell in love as girls overcome the hurt caused by the father who tore them apart? (978-1-63555-421-2)